Since winning the Catherine _____
for her first novel, *The Hu* _____
become one of the most popu_____

Born in the mining town of Castleford, Val came to East Yorkshire as a child and has lived in Hull and rural Holderness where many of her novels are set. She now lives in the market town of Beverley.

When she is not writing, Val is busy promoting libraries and supporting many charities.

Val has now written twenty-five novels and has no intention of stopping!

Find out more about Val Wood's novels by visiting her website at www.valeriewood.co.uk

Have you read all of Val Wood's novels?

The Hungry Tide
Sarah Foster's parents fight a constant battle with poverty – until wealthy John Rayner provides them with work and a home on the coast. But when he falls for their daughter, Sarah, can their love overcome the gulf of wealth and social standing dividing them?

Annie
Annie Swinburn has killed a man. The man was evil in every possible way, but she knows that her only fate if she stays in Hull is a hanging. So she runs as far away as she can – to a new life that could offer her the chance of love, in spite of the tragedy that has gone before . . .

Children of the Tide
A tired woman holding a baby knocks at the door of one of the big houses in Anlaby. She shoves the baby at young James Rayner, then she vanishes. The Rayner family is shattered – born into poverty, will a baby unite or divide the family?

The Gypsy Girl
Polly Anna's mother died when she was just three years old. Alone in the world, the workhouse was the only place for her. But with the help of a young misfit she manages to escape, running away with the fairground folk. But will Polly Anna ever find somewhere she truly belongs?

Emily
A loving and hard-working child, Emily goes into service at just twelve years old. But when an employer's son dishonours and betrays her, her fortunes seem to be at their lowest ebb. Can she journey from shame and imprisonment to a new life and fulfilment?

Going Home
For Amelia and her siblings, the grim past their mother Emily endured seems far away. But when a gentleman travels from Australia to meet Amelia's family, she discovers the past casts a long shadow and that her tangled family history is inextricably bound up with his . . .

Rosa's Island
Taken in as a child, orphaned Rosa grew up on an island off the coast of Yorkshire. Her mother, before she died, promised that one day Rosa's father would return. But when two mysterious Irishmen come back to the island after many years, they threaten everything Rosa holds dear . . .

The Doorstep Girls
Ruby and Grace have grown up in the poorest slums of Hull. Friends since childhood, they have supported each other in bad times and good. As times grow harder, and money scarcer, the girls search for something that could take them far away . . . But what price will they pay to find it?

Far From Home

When Georgiana Gregory makes the long journey from Hull for New York, she hopes to escape the confines of English life. But once there, Georgiana finds she isn't far from home when she encounters a man she knows – who presents dangers almost too much to cope with . . .

The Kitchen Maid

Jenny secures a job as kitchen maid in a grand house in Beverley – but her fortunes fail when scandal forces her to leave. Years later, she is mistress of a hall, but she never forgets the words a gypsy told her: that one day she will return to where she was happy and find her true love . . .

The Songbird

Poppy Mazzini has an ambition – to go on the stage. Her lovely voice and Italian looks lead her to great acclaim. But when her first love from her home town of Hull becomes engaged to someone else, she is devastated. Will Poppy have to choose between fame and true love?

Nobody's Child

Now a prosperous Hull businesswoman, Susannah grew up with the terrible stigma of being nobody's child. When daughter Laura returns to the Holderness village of her mother's childhood, she will discover a story of poverty, heartbreak and a love that never dies . . .

Fallen Angels

After her dastardly husband tries to sell her, Lily Fowler is alone on the streets of Hull. Forced to work in a brothel, she forges friendships with the women there, and together they try to turn their lives around. Can they dare to dream of happy endings?

The Long Walk Home

When Mikey Quinn's mother dies, he is determined to find a better life for his family – so he walks to London from Hull to seek his fortune. He meets Eleanor, and they gradually make a new life for themselves. Eventually, though, they must make the long walk home to Hull . . .

Rich Girl, Poor Girl

Polly, living in poverty, finds herself alone when her mother dies. Rosalie, brought up in comfort on the other side of Hull, loses her own mother on the same day. When Polly takes a job in Rosalie's house, the two girls form an unlikely friendship. United in tragedy, can they find happiness?

Homecoming Girls

The mysterious Jewel Newmarch turns heads wherever she goes, but she feels a longing to know her own roots. So she decides to return to her birthplace in America, where she learns about family, friendship, love and home. But most importantly, love . . .

The Harbour Girl

Jeannie spends her days at the water's edge waiting for Ethan to come in from fishing. But then she falls for a handsome stranger. When he breaks his word, Jeannie finds herself pregnant and alone in a strange new town. Will she find someone to truly love her – and will Ethan ever forgive her?

The Innkeeper's Daughter

Bella's dreams of teaching are dashed when she has to take on the role of mother to her baby brother. Her days are brightened by visits from Jamie Lucan – but when the family is forced to move to Hull, Bella is forced to leave everything behind. Can she ever find her dreams again?

His Brother's Wife

The last thing Harriet expects after her mother dies is to marry a man she barely knows, but her only alternative is the workhouse. And so begins an unhappy marriage to Noah Tuke. The only person who offers her friendship is Noah's brother, Fletcher – the one person she can't possibly be with . . .

Every Mother's Son

Daniel Tuke hopes to share his future with childhood friend Beatrice Hart. But his efforts to find out more about his heritage throw up some shocking truths: is there a connection between the families? Meanwhile, Daniel's mother Harriet could never imagine that discoveries about her own family are also on the horizon . . .

Little Girl Lost

Margriet grew up as a lonely child in the old town of Hull. As she grows into adulthood she forms an unlikely friendship with some of the street children who roam the town. As Margriet acts upon her inspiration to help them, will the troubles of her past break her spirit, or will she be able to overcome them?

No Place for a Woman

Brought up by a kindly uncle after the death of her parents Lucy grows up inspired to become a doctor, just like her father. But studying in London takes Lucy far from her home in Hull, and she has to battle to be accepted in a man's world. An even greater challenge comes with the onset of the First World War; will Lucy be able to follow her dreams – and find love – in a world shattered by war?

A Mother's Choice

Delia has always had to fend for herself and her son Jack, and as a young unmarried mother, life has never been easy. In particularly desperate times, a chance encounter presents a lifeline. Delia is faced with an impossible, heart-wrenching choice. Can she bear to leave her young son behind, hoping another family will care for him? What else can a mother do to give her son the life he deserves?

A Place to Call Home

When Ellen's husband Harry loses his farm job and the cottage that comes with it, they have to leave the countryside they love in order to survive. Harry sets out to find a job in the factories and mills of nearby Hull, and Ellen must build a new life for her family on the unfamiliar city streets. But when tragedy threatens Ellen's fragile happiness how much more can she sacrifice before they find a place to call home?

FOUR SISTERS

Val Wood

CORGI BOOKS

TRANSWORLD PUBLISHERS
61–63 Uxbridge Road, London W5 5SA
www.penguin.co.uk

Transworld is part of the Penguin Random House group of companies
whose addresses can be found at global.penguinrandomhouse.com

First published in Great Britain in 2019 by Bantam Press
an imprint of Transworld Publishers
Corgi edition published 2020

A CIP catalogue record for this book
is available from the British Library

ISBN 9780552176699

Typeset in 10.46/12.86 pt New Baskerville ITC Pro
by Integra Software Services Pvt. Ltd, Pondicherry.

Printed and bound in Great Britain by Clays Ltd, Elcograf S.p.A.

Penguin Random House is committed to a sustainable future for
our business, our readers and our planet. This book is made
from Forest Stewardship Council® certified paper.

1 3 5 7 9 10 8 6 4 2

For my family with love and for Peter as always.

PROLOGUE

The news spread rapidly in the ancient market town. The family were well known. Beverley people.

It was a tragedy, everyone agreed. Such a waste. Especially a woman like her. A beautiful woman, kind too, it was said. So much to live for; and her young children – the youngest still an infant – all girls, left behind: how would they manage, the whispers went, without a mother's direction to guide them?

They'd grow wild and tempestuous, someone said, for their father, as everyone knew, was inconsolable in his grief and might never recover from the loss of his wife and baby son.

CHAPTER ONE

Matty

April 1852

'It's not fair! Becca gets away with everything.' Becca had not dared to leave the house until Papa had driven off to Hull to collect his sister, their aunt Gertrude, and bring her back for luncheon, but now Matty had seen her sister skipping down the house steps and rushing across the York Road.

'I know where she's going,' Matty continued. 'She needn't think I don't, and if she's late back for luncheon I'll be the one to get into trouble for allowing her to go; as if I had any control over her!'

'Are you talking to yourself again, Miss Martha? You know what happens to people who do that?' Mrs Nunnington, otherwise known as Nunny, housekeeper and nanny, confidante, keeper of secrets, wiper of tears and soother of the aches and pains that four growing young ladies were prone to, had opened the door to the sitting room without Matty's hearing her. 'Has Becca escaped again?' She joined Matty by the window and looked out. 'She's a wild one, there's no escaping the fact. But she'll be back in time for luncheon; she always is.'

Matty turned to her. 'How is it, Nunny, that you call Rebecca Becca but you call me Miss Martha? You know how I hate it. I much prefer Matty.'

'That's because she's the youngest and you're the eldest and therefore deserving of respect, and,' Mrs Nunnington added, 'with more responsibilities. Come your birthday in May, you'll be called Miss Maddeson.'

'Another month. It will be nearly ten years then, won't it?' Matty's hot scalding tears fell unbidden on to her cheeks; every day recently they seemed to lie in wait beneath her lashes, and, like a tap loosely turned, a chance casual remark opened the valve, allowing the tears to flow. Whatever was the matter with her?

'Since your mama died? Yes, almost.' Mrs Nunnington nodded and put her hand on Matty's arm. 'You're allowed to cry. It's perfectly natural; there's no need to hold back 'tears, except of course in front of anyone else. Sorrow is best kept private if possible, m'dear, so cry now before your papa and aunt arrive home.'

Matty sat down in the nearest chair, feeling Nunny's sympathetic eyes upon her; Nunny understood her feelings, she knew that. It was Nunny who had comforted her on her mother's death; Nunny who'd held her hand at her mother's bedside when her father and the doctor had said that she should go in and say goodbye.

At eight years old she had been told and understood that her mother wouldn't be coming back, and neither would the baby brother who had died with her. She had thought for a long time that perhaps it had been her fault, that she had done or said something wrong or bad, even though Nunny had told her that she hadn't, that her mother's death had been a natural occurrence because Mrs Maddeson hadn't been strong. But even now, almost ten years on, she often worried that perhaps she hadn't always been as obedient as she might have been, and so felt an overwhelming desire to please.

Her sister Julia, who at only six years old had been considered too young to sit by her mother's side and see her pale and beautiful waxy face and her father's inflexible one, was convinced for a whole year that her loving mama had gone

4

away on holiday without them, and refused to accept that she wouldn't be coming home. Gradually, she stopped mentioning her and didn't join in any conversation about her, and it was as if she had totally forgotten her existence.

Faith, who had been only four, had at that time been confined to bed with a heavy cold; once recovered she had searched all the rooms in the house, including the cupboards and closets, and discovering that her mother wasn't in any of them went back to her cot and slept sporadically for a week, watched over by Nunny and a nursery maid who had been hired to look after the new baby when it arrived. The young est daughter, Rebecca, had only recently been weaned at two, and had screamed constantly until Nunny, in despair, and wretched herself over the death of her mistress, had laced her bottles of warm honey-sweetened milk with the smallest of drops of laudanum to make her sleep and give them all some rest.

'How would it be if I brought you a strip of willow bark and a cup of camomile tea?' Nunny asked Matty now. 'Then you could put your feet up for half an hour before getting ready for your aunt.'

Matty leaned forward and put her hand out to touch her. 'Thank you, Nunny,' she said, her lips trembling. 'I'm sorry I'm such a crosspatch. I don't mean to be.'

'I know, m'dear. It's only your flux on 'verge of making its monthly visit, you do know that?'

'I'd forgotten,' Matty said tearily. 'It seems to come round so often.'

Nunny raised her bushy eyebrows. 'You don't need to tell *me* that!' she groused. 'Three young women, two of you about to start or finish and 'other one on 'brink of womanhood ready to blow her top; it's like living in 'middle of a volcano.'

Matty laughed in spite of herself. How lucky they were to have Nunny still with them; she had never been married but like most housekeepers was referred to as Mrs, and Matty remembered how she had once heard a whispered conversation between her parents on whether to keep her or manage with just the new nursery maid when the baby arrived. The girls would have been lost without her; she was their surrogate grandmother, their mentor and friend, and they loved her as if she were family.

Certainly their father couldn't have managed four daughters alone; when his wife died he was completely lost, silent, and unable to think straight or communicate with his children. Matty had heard her mother crying in their bedroom one day after the doctor had visited, telling Papa that it was too soon to have had another baby; that they should have waited. Matty had been a child who overheard conversations, and not always understanding their meaning kept them firmly trapped in her head until she did.

Nunny plumped up a cushion and put it behind Matty's back. 'There now,' she murmured. 'You rest while I make your tea and you'll soon feel as right as ninepence.'

I feel guilty, Matty thought. It's normal, I understand that, and I wonder if this is how women feel if they are expecting a child. If it is, then I don't want any. And yet I used to think I'd like to fall in love and marry, but now I'm not so sure. If there's a chance of dying in childbirth then I think I won't take that step. I'd rather not risk it. She sighed. I wish I had someone who could advise me, but such matters are not open for discussion.

Her thoughts drifted to her father, who had remained widowed, for which she was eternally grateful. She would not have liked another woman taking her mother's place, but sometimes he seemed morose and, as if impulsively, would come out of his study, run upstairs to change and either saddle up his horse and ride out across the meadows of Westwood or go out to his club.

He should have an occupation, she considered, smoothing out the skirt of her plain grey morning dress. Something to fill his leisure time rather than sitting alone in the library reading his newspapers or studying the politics and economics of the world and how his stocks and shares were affected; it must be very boring being a gentleman with nothing much to do. I wouldn't mind if he would discuss world affairs with me; there must be many questions I could ask which he would find interesting to talk about, and could help me to understand. I feel sure he would have done so if I had been a son.

Nunny brought up her tea and a small strip of willow bark to chew on. 'Just gently run your teeth along it, m'dear,' she said. 'It's very effective when you're feeling a little under the weather. Now if you'll excuse me I must prepare 'luncheon table before your papa and Miss Maddeson arrive back or she'll want to do it for me.'

Matty smiled. How well Nunny knew them all. Aunt Gertrude, unmarried and living alone in Hull, apart from a few faithful retainers to carry out her every whim, was a stickler for everything's being just right; when she came on her monthly visit her brother's servants made sure there wasn't a speck of dust anywhere, and that the table linen was washed and ironed without a single crease and laid out exactly as she would wish it, for she would, for sure, spot any sign of disorder.

Their father always drove into Hull to collect her, and Matty had long ago deduced it was so that he could listen and nod to all of her opinions on the journey back so that he didn't have to do so at the luncheon table. Their house stood adjacent to the grassy Hurn with the Beverley York Road dividing it from Westwood; both areas were pleasant green common pastureland where cattle and some sheep grazed unrestrained and now, in April, the buttercups were unfolding their bright golden flowers and abundant trees were greening.

When Aunt Gertrude was ready to leave, their coach driver, Sam, would drive her home in the brougham, which was warmer than the chaise Mr Maddeson had bought on a sunny day a year after his wife's death. Matty, listening again to Cook and Nunny talking in the kitchen when they thought she was engrossed in shelling peas, realized they thought it was so that

7

he could drive alone sometimes, as there wouldn't be room for his daughters.

One of the junior maids knocked and came in with a stone hot water bottle wrapped in a thick cloth. 'Mrs Nunnington asked me to bring this up to you, miss,' she said meekly. 'She said as you weren't well and were feeling a chill.'

Matty took it from her. 'Thank you, Brown,' she said. 'How kind. That will help, I'm sure.'

The young maid, a slip of a girl who must have been about the same age as Faith, was dressed in black with an overlong white apron and a white cap which slipped over her forehead as she dipped her knee and turned to leave, and Matty thought how lucky she and her sisters were to be living at home and hadn't been sent out to work in service.

'Brown,' she called after her, and the maid looked anxiously back at her.

'Yes, miss?'

'What's your name? Your first name, I mean? Your Christian name?'

The girl licked her lips and pushed the too-large cap up from her forehead. 'Betty, miss. Cook said there'd been a Betty here before so I should answer to Brown.'

'And do you mind?' Matty frowned.

'I didn't think I had a choice, Miss Martha. That's what Cook said I should answer to.'

Matty considered. Names were very important. 'Would you prefer to be called Betty?'

'Yes, miss,' she mumbled. 'Brown could be a lad, couldn't it?'

'Yes, it could. Very well. I shall call you Betty. It's from Elizabeth, isn't it?'

'Yes, mum – I mean miss. My ma's called Elizabeth; that's why I'm Betty, so we don't get mixed up, though now I'm not living at home it don't matter so much.'

Matty nodded solemnly, trying to be grown up and behave as her mother might have done. 'Mmm, well, Cook is in charge of her kitchen, so Brown it is, but upstairs it's to be Betty, and I'll make sure my sisters call you that too.'

'Thank you, miss.' Betty bobbed her knee. 'Much obliged.'

There, Matty thought. I've asserted my authority. I don't suppose Papa will mind one way or another, as he rarely sees the maids, but I'll tell him as soon as there's an opportunity. Perhaps I'll tell Aunt Gertrude too. She breathed in and then out. If I dare. Getting up from her chair, she left the room clutching the hot bottle to her aching abdomen, and lifting her hem walked upstairs to her room.

CHAPTER TWO

Julia

Julia had also seen Becca escape from the house and run in the direction of the stables on the other side of the York Road, her skirts flying, showing the lace around the ankles of her cotton drawers. Julia had a legitimate reason for being out alone, for today was Saturday and the weekly market was in full swing. Had her papa known she was unaccompanied he wouldn't have objected, for he was liberal-minded and liked to think his daughters were living useful lives; she had heard him say so to Aunt Gertrude, no less, when she had been pontificating one day about young females on the brink of womanhood not behaving with the decorum she had shown when she was a gel. That was how she'd pronounced girl, and Julia had rolled the word around her tongue like an aniseed ball before looking up *liberal* in Mr Johnson's dictionary in her father's study and discovering it meant tolerant or broadminded.

I'm not sure he's so liberal-minded that he would approve of Becca's being out alone, she reflected as she came to the historic brick-built North Bar, which in ancient times was the principal gated entry into the town; when she was very young, four or five, she and Matty used to pause here when out with their mother, for she had told them that outside the bar they were *without* and once they had stepped through they were *within*: and they would make a ceremony of passing through and giggling on the other side. She didn't giggle now, of course, but try as she might she couldn't erase the memory and still looked up as she passed into the old town.

She crossed over to be on the same side as St Mary's church and paused by the haberdasher's window, her thoughts still on Becca's behaviour. She's young, Julia considered, with the wisdom of a not-quite-sixteen-year-old, and will get into mischief with those friends of hers, mostly boys, who are not really suitable companions. I'll have to talk to Nunny, I think, and then she can decide what to do. Julia frequently had interesting conversations in her head where she discussed alternative and sometimes opposing views.

She regularly came for a stroll into Saturday Market; she liked the bustle of it, particularly on market day itself, and the cries of the traders extolling their wares to those who came from outlying villages such as Leconfield and Arram, Etton and Cherry Burton that hadn't a market of their own. It meant that she could be truly independent and walk wherever she wanted to, indulging in conversation with other visitors if she wished, or not, as the mood took her. On this occasion, she was also quite legitimately shopping for odds and ends that Nunny had asked her to buy for the household, and for thread and patching material that the seamstress who came once a month to attend to their dresses had requested that she obtain. She was entrusted with money from the household fund and as always would take home the receipts.

'Julia!' a voice breathed just above her ear. 'Out alone?'

'Good morning, Adam.' She would have known his breaking voice anywhere. Sometimes cracking, sometimes deep, he was always embarrassed by it. Adam was the older brother of her friend and confidante Eliza Chapman, and she was quite sure he had designs on her. If he should ever make any obvious odious signs that she was right he would feel the sharpness of her tongue. It wasn't that she didn't like him, but sometimes he annoyed her.

'Why, I wonder, should you seem surprised that I am on my own?' She arched her eyebrows in what she intended to be a confrontational manner. 'I am a liberated woman.'

'Ha!' he snorted, which he was apt to do when he was lost for words, and drew back his shoulders on his lanky frame. 'Begging your pardon, but you're the same age as Eliza and she hasn't put her hair up either.' He glanced at her long dark braid. 'So neither of you is a woman yet.'

'Any more than you're a man,' she responded sharply, and was immediately regretful, for he blinked and flushed. He stepped back, and before she could say any more he gave a short bow, muttered 'Miss Julia' and turned away.

She breathed out, watching his straight back as he walked off. I shouldn't have said that. I always seem to put my foot in it with Adam, and he's harmless really. Just being friendly, I suppose.

She'd known him and his sister since they were all small. A memory came back of when she and Matty had been taken to their house to play and the Chapmans' nanny had patted their heads and given them lemonade and cake; she quickly pushed the recollection away.

She turned and walked into the haberdashery. The bell above the door jangled as she pushed it open. Mrs Shaw looked up; she had folds of woollen material on the counter in front of her and a box of lacy trimmings in her hand. 'Good morning, Miss Julia. What can I do for you today?'

'May I sit down, Mrs Shaw? I feel a little dizzy.' Julia leaned on a bentwood chair that stood by the counter. 'I've hurried from one end of town to the other and I don't know why.' She sat down, thanking the draper with a smile. 'Well, yes, I do. My aunt is coming for luncheon and I should get back to help.'

It was a blatant lie; she hadn't been into Wednesday Market yet and she didn't need to help at home; Nunny and her staff could manage perfectly well without her assistance. She was just cross with herself because she'd upset Adam. Mrs Shaw leaned across the counter and whispered confidentially, 'I used to feel faint when I was your age, m'dear, especially at certain times of 'month.' She straightened up. 'I'm done wi' all that nonsense now. There's summat to say for getting older and not having to put up wi' it.'

Julia quickly told her what she needed and paid for her purchases, thanked her for the offer of a cold drink, which she refused, and went back into the market to do the rest of the shopping. She didn't need much, and reflected that because of her silliness she had completely ruined her morning. She saw Adam again outside the Corn Exchange, chatting to friends whom she also knew, but she didn't approach them as she was sure that Adam had seen her but hadn't made any sign to acknowledge that he had.

She walked slowly down Toll Gavel, idly looking in shop windows, on her way to Wednesday Market, where she realized that she was merely killing time and turned back for home. Avoiding the town centre in order to decrease the chances of bumping into Adam again, she pondered their conversation once more.

I'm not grown up, of course, she thought dismally. If I were, Mrs Shaw wouldn't have mentioned such personal things. She did so because she thought perhaps I hadn't been informed because . . . *because*; and of course I do know everything I need to know. The irritability that she had felt earlier began to quicken again. I am perfectly capable of discovering anything. I can read! And in any case, I didn't really feel faint, even though I do have a headache coming on.

She cut across the roads behind North Bar Street and along Pasture Terrace towards the buttercup-dappled grass of Westwood, and as she approached their house she saw Becca again on the other side of the road. Her coat was hanging half off her shoulders and her hair had come undone from its plait. She held a shopping bag in front of her with both hands as if it were a precious parcel.

'Becca,' Julia called. 'What have you got there? Where have you been?'

Becca slowly turned and gazed at her sister. With her fair skin and blonde hair she always looked innocent, yet guilt could never be quite disguised. It was clear in her winsome blue eyes and softly parted mouth.

'Nowhere,' she said meekly. 'Just about, you know, meeting friends.'

'And what's in the bag?' Julia frowned, crossing over to walk beside her. 'It's wriggling. What have you got? It's not a snake, is it?' Becca had once 'rescued' a grass snake and brought it home, tipping it out of a box on to the sitting-room carpet.

'No.' Becca pouted. 'Of course not.' She lowered her voice to a whisper. 'It's just a puppy.'

'A puppy? Let me look! You know you can't take it home.'

'I can.' Becca turned her angelic face up to Julia. 'You can't say if I can or not. Besides, he's for me and Faith to share, not for you or Matty, and if we don't have him he'll be drowned and die.'

'What will Papa say – or Aunt Gertrude?'

Becca's sweet mouth turned into a pout. 'We won't tell him until after Aunt Gertrude has gone home. He can sleep in my bedroom. I've got a bottle for him because he's still a baby and needs milk. I'll put some paper down in case he makes a mess.'

'What about Nunny?'

'What about her?'

'She'll find out,' Julia said.

'Not if you don't tell her. You won't, will you, Julia? I'll train him. He'll be a good house dog. We'll never get any vandals.'

'Burglars, you mean.' Julia knew she wasn't going to win this battle.

'Burglars or vandals, they won't come near the house if they know we've got a dog.'

The puppy raised a kinked listening ear. He was rather sweet, Julia thought. 'Come on then,' she said, capitulating. 'We'd better go through the garden and in the back door,

14

and whilst I'm giving Nunny the shopping you can slip up the back stairs.'

'Oh, thank you, Julia.' Becca's face lit up with delight. 'I knew you'd love him. I'd give you one of my humbugs, but they've been in my pocket and have bits of straw and grass stuck on them. Still, you can have one if you like. The bits will suck off.'

'Thank you, but no, you keep them,' Julia said hastily. 'Now, ought you to cover him up again?' She opened the garden gate and dropped her voice to a whisper as they reached the back door. 'You'd better go straight upstairs. Cook won't want him in the kitchen whilst she's preparing luncheon, and whatever you do make sure Aunt Gertrude doesn't see or hear him.'

Becca shook her head conspiratorially and tiptoed inside. Julia couldn't help but think her sister was enjoying this. She sighed. *It's been a strange morning. Why do I feel that I've been at war, and lost all the battles?*

CHAPTER THREE

Faith

The third child had been christened Faith. Her mother had been plagued with sickness throughout her pregnancy and had been convinced that both she and the infant would die. Her husband expected the worst; it was Nunny who had constantly implored her only to have faith and they would both live and thrive.

It had been risky and the doctor had been uncertain of the outcome, but the baby was small and came early, giving a weak cry and a sneeze as she entered the world. The doctor said she wouldn't live and was astonished when she did, and Nunny was triumphant.

Little Faith had a poor appetite and was late to walk; she appeared so fragile that it seemed as if the slightest breeze would blow her away, but she had a resilient nature despite being prone to catch every childish ailment that came her way. She had a bout of pneumonia at two, whooping cough at three and heavy colds throughout her fourth year, so wasn't allowed near her baby sister, or her mother either during the final stages of that tragic last pregnancy.

At thirteen she was slim, dainty and sweet-tempered, able to see both sides of every argument, and her father agreed solemnly with his sister's statement that she wouldn't 'make old bones' while at the same time nodding when Nunny said that she had a cast-iron constitution. Her sisters doted on her, for she could always be relied upon to repair a droopy hem or find and sew on a missing button for the older ones, and invent excuses acceptable to adults for the misdeeds of the younger one.

She was sitting in her bedroom reading when Becca arrived home with the wriggling shopping bag. Faith had had her own small bedroom since she was a child, when she was supposed to be kept away from her sisters in case they caught any of her ailments, though they could often be found lying on her bed whilst she occupied a chair. Matty and Julia shared a larger room, and Becca was still in what had been the original nursery.

'What have you found?' Faith put down her book. 'Not a kitten? You know Papa said we can't have any more cats.'

Their father, usually so temperate and understanding, had put his foot down when one of the many cats that Becca had adopted gave birth to six kittens in the wardrobe where he kept his formal black tailcoat and trousers, silk top hat and white gloves.

'It's not a cat,' Becca said, tipping the puppy out unceremoniously on to Faith's bed. 'Isn't he lovely? He would have been drowned if I hadn't rescued him.' She couldn't resist retelling the tale.

'No he wouldn't,' Faith said calmly. 'Whoever told you that was telling fibs. He's too big to drown. Pups and kittens are drowned just after they're born if no one wants them. They don't get drowned after they've been fed like this one.' She bent as the pup rolled over, and tickled his tummy. 'Look at this fat tum,' she crowed. 'You've been well fed, haven't you?'

The pup tried to bite her hand and she exclaimed at his sharp little teeth, then watched him as he gambolled about the room. Suddenly, she called to Becca. 'Quick, quick! He's going to make a mess. Take him out. He'll make such a stink; take him into the garden.' She jumped up and dashed to open

17

the door and the pup headed towards it. 'Show him where to go. Go on!'

Becca pulled a face and followed the little dog, who was already scampering down the back stairs. Faith closed the bedroom door behind them and went to the window to look out into the back garden. The pup had already reached it; someone, probably Becca on her way up, had left the door open.

'The trouble with you, Becca,' Faith murmured, before picking up her book and sitting down again, 'is that you have these wonderful ideas and then expect everyone else to carry them out for you.' I wouldn't be surprised, she thought, if you intended sharing the puppy with me so that I can house-train him for you and you'll just take him for a walk now and again when the mood takes you. She opened the book to the page she had been reading before Becca interrupted her. Well, no. I won't.

Faith had fleeting memories of her mother. They came back at odd times and were often totally unexpected. It was usually an aroma that reminded her. Apple blossom or the smell of fresh new growth on a privet hedge, and sometimes the fragrance of a spiced Christmas pudding. They were happy scents, she always thought, for she often felt that she sensed her mother's presence then, even though she didn't have a physical picture of her, except for the painting that her father had hung in the sitting room. But she remembered that her mother had sat with her on her knee if ever she had been ill, gently rocking her until she fell asleep.

Poor Becca, she thought compassionately; she doesn't have any treasured memories. Neither does Julia, or at least she says she doesn't, but she wouldn't admit it even if she had. Matty does, she thought, but is afraid to talk of them in case she cries and upsets everyone.

Dear Matty, she tries so hard to take our mother's place and doesn't realize that she can't; she's our lovely warm beloved sister and that's enough. We all have each other.

CHAPTER FOUR

Becca

Becca stood with her arms folded across her chest waiting whilst the pup tidied up after himself; he was making a really good job of it by scattering dead leaves in all directions. The gardener might not be very pleased, she considered, nor Faith as she said they should always be piled up for hedgehogs and other creatures to shelter in.

'Come on,' Becca said, 'hurry up. I have to get changed before Aunt Gertrude gets here.'

The pup looked up at her with his head on one side and then, as if making up his own mind, scampered into the small copse which backed on to the garden to explore. Becca heaved a great sigh and followed him. It was her own fault, she supposed, but Owen Field at the stables had definitely told her that the pup was going to be drowned. She realized now that Owen must have rescued the pup from drowning himself and had probably hidden him from Mr Lawrence, who owned the racing stables, for as long as possible. Owen had a dog already, so he would have known he couldn't keep another one.

What's Papa going to say? Maybe I won't tell him until Aunt Gertrude has gone home, because she always says that I'm a spoilt child. And I'm not, she thought mutinously. I'm the youngest and I haven't got a mother.

She often used her situation when she wanted her own way over something, and if chastised over some misdeed would lower her long fair lashes on to her cheeks and let her mouth tremble. Sometimes she would practise in her looking glass, bending her head to let a lock of blonde hair cover her face. The performance didn't work with her sisters, but it often did with her governess and friends of her father, especially the gentlemen, who didn't recognize her acting ability or know that she had perfected the skill of getting exactly what she wanted nearly all the time.

She didn't remember her mother at all and felt resentful about that, as though it were somehow a slight, although Faith said that she didn't always remember how she had looked either, except sometimes when she recalled someone dark-haired looking down at her in her cot when she was very small. But Becca didn't have a single memory of her mother, and although her father had a painting of her, it didn't mean anything at all to Becca. 'I'm half a norphan,' she'd once complained and was peeved when Faith and Matty, but not Julia, had chorused that they were too.

'Come on, Pug,' she called to the puppy. 'I'm going in now. Here.' She patted her thigh and turned away, and to her surprise the puppy chased after her, overtook her, pushed open the kitchen door and raced upstairs to scratch on Faith's door.

'Go away,' Faith called from inside. 'I'm getting ready to help downstairs. Aunt Gertrude will be here in twenty minutes.'

'It's not me scratching on the door,' Becca complained. 'It's Pug. He must think this is his room.'

Faith opened the door and put her foot out to stop the dog coming in. 'Well, it's not. Take him to your room and put some paper down.'

'He's been,' Becca said. 'In the garden. He just thinks that this is his room.'

Faith pointed a long slender finger towards the old nursery. 'That way,' she commanded, but couldn't help the twitch of her lips. Shaking her head, she marched down the corridor, Becca trailing behind, and opened the door. 'In,' she said. The dog raced in, bounced on to the bed and sat looking at them. 'You've just got to be firm with him,' Faith said, turning away.

Becca folded her arms. 'You're for sharing,' she whispered to the dog, who woofed at her and jumped down to race after Faith and settle himself outside her door. She gave a sigh. 'I tried my hardest,' she murmured. 'But he doesn't want me. Nobody does. I'll just have to tell Papa that he followed me home.'

She didn't always get her own way. The governess, Miss Hargreaves, was strict with her and it was boring doing lessons on her own, for Faith was given different studies now and did them in her bedroom, where she had a desk with an inkwell and a chair and always a fire lit in the grate. Miss Hargreaves had told their father that Faith could be trusted to do the lessons without supervision, and Rebecca could not; which was probably true, Becca admitted, for she would rather be at the Westwood stables, playing with the cats and dogs or helping Owen to groom the horses.

Owen didn't always want her there either; he sometimes said she got in the way of his routine. He was sixteen and would have been more interested in Julia, except she always completely ignored him and didn't ever speak, even if he passed her on the street and *always, always,* tipped his cap or forehead at her. But Becca had seen with her very own eyes that Julia simply sailed past him as if he were completely invisible.

He told Becca that her sister was 'stuck up', and Becca hesitated over agreeing with him as she wasn't quite sure what he meant. Besides, Julia was her sister after all, and Aunt Gertrude had said that, like it or not, blood was thicker than water as far as family relationships were concerned, which of course she knew, but didn't quite understand what it had to do with anything.

Of all the people they knew in Beverley – and there were lots, as her father had been born in the town – Becca's favourites were the Lawrence family and especially the twins Frances and Roger, who were her best friends in the world. She had felt deprived last year when they had gone away to separate schools, and they had hated it too because they had never been parted before. Their father was a landowner and farmer and owned the racing stables where Becca spent as much time as possible, for Mr Lawrence had said that she might when she'd cried over the twins' leaving.

She groomed the horses and mucked out the stables and played with the kittens and puppies when she got bored, and often followed the horses and jockeys on foot to watch them in training before wandering home again. She wished that she could live and work there with the horses but she wouldn't be allowed to. She was a girl, after all, and girls couldn't; but she could ride if she wanted to and she had seen pictures in magazines of young women sitting on horses while dressed in fine costumes with tiny hats perched on their heads. But she wanted to sit astride, not side-saddle as they did; and she supposed that she would never, ever be allowed to race on the racecourse which she could see from her bedroom window, which was what she wanted more than anything in the whole world.

CHAPTER FIVE

Roland Maddeson heaved a sigh as he shook the reins and Star moved on in response to his sure touch. He cherished this time of solitude, for although he was often alone, spending his time in his study with his books, his certificates of stocks and shares and his notes of interest rates, he was always conscious of the hum of his daughters' voices, their laughter or the clatter of their feet on the stairs, and the sounds of his domestic staff going about their business of keeping the household running well.

This journey once a month to collect his sister and bring her back for luncheon enabled him to clear his head, put his thoughts in order and look towards the future. Not his future; that was fixed, immovable and most unlikely to change, and he had accepted it as his lot without any expectation of variation. Except that, sometimes, he longed for female companionship other than that of his daughters.

And it was his daughters' future that concerned him; he knew that he should be setting out the course of their lives, planning to do what was right for them. Had his wife lived they would have done it together, or at least she would have made plans and he would have carried them out, for she had ambitions that would have encompassed them all. She would have made sure they met the right people, who in turn would introduce them to others and possibly present them to their future husbands.

But I can't do that, he thought, leaving the town behind and picking up speed on the open road. It is a woman's role more than a man's, for no suitor would be good enough for a doting father. My introduction to Constance came through one of my father's sisters. His mouth lifted into a smile. His lovable extrovert mother would not have found anyone *suitable*, but someone beautiful who would have entertained him but had no brain for conversation.

Constance, on the other hand, had been beautiful and intelligent too, and he still missed her. Their eldest daughter, Matty, was most like her in demeanour, always careful not to upset or annoy anyone; she was discreet and helpful, always aware if anyone was unhappy, and although only young took care of all her sisters. Julia was most like Constance in looks, with her dark-haired beauty and fine bone structure, but withdrawn and inclined to be critical of inadequacies, her own as well as those of others.

Faith, he sighed, was a model of a child, who seemed so fragile and yet contained an inner strength that belied her slenderness and air of quiet repose. She, of all of them, would perhaps not thank him for searching out a suitable husband for her. Doubtless Becca, energetic yet lazy, rebellious Rebecca, would head off in her own direction, unheedful of any path that he might recommend. She had been brought up by her sisters and the household staff as he'd battled with his despair and guilt at his wife's early death, and thus was already independent of him.

Perhaps if I'd married again. He slowed as a coach and four came towards him down the middle of the road and he pulled over to let it pass. The girls might have taken heed of another woman, but what woman would take on a man with four ready-made daughters who might, or more likely would, resent and resist her? And, as I have never yet met anyone who could take Constance's place, the matter is irrelevant in any case.

The top road into Hull from Beverley was tree-lined and rural until he reached the crossroads leading to the village of

Cottingham in one direction and towards Newland Clough in the other. Continuing on, he came to a second crossroads where country lanes ran off on each side and isolated farmland and buildings seemed trapped in time. Roland recalled the great plans for development that had been put forward and that he had toyed with the idea of investment. Industry had arrived in Hull: the railways and docks were already thriving and further down towards the town individual villas and terraces of substantial housing stood on both sides of Beverley Road, wide boulevards being planned for the bourgeoning town. Businessmen and political idealists were even discussing a possible invitation to the Queen.

Approaching the town Roland reined Star to a walk as the traffic of mules, horses and drays, carriers' carts and coaches became heavier. Fortunately, it was not long before he was able to turn into Albion Street and draw up in front of his sister's house.

This was one of the more prosperous areas in Hull, with its elegant Georgian terraces within easy reach of the museums, the well-established General Infirmary and the shopping area of Whitefriargate. It was also within walking distance of the Paragon railway station, which had been opened only four years before and suited his sister very well, as she was rather enamoured of this method of transportation and quite brave enough to take short journeys on a train, alone or with a friend.

Gertrude had moved to the house with their mother Henrietta after their father Henry had died an early and unexpected death, leaving their Beverley home in the possession of Roland, the eldest son, who being already married with one child and his wife expecting another was certainly more in need of the larger house than his mother and her unmarried daughter could claim to be. Henry's second son, Albert Fisher Maddeson, then unmarried, was given a house in the heart of Beverley, smaller than the family home yet large enough to accommodate a wife and family if he should have one, which a few years later he did.

Henry Maddeson had always been a man of property and had asked his wife early in their marriage where she would like to live if he should die before her.

'I would like a villa in Italy, darling Henry,' Henrietta had declared, 'so that I can have warmer winters, and a house in Hull for when I visit. My papa was always sad that I had left Hull for Beverley when you and I married, for his family had lived in the same house for *centuries*, but what can a woman do? We have no voice and must live where our fathers and husbands decree.'

Henrietta was prone to exaggeration, as her husband well knew; her father's house was minuscule compared with the Maddeson house and was home to many siblings; her father and grandfather had risen from lowly positions in the fishing trade to being the owners of several successful and profitable shipping fleets in the port town, a direct result of hard work, energy and enterprise and not the result of being born with the legendary silver spoon as Henry Maddeson, his father and his grandfather had been.

When Henrietta met Henry on a chance occasion he immediately fell for her considerable charms and love of life; her father was agreeable to giving her and her substantial dowry to a man who so obviously adored her happy nature, her fine figure and beauty, and didn't mind too much her lack of gentility or propriety; indeed would take her up the ladder to become a gentleman's wife. She never did quite become a lady, being far too familiar and friendly with everyone she met, but their sons Roland and Albert were gentlemen and their only daughter Gertrude had the manner of a dowager from the age of six, when she realized she was the daughter of a gentleman and that more was expected of her than was of her mother.

Gertrude now lived alone in the elegant Albion Street house, as after a few years of widowhood her mother had decided that she preferred living in the villa overlooking the sunny shores of Lake Maggiore to being in the town of her

26

birth. She packed her considerable wardrobe, left her daughter to look after herself and the house, and took the journey to Italy alone, but for one maid and a butler to look after the luggage. She quickly learned as much of the language as would be needed to entertain the many friends she made, never begrudged hospitality to English visitors who might once have looked down on her, and joyously received occasional visits from her grandchildren once they had grown out of babyhood and could be trusted not to break anything valuable.

'You're late,' Gertrude greeted her brother, pinning her hat on her upswept hair as she gazed into the hall mirror. She was dressed plainly as usual; she had no truck with fashion, though she liked to look well and today was wearing a dark green fitted two-piece gown with a slight bustle and matching high-necked jacket.

'I don't think so,' Roland replied; he was given the same greeting on every visit and each time made the same bland riposte, which she ignored. He and Gertrude had always played cat and mouse; she was the elder by three years and had always considered herself the equal of Roland and the superior of Albert, who was not only younger but also less able to find a suitable response to her mercury-like tongue.

She gave directives to her housekeeper as the woman opened the door for them with a discreet smile of appreciation to Roland as he escorted her mistress down the steps towards the chaise, and he thought that she must look forward to this one afternoon every month when she and the cook could put their feet up and have a few easy hours to themselves once she had given the daily maid the afternoon off.

'Hah,' Gertrude remonstrated as he helped her into the chaise. 'I don't know why you like this carriage so much. The brougham is much more comfortable.'

'It's very well sprung,' he retaliated as he walked round and climbed up into the driving seat. 'The old brougham is very creaky nowadays. We've had it a long time. But Sam will drive you back in it as he usually does.'

'Hmm,' she sighed. 'He's inclined to drive more slowly than you do – not quite so dashing.'

'I've not been called *dashing* in a lot of years. If only it were so!' He grinned, and Gertrude arched her eyebrows at him.

'Too late now,' she said. 'You took too long grieving; you'll need to marry off all your daughters first before thinking of *dashing* anywhere. Still, you'll have all female eyes upon you once you are without dependants; and that might not be so far away. Martha has her eighteenth birthday coming up next month; she'll be of an age to prepare for marriage.'

'But she won't!' he said. 'Matty won't leave her sisters. She's their rock. They'd be adrift without her influence.'

'Julia, then. She'll soon be sixteen and then you can start looking.'

'I don't understand you, Gertrude. Why would I marry off my daughters just so that I can marry again? I don't want another wife. I had the perfect one and no one will replace her. *You* chose not to marry; perhaps the girls will do the same.'

Gertrude gave a chuckle. 'I chose independence,' she said. 'I knew Mama wouldn't stay long in Hull. She had tasted life in Italy when Papa bought the villa and she fitted in well with the free and easy lifestyle. I'm satisfied with my genteel life in Hull, although I often think of our childhood in Beverley. We were given more freedom than many of our contemporaries.'

She was silent for a few miles and then said, 'And in any case, I haven't met anyone with whom I want to share my life or my fortune.' She turned to him and he reflected that she never looked at the countryside, but always wanted to talk; he wondered if perhaps she was sometimes lonely. 'I suppose you've made adequate provision for your daughters in the event of your early demise?' she asked. 'After all, the Beverley property is entailed; you can't leave it to them.'

He muttered beneath his breath and she interrupted, saying caustically, 'Our father died before his time, so don't think it can't happen to you! If it did, Albert would most definitely want the house and then his scatterbrained son Ralph would have it after him.'

'I know, I know,' he said testily. 'There's nothing I can do about that, but the girls are provided for.'

His daughters each had a settlement, but his sister was right: they wouldn't have property, and if his brother and his wife weren't willing to allow them to stay in the house after they moved in, where else would they live? With Gertrude? They wouldn't like that. With his mother, their grandmother, in Italy? *She* wouldn't like that. Constance's parents had taken themselves off to live in a cottage in the Dales or somewhere, but the girls didn't really know their maternal grandparents, and in any case their house was too small to take them all, and they wouldn't like to be separated.

Then there was Louisa, his sister-in-law in Scarborough, in her rambling old house which they all loved and visited twice a year for a month at a time. She would always watch over them.

He brushed away the very idea. How ridiculous. It wasn't going to happen. He was only forty-three. He was in his prime.

CHAPTER SIX

Matty and Faith were waiting at the door as the chaise drew up. Although they were too young to wear crinolines or hooped skirts both were dressed in their prettiest muslin gowns with several stiffened petticoats beneath them and lacy shawls draped about their shoulders. Matty's patterned gown was strewn with pale pink flowers and ribbons, and Faith's similarly scattered with light green leaves and closed white buds reminiscent of snowdrops. Matty's hair was dressed in a chignon beneath a lace cap and showed tendrils of curls on her cheeks, whilst her sister's was looped into a loose braid.

They ran down the steps to greet their aunt. 'So lovely to see you, Aunt Gertrude.' Matty dipped her knee and kissed their guest on the cheek.

Faith too dipped her knee and put her face up to receive her aunt's perfunctory peck. For as long as she could remember Aunt Gertrude was always the one who offered the token of affection, rather than the other way round; Faith had decided when she was a child that her aunt didn't like to be kissed, but as she grew older she started to believe that perhaps it was only from her that Aunt Gertrude didn't like to receive a caress, in case she caught some malady.

It didn't bother or offend her; she had been an amiable child and merely supposed that her aunt was being cautious. She was old, of course, at least three years older than Papa, and might therefore be vulnerable to illness, although it was noticeable too that her sisters had never caught her colds or ailments and they'd sat by her bedside and kissed and hugged her often.

'Where are your sisters?' Gertrude asked the pair. 'Are they not here to greet me?'

'Just coming, Aunt,' they chorused, and on cue Julia appeared, dressed in mid-blue under a grey silk shawl and a bonnet on her dark hair, a complete contrast to her sisters. She was carrying a small posy of mimosa and hypericum, and Matty glanced sideways at Faith; she knew that Faith had picked the flowers from the garden only that morning to place on the dining table, and now Julia had filched them.

Julia presented them to her aunt, thus avoiding having to kiss her as she dipped her knee and said, 'So lovely to see you, Aunt Gertrude. It seems an age since you were last here.'

'Thank you, dear,' her aunt murmured. 'How very kind, but it is only a month.' She handed the flowers back. 'Be so good as to put them in water for me, would you? I'll take them home with me.'

They all smiled and nodded, and knew that she would forget. 'I'll put them on the luncheon table,' Julia said demurely. 'Then you can see them whilst we are eating.'

'Look after your aunt whilst I drive round to Sam,' their father interrupted. 'And make sure that Nunny has brought out the sherry decanter and glasses.'

'She's done so already, Papa,' Matty said to his back as he climbed into the chaise. 'She never forgets,' and tucking her hand through Aunt Gertrude's arm she led her into the house, where Nunny had already poured a sherry and placed the glass on a side table set by the visitor's chair.

'Are you keeping well, Miss Maddeson?' she enquired. 'We've got off quite lightly this winter, have we not? March wasn't bad at all, although I admit February was rather cold. You didn't visit us that month, as I recall.'

'I did not.' Gertrude took a sip of sherry. 'I don't care for the month of February and I barely leave the house. Such a damp, dreary month.'

'It is indeed, I quite agree,' Nunny answered. She mostly agreed with this particular visitor, since the alternative suggestion or theory she had occasionally been known to offer was rarely acknowledged.

'Is this the same sherry as usual, Mrs Nunnington? It seems to have a different bouquet from the one my son generally keeps.'

'It's from the same cellar, ma'am, although whether it's a different grape or year I wouldn't know. The master will be able to tell you.' The housekeeper dropped a curtsey. 'Will you excuse me?'

Aunt Gertrude humphed and sat back in the chair. 'I believe there is a niece missing. Where is the young sprite?'

'We've sent the military to look for her, Aunt,' Matty said placatingly. 'She's probably lost a hair ribbon and is looking for another to replace it.'

They heard a whispered commentary coming from the stairs and then running feet and scampering paws, and the three sisters slid eyes towards each other. Faith half rose from her chair but then sat down again as the door to the sitting room opened and their father came in. He looked at the three of them sitting so innocently and shook a finger at each of them in turn.

'So who was going to tell me about a dog in the house?'

Matty parted her lips, although she had no answer to give, but the sound of yapping stopped her in any case. She glanced at Faith, and then Julia, who shook her head and remarked, 'It sounds like a young puppy, Papa.'

'It is,' he said. 'It's racing up and down the stairs and Becca is trying to catch it. Where has it come from?'

'I believe that Becca saved it from drowning, Papa,' Faith offered.

'And it followed her home,' Julia added. 'That's what . . . I understand.'

'Drowning! Please don't tell me that Becca has been down to the Beck?'

'Oh, I don't think so, Papa,' Julia quickly responded. 'She wouldn't go so far on her own. Perhaps one of Westwood ponds.' She felt that she was digging her own hole in the ground and was about to fall into it.

'No,' Faith butted in. 'One of the stable lads told her that it was going to be drowned if a home wasn't found for it, and – well, Becca is so soft-hearted . . .'

'It must be all of six months old!' their father admonished. 'It wouldn't be drowned at that age.'

He was stopped from saying more by the door's being pushed wide open by the pup, who greeted them all in turn with much wagging of his tail and many licks until, stopping in front of Aunt Gertrude, much to her alarm, he put his front paws on her knees.

'I'm so sorry.' Becca followed him in. 'I tried to stop him but I couldn't catch him. He thought we were playing a game.'

Her sisters were bursting with laughter and trying to contain it, and even their father had his lips pressed tightly together at the sight of Aunt Gertrude leaning back in her chair with the glass of sherry held high in one hand as the pup tried to climb up on her knee.

'He likes you, Aunt Gertrude,' Becca said innocently. 'He won't sit on my knee, even though I'd like him to.'

'Well, I don't want him on my knee, thank you, so please take him away,' their aunt said. 'I'm not overly fond of dogs.'

Their father raised a forefinger again. 'You can keep him, Becca,' he said, and Becca's eyes lit up as she began to smile. 'But not in the house. You must find a place for him outside until he's house-trained.'

Becca started to pout and her father went on hurriedly, 'He's probably used to being outside anyway, so he won't mind. What's his name?'

'Pug,' Becca said, appeased. At least she could keep him, and she thought that when he was trained perhaps he could come in and sleep on her bed.

'Pug!' Aunt Gertrude sat forward. 'What a ridiculous name! Call him Rover or something doglike.' The pup cocked an ear at her again.

'He doesn't look like a Rover to me,' her brother said. 'He's a mixture of breeds, I think.'

Aunt Gertrude sighed, bored with the conversation. 'Well, I don't know. Something commonplace like Charlie, then.'

Pug looked at her again and woofed loudly, as if in disapproval. Becca, sensing that it might be wise to move him now before her father changed his mind, clicked her fingers and said 'Come on', and obediently the pup followed her out of the room.

'You see how it is,' Roland sighed to his sister. 'All the difficulties I have in bringing up four daughters?'

Aunt Gertrude glanced sceptically at him. 'If these are the worst of your troubles' – she turned to look at the three remaining girls sitting quietly with their hands clasped on their laps as if they were the most obedient of females – 'I think you have little to concern you.' She glanced from one to another, murmured 'They're good girls on the whole', and, tipping her head back, drained her sherry glass.

'That was quite a compliment,' Matty murmured to Julia after luncheon as Faith led their aunt to the garden to show her the early blossom on the old apple tree and the primroses beneath it. Becca had followed them out of the house but then disappeared in the direction of the stable, where she had left Pug.

'Yes. I wonder what prompted that? Were we on especially good behaviour?' The girls had removed the last of the condiments from the table and were now folding the tablecloth ready for Nunny to put in the laundry basket.

Their father had come in as Julia was speaking and had caught the end of the conversation. 'No,' he said. 'You are growing up and learning how young women should behave.'

He smiled at them. 'You have inherited your mother's sense of grace and decorum.'

Matty returned his smile, but Julia didn't. It was as if she hadn't heard his comment. She turned and picked up the tongs from the hearth to take a lump of coal from the scuttle and place it on the fire. The maid had prepared the grate first thing that morning, as instructed by Nunny; Miss Maddeson, she'd been told, felt the cold.

'We'll go upstairs,' Roland said. 'It's warmer up there and there's a good fire. When Faith brings your aunt back in, there's something I'd like to discuss with you. About Italy,' he added. 'And your grandmama.'

'Are we going to visit her?' Julia's eyes brightened, but Matty's did not; she breathed in, looking anxious.

He nodded. 'Yes, but we'll wait for Faith and Becca to discuss it. And your aunt.' It was a palpable afterthought.

'You don't think that Aunt Gertrude will want to come?' Julia questioned. 'She hasn't been in a long time.'

'I know.' Their father gazed at them both. 'All the more reason why she should; Grandmama is almost seventy. One of us should visit her. Your uncle Fisher goes more frequently.'

Their father's brother had been christened Albert Fisher Maddeson after relatives from each side of the family, but when Queen Victoria married Prince Albert he announced that he no longer wished to be called Albert, as every commoner in the land would now be given the same name. In future he was to be known as Fisher Maddeson. His doting mother said he could be called anything he wished, and didn't seem to notice the slight on the uncle after whom he had been named. His sister Gertrude continued to address him as Albert.

Julia disliked Uncle Fisher; neither did she care for his wife Caroline or their children, their cousins Ralph and Rosalind. Fortunately, because they were both younger than she was, nearer Becca's age, she could ignore them whenever she felt it appropriate to do so.

'It's still a little chilly,' Aunt Gertrude said, shivering slightly as she came in with Faith. 'There's not much heat in the sun.'

Matty and Julia both rose from their seats. 'We'll go upstairs, Aunt,' Matty said, taking her arm to lead her out of the room and up the stairs to the larger of the two sitting rooms. Their father claimed the smaller one as his own when he wanted to sit quietly and read his newspapers.

'Where's Becca?' he asked Faith as they followed the other three upstairs. 'Is she coming in?'

'I think so, Papa.' In the sitting room Faith took the chair opposite Aunt Gertrude and smiled her thanks to Matty who had left it for her, closest to the fire. 'She was chasing after the puppy, but said she wouldn't be a minute.'

'All right, we'll start without her.' Roland sat on one of the small sofas and Matty sat next to him, while Julia sat sideways on the wide windowsill where she could see both the green pastureland of Hurn and the racecourse as well as the occupants of the room. 'I wanted to ask all of you if you'd like to visit Italy and see your grandmother, and celebrate Matty's eighteenth birthday at the same time? It won't be too hot in May and we could perhaps spend a month there; we could rent a villa so as not to disturb your grandmama too much. What do you think? Matty? Gertrude?'

'Were you thinking of including me?' His sister seemed alarmed. 'I don't think so! It will be far too hot for me; you know I can't stand the heat.'

'That's why I suggested we travel in May,' he said patiently, and was about to say more when Becca burst into the room.

'Sorry,' she said breathlessly. 'Pug had got out. He was heading back towards Westwood and the stables but I managed to catch him.'

'You'll have to tie him up, Becca,' her father told her. 'If he goes near the cattle he could cause havoc. Sit down, please.'

She sat cross-legged on the rug with her skirts pulled down to her ankles and glanced guiltily at Aunt Gertrude, who was shaking her head at her.

'I was asking everyone if they'd like to visit Grandmama in Italy and celebrate Matty's eighteenth birthday whilst we're there,' her father repeated.

'Oh!' Becca's eyes lit up. 'Would she mind? Grandmama, I mean? There are quite a lot of us.'

'We'd take a villa close by,' her father told her. 'Then we wouldn't be a nuisance.'

'I couldn't possibly stay for a whole month,' Gertrude cut in. 'Two weeks would be the absolute maximum. I'm far too busy to be away for any longer.'

Her brother sighed. He couldn't imagine what she would be busy doing.

'I'm not sure whether I'd like to be away for my birthday, Papa,' Matty said anxiously. 'I always have it at home.'

She'd feel strange being away, especially on such a special day. It wasn't her coming of age, of course, but nevertheless it meant that she was almost grown up and, as Nunny had told her, would be addressed as Miss Maddeson. Like Aunt Gertrude, she thought.

'Wh-what about Nunny?' she asked. 'She won't want to miss my birthday.'

Her father frowned slightly. 'She won't, will she?' he murmured, and thought that he'd be lost without the housekeeper, the surrogate grandmother who had kept his family on an even keel for so long.

He had taken Matty and Julia to Italy when Matty was ten and Julia eight, then Matty and Faith the following year. Faith loved the warmth and seemed to thrive in the time they were there, but Matty was always happier once they were home again. Becca hadn't been at all, but had been left at home under the care of Nunny.

He considered. 'I suppose we could ask her if she'd like to come.'

'And Cook?' Becca said eagerly. 'She'd want to come and make a birthday cake.'

Breathing out, her father put his head back and said wryly, 'And I suppose you want the housemaid, the laundry woman, the boot boy, Sam, and Uncle Tom Cobley and all?'

Becca gazed open-mouthed at her father. 'Erm – I'd have to ask one of them to look after Pug,' she said. 'I don't suppose we could take him with us.' And then she frowned. 'I didn't know we had an Uncle Tom Cobley. I don't remember him at all.'

Aunt Gertrude intervened. 'Your papa is joking, Rebecca. Tom Cobley is a fictional person. Or I suppose he might be real,' she conceded. 'He's featured in an old Devonshire song.'

Matty gave a wistful half smile. She remembered the song; her mother used to sing it to her sometimes when she was little, and make her laugh as she tried to recall all the characters' names. *Tom Pearse, Tom Pearse, lend me your grey mare.* But she never told me the whole story of Widecombe Fair, and never finished the song, and now I know why, she reminded herself. For I found it for myself, and it has a sad ending, and Mama wouldn't have wanted me to be sad.

'We should go!' she said suddenly, wanting to dispel the image of bouncing on her mother's knee. 'And take Nunny; she would love to come, I'm sure. We could hire a cook, couldn't we, Papa? Grandmama will be sure to know someone.' She thought for a moment. 'Unless we can take a villa with a maid, perhaps we could take Betty with us – although I suppose Nunny might want her to do spring cleaning or something whilst we're away.'

Her father leaned forward and gazed at her. What had suddenly motivated her eagerness to plan when just a minute earlier she'd said she wasn't sure if she wanted to be away on her birthday? Females, he thought; he'd never understand them. Was she missing her mother? Was she thinking that her mama wouldn't be here for her special day and her loss wouldn't be as sharply felt in different surroundings as it would be at home?

But it will be, darling Matty. He felt a lump in his throat as he thought of his own grief and the difficulties of coming to terms with it. It will, my dearest girl, and I understand completely.

CHAPTER SEVEN

When finally they were in agreement, Matty suggested that they should bring Nunny in to put the idea to her. She didn't usually come with them on holiday, but this year, with Matty's birthday celebration imminent, it seemed right to ask her to share it with them.

After an initial hesitation, Nunny said she would be delighted to travel with them. When Miss Maddeson again adamantly refused to stay in Italy for more than two weeks, the housekeeper suggested that she too might stay for the same period, and she and Miss Maddeson could then travel back together whilst the rest of the party stayed on.

'What an *excellent* thought, Mrs Nunnington,' Aunt Gertrude declared. 'One of the reasons I don't go to see my mother very often is because I don't have a trustworthy companion who can see to the tickets and so on.' She waved a nonchalant hand in the air. 'I really can't be bothered with such para-phernalia, and as I know how efficient you are with household detail, I'm sure you will be perfectly able to deal with all the arrangements.'

'Which *I* will make, Gertrude,' Roland broke in, thus reassur-ing his sister, but mainly his housekeeper, who had never in her life travelled abroad, that all would be organized beforehand. It would be a long journey, with several changes of train and carriage on their journey from Italy across France to Le Havre.

'How lovely!' Faith declared. 'We can all look forward to it now. Goodness, it won't be long, will it, if we're to travel in May? Only a month!'

'Time for it to warm up before we leave, then,' said Nunny. 'But be sure to ask your maid to pack a warm coat or cloak, Miss Maddeson.'

'I was too hot last time I was there, but that was during July,' Aunt Gertrude replied, 'but yes, I will. One can't be too careful,' and the three older girls and their father glanced at each other as if agreeing that their aunt and Nunny would get along most suitably.

But April was still rather cold at home. They had occasional bouts of sleet and rain; their father told them that he had read there had been snow in Ireland, and they had all heard of last year's earthquakes in Scandinavia, Hungary and Italy.

'I hope we don't fall into a great crevice, then,' Becca responded. 'Do you think there'll still be snow on top of the mountains when we're in Italy, Papa? That would be strange, wouldn't it, sunshine and snow?'

'There's often snow on the tops even during the summer,' her father told her. 'When I was a young man, before I met your mother, a friend and I travelled to Switzerland; the heat was wonderful, but we scaled the heights and found snow. The snow had been so deep during the winter that it hadn't melted in spite of the sun.'

Becca jumped up. 'I'm going to look through my wardrobe now. I think I might need some more clothes.'

Her father reminded her that Aunt Gertrude was here to visit them, and she could perhaps do that later, so she sat down again.

'Let's make notes of what we might need,' Faith suggested, seeing Becca beginning to pout, and got up to fetch pencil and paper. 'Aunt Gertrude will need a warm coat, but a sun hat as well . . .'

She licked the end of the pencil, and Nunny smiled, bobbed her knee to Miss Maddeson, and withdrew from the room.

She knew what she had to do before thinking of what to wear, and that was to draw up instructions to leave the household staff for jobs to be done whilst she was away.

She would ask Betty Brown to take down all the curtains, the muslin ones to be washed, the heavy brocades and velvets to be put out on the washing line to be beaten with the carpet beater until all dust was removed. The rugs must be taken up to be given the same treatment and floors washed or polished. Windows and paintwork to be washed down with soda crystals and soft soap before the clean curtains were put up again. Silver and copper to be given an extra special clean and polish – the scullery maid can do that, she mused – and furniture to be polished and buffed.

Hmm, she thought. I'll be quite sorry to miss that, for I love to see everything shiny and clean after all the effort. Still, I'll inspect it thoroughly on my return and perhaps bring everyone little presents back from my travels.

Matty was wondering if she would have to organize her own birthday celebration. She and Nunny had always arranged her sisters' birthday parties; they enjoyed planning the games they would play, finding suitable piano music for musical chairs, and deciding on the food they would eat and whom they would invite. Matty always felt that it was polite to invite their cousins, Ralph and Rosalind, but they didn't always attend, their mother usually giving some excuse or other, and rarely were the sisters invited to their home. Matty could never understand why.

But, she thought, it would be different this year. She wondered if their grandmother would want her to have the celebration in her villa; certainly there would be plenty of room for guests. Then she thought of her own and her sisters' friends: would they be able to come? Eliza and Adam Chapman had always shared celebrations with them; Eliza was really Julia's closest friend, but they had all known each other since early childhood.

Then there was Sybil, who had been Matty's best friend until she went off to boarding school and would write to say how much she hated it. I don't suppose she will be allowed to come; her parents wouldn't let her travel even with a maid. Then there's Dorcas. Perhaps if her brother Timothy could accompany her? She thought that Dorcas's father, Mr Garton, would allow that if Timothy were willing. But he was already twenty-two and studying law. He might not be free, but perhaps Dorcas could travel with us. I must ask Papa. She looked up to find that her father was already smiling at her.

'Something troubling you, Matty?' he asked.

'Not exactly,' she murmured. 'But I was wondering about the friends we have always shared our birthdays with; would they be able to come?'

Her father pursed his lips and nodded. 'That's why I suggested we have our own villa; we can't possibly expect your grandmama to have everyone to stay. But if we have our own, then you can invite whoever you like, and I was thinking that you might like to ask your aunt Louisa to join us. She would be a suitable companion for any young lady who might like to come without her mama!'

Matty clasped her hands together. 'Oh, yes! Aunt Louisa must come.' She caught sight of Aunt Gertrude's tight-lipped expression, and added, 'Because while you are with us, Aunt Gertrude, my friends' parents will be assured that they are safe, and then when you leave Aunt Louisa will still be there. I must write to everyone at once,' she went on eagerly. 'We have so little time.'

That was true; Roland was beginning to wonder whether to use an agent to make the arrangements for travelling as well as finding a villa. The foreign excursions arranged by Mr Thomas Cook were proving successful with his customers and other agencies were now following suit, booking not only travel but also accommodation, in this country as well as abroad, for those who wanted both.

Roland didn't know of such an agency in Beverley, but there surely would be one in Hull or York; I must ask about, he thought. Such an opportunity for some enterprising well-travelled person, for more people are beginning to venture further, to discover other countries as well as places in their own country that they may never have seen. Even some employers were hiring charabancs to take their work-force and their wives and children out for a day at the seaside, somewhere they perhaps would never have been able to visit for themselves. The world is changing, he thought, and Prince Albert had a hand in it when he designed the Great Exhibition.

Roland had been to the opening of the exhibition the year before and had marvelled at the exhibits brought from across the world as well as those which showed with great pride just what Great Britain, at the forefront of industry, could do in the world of engineering and science.

He had told his daughters what he had seen and described the enormous glass palace that had surrounded the exhibits, the trees and shrubs in the giant glasshouses; he had recognized the wonder in their eyes as he talked and wished then that he had taken at least one of them to see it. I could have taken Matty, he thought now. Why didn't I?

He forgot sometimes how his daughters were growing up, but with Matty's eighteenth birthday coming up so fast he reminded himself again that he must plan their futures.

'Papa! Papa! Where are you?' Faith said urgently. 'Come back. I'm making a list of the friends we might bring if they're allowed. How many can we accommodate? How many rooms will we have in the villa?'

'Ask them first,' he suggested, coming out of his reverie. 'When we know who's coming we can plan accommodation.' He wrinkled his brow. 'I think it will be best if they make their own travel arrangements. I can't be responsible for them all. Tell them I'm probably going to use an agent to arrange the travel, and perhaps they would like to do the same.'

He had no doubt that all the parents could afford to let their children travel to Italy – they were professional people or farmers and land owners, after all – but whether they would be willing to spend their income on what some of them might think a frivolous birthday party abroad when one at home would be less expensive was another matter. He, on the other hand, felt that this celebration for his eldest daughter would mark a very important occasion; somehow he wanted to make up to all his girls, but Matty in particular, with a longer memory of their mother, for being deprived of her love.

Matty wanted to invite their aunt Louisa more than anyone else; the occasion wouldn't seem so special if she were not there. She had a special bond with her, not only because she looked like Constance – although Matty's impressions of her mother's appearance were fading – but because Aunt Louisa was full of fun and yet would enter into serious discussions too, and there was not a single subject on which she couldn't be asked for her opinion or advice.

I'll write to her later this afternoon, she thought, once Aunt Gertrude has left for home. She had often seen the tightening of lips and twitch of her maiden aunt's nose when Louisa's name was mentioned, as if she didn't wholly approve of the connection. Matty was above all very receptive to others' sensibilities and would hate to upset the feelings of anyone, least of all Aunt Gertrude.

'Julia?' Matty gazed at her sister. 'You're very quiet. What are your thoughts?'

Julia took a deep breath and turned her gaze towards the window, avoiding looking at anyone directly. '*My* thoughts! My thoughts, if anyone is sufficiently interested' – she was suffering a fit of pique and her voice cracked slightly as she went on – 'are that no one has given any consideration to the fact that I too will be having a birthday, *before* Matty has hers.'

There was a sudden silence, broken by Faith. 'That is simply not true, Julia.' She got up from her chair and knelt at her sister's feet. 'If I were to show you my sewing basket it would completely spoil the surprise that is hidden in there, especially for you.'

44

Matty broke in to say that she too had something hidden away, whilst Aunt Gertrude leaned to reach into her capacious handbag and withdrew a brown envelope. 'I was going to leave this before I left, my dear, for you to open on your birthday, in case I couldn't come for any reason, but you may open it now if you wish.'

A tear slipped down Julia's cheek; she had been so sure that they had forgotten her in the excitement of planning Matty's party.

'How could we forget, Julia?' Matty whispered, and Julia saw that she was really distressed that she could ever think it.

'Sorry,' she murmured. 'I'm so sorry for doubting you.'

Her father got up from his chair and came to drop a kiss on the top of her head. 'As if any of my lovely daughters could be forgotten!' He blinked, suddenly consumed by a great sense of loss and regret. 'You are all so precious to me. My life would be worthless without any one of you.'

CHAPTER EIGHT

Louisa Walton woke early, as she often did, slipped out of bed and into her pale cream peignoir and walked barefoot to the window. She gave a shiver. It was cooler this morning with a hint of ground mist lingering, and perhaps, she thought, it was not yet warm enough to be wearing silk.

The negligee had been a present from her late husband, Arnold, who always insisted that she wear it whatever the weather. Now she could please herself what she wore, and usually she chose something warm and comfortable, but from some slight persistent sense of regret she occasionally wore the pretty garment, if only in the summer months.

The herring gulls had wakened her with their noisy screeching cries. There were two nesting pairs in the gutter below the roof, and sometimes they would squabble over a snatched piece of fish or some discarded bread that would be considered a tasty morsel for a hungry chick and feathers would fly. She often collected these feathers if they flew to the ground, and dipped the clean ones into the juice of beetroot, raspberries or blackcurrants, dried them and combed them and used them to decorate a hat. She had a flair for fashion and liked to be creative.

She had chosen this attic room after she had become widowed, and allowed her housekeeper, Mrs Birch, who used to sleep there, to use the room alongside the kitchen. It had formerly been the butler's pantry, but as Louisa hadn't any use for a butler it had been converted into a sitting room cum bedroom. Mrs Birch was delighted, as it was warmer than the attic and she no longer had to trail all the way to the top of the stairs. Louisa brought in a handyman to knock through the wall into the other small attic room and fit a larger grate, and now she used it as a bedroom and cosy sitting room for her own use only. When she had visitors, which was often, as she liked to entertain, she invited them into the drawing room on the first floor, and those staying overnight, such as her nieces, slept in the bedrooms between.

It is my house again. She had breathed a sigh of pleasure when the renovations were finished, for she and her sister Constance had been brought up here in this tall house in Scarborough and when they had both married and their parents moved to the Yorkshire Dales Louisa had persuaded her husband to buy back the family home, which became hers after his death.

She sat now in the window seat, sipping on water and looking out at the view across Castle Road to St Mary's church, over the ancient graveyard and beyond, down to the rooftops of St Sepulchre and the boat builders' yards. If she had been up early enough she would have seen the fishermen trundling their boats down the hill towards the Sandside cottages, workshops and slipway. She never tired of the view of the lighthouse and harbour, and if she tilted her head sideways she could see almost to the top of the hill, and the entrance to the castle where she and Constance had played on the crumbling ancient walls which still stood proudly watching over the headland.

Sometimes the girls would slip out during an afternoon after lessons, when their parents weren't looking or were entertaining, and as long as they were not late coming back in no one seemed to notice they hadn't been playing indoors, except perhaps the young maid, who would wink at them but never ever told on them.

She heard the rattle of the letter box as the postman dropped in the morning post, and changing into a warmer dressing gown she slipped downstairs to collect it.

'I was about to bring you a pot o' tea, ma'am.' Mrs Birch greeted her at the bottom of the stairs, with a tray in her hands.

'I'll take it up,' Louisa said. 'Just wait there a minute whilst I collect the post.' Side-stepping the housekeeper, she crossed the hall to pick up the single letter from the letter box behind the door and smiled as she glanced at the postmark.

'Don't scald yourself, ma'am,' Mrs Birch murmured in her North Yorkshire accent. 'I've only just mashed the tea so it's red hot.'

'Good.' Louisa put the letter in her pocket and took the tray. 'Just as I like it. You go and enjoy yours too, Mrs Birch. We're both up early.'

In her room, she placed the tray on a small table by the window, gathered up a blanket from the top of the ottoman to put over her knees, and sat down to pour her tea. Bliss, she thought as she sipped and gazed again at the view. I'm so very lucky. She made herself bring that thought to mind every morning. She had her own house, an income to sustain her although it wasn't excessive, many enduring friends and the family of her much missed sister; true, she had a widow's status and at thirty-six years old was considered by some to still be a marriageable prospect, but the widowers who had shown an interest were twice her age and had nothing to offer her but the opportunity of being available to look after them in their declining years. When she was young there had been only one man she had held a candle for, or felt she might have loved, but he was totally unobtainable, even now, many years on. Now, she considered Roland to be a loving friend.

Her marriage had been adequate, but not exciting; Arnold Walton had asked her father for her hand in marriage and it had been settled between them before she had been aware of any interest. She had met him twice at the home of a friend of her parents, and when told of the proposal had difficulty in bringing him to mind, but agreed to meet him. He was pleasant enough, and as the man of her choice would never be available she decided to settle for second best.

She finished her first cup of tea and opened the envelope before pouring another, sitting up straighter as she read the letter. Well, here's a thing! How lovely that dear Matty wants me there. What an absolute treat! She read on: her brother-in-law was booking a villa through an excursion agency – mmm, she pondered – and the girls' aunt Gertrude had agreed to join them. Well, I won't be put off by that, although I always suspect that she doesn't quite approve of me. Louisa gave a little laugh. I can't think why.

There was nothing in her diary that couldn't be changed, but in any case she was extremely fond of Matty and her sisters and they would always come before anything or anyone else. Poor Roland, she thought, having to arrange what would have been Constance's joy: making sure everything was just right for her eldest daughter's birthday. I hope he isn't considering marriage prospects for her yet. She is so young; she needs freedom before she thinks of tying herself in marriage. Perhaps I'll write to him and offer to arrange a party before either his mother or Gertrude does.

She knew Roland's mother and liked her; she was jolly and kind but totally impulsive, unrestrained and capricious, and might want to take over. So strange, she mused, that Gertrude is so unlike her. She began planning in her head what kind of birthday party Matty would like. It would be so much easier to arrange in a separate villa, with much more freedom than if they used their grandmother's house, and especially if, as Matty had said, some of her English friends were able to come over too. I could offer to escort them, she supposed, if their parents don't want to or can't travel.

She was so busy making plans that at first she didn't notice a man on the other side of the road signalling to her, waving both arms from side to side. A dog stood at his heel. Stephen! She leaned over and opened the window.

'Are you deaf and blind?' he called. 'I've been standing here waving like a madman this last half hour.'

'Liar,' she called back. 'No, you haven't.'

'Ten minutes then. Five maybe. I'll be round later. Your grass needs a trim.'

'All right,' she said. 'I'm not going out.'

Smiling, she waved back and closed the window. Stephen Nielsen. Her immediate neighbour and good friend never failed to make her smile. He wasn't a gardener, but he liked gardening, and when he ran out of things to do in his own garden he came and did hers, turning up from time to time with a shrub, a rose tree or bulbs that he knew just the place to plant in her garden so they would grow and flourish and withstand the brunt of the coastal winds; and generally they did, bringing colour and fragrance to her garden, which she loved.

So, too, did he fix things that would normally require a workman: a broken lock, an unsafe shelf, a curtain rail that she couldn't reach; and he noticed things that needed attention which she would ignore, hoping they would go away until she had time to do something about them. It wasn't that she was lazy, it was because there were more interesting things to do, such as the drawing and painting she began when the mood took her and which she had to complete before she lost the urge or the inspiration.

To compensate him, for he would have been affronted if she had given him a gift in return, she would give her cook the night off and prepare dinner for the two of them, something simple and delicious and always accompanied by a good bottle of wine or two; afterwards they would sit by her fire with a tot of the best brandy or liqueur in conversation or companionable silence.

One evening she had returned from the kitchen after making coffee to find him fast asleep in his chair. She silently put down the tray and gazed at him; she had once asked him why he had never married, but didn't get a satisfactory answer. He would make someone an excellent husband, warm and companionable, knowledgeable on so many subjects yet never boring in discussion, and handsome too, with dark curly hair streaked with a few strands of grey, a neatly trimmed beard and a ready smile. Those ideals were a necessity for some women, not that they were for her, she had thought, turning away her eyes as he started to stir, and began to pour the coffee.

There would, of course, be much talk if it were ever discovered that she had entertained a man alone in her home, but she gave not a fig for idle gossip and as far as she knew neither he nor her housekeeper had ever whispered a word. He was a friend of many years, after all, and had been a frequent visitor even before her husband had died, as well as a source of great support when he did.

When he called in later in the day, she told him of Matty's letter, the proposed visit to Italy and the party.

'Will you go?' he asked.

'Most certainly,' she said. 'I wouldn't miss it for anything. I love those girls as if they were my own, and especially Matty. I remember how brave she was when my sister died. How she gathered her sisters together and took care of them, trying to be the little mother when she was a mere child herself.'

She swallowed hard, holding back her own tears, and thought of her parents. They hadn't come until the day of their elder daughter's funeral, her mother writing a note to Louisa saying she was too upset to travel. She brushed away the memory, which still irked her, even after so long. 'Besides,' she said thickly. 'Who could possibly miss a party by the side of Lake Maggiore? If you're travelling abroad, Stephen, perhaps you might call in? You know my nieces.'

He nodded, giving her a gentle smile. 'I do,' he murmured. 'Most charming. I had thought of visiting Switzerland this year, so perhaps that offer might spur me on to make my travel plans and arrange a detour.'

'That would be lovely,' she said. 'I'll write to Matty and Roland today. But we will be going soon. Her birthday is in May.'

He nodded solemnly. 'I can rearrange my plans. I have no difficulty with that.'

CHAPTER NINE

Julia said she would like to go out to tea for her birthday; their father packed them all into the brougham and drove them into Hull to a teashop near the Market Place which they had visited before. It was close by the Holy Trinity church, so they went inside and lit a candle for their mother.

Matty took Julia's arm when they came out and tucked it into hers. Intuitive as she always was, she had noticed that Julia had become withdrawn. It was a warm, sunny day and Matty had suggested that they should stroll as far as the pier; the estuary waters were high and were drenching everyone who stood close to the edge and children were running back and forth, escaping or not the chance of a soaking.

Many people were out making the most of the sunshine; gentlemen tipped their hats as they passed and their ladies smilingly acknowledged the handsome gentleman with the group of pretty daughters as they walked back again towards the long shopping street of Whitefriargate.

There were many fine shops here. Julia saw a pretty scarf that she craved, so her father took her inside to look at it and bought it for her whilst her sisters waited outside; when they came out Matty noticed that Julia's dark mood had disappeared, or at least wasn't so obvious.

The weeks soon passed. Roland had found an excursion agent in York who booked their first class train tickets from

Hull to London and then on to Dover. From there two cab-riolets were reserved to take them to the port, where their luggage would be taken on board the ferry; they would also be meeting Eliza and Adam Chapman and Matty's friend Dorcas, who was travelling with them. Tables were reserved for the whole party to eat dinner in the dining saloon, and shared cabins would be prepared for them to rest in overnight dur-ing the crossing to Le Havre.

'Roland,' Gertrude muttered during their final luncheon before setting off on their journey, 'this must be costing you a fortune. You have booked first class?' She pinched her lips together. 'Of course, I will pay for my own passage, and I have already arranged for my regular cabbie to pick me up from home and take me to the railway station. I could really do with Mrs Nunnington to help me, but I suppose she'll be busy here?'

'She will,' Roland said firmly, knowing full well that his sis-ter's own housekeeper was perfectly capable of packing her trunks, and that he would be taking care of her tickets along with everyone else's. 'We'll meet you at Paragon railway sta-tion and a porter will load all our trunks in the luggage com-partment, so we'll have nothing to do, even at King's Cross. Of course we have two changes to make, but everything will be taken care of all the way to the ferry at Dover.'

'Oh, no!' Gertrude protested. 'I want my luggage in the railway carriage with me where I can see it. Otherwise it might be put on the wrong ship.'

'It will not,' Roland insisted. 'Everything will be clearly marked. Look.' He got up from the table and went to the man-telshelf. 'Here are your luggage labels; they have your name and destination clearly written on them. Matty has done them, and very neatly too. There won't be room for any luggage in the compartment.'

His sister humphed her disapproval, but having examined the labels couldn't think of a further rejoinder and said, reluc-tantly, 'Thank you, Martha. Well done. I'll make sure they are firmly fastened on.'

Matty was very excited about the impending journey and the holiday party. She and Julia had endless discussions about what gowns and accessories they would take, and asked Faith what she would like to wear. Faith liked soft, comfortable, plain dresses; at thirteen she wasn't thus far interested in fashionable clothes, and yet she managed to look graceful in whatever she wore.

But then they realized that she too would be having a birthday whilst they were away, so she must take her prettiest gown, even though she insisted she didn't want a fuss; this was to be Matty's special time. Finally, the three of them decided that they would choose what Becca should take with her and make sure everything was clean and pressed, for otherwise she would push all her favourite old clothes she wore for helping out at the stables into her portmanteau.

Matty was particularly happy that Dorcas Garton, whose brother Timothy couldn't take time out from his studies to join them, had been given permission to travel with the Chapmans, who were sufficiently experienced travellers to be allowed to journey without an adult escort. Adam was almost eighteen and after the summer break hoped to be going away to university, so he was looking forward to this chance of a holiday abroad before leaving home to continue his education.

Matty had not yet received a reply from Sybil, and feared that she wouldn't be allowed to come with them. She was sad about it, knowing how unhappy her friend was at boarding school; Sybil had also said in an earlier letter that when she finished school at eighteen, only a few months away, she would be sent to a finishing school in France, and she didn't want to do that either as her French was practically non-existent and she was sure she would only be laughed at.

Matty sighed. It was such a pity, but there was nothing she could do about it, except to write to Sybil giving her their address in Stresa, in case at the last minute her parents agreed that she could join them. She also wrote to her grandmother to say how much they were all looking forward to seeing her again.

Aunt Louisa arrived on the day before departure, having come on the train from Scarborough, and said how thrilled she was to be going with them.

'I am too,' Matty told her. 'The agent has written to us and explained about the villa, which will be more than big enough for all of us, and we have lovely gardens which overlook Lago Maggiore.' She took a breath, and Louisa smiled at her enthusiasm. 'And seemingly from the top floor of the villa there's a view of Isola Bella. I went there when I was a child when we visited Grandmama, and I can remember the flowers and the statues in the palace gardens.'

'I've never been,' Louisa remarked. 'I shall look forward to seeing it. It's one of three islands, isn't it? The Borromean Islands?'

Matty nodded and bent her head to her aunt's. 'I'm going to ask Papa if we might have a private visit,' she whispered, 'seeing as there're so many of us. I'm looking forward to showing it to Nunny. She won't have seen anything like it in her life!'

Louisa thought how lucky her nieces were to have such advantages and no money worries. She and Constance had been quite restricted when they were growing up, their father telling them that Scarborough was as good a place to live as anywhere in the world, and although Constance had no quarrel with that she had always longed to travel abroad.

Unfortunately, her husband Arnold was of the same mindset as her father, and the nearest she ever got to achieving her dream was on her honeymoon, when he arranged a visit to the Isle of Man.

She remembered that the journey to Liverpool to catch the ferry had been long and arduous and she'd been seasick on the short sea crossing. It was beautiful, she agreed, when Arnold told her to buck up, for the scenery was worth the journey, but they never went again, Arnold's preference being Scotland during the shooting season.

Now she was a wealthy widow she could afford to go wherever she wanted, but her women friends were tied to their own husbands and families and it was not considered seemly for a woman to travel without an escort. Even for the journey from home to the railway station in Scarborough, Stephen had insisted on going with her in the hired cabriolet to see her safely on board with her luggage.

'I could have come with you on the train,' he'd remarked as they trundled down the steep hill towards town. 'It would have been no trouble.'

'Thank you, Stephen, but there was really no need,' she'd protested. 'I don't have to change trains, and Roland and Matty will meet me on arrival.'

'And how long will you be away? A month? Will you last that long with all that company? If you want to come home, I can always come and fetch you, you know. You only have to write. I could be there in just a few days.'

Louisa laughed. 'I won't want to shorten my holiday! Why would I? I'm really looking forward to visiting Italy.'

'Yes, of course you are,' he'd murmured. 'Of course you are. Indeed, why wouldn't you?'

'What are you going to be doing? Are you still planning a trip to Switzerland?'

'Mmm, I might.' He'd pursed his lips and nodded nonchalantly. 'I've written to a friend, a single man like me, to ask if he fancies a trip to the Alps. We used to travel together when we were students: walking, climbing, that sort of thing, you know. But the last I heard was that he'd met someone, a young woman, quite a few years younger than him . . .'

His voice tailed away and he didn't finish what he was saying. She'd gently patted his hand. 'You should go anyway, Stephen. It would be good for you, and you might meet a young woman too.'

'I'm nearly forty, Louisa,' he'd said rather abruptly, snatching his hand away and crossing his arms over his chest. 'I'm no longer interested in young women. I like the company of women I can talk to, discuss issues with; who understand my sense of humour as I understand theirs.'

'There'll be someone—' she began.

'As there is for you?' He'd turned towards her with a forced laugh. 'Here's the pan calling the kettle black!'

She'd nodded. He was right, of course, but the conversation had disturbed her, staying with her for the whole of the journey, and she thought he had seemed rather wistful as she waved goodbye, the train pulling away with a hiss of steam and leaving him standing alone on the platform, his hand raised in farewell as if carved in stone.

They were up very early the next morning, and miraculously Mrs Nunnington had organized Cook to prepare a cooked breakfast of bacon, kippers, kidneys and scrambled eggs which were waiting under covered dishes in the dining room.

'Now tuck in,' the housekeeper urged. 'We don't know how long it will be before the next meal.'

Everyone hid a smile and Roland solemnly agreed with Nunny. 'Very true,' he conceded. 'We don't know if there will be a restaurant car . . .'

'That's why I've taken the precaution of packing a hamper.' Nunny wore a complacent look of satisfaction on her face.

Becca looked up from her breakfast. 'The trains travel at fifty miles an hour, Nunny; Mr Lawrence told me that when I said we were going all the way to Dover, and he said that the north-eastern railways were not known for their punctuality.' She cut into her crispy bacon. 'I hope we don't crash into anything.'

Her sisters groaned and their father said, 'Come along, eat up, everybody. You too, Nunny: don't forget that you're coming with us, so go and have a good breakfast yourself. We've got three quarters of an hour before the cabs arrive for the luggage.'

'Oh, my word,' Matty breathed. 'Italy! We're on our way.'

Becca looked across at her sister and bit into a piece of toast. 'Matty?' She chewed and swallowed and wiped a crumb from the corner of her mouth. 'Seeing as you're going to be eighteen in another week, and you're very pretty, do you think you'll fall in love with an Italian man whilst we're there and marry him and live in Italy?'

'Silly goose, of course not,' Matty said, though her cheeks turned pink. 'Whatever made you think that?'

'Well.' Becca paused and put her head to one side. 'I just hoped that you wouldn't, cos I'd miss you if you did.'

CHAPTER TEN

On the ship they divided themselves up. Aunt Gertrude had her own cabin; Aunt Louisa was happy to share with Nunny, who hadn't sailed before and had confessed to being very nervous. Matty shared with Faith, and Julia with Becca, whilst their father had a single cabin further along the corridor. Their friends Eliza and Dorcas shared a cabin and Adam hadn't said where he would be. Faith hadn't invited anyone as she said that it wasn't her birthday, and that she knew Matty's friends in any case.

It wasn't rough but Julia was sick, much to her annoyance, whilst Becca was thrilled when the ship pitched and rolled once they left the harbour; she climbed into her bunk and went to sleep almost immediately.

Louisa couldn't get to sleep, and once Nunny was settled and beginning to snore a little she got out of her bunk, slid her feet into her slippers and put her cape on over her nightgown, draped a shawl over her shoulders and quietly stepped out of the cabin, leaving a nightlight burning safely while she walked along the corridor to the saloon to get herself a tot of brandy.

There were only a few people in there and one of them was Roland, sitting at the bar counter. 'Louisa!' He'd glanced at the lone woman and turned on his stool in surprise at seeing her. 'Are you all right?'

'Yes, perfectly,' she said, pulling her shawl closer to her; not that anyone would have guessed that she was in her night attire, as her cape covered her completely. 'I couldn't sleep, and I thought a brandy might help.'

'I'm sure it will.' He was drinking a glass of red wine and beckoned the barman over to order a brandy. 'Not nervous about sailing, are you?' A little frown pinched the top of his nose.

'No, not a bit, although I have been known to be seasick.' She smiled a little. 'I haven't sailed for a while, apart from on our local tourist steamers, which I do from time to time. I love that; seeing Scarborough from outside the harbour is a different vista entirely. What about you?' She was making conversation and finding it difficult. 'Are you a good sailor?'

'Not bad. I should visit my mother more often than I do; I shouldn't wait for a special occasion such as a birthday.'

'She must miss you,' Louisa murmured as she sipped her brandy. She sighed. 'I don't visit my own parents more than once a year,' she admitted, 'even though it's only as far as the Yorkshire moors. Truth to tell, I'm not sure if they would appreciate it if I did. They have a good social life, especially since my father took up shooting, and last year when I went to stay they insisted I went with them up to the North York moors to visit friends who had arranged a shoot. They and their hosts seemed surprised and not a little offended when I declined the prospect of partaking in a picnic of tea and cake whilst sitting on a blanket watching men kill birds. My father thinks I'm quite mad when I feed the gulls who nest on my roof.'

He nodded vaguely, and she wasn't sure if he were listening until he murmured that he hadn't seen her parents for a long time, and didn't think they were in touch with his daughters very often. He finished his wine and ordered a brandy for himself, raising his eyebrows questioningly at Louisa, who refused another. She would have expected her mother, at least, to keep in touch with her granddaughters, and was mildly shocked to hear that she didn't, although not totally surprised. Both her parents were, she had decided a long time ago, totally self-centred.

'Are you happy with your life, Louisa?' Roland asked suddenly, breaking into her thoughts. He took a sip from the glass that the barman had placed before him. 'Are you content to be living alone? I always thought that you would marry again. It's a while since Arnold died, isn't it?'

She nodded. 'I haven't found anyone with whom I would wish to share my life, although . . .' She hesitated over her confession. 'I would have liked a child. I – I have a good friend; you've met him, my neighbour, Stephen.' Strange, she thought, how I always think of him whenever I'm away. 'We have a companionable relationship without love or marriage getting in the way.' She paused reflectively. 'Besides, I'm in charge of my own life; I can do as I wish without having to consider anyone else.'

'And did you not do that with Arnold?'

'No. He made the decisions, just as my father did and still does with my mother; indeed, Papa still gives *me* the benefit of his advice sometimes. Not that I take it. He and Arnold might occasionally have asked for my opinion, but neither of them actually expected me to have one, or would have listened to it if I did.' She gave a contemplative smile, finished her brandy and slipped down from the stool. 'It's the way married life works.'

Roland stood up and drained his glass too. 'No, not all marriages are like that, Louisa. Ours wasn't, mine and Constance's. We were equal.'

She looked up at him and searched his face. 'Then you were both lucky,' she murmured. The perfect husband, lover and companion? Is that why I never found anyone quite like you? My sister found you first, and poached you from right under my nose. And has the loss of Constance made her seem to have been the perfect wife?

He took her elbow to escort her back, but as she turned she paused, looking in the direction of the seating at the back of the saloon where a figure was coiled up in a chair, seemingly fast asleep. 'Isn't that – Adam?'

He glanced in the direction she indicated. 'Yes, it is.' He dropped her arm and walked towards the unconscious young man. 'Why is he sleeping here, I wonder? He could have shared my cabin.'

'Independence?' she suggested, gazing at the slumbering youth in such tranquil repose, and thought him bordering on handsome manhood.

Roland nodded agreement. 'Excuse me for a moment.' He strode off towards the barman and she saw him speaking to him, the man listening and then summoning one of the waiters.

'What did you ask him?' she said on his return.

'Just to bring Adam a couple of blankets and a pillow; he'll have a crick in his neck by morning and it will get much colder during the night.'

'It will,' she said in some concern. 'But he's young and resilient. Do you think that he couldn't afford the cost of a cabin?'

'His father certainly could. Independence, as you suggested, I think.'

He took her arm again and led her back towards the corridor and her cabin. There was a high-pitched whistle coming from inside.

'Whatever is that?' he said, perturbed.

She laughed. 'Nunny and her orchestra. She's in full harmony by the sound of it.'

'What? She's snoring? Will you be able to sleep through that?'

'I will,' she said. 'Especially after the brandy. Thank you, Roland.' She put her hand on the door handle. 'Good night. Sleep well.'

'You too.' He dropped a chaste kiss on her other hand, and it was as if he were saying goodnight to one of his daughters. 'Goodnight, dear Louisa.'

She closed the cabin door behind her and put on the safety chain, then sat on the edge of her bed. Nunny was lying on her back in the opposite bunk with her mouth partly open, and Louisa leaned towards her to gently move her head to one side and close her mouth. The snoring stopped as Nunny turned over on to her side and settled back into sleep.

Louisa took off her slippers and cape and put them at the bottom of the bunk. So what did you expect? she asked herself. He still grieves for Constance, but I don't believe what he said about them being equal. I believe that he's feeling remorse. He's a kind man, no doubt about it – she thought of his concern for Adam – and yet I have a feeling that he may not be as perfect as he appears to be. You're a cynic, she told herself, but anyway it doesn't matter what I think. He's unattainable in any case.

In the cabin next door Matty had plumped up Faith's pillow and placed another blanket over her.

'I shall be too hot,' Faith said, though not in a complaining manner. 'I'm not an invalid, Matty. You really must stop worrying over me; I've outgrown all that.'

'Sorry.' Matty sat back on the edge of her own bunk. 'I know I fuss.'

'I didn't say that.' Apologetically, Faith reached for her hand and patted it. 'I'm nearly a grown-up,' she said. 'I'll soon be fourteen. Some girls are working at my age.'

'That's true,' Matty agreed. 'I suppose Betty Brown is no older than you. But not girls like us. We've been cosseted since we were children; especially since – since . . .' She stopped, and Faith finished the sentence for her.

'Since Mama died,' she said. 'It's all right, Matty. I'm able to talk about her much more easily than you can because I barely remember her. She's a cloud of dark hair and a sweet perfume to me, and that's lovely; it's a happy memory. It's Julia who's the worry for us. But we're going to think of happy times, aren't we? It will soon be your birthday and I'm so excited that I shall have a grown-up sister.'

'But I'm not!' Matty exclaimed. 'Another few days is not going to change me from who I am now to someone else. I'm petrified, to be honest,' she confessed, climbing into her bunk. 'What will I have to do to prove that I'm grown up?'

Faith yawned. 'Just be yourself, I suppose, though perhaps you'll have to decide who you want to marry. Shall we make a list of all the young men we know? Or maybe you'd like to remain single, like Aunt Gertrude? Do you think' – she yawned again, and slid down beneath the blankets – 'that she ever considered marriage when she was young? Has she ever mentioned that someone wanted to marry her? I don't want to be,' she went on drowsily. 'Married, I mean. I don't think it can be up to much; look at Aunt Louisa. She hasn't married again and she's very pretty, so she must have had some suitors. Perhaps . . .' She closed her eyes. 'Perhaps we should . . .' She gave a big sleepy sigh. 'Perhaps we should . . .'

'Ask her?' Matty blew out the night light. 'Yes, perhaps we should. But not tonight . . . tomorrow . . .' She too snuggled down, felt the rocking of the boat and hoped it wouldn't tip her out of the bunk, and was asleep in minutes.

Julia, in the next door cabin, was sitting up on her bunk bed with a blanket wrapped around her shoulders; she didn't dare to lie down in case she felt sick again. It must be terribly rough out there, and we've ages to go before we reach France. She had brought a book to read but the words swayed in front of her, making her dizzy. She reached out to take a sip of water from the glass on the shelf beside her, but the water slopped about and she had to lean over to drink in case she spilt some on the sheet or the blanket.

I have to overcome this, she thought, or else I'm never going to be able to travel when I'm old enough. She thought of her friend Eliza. When they'd first come aboard they'd chatted excitedly about the places they would visit when they were grown up; Eliza had said that perhaps they wouldn't be allowed to travel without an escort, and then Adam had joined in the conversation and said that if they waited until they were twenty-one, then they could go wherever they liked.

'You've forgotten something, dear brother,' Eliza had commented, raising her eyebrows wryly in Julia's direction. 'We won't have any money. *You* will; when you reach twenty-one you'll receive your allowance and be on your way towards a profession or a vocation, but mine will be tied up ready for when I marry, and I expect yours will be the same, Julia?'

Julia hadn't answered. It wasn't something she'd even considered, and no one had mentioned anything about money as far as she was aware, not even to Matty.

Eliza had thrust her chin into her hands and said gloomily, 'That's if I'm not already married off by then, and if I'm not then I'll be an old maid and Mama will be so disappointed!'

Is that true, Julia reflected now; will Papa expect us to marry? Does he expect some gentleman to take each of us off his hands, and does he have enough money to marry off four daughters? Will we all receive the same dowry, and is it true that our husbands keep it? Can they do that? I must ask Matty if she knows, for if they do, it seems to me to be entirely, utterly unfair. Perhaps we should ask Aunt Gertrude – or Aunt Louisa. Yes, Aunt Louisa will definitely know.

She risked feeling sick and carefully slid down between the sheets. Is that perhaps why Aunt Louisa hasn't married again? Mmm, I rather think that might be the reason.

CHAPTER ELEVEN

They arrived at Le Havre early the following morning, all sleepy and disorientated and staggering towards the waiting carriages which would take them to the railway station in the town where the train to Rouen was waiting. Mrs Nunnington told Miss Maddeson that she hadn't slept a wink all night, causing Louisa to give a wry smile that she hid behind her gloved hand.

They were able to buy hot drinks before the train departed, and Nunny, with a smug smile, opened up the hamper she had brought for their breakfast. Cook had made bread rolls and filled them with smoked salmon drizzled with lemon juice and thinly sliced spring onions, egg mayonnaise or, especially for Mr Maddeson, cold bacon, sausage and mustard; she'd also packed tomatoes and fruit, a sponge cake, a fruit cake and a slab of Cheddar cheese.

'Goodness,' Aunt Gertrude exclaimed. 'There's enough food here for an army.'

'There is,' Matty agreed. 'I'm going to take some to the next carriage. Eliza, Dorcas and Adam will help us eat it.'

Their friends had been lucky enough to book the adjacent carriage, but there was no interconnecting door. Matty's father told her not to dally as the train was due to leave in five minutes.

'I'll help you, Matty,' Aunt Louisa said. 'If we leave the door to this carriage open there'll be no fear of the train's setting off before the guard comes to close it.'

'Besides,' Becca was about to bite into a bread roll, 'you'll hear the whistle and see him wave the green flag.'

'And see the head of steam.' Aunt Gertrude, who regarded herself as an experienced traveller, pondered the selection of breakfast food, her fingers hovering between salmon and egg mayonnaise. 'It will be so thick that we won't be able to see through it.'

In the end they had to wait another fifteen minutes before the train drew out, with, as Aunt Gertrude had predicted, a huge head of steam as well as a succession of whistles and shouts before they finally started to move. Becca and Faith, and then a reluctant Julia, waved to the people on the plat-form who were fluttering handkerchiefs and gloves to speed the departing passengers on their way.

The train would take them to Paris, where they would board another at the Gare St Lazare for an even longer jour-ney through Switzerland, entailing several changes, before a late arrival at the Italian border. They were to stay over-night in a *pension de famille*, or small hotel, as Aunt Gertrude explained to Nunny.

'Oh!' Faith let out a breath of excitement. 'I really feel as if we're on our way at last.'

'Did you not feel that yesterday on the ferry?' her father asked as he helped himself to more food.

'No, not really,' she said. 'I fell asleep almost immediately I climbed into my bunk. But now, hearing the foreign voices, I feel as if we're truly on holiday.'

Her father smiled. 'Except that we are the ones with the foreign voices, are we not?'

Faith gazed at him blankly, and then said, 'Oh! Of course we are! I quite forgot. I suppose we should practise our French or German in readiness for our next stop.'

'I can't speak Italian,' Becca said. 'Or understand it either. What will I do if someone asks me a question?'

'You'll say *Non capisco*,' her father advised her. 'That means "I don't understand Italian." '

'And what will happen then?'

Her father laughed. 'You will be quieter than you have ever been!'

Becca looked at everyone in turn and saw they were all smiling except Aunt Gertrude and Nunny. Nunny was looking very confused, whilst Aunt Gertrude said very firmly, 'I always make them understand what I want. I just wave my arms about and speak very loudly.'

Roland explained to his daughters and housekeeper that the French railway system had not progressed as quickly as the British one. 'Many people were against it; some still are, and prefer to travel by boat: there are many waterway and river systems in place here. Also, during the Napoleonic wars the infrastructure suffered a great deal of damage which, even after so many decades, still inhibits the laying of railway lines.'

Both Aunt Gertrude and Nunny nodded off during the journey, only to waken with a start when each train drew to a halt with much screeching and clanging of brakes, and they had to gather up their belongings to change to another. 'Don't rush,' Roland had told his sister. 'The next train will wait for us.' He checked with the porters each time that their baggage would be transferred with them, and it always was.

Matty woke Nunny when they crossed into Switzerland. She didn't want her to miss the wonderful view of sun-sparkling snow-capped mountains and steep green valleys below them.

'My goodness,' Nunny exclaimed, gazing out of the window. 'However did we get up so high? And how will we get down?'

Roland Maddeson smiled. 'That's the power of engineering.'

'Well,' she breathed out. 'I would never have believed it if I hadn't seen it for myself. It must be like looking down from heaven.'

*

'We're almost there, ladies and gentlemen,' Roland announced. They were sitting on a steamer travelling across Lake Maggiore, and would shortly arrive at their destination of Stresa, on the western shore of the lake which touched both Switzerland and Italy.

Nunny said she was lost for words as she stood on deck next to Matty, watching the shoreline coming nearer. 'This is something I'll remember for 'rest of my life, Miss Matty.' She wiped her eyes. 'I'm Beverley born and bred and think it 'best town in 'country and it probably is, but this . . .' She lifted her hands to encompass the scenery. 'This is something I'd never dreamed of; such beauty.' She lifted her face to the blue sky and the towering mountains across the water. 'It's just wonderful, and I might never want to go home – and not just because I'll worry about managing 'trains on 'way back.'

'Please don't worry about that, Nunny,' Matty reassured her. 'Aunt Gertrude has done the journey before and between you you'll manage perfectly. Papa will draw up a plan for you to follow.'

'Will he? Oh, that's a relief.' Nunny breathed out a sigh. 'I thought we might get on 'wrong train and finish up somewhere we didn't want to be.'

It was a big undertaking for someone who had never travelled, Matty realized, but Aunt Gertrude is very efficient; she just doesn't like to travel alone, which is right and proper for an elderly lady who might be vulnerable. But then she thought that if anyone tried to take advantage of her aunt, they would soon back away if they felt the sharpness of her tongue; and she always carried an umbrella with a pointed tip. She was quite sure that her aunt and Nunny would be very comfortable together on their journey home.

A carriage was waiting for the passengers as they disembarked, and a horse and trap to collect their luggage. 'We'll need another trap,' Roland told the driver. 'Or a wagon . . . erm, *un cavallo*.' He had forgotten for a moment that the driver might not understand English, but fortunately he did. Roland recalled that many English tourists came to this most lovely part of Italy, and that those supplying a service would probably have a better smattering of English than he had of Italian.

He suggested to his sister that she, Mrs Nunnington and Faith might like to drive to the villa in the carriage while the rest of them walked. They could see the house only a short distance away, standing back from the road on a slight incline, which would give a clear view of the gardens and the lake.

'This is just lovely, Roland,' Louisa said, walking alongside him with the young people in front. 'There's no wonder that your mother prefers to live here. I've always thought that she looks slightly Italian with her dark hair – and her manner, of course.' She smiled as she thought of the exuberant Henrietta.

'It suits her very well,' he agreed. 'The lifestyle, as well as the weather. In the winter, when it snows or thunderstorms are pending, she either shuts herself indoors or closes up the villa and goes to live in a hotel away from the lake for a few weeks.'

'Very sensible,' Louisa said. 'I wonder that your sister doesn't join her here.'

'Oh, no! It wouldn't suit Gertrude. She's far too English to live in Italy; too strait-laced and puritanical.' He wasn't criticizing his sister exactly, but explaining how she was. 'She's totally different from our mother.'

Matty, Julia, Becca and their three guests stopped opposite the wide drive leading up to the villa. From here they could see a terrace and marble statues and spouting fountains, and a wide grassy lawn in front. A wooden sign proclaimed *Vista Lago*.

'Papa, is this really it?' Matty called. 'It's very grand.'

Roland turned his head as the carriage bringing Gertrude, Nunny and Faith caught up with them and turned up the drive towards the villa, followed by the cart with all their luggage. 'Yes indeed. It would seem so,' he said, adding, 'It looks very impressive.'

As they walked up the drive Louisa turned to look back. 'How superb,' she murmured. 'I do like being close to water. There's movement changing the atmosphere at all times of the day.'

'You're very fond of your own town, aren't you?' Roland said.

'Oh, I love it; the outlook changes constantly according to the mood of the sea.' She smiled. 'In Scarborough there's always the sigh of the sea and the cry of the seabirds, and the sound of the wind singing in my ears.'

He looked fondly down at her. 'You wouldn't be tempted by such a place as this?'

'Tempted? Yes, but would never move. I'm very comfortable in my own home. And you?'

'Not sure.' He hesitated. 'Sometimes I think it would be good for my girls to move elsewhere, but they're safe in their own home, they're familiar with it, and for Matty and Julia, well . . .' He gave a small sigh. 'They still have memories of their mother living there.'

Louisa nodded, but wasn't sure if she agreed with him. She worried sometimes that her nieces wouldn't be able to take control of their own lives whilst they were tied to the memory of Constance, who still held them fast and lovingly – as she held Roland.

The girls all rushed around the villa, shrieking at the rooms and the view from the wide windows, the marble floors and the magnificent staircase, and trying to decide which room they would have and how they would share. Adam took a brief look round and then stepped out on to the terrace where Miss Maddeson, Mrs Walton and Mr Maddeson were sitting at a table under a large umbrella.

'It's very kind of you to invite Eliza and me, sir,' he said to Roland, and sat beside them as his host suggested. 'We haven't visited this part of Italy before. We've been to Rome and Pisa and Genoa, but not the lakes, and I'm quite dazed by what I've seen so far. It's beautiful.'

'You're very welcome, Adam,' Roland told him. 'Have you chosen a room yet, or have you been confined to the boot room by the girls?'

Adam grinned. 'They're all so excited that I decided to leave them to it and just take what's left. It will probably be a broom cupboard!'

A young maid came out carrying a tray of wine glasses then brought through a bottle of red wine, and Roland stood up to open it. 'I think you'll find that Mrs Nunnington will have followed them and made the decision for them. I asked her to make sure that Miss Maddeson and Mrs Walton had rooms with a view of the lake. Will you take a glass?'

Adam hesitated. 'Erm, just a small one, sir, thank you. I rarely drink, except sometimes at dinner. My mother doesn't approve; she says I'm not yet old enough.'

Louisa smiled at him. 'I would agree with your mother. It's best to start slowly, but one small glass won't hurt.' She nodded her thanks to Roland as he poured one for her. 'And you'll find out whether or not you have a taste for it.'

'I'd rather have a glass of sherry, if you have it,' Gertrude commented, 'but I'll have a small one if not.'

'I'll have to find out what's in the cellar,' Roland said to her, poured her a glass of wine and then lifted his to them all. 'The agent arranged two days' food and drink for us, and then we must order the commodities we need. So, here's to a lovely holiday and birthday party. Ah, Nunny,' he went on, as his housekeeper came to find them. 'Come and join us. Will you take a glass of wine?'

She seemed startled, for she had resumed her role as house-keeper and did not expect to be invited to sit with members of the family.

'Well, I . . .' She took a breath. 'Thank you, sir. Just a small glass, if you please.'

Louisa patted the chair next to her. 'Come and sit down, Mrs Nunnington. How did you get on with arranging bed-rooms? Are the young ladies squabbling over them?'

Nunny laughed and took a sip of wine, and then drew in her cheeks as if it were sour. 'They all wanted rooms over-looking the lake, of course, but I pointed out that you and Miss Maddeson will have two of those, and Mr Maddeson and Master Chapman need separate ones as well, so there aren't enough rooms left for them to have one each. I left them to decide who shares which rooms.'

Louisa saw Adam grimace slightly at being called Master, as if he were still a child, and he wiggled his eyebrows at her when he saw that she had noticed. 'And where have you put this young man, Mrs Nunnington?' she asked mischievously.

'In one of 'two best rooms in the house,' the housekeeper said roguishly, 'and I'm having 'other one. They're right at 'top, under the roof; small, with just a bed and a chest o' drawers in each, but I reckon that at night it'll be like sleep-ing under 'stars.'

They all saw her eyes well up with tears, and she pressed her lips together before saying, 'When I was a young house-maid in my first position, I slept in 'attic under the roof and it was nothing like this, just dark and cold and damp, and these rooms are warm and full o' light, and so I hope, young master, you'll like your room as much as I will like mine.'

Adam got up from his chair. 'Thank you very much, Nunny,' he said softly, and the name he gave her seemed perfectly all right, for he had known her most of his life. 'I can't wait to see it.'

CHAPTER TWELVE

Adam ran upstairs to the first landing and paused. Windows with stained glass borders occupied the walls like landscapes, the clear centres giving a view of the lawn, the terrace and the fountains at the front of the villa. Turning to face the other way, he saw through the opposite window a cobbled yard where the maid was hanging out washing cloths and dusters. He tilted his head and the maid became blue; tilted it the other way and she wore gold.

On this floor were bedrooms; a door was open and he saw a wooden trunk belonging to Miss Maddeson. The door to the next room was also ajar, and Mrs Walton's trunk and valise were set inside next to a canopied bed with hangings.

He turned away, not wanting anyone to think he was prying, and ran up on to the next landing where there were more rooms with the doors firmly shut and the voices of his sister and Julia coming from one of them and the chatter of Matty and Faith and, he thought, Dorcas and Becca from the one next door. This floor also had windows running around the perimeter, affording an even better view from the higher vantage, and three more doors set closer together, which he assumed were two more bedrooms and a wash room.

He looked up into the centre of the dome, which was filled with bright blue sky with only one small white fluffy cloud barely drifting across it, which did not detract from its calm perfection.

Surrounding the circle was stained glass inserted between thin slivers of silver-grey lead in various shapes: oblongs, triangles and small squares created a kaleidoscope of colour that almost took his breath away. He sank down on the stairs and marvelled at the artistry.

This is where I shall sit tonight and watch the stars, he thought. They'll be trapped within the circle. He looked around him again and saw a short, narrow staircase to the left of the one he had ascended, which led up to a small landing and a door leading off it. He smiled as he realized that this was where Mrs Nunnington had found the two small bedrooms.

They were not under the roof, as she'd described, but to the side of it; at the top of the narrow staircase and through the door was a large flat roof. He thought it was probably over the kitchen and other servants' quarters, for there was a chimney exuding smoke, and here had been built a brick and glass structure divided into two rooms.

He opened the door of one and saw that Mrs Nunnington had laid claim to it already, for her cloak was hanging inside the door and her small trunk was on the floor by the window. He closed the door and went to the next one, and he saw now why she had left this room for him.

A glass roof covered the small bedroom with its single bed and chest of drawers, as Nunny had described; another door led out to the open area, which was surrounded by a white waist-high wall. Pots of jasmine and lavender filled the air with their perfume, and crocus, cyclamen and geraniums in every possible riotous colour filled each corner. Cane chairs and small tables were set out as if waiting to be filled with people.

'It's a rooftop garden room,' he murmured. 'How absolutely perfect.'

Downstairs Roland pushed back his empty glass and rose to his feet. 'I'm going to see Mother.' He turned to his sister. 'Would you like to come? It will be about a ten-minute walk.'

'Oh, no thank you,' Gertrude said. 'I need to rest, and intend to retire to my room for a while. I will visit her tomorrow,'

'Very well. I won't be long – I'll just let Mother know we have arrived and we'll all come tomorrow.'

'All of us!' Gertrude exclaimed. 'We'd be better going in small groups, surely? I wouldn't like so many people descending on me.'

Roland wanted to say that she wasn't anything like their mother, who loved having people around, and a group of relatives descending on her wouldn't daunt her in the least; but he didn't say so – merely nodded and repeated that he wouldn't be long.

Louisa was on the point of offering to accompany him, but held back; perhaps it wasn't appropriate, and Roland probably wanted a quiet time to himself after the hustle and bustle of travelling and making sure that everyone had picked up their belongings.

Louisa had been right: Roland had wanted this quiet time and he exhaled a breath once he was outside. The air was still and warm, with the sun going down and the sky filled with colour. At the bottom of the long drive he crossed the road and then, picking up a faster pace, started walking by the side of the lake in the direction of Stresa. His mother had chosen this particular area as she and his father had spent their honeymoon here, and she had fallen in love with the location and the people. They'd visited often during their marriage, and it was the obvious choice when Henry had asked her where she would like to live if he should precede her. Now, the lake shimmered with reflected colour and Roland looked across to the opposite shore, which was darkening as the sun was sinking. Pleasure boats with their passengers were heading back to their moorings on this side, the sails showing white against the sky.

His mother's villa was also set back from the road, though not as far as the one they had hired, and in each front window lamps had been lit. The terrace in the front showed several tables with oil lamps glowing on them, and at one of them he saw his mother sitting with a warm shawl wrapped about her shoulders.

'Mama,' he called out so that he didn't startle her. 'It's Roland.'

'Oh!' She rose to her feet. 'My darling Roly, how lovely to see you. I didn't expect you until the morning.'

She put out her arms and he stepped into her embrace. 'Lovely to see you too, Mama.' His voice was muffled in her thick, still-dark hair as she held him to her ample bosom. 'I wanted to let you know we'd arrived. Gertrude will come in the morning. She's tired after the long journey.'

Henrietta sank back into the downy cushion of the chair, reached for a small handbell and shook it vigorously, then laughed as she waved her hand for him to take a seat. 'That's what she would say. She'll want to prepare herself before coming to see me; we don't have a great deal in common, my daughter and I. She's years older than me, you know.' She laughed again, throatily and heartily. 'Not as much stamina.'

Roland gazed at her and smiled; she looked the picture of health, and she still had the great spark of life in spite of her maturity. Was it the effect of being here in Italy? But no, he reminded himself, she had always had a huge zest for life even when he was just a child. There was no palming them off on a nursery maid or governess; she always came up with ideas to entertain him and his brother, although eventually his father took control and said they would either have a home tutor or be packed off to boarding school when they reached eight. His mother had succumbed then, and as they grew older agreed that first Roland and then Albert should go away to school, although only as far as York, where she could visit them or they could come home at weekends. Now her heart was in Italy and she rarely came back to Yorkshire.

'So tell me about our birthday girl. Matty, she calls herself, doesn't she? Quite right. Martha is too old a name for a young woman. Does she have a husband in mind? No?' she said, as

Roland shook his head. She poured him a glass of wine from the carafe a maid had brought. 'Good. She's too young, and needs to live a little. Although here in Italy young unmarried women cannot go very far without their mamas hanging on to their arms; possibly the Italian men can't be trusted.' She sighed a gusty sigh. 'They are very handsome, of course, or most of them are, and have such a way with words.'

He laughed. She was incorrigible, and quite right about Gertrude, who was nothing like their mother. Henrietta would play her male Italian visitors at their own game: they would probably give grand compliments about her mature beauty and she would accept the proclamations as her right without believing a word they uttered. Gertrude would be horrified.

'Well, my dear,' she said, after fifteen minutes or so, 'I'm going to send you off to your villa now, as it's time I went up to my room. I like to spend an hour reading and resting before taking to my bed. I wake to see the dawn come up, and unless there's a party or I have people visiting for supper I retire early.'

'Of course, Mama, I understand. I'll take a quiet stroll back and after supper might have an early night too. I am quite tired after our journey. It's a lovely villa, by the way, and I'm delighted with it.'

'Good,' she said, as he helped her out of her chair. 'I know the owner and told him that you would only want the best.' She leaned towards him so that he could kiss her cheek. 'I'll look forward to seeing your darling daughters tomorrow.' She paused for a moment. 'You were fortunate to have daughters,' she murmured. 'Such a comfort when you're alone.'

He gave a puzzled smile. 'You have a daughter, Mama.'

'Hm? Oh, Gertrude, yes. But she's not at all girlish, is she? She never was. We never had discussions about gowns or hairdos or balls and parties, let alone husbands. No, Gertrude was born an adult. I love her all the same,' she added softly. 'Even if she doesn't know it.'

He left her then and began his stroll back alongside the lake to the villa, where supper would be waiting.

There was a chill in the air now that the sun had disappeared – quickly as it always did here – and he gave a slight shiver. He wore only a thin jacket and trousers, not having brought his summer overcoat out with him. He quickened his step; it could be that they were holding supper back until he arrived, although it wasn't late, perhaps only eight o'clock. One or two couples walked towards him murmuring *Buona sera* as they passed, and he replied in kind.

He passed the landing stage where the sailboats were safely berthed, anchor lights fixed on the mastheads, and wondered if any of his daughters might like to take a sail on the lake. Becca, perhaps; she was the adventurous one in the family and had said when she was very young that she wanted to be a horsewoman when she was grown up, and indeed spent most of the time when she wasn't with her governess grooming the horses at the Westwood stables. He had approached Mr Lawrence, whom he knew well, and asked if she were a nuisance, and Mr Lawrence had said that she wasn't at all and was actually very good at handling the horses.

He walked on, and as he was about to cross the road a figure rose from one of the wooden benches that were placed strategically by the lakeside and took a step towards him. It was a tall man dressed in a shabby black coat with a woollen cap on his long hair, holding out his hand.

'*Buona sera, signore. Come stai?*'

'Good evening. Yes, I am well, thank you,' Roland replied in hesitant Italian, and rebuked himself for not bringing any currency out with him. He had not a single coin in his pocket. He pulled out the lining from his jacket pockets to show the man; he had no pockets in his trousers.

The man kept out his hand. '*Per piacere, signore.*' If you please, sir. There was a pleading tone to his voice.

Roland held out both hands to show him they were empty. '*Scusate,*' he apologized, and the man turned away, shrugging his shoulders as if to say it was only what he expected. He sat down again on the bench, both arms stretched across the back rest, his eyes following Roland as he passed him.

There was a dignified bearing to the man's posture in spite of the shabby coat he was wearing, Roland thought as he crossed to the other side, and he wondered how the fellow had come to be begging. His own Italian wasn't good enough to hold a proper conversation. Perhaps he should have asked him if he spoke French; his own French was fluent, but he still couldn't have given him anything, and the fellow might not have appreciated the reason why he was out in the early evening without any money on his person, not a copper or a *scudo*.

The encounter had disturbed him, and he felt a cold shiver down his spine. As he walked up the long drive to the villa, where lights glowed in the windows, he wondered how anyone managed without any money to buy even a hot drink or a chunk of bread, wherever in the world they lived.

CHAPTER THIRTEEN

They proceeded towards Grandmama Maddeson's villa on foot late the next morning, after a delicious breakfast of freshly baked bread, sweet cake filled with apricots, and piping hot coffee.

'We will *fare passeggiata*,' Roland pronounced as they walked down the long drive, 'and I don't know if that is grammatically correct or not!' He laughed. 'But it sounds more exciting than taking a walk.'

He seemed much more cheerful this morning than he had been last night when he arrived back from his mother's house, and Matty, who was always sensitive to others' emotions, had asked him if he were feeling well. He had proclaimed that he was perfectly fine, but in truth he had not slept well. As they walked he kept glancing about, but there was no sign of the man who had approached him and disturbed his sleep. The road was busy with horses pulling carts and wagons in the direction of Stresa, men trundling barrows laden with boxes of fruit and vegetables, and many cabriolets and tourist omnibuses. Some of the passengers waved to them, and Becca and Faith cheerfully waved back.

'Everyone will know that you and I are not Italian, won't they?' Becca asked. 'Do you think there are any blonde Italians?' Both girls wore their hair in plaits that fell below their sunhats.

'I don't know,' Faith said. 'I shouldn't think so; they're generally dark-haired, I think.'

They were walking in front of everyone, with Matty, Dorcas and Adam behind, Julia and Eliza behind them, and the grown-ups, as Becca had named them, bringing up the rear. Nunny had had to be persuaded to come with them, insisting that she wasn't family and wouldn't be expected at Mrs Maddeson's villa.

'I told her that you'd be coming with us.' Roland offered the lie affectionately. 'She's expecting you, and besides, she hasn't seen you in such a long time.'

'That is true, sir, but even so—'

'It's a holiday, Nunny. How long is it since you took one?'

'Well, as for that, Mr Maddeson, I couldn't say, for I'm not sure if I've ever had one. Mrs Maddeson took me for a day out to Scarborough many years ago when Miss Martha and Miss Julia were just tiny tots, and we went to visit Madam's sister.'

'So you did, Nunny. I remember that,' Louisa agreed. 'You took the babies for a walk in a bassinet that I'd borrowed from a friend, and Constance and I sat in the garden.' She sighed. 'It was such a glorious day: sunny, and unusually for Scarborough there was barely a breeze.' I told Constance about Arnold's proposal, she recalled, and she advised me not to marry him if I hadn't any affection for him, which I hadn't. But it was too late. Our father had decided.

'So long ago,' Nunny reminisced. 'I remember the steep hill as I came back to the house, and how out of puff I was!' And then she changed the subject to the view across the lake, for she didn't want to bring up sad memories for anyone.

'Yes, indeed.' Louisa smiled. 'A lot of breath is needed for Scarborough!'

The sailing boats were being prepared for visitors to be taken across to the three Borromean islands, and the crews were calling out their prices for a voyage to Isola Bella, Isola Madre or Isola dei Pescatori.

'Oh, Papa, may we go?' Julia begged. 'I've been reading about Isola Bella. The palace was built by a prince for his bride.'

Faith turned round on hearing the request and added her plea to Julia's. 'How *romantic*! Oh yes, please, Papa, we must go. I'll take my sketch book.'

'Pwh,' Becca said derisively, blowing out her lips, whilst Adam said something that made Matty laugh and he turned to her, smiling, and put his arm round her shoulder. Julia saw it, and froze.

She knew she had been cold and rude to him that day in Beverley and had seen him draw away, yet on her birthday he and Eliza had brought her a gift of a silver pendant and Eliza had told her that Adam had chosen it. On the final leg of their journey yesterday she had thought that she and Adam had reached a more friendly understanding, but had he now become Matty's friend and not hers? He has never put his hand on my shoulder, or at least not since we were children when he sometimes took my hand while playing games. But perhaps he no longer thinks of me as a best friend.

Eliza nudged Julia and whispered in her ear. 'Did you see that? Is my brother becoming amorous? It must be the notion of a prince building a palace, but I can't see Adam in that role, can you, Julia? Or falling in love either, for that matter, and certainly not with Matty.'

'Why not with Matty?' Julia said defensively, *sotto voce*. 'She's very lovable.'

'I didn't mean that she isn't,' Eliza whispered. 'Of course she's the most lovable person in the world; everybody loves her. No, I meant with Adam! He's my brother, after all, and I know him better than anyone, and Matty is far too good for him.'

Adam had dropped his arm and put his hand to his forehead to look more intently at the view across the lake. 'Wonderful,' he said softly, and turned his head to address his sister. 'What are you whispering about, Eliza? Plotting something?'

'Not at all.' Eliza put her nose in the air. 'And I wouldn't tell you if we were,' she said mischievously, glancing at Julia, who saw Adam grin at his sister and wondered if she had misread the situation once again.

The Maddeson girls were greeted enthusiastically by their grandmother, who was sitting on the terrace in a black velvet peignoir drinking coffee and nibbling cake.

'My dearest darlings,' she crowed. 'How wonderful to see you. How lovely you all are, and so grown up; come here, all of you, and give me a kiss,' and they all complied. Matty introduced Eliza and Dorcas, and Henrietta exclaimed at their beauty before greeting her daughter Gertrude, who gave her a small peck on the cheek, and Louisa, who gently took her hand and said how nice it was to see her again.

'And who is this most handsome young man?' she asked of Adam. 'I haven't met you before, have I? No,' she said naughtily, 'I would most certainly have remembered.'

Adam gave a small bow. 'I think not, Mrs Maddeson,' he agreed politely. 'I too would have remembered the occasion.'

'Most charming,' she murmured, fluttering her eyelashes. 'And are you a friend of all my granddaughters or is there a special one?'

'They are all very special to me, Mrs Maddeson.' He smiled. 'They all have exceptional attributes.'

'Is that so?' she said mischievously. 'Then you must tell me when we are alone.'

He bent to whisper in her ear, just loud enough for the others to hear. 'I don't think I could do that, ma'am. I would be giving away secrets.'

She laughed heartily and told them all to find chairs and sit down and that coffee would soon be on its way, and then signalled to Nunny to come and sit next to her.

'My dear Mrs Nunnington. How good it is to see you again. It has been many years since we last met. The last time must have been when one of my brothers died and I came to

England for the funeral; I stayed with my daughter in Hull and then made a brief visit to Beverley to see Roland and Albert and their families. It was a bitterly cold November, I recall. I won't do that again. Not unless my relatives die in the summer months, and then I might.'

Nunny's mouth quivered. Mrs Maddeson was even more eccentric than she remembered, and she obviously intended to outlive all her relatives. 'You look very well, ma'am. The Italian climate appears to suit you.'

Mrs Maddeson did indeed look very healthy; she had put on weight since Nunny had last met her, and she had more streaks of silver in her dark hair than before, but she had very few wrinkles in her plump cheeks and an enviable appearance of gaiety about her as she sat comfortably on the sun-filled terrace.

'I am well,' she agreed, 'and who wouldn't be, living in such a place as this?' She lowered her voice. 'My only problem, in truth, Mrs Nunnington, and I'm sure you will understand when I say this, is that I am a young woman masquerading as an old one and it is hard sometimes to keep up appearances.'

The party chatted and drank coffee and ate more cake and then the young ladies, Adam, Louisa and Roland went inside to look at the villa, leaving Becca, who couldn't remember her grandmother at all, standing in front of her whilst she finished a conversation with Aunt Gertrude.

Henrietta looked up at her and smiled fondly. 'Do you want to ask me something, *amore*?'

Becca nodded. 'Yes, please.' She hesitated for a moment, and then asked, 'Do you remember me?'

'*Si, mia cara*,' she said softly. 'You were only a *bambina* when I last saw you; you were getting into mischief, crawling into cupboards or sitting under tables where we couldn't find you. You were just beginning to chatter and to make yourself understood, and running circles around Nunny. Isn't that so, Mrs Nunnington? You were a beautiful child,' she went on as Nunny nodded, 'and now . . .' She paused for a second only.

'And now you are on the brink of being a beautiful young woman just like your sisters.'

Becca pressed her lips together. 'Thank you, Grandmama,' she said. 'You see, I don't remember you at all, and the others do, even Faith, because Papa brought her and Matty here one year, but I was too young for the journey. So I felt left out.'

'Well, you don't need to feel left out at all, because I remember you very well indeed,' her grandmother said emphatically. 'You were just at the age when life was becoming interesting to you. But now we must get to know each other better, don't you think, and perhaps,' she dropped her voice, 'I could teach you a few words of Italian?' She put her fingers across her mouth and whispered, 'I know a few words that polite people don't use.'

Becca's mouth shaped into an *oh*. Julia said she knew some English words that you could use when you were angry but not when you were in company. But to know Italian ones would be better, she thought, especially as no one else would understand them. Her eyes sparkled and she nodded. Just wait till I tell the others.

CHAPTER FOURTEEN

'What was Adam saying to make you laugh?' Julia asked Matty later, back at Vista Lago.

'Mmm? When?' Matty said.

'When we were walking to Grandmama's. Faith had said something about taking her sketch book to Isola Bella.'

Matty began to shake her head. 'I don't—' she began, and then laughed. 'No! It wasn't Faith; it was what you said about the prince building a palace on Isola Bella.' She laughed again. 'He's so funny, isn't he – Adam! He said we should try to find a prince and ask him to come to my birthday tea! I said he would run a mile if he were confronted by four English sisters, and Adam suggested that we could tie him up and keep him prisoner until he'd chosen one of us to be his bride!'

'How silly he is,' Julia agreed. 'Such a joker.' Why don't I see his humorous side? she wondered. I read so much into what people say or do, and I get it wrong so many times. 'Do you think the prince's bride is a captive on the island?'

'No,' Matty said. 'It happened a long time ago and I expect they're a boring married couple now with lots of children and grandchildren.'

'Well, you're not romantic at all, are you?' Julia chided. 'I'm so excited about going to see the palace. Wasn't it nice of Grandmama to book a private tour? You'll remember this birthday for ever.'

Their grandmother had booked the tour as a birthday gift for Matty, and it would take place at the beginning of the following week. In the meantime Nunny, Aunt Louisa and Aunt Gertrude, with Roland and the hired cook, were planning the party, which was to be held on Sunday. The girls and Adam took themselves off to look round Stresa, which because of its wonderful views of Lake Maggiore and the glorious weather was fast becoming popular with English tourists as well as with wealthy Italian holidaymakers. It was also known as the home of the Borromeo family, who owned the famous islands. Before they set off, Adam had been charged with escorting all the young ladies, and especially with watching over Becca, who had a habit of wandering off on her own adventures.

'You're not in Beverley now,' her father warned her, 'and an Italian *signorina* is not allowed out on her own.'

'Oh!' Becca said. 'Well, I shan't want to come and live here.'

'You shouldn't be allowed out on your own in Beverley either,' Aunt Gertrude told her. 'You are given far more freedom than is becoming in a young lady.'

Roland raised his eyebrows at his sister. 'They are perfectly safe in Beverley. Everyone knows them and they know everyone, and,' he added, 'there are many children who are given even more freedom.'

'Hmph,' said Gertrude. 'But not daughters from families such as ours!'

'I'll take great care of them all,' Adam said earnestly, though his eyes were merry, 'and not let anyone out of my sight.'

Aunt Louisa called after him, 'You'll be the envy of all the young men in Stresa,' and as he turned round to smile at her comment she winked at him, which completely unnerved him. He had never seen a woman do that before, not even his mother, who was considered by many to be unconventional.

The sun was already hot, even though it was only just after ten o'clock. Faith put up her parasol and urged Becca to do the same, as they were both so fair. Then Matty did too, as she was inclined to burn even though darker-haired than her younger sisters; Eliza and Dorcas followed her example, but Julia airily dismissed the idea, saying her sunhat would protect her face. Adam, walking between Faith and Becca, pulled a cream fedora from his pocket and placed it at a jaunty angle on his fair hair.

The group caused quite a stir as they entered the lakeside village and many local people turned to gaze at them, murmuring to one another '*l'Inglese*'.

Adam lifted his hat and greeted those who stared with *Buongiorno, signora, signore* or *signorina*, pronouncing his 'r's appropriately.

'I'm impressed, Adam,' Matty commented. 'I hadn't realized you were a linguist!'

'He's not,' Eliza said cynically. 'He's been practising ever since you asked us if we'd like to come.'

'You're only jealous,' he teased, 'because your accent is not as good as mine.'

'I do wish that Timothy could have joined us,' Matty said, speaking of Dorcas's brother, as she linked arms with her friend. 'That would have been nice, wouldn't it? He and Adam get on so well, they would have been company for one another.'

'It would,' Dorcas agreed. 'He would have liked to have come, but he's very busy studying. It's a crucial time for him. Exams are looming and he wants to do well.'

'Of course,' Matty murmured, and thought of how life was changing for all four of them. They were all coming into adulthood, and their carefree existence was slowly dissolving. They had been friends since childhood, and although she and Dorcas would always remain close, Timothy, already at university, and Adam, who would soon be following the same path, would move out of their sphere, make other friends and meet other young women, perhaps choose a wife, and then nothing would ever be the same again. Matty didn't care for change. She liked life to be consistent, to follow a similar pattern without disruption.

Adam suggested that they sit in a local café and he would buy them all coffee or lemonade. 'We can sit and admire the view and watch the locals,' he said, 'and then take a walk and look at the villas on the hillside.' Some of the villas, he had noticed, were having work done on them, extensions and terraces built, and he guessed that they were being enlarged to accommodate the visitors who were attracted here. He had also read that a railway tunnel through the mountain had been suggested, to make a faster route than the present long and dangerous Simplon Pass which was so hazardous in winter.

'You're very clever, Adam,' Becca said. 'How is it you know so much?'

'I'm not especially clever,' he told her. 'But I read the newspapers and I have a good memory, and I find progress in other countries as well as our own very interesting. If we come back to Stresa in, say, another twenty years' time, we'll see a huge difference with regard to visitors, especially if it is decided to build the Simplon tunnel, though that of course could take decades and not be finished until we are old and grey.'

'We'll bring our grandchildren, then,' Eliza commented.

'I hope it won't be spoiled,' Faith added. 'It's lovely as it is.'

'Then you must sketch it, Faith,' Eliza told her. 'And then paint the picture as a reminder when you return home. You have a very good eye for detail.'

Faith smiled her thanks and lifted her sketch pad to show she had brought it with her, with those exact intentions. She was very aware of local natural beauty and had an affinity with it, as well as with art and music, and was the only one of the sisters who played the piano every day.

They moved on after a while and strolled about the village, seeing, as Adam had mentioned, the changes that were being made.

'Let's call on Grandmama,' Becca said eagerly as they left the village to walk back. 'She'll be pleased to see us.'

'All right,' Matty agreed. 'It's too early for her luncheon as she's a late riser, so I don't think we'll be disturbing her. But we mustn't stay long as lunch will soon be ready at Vista Lago.' She giggled. 'I love saying that!'

Grandmama was not out on the terrace today, and the young maid who opened the door to them said something quite incomprehensible as she led them to the drawing room, where she knocked and opened the door.

Eliza excused herself and disappeared down the hall to the bathroom, whilst Dorcas, in her usual manner, held back behind the others and brought up the rear with Adam. Becca led the way, but dropped her parasol on the threshold and had to bend to pick it up. Her mouth opened as she stood up and saw her grandmother reclining on a chaise longue with two young men sitting on the floor at her side.

Behind Becca, Matty blinked and her lips parted. Faith gave an amused smile, whilst Julia opened her eyes wide and gazed curiously at the young men as they rose from the floor, looking towards the door as they all stood as if in a tableau, waiting for someone to speak.

'*Miei cari!*' their grandmother exclaimed exuberantly. 'My darlings. I was only this second telling my young friends about my beautiful granddaughters and their friends. Come in, come in, and I will introduce you.'

Dorcas and Adam hung back, Adam turning to his sister as she returned from the bathroom and giving a helpless facial gesture which made her smile. Moving forward, Matty put a hand to her throat, Julia steepled her pale fingers together, Faith kept on smiling and Becca simply gazed at the young men before them.

'This most handsome one,' their grandmother pronounced, 'is Antonio Rosso; my granddaughter, Miss Martha Maddeson.'

And he was indeed handsome, as they all agreed later, as he put his hand to the front of his cream jacket and gave the slightest of bows whilst gazing at Matty from the darkest eyes and longest eyelashes she had ever seen in a man. '*Buongiorno, Miss Maddeson,*' he said softly. '*Come sta?*'

This at least she understood: good morning and how are you, she thought as she held out her hand to him and bent her knee. '*Molto bene, grazie, signore.*' She turned to Julia and introduced her. '*Le presento Julia.*' She did the same for Faith, and Becca, who gave him a cheeky grin, and then Dorcas and Eliza, both of whom dropped a neat curtsey, whilst Adam offered a formal handshake and a short bow, which were returned.

It was then the turn of Mario Alfonsi who, if it were possible, Matty thought, was even more handsome than Antonio, with his dancing eyes, dark curly hair and darker skin. He raised her hand to his lips and murmured '*Sei bellissima*', which quite took her breath away.

When the introductions had been made, Henrietta clapped her hands to summon her maid and ask for refreshments to be brought.

'Oh, but we are on our way back to Vista Lago,' Matty said hastily. 'We are expected for lunch. We called on a brief visit only, and—'

'Signorina Maddeson, in Italy,' Mario Alfonsi implored, interrupting her excuses, 'luncheon can be at any time. You must not hurry away from us.'

She was trapped in a chair by the window, with Mario by her side. Faith, Julia and Eliza were similarly imprisoned by Antonio, who was in earnest conversation with them, whilst Becca sat by her grandmother, and Dorcas and Adam gazed out of the long windows on to the terrace.

'Sorry that you're stuck with me, Dorcas,' Adam murmured. 'What shall we talk about?'

'It can only be the weather,' Dorcas murmured back. 'We know each other too well to discuss anything else.' She wanted to giggle at the pickle her friends were in; she knew that Matty would be embarrassed and that Julia was loving it. 'I think we might have lost Julia.'

'Hm.' Adam pursed his lips. 'I rather thought so. I have nothing to offer in resistance. In fact the fellows are so handsome that I could fall in love with either of them myself. Either that or I'll have to assassinate them.'

Dorcas spluttered and turned away to find something fascinating outside.

Antonio was asking Faith what was in her sketch book. 'Nothing yet,' she admitted. 'I brought a new pad with me. But I shall sketch the lake, I think, or perhaps wait until we go to Isola Bella.'

'Ah, you go there, yes? The palace is beautiful, built for a beautiful lady.' He curled his fingers together and threw a kiss into the air in an extravagant gesture. '*Bellissima.*'

Eliza excused herself and moved to sit by their hostess, and Becca took her place. Antonio leaned towards Faith. 'Signorina,' he murmured. 'I too am artist.' He turned to Julia and Becca and looked across at Matty in conversation with his friend. 'May I ask, *mi scusa* – erm – poor *Inglese* – if I could paint – you and your –' He interrupted himself to ask Mario something, who called back to him '*tu e le tue sorelle*', and then Grandmama Maddeson said, 'He is asking if he can paint you and your beautiful sisters, my dear, and you should say yes, as he is a most accomplished artist. I will be delighted to pay his fee, even though he will say he doesn't want any payment.'

'It is most kind of you, Signore Rosso,' Julia answered for them all, 'but we must first ask our father for permission. If he agrees,' she glanced towards her sisters and saw their eager response, 'I am sure we will all be delighted.'

CHAPTER FIFTEEN

Their father gave his reluctant assent, although the fact that his mother had vouched for the young men didn't give him any comfort or reassurance whatsoever, and when Gertrude was told of the suggestion she was appalled, saying that the girls would have their heads filled with romantic nonsense.

'There's no harm in a little romantic nonsense,' Louisa commented, expecting and receiving a sharp stare from Gertrude. 'It's harmless fun. I'd be happy to be chaperone,' she told Roland later, 'and I hardly think that either of the young men would attempt to seduce any of them under the eye of your mother. She is perhaps the young men's patron?'

'She might well be,' he said. 'Surprisingly, perhaps, she is a lover of the arts – and handsome young men too.' He smiled. 'I suspect they make her feel young again.'

'Well, nothing wrong with that,' Louisa agreed. 'Better than growing old and grumpy.'

So it was agreed that Antonio would come to Vista Lago to sketch and then paint the Maddeson sisters, and when he came with Mario to be introduced to Roland he told him he was enthralled by the villa, especially the domed roof and Venetian glass windows. When Adam, deciding to forgive him for being so handsome and charming, took him up to see the roof garden, Antonio vowed that one day, if he ever became rich, he too would build such a house.

He explained that today he would sketch the *signorine,* and requested that when he came back to paint them they wear white gowns, all but Julia, whom he asked to wear deep red, 'to show off your dark beauty, signorina,' he said.

Then he asked if they would group themselves a few steps up the staircase, Matty at the head, with one hand on the balustrade, Julia one step below, and Faith and Becca side by side one step below Julia. To their surprise, Mario produced a sketch book of his own and began to draw swiftly, while Antonio studied them through half-closed eyes and asked Becca if on his return she would wear a simple ankle-length gown with ballerina-like slippers.

'He's going to portray me as a child, I just know it,' Becca grumbled later to Aunt Louisa, 'and the others will be grown up.'

'I think he will portray you as you are now, Becca,' Louisa said soothingly. 'Coming out of childhood and growing into the charming young maiden you will become. I think that is why he grouped you in such a way.'

She had taken a surreptitious peek over Antonio's shoulder and thought how quickly he worked to capture the sisters on paper, even though only in pencil. He had then released them from their places on the stairs, and whilst they chatted and laughed together as they sat on the terrace with the others, disregarding his presence, he sat at another table with a pot of coffee and his sketch pad and outlined their features individually.

Adam came quietly to his table and asked if he would disturb him if he sat there. Antonio shook his head. 'No, signore,' he answered mildly. 'Today I outline only. Tomorrow, or perhaps tonight if the light is good, I will start to paint.' Then he added, 'You are family of these beautiful English *signorine,* yes?'

'No,' Adam answered. 'We are friends. Friends since childhood. My sister Eliza,' he pointed her out, 'is Julia's friend, and—'

'Ah! Julia. *Bella signorina*, yes.'

'She's sixteen,' Adam pointed out, wanting to make it perfectly clear that she was very young. 'They are all young.'

Antonio gave a slight shrug. 'They will grow up very soon.' He glanced at Adam. 'You are also *giovane*, I think – erm – a young man?'

'I'm eighteen,' Adam said matter-of-factly.

'Ah.' Antonio kept his eyes on his pencil and pad. 'Your Englishman, Shakespeare, he wrote of young love, did he not?' He gave Adam a swift glance. 'Romeo and Juliet, you are like that, yes? You and your Julia?'

'She's not *my* Julia,' Adam said in a terse mutter. His cheeks had flushed. 'She's not anyone's Julia. She's sixteen, as I said, and her own person.'

Antonio smiled and closed his pad. 'Then you would not mind too much if she fell in love with me?'

'I would mind very much.' Adam clenched and unclenched his fists. 'She is not ready for love. She's only a girl. How old are you, anyway?'

'I am twenty-two,' Antonio said, getting to his feet. 'We will see if she is ready for *romanza*. I will do her no harm. She is not very 'appy, I think; she needs a leetle *amore* in her life.' He nodded and smiled down at Adam. '*Ciao*, young man. We will meet again soon.'

There was great excitement on the Sunday morning as everyone looked forward to the luncheon that was being prepared. Matty had decided on luncheon rather than an evening, as she thought with the perfect weather they could sit outside on the terrace; parasols had been put up over the long table where they would eat and side tables where dishes of salad and fruit were to be laid out were decked with matching cloths and parasols. Another table would hold glasses and jugs of lemonade and ice buckets for the wine and Italian prosecco that Roland thought more appropriate than French champagne.

'It's all so lovely,' Matty said, putting her arms around her father's waist. 'Thank you, Papa.'

He kissed the top of her head. 'You deserve the best, my dearest Matty. I have so much to make up to you; to you all.'

Matty choked back a sob. Now wasn't the time for tears, but they were not far away. She could tell that her father was emotional too, although he hid it well.

'You know that you will have to do the same for my sisters, don't you?' she teased. 'In two years' time we'll be coming back for Julia's eighteenth birthday.'

Her father gave a mock groan. 'I'd better check my shares,' he said, 'and speak to my bank manager. With four daughters I shall soon be bankrupt!'

She was sure that he was joking; he never questioned them if they said they were in need of material for a new gown or coat or leather boots. We have always assumed that there was no need to do so, she thought.

'I'm going upstairs to change,' she told him. 'Grandmama will be here soon and I want to be ready to greet her.'

She left him to drink the coffee that one of the extra maids he had hired had brought him and went indoors, where she heard Nunny, who was having a lovely time organizing everyone and coping with their complete lack of English by calling out '*Andiamo!*', a word that the cook had taught her and she used often and to great effect when she wanted them to hurry up.

Matty laughed as she ran upstairs. Everything was going to plan, and, she thought, although her party would be small in numbers – her uncle Albert's family had failed to respond to the invitation – she would be surrounded by friends that she cared about.

She changed into her party dress – white muslin with pale blue embroidered forget-me-nots strewn across the skirt – and called Julia in to dress her hair. Julia was wearing her deep rose gown, the nearest thing she had to the dark red that Antonio had requested, for she had never worn such a colour.

Dorcas came in wearing blue, and then Faith in a white dress with a blue sash, a matching blue ribbon in her hair.

'Where's Becca?' Matty was anxious. 'Is she not ready yet?'

'Yes, don't worry. Eliza is curling her hair; they're just about ready,' Julia told her, and then Dorcas piped up from the window where she stood looking out.

'Here's your grandmother arriving, she's just getting out of a chaise.' She began to laugh. 'You'll never guess who is escorting her! Antonio!'

They all squealed and rushed to the window to look out, as Eliza and Becca appeared in the room. 'Oh, goodness,' Eliza giggled when she was told what the fuss was about. 'Adam is going to be furious.'

'Is he?' Julia turned to look at her. 'Why? Can he stay, Matty? Did you invite him?'

'No, I didn't.' Matty spoke from the window. 'But' – a smile curled around her lips – 'I don't see why not.' She saw her father stand up to greet his mother and shake the young man by the hand before indicating that they go inside. 'Perhaps I'd better go down,' she said hurriedly. 'Do I look all right?'

'You look lovely.' Julia gave her a kiss on her cheek and then Faith said, 'Happy birthday, dearest Matty,' while Becca muttered, 'You're a proper grown-up person now, aren't you?' Tears glistened. 'You won't change though, will you, Matty?'

'Course I won't, you goose,' Matty said affectionately. 'I'm the same today as I was yesterday. Just a day older.'

'That's all right, then.' Becca sniffed. 'And you won't marry Antonio or Mario, will you, because I told you before that I'd miss you if you left home.'

'I won't,' she said. 'If I find a nice Englishman I'll ask you first if you like him.'

They trooped towards the stairs and Adam, coming down from the roof, thought they looked like a throng of fluttering butterflies in their pretty gowns. Julia, the last to leave the room, closed the door and looked up.

'Julia,' he said, and smiled. 'You look lovely.' She gave him a demure smile and he held out his hand. 'May I walk you down?' Julia nodded, but instead of taking his hand she tucked hers under his arm. I'm in heaven at last, he thought as they turned to the stairs, until he saw the bevy of young ladies around Antonio and inwardly groaned.

Their father proposed that Matty invite Antonio to stay for the luncheon. 'It would be discourteous not to,' he whispered to her. 'Especially as he was kind enough to escort your grandmother. He would have to come back for her later in any case. Are you happy with that?'

Matty murmured that of course he was quite right, and as it was an informal gathering one more person would not make any difference to the catering.

She curtsied to her grandmother, kissed her cheek and thanked her for coming, and turning to Antonio, who was standing by her side, dipped her knee, thanked him for bringing her grandmother, and asked if he would give them the privilege of his company.

He put a hand to his chest and gave her a formal bow. 'Signorina Maddeson,' he murmured. '*Con piacere.*' Matty understood – 'with pleasure' – and blushed when from behind his back he produced a bouquet of flowers with a heavenly perfume.

Adam, watching with Eliza and Julia, muttered in Eliza's ear, 'Scheming Machiavellian. He knew he'd be invited if he brought Mrs Maddeson.'

Eliza gave him a sideways glance. 'Listen who's talking!' she murmured. 'You would have been heartbroken if you hadn't been invited.'

'But I'm a friend,' he hissed back.

Julia glanced at them both. 'What are you two muttering about?'

She was interrupted by a shout from Becca. 'Someone else is coming! Look.' She pointed towards the drive, where a tall man with a rucksack on his back was striding towards them. 'I don't know who it is.'

They all turned to look. Adam began to grin.

'Who is it?' Matty asked, shielding her eyes from the sun's brightness. Dorcas gave a sudden shriek and darted away towards the drive. 'It's Tim! My brother! Timothy,' she shouted, waving her arms. 'It's me!'

Tim Garton slipped off his rucksack and placed it on the ground, then put out his arms and wrapped them around Dorcas, lifting her off her feet. 'Hello, little sister.' He put her down and waved one arm to the assembled company. 'I know I said I couldn't come, but . . . Am I gatecrashing?'

They walked up to the terrace where Matty was waiting. 'Matty,' he said. 'I wouldn't have known you. It's been such an age since I last saw you.' He reached for her hand. 'Happy birthday, dearest Matty,' he said, and kissed her fingers. 'It's so good to see you again.' He glanced round at the smiling sisters and their father. 'All of you.'

He spotted Adam, who was still grinning, and who, lifting his right thumb to him, murmured to Eliza, 'Thank heavens. The cavalry has arrived!'

CHAPTER SIXTEEN

'I have to leave tomorrow,' Tim told Adam as they sat outside together and chatted whilst waiting for the food to be brought out. He'd dumped his rucksack in Adam's room, had a quick wash and changed his shirt; a palliasse was going to be brought up for him to sleep on that night.

'It's a long way to come just for one night,' Adam commented.

'It was a quick decision,' Tim told him. 'I was so bogged down with work that I felt I needed a break, so I decided to come. Fortunately it's not such a long journey for me from London to the port so I packed a bag and set off to catch the overnight ferry on Friday. I was lucky that all the trains were on time and I'd very little waiting between connections.'

'Well, I'm glad to see you,' Adam said mournfully. 'I'm overrun by handsome Italians.'

'I only see one!' Tim joked. 'But I can quite see he'll be fully engaged; the girls are like bees round a honey pot. But here's Matty coming to console us,' he added as she strolled over to talk to them and they both stood up.

'I'm so pleased that you could come after all, Tim,' Matty said. 'Dorcas never said there was even a possibility.'

'There wasn't.' He grinned, taking her hand affectionately. 'I'm just saying to Adam that it was a last-minute decision.'

'And he's leaving tomorrow,' Adam broke in.

'Oh, no!' Matty's forehead creased. 'Oh, must you, after such a long journey?'

'I must,' he said. 'But worth every minute to see you, Matty. It's been so long. Must be two years since we last met, isn't it?'

'More than that, I think. We've met only once since you went to university – the first Christmas, I think.'

He pursed his lips. 'So two and a half years ago,' he said. 'I came home each Christmas, but I stayed on in my lodgings and took casual work each summer to earn some money.' He turned to Adam. 'I suggest that's what you do, Adam. It's the start of independence. Can't rely on our fathers to pay for everything.'

'I suppose that's right,' Adam mused. 'Though I'll try to get home as often as I can.' He cast a glance towards where Julia was standing talking to Antonio.

Tim followed his gaze but made no comment, instead turning to Matty as she spoke. 'You look different, Tim,' she was saying. 'I can't think what it is.'

'I've grown taller,' he laughed. 'But you've changed too; quite the young lady, aren't you? You were, what, fifteen or so when we last met up?'

She nodded. 'The same as Dorcas, more or less.'

'Mmm,' he mused. 'But Dorcas is still a fledgling, a schoolgirl, compared with your . . .' His scrutiny was quite penetrating, but he seemed to run out of words of comparison and she felt herself flushing.

'Come on,' she said hastily. 'The food is ready; let's all find seats together.'

Not me, Adam thought; I'm the gooseberry here. I'll try to get between the Italian Lothario and Julia and scotch his romantic notions. He fell behind Matty and Tim, but to no avail: he heard his name called and turned to see Grandmama Maddeson beckoning him to a place between herself and Aunt Gertrude. Roland was at the head of the table, Becca on his left and Faith next to her. Matty was opposite Roland, with Tim on her right and Julia on her left, Antonio next to her.

Louisa, who was sitting in the middle with Eliza and Dorcas, looked across at him and smiled. Catching his eye, she raised her glass and mouthed, 'Good luck!'

She knows, he thought. How does she know? How humiliating.

Roland made a short speech about his beloved daughters and Matty in particular, who had been the anchor in their lives for the last ten years, and they all raised a glass to wish her a happy eighteenth birthday and all the best for her future.

Adam saw how solicitous Tim was being towards Matty, which raised a question in his mind; but we're too young, he thought. We're all too young. I've held a torch for Julia since she was six years old, and she never notices me. I'm just someone she knows.

When I leave for university, he decided, I will lead another life. I'll meet other people, join societies and expand my mind and outlook and fall in love with other young women; young women who want to make their mark in the world if they are allowed to. I won't forget my old friends, who'll always have a special place in my life, but I must look forward; there's a whole new world waiting. And with a single-mindedness he didn't know he had, he turned his gaze away from Julia and began a conversation with Mrs Maddeson and Miss Gertrude Maddeson.

Faith too had looked around the table, observing her family and their guests. She wondered about Antonio, who seemed to have insinuated himself into the party. Had it been intentional? Had he offered to bring their grandmother in the hope that he would be invited to stay for the luncheon? If that was the case then she thought it presumptuous. Faith had a fine regard for what was right and proper and didn't believe in anyone's taking advantage of someone else's generosity.

Their grandmother would have thought nothing of it. She was open-hearted and entertained lavishly, but this wasn't her party to which she could invite people as she wished. Antonio, she decided, had inveigled his way in to be with Julia, whose attention he had claimed – and, she remembered, he'd brought Matty flowers, so he had been expecting to be invited to stay.

Julia was flattered to have been singled out by Antonio, and she had noticed the glowering expression on Adam's face when he saw the Italian sitting next to her. I don't know what Adam expects; just because we have known him for ever doesn't mean that we can't have new friends as well as our old ones. It's right that we make new friendships; we must stretch our minds. Be more *liberal*. There, that word again. It's always cropping up. I'm sure that's what I mean – more open-minded, and especially with someone from another country; that, I think, is extremely important.

'Sorry?' she said. 'I didn't catch . . .' Antonio was whispering something in her ear. He whispered again and she turned towards him, her eyes wide and her lips parted.

'I would like to walk with you in the garden later,' he had said, and she was astonished. How could he say such a thing in hearing distance of her father, her aunts and sisters?

'No,' she murmured, feeling a frisson of danger run through her. 'That won't be possible.'

'There is a moon tonight,' he said, still in that smooth whisper. 'I would like to show it to you over the lake.'

'It is my sister's birthday,' she murmured in reply. 'I can't possibly—'

'We would not be long,' he interrupted. 'No one would miss us for five minutes,' he added persuasively.

'Perhaps,' she said, laughing in what she hoped was a coquettish manner. It was a long time before darkness. It was a glorious day now, the sun beating down, and she knew that soon they would have to retreat indoors to escape it. It won't do any harm to tease him a little, and besides, she thought, Grandmama won't stay long. She will want her afternoon nap and Antonio will have to take her home.

She was quite right. The luncheon took time, for there were many courses of pasta, tiny potato dumplings, salads with dishes of tomatoes drenched in oil, garlic and basil, cured meats and pâtés. The young maids were run off their feet by Nunny, who had refused Matty's entreaty to eat with them and was constantly urging the maids to hurry, to bring fruit, or sweet cake, ice cream, or jugs of lemonade, clapping her hands and urging them on with frequent cries of '*Andiamo!*' The sun became hotter and some retreated indoors or went to fetch parasols, and finally Grandmama called for Antonio to fetch the chaise to the front and take her home.

'It was so very good of you to come, Grandmama.' Matty kissed her grandmother's cheek. 'We will come to visit you tomorrow after we have been to Isola Bella; we are all looking forward to seeing the palace.'

She turned to Antonio and thanked him for bringing her grandmother, and added that they were all eager to see his sketches and the subsequent painting. He bowed and kissed her hand and thanked her for her hospitality, and had he been hoping for an invitation to come back he would have been disappointed, for Matty didn't even think of it.

The chaise was waved off from the terrace and then everyone who was still outside disappeared indoors, for it really was very hot, more so than was expected so early in the year. 'It's bound to rain,' Aunt Gertrude said, hurrying indoors to find a cool corner. 'I can feel it in the air.'

Nunny appeared in the front lounge and asked if anyone would like a pot of tea. Everyone said yes except Louisa, who said she would drink a glass of water and then take a stroll down to the lake.

'Anyone care to come? Adam?'

'Yes, I would,' he said. 'I'll just get my hat. Anyone else?'

No one else volunteered. Tim sat down between Matty and his sister, Faith said she was going to take her tea and lie on her bed to cool down, and Becca asked if she might go on to the roof. Her father agreed, providing she took a parasol or umbrella, and then he and everyone else simply sought a comfy chair where they could relax out of the heat.

'Are you sure it's not too hot for you, Mrs Walton?' Adam asked as they walked across the grass towards the bottom of the garden.

'I'm all right under the parasol,' she said, 'and my shoulders are covered.' She'd picked up a silk shawl on the way out. 'Let's sit under the tree near the statue for a while before we go down to the lake. And do call me Louisa,' she added, 'at least whilst we're alone. We don't want to upset anyone's sensibilities.' She glanced at him and smiled. He was perspiring under his hat. 'It will make me feel young again,' she told him, 'and you grown up!'

'You're hardly old,' he said, bravely gallant. 'And I'm not sure if I'm ready for being completely grown up yet.'

She led him across the grass towards an ancient olive tree with untidy branches which sheltered a bench seat and a marble statue. Louisa was pleased to see that the woman depicted was fully clothed. She had seen much statuary and some, such as *Venus of the Bath*, did nothing to hide the naked form of a woman. She wouldn't have been embarrassed for herself, but was glad to have spared the blushes of this very young man. This image, she thought, could be discussed dispassionately in spite of the bird droppings which adorned her coiled ringlets.

Adam gazed at the statue before he sat down next to Louisa. 'She's a fine specimen of womanhood, isn't she? Though very petite.'

So he's noticed her small breasts and isn't embarrassed. Louisa gazed at the statue and brought out her fan and cooled herself. 'It seems that Grecian women are mostly diminutive in statues.'

'More expensive to create voluptuous women,' he said without thinking, and turned a flushed, mortified expression towards Louisa. 'I do beg your pardon,' he stammered. 'A schoolboy joke.'

Louisa laughed. 'Yes,' she said, 'much more marble needed. Don't be embarrassed. I'm not a prude, but be careful in front of Miss Maddeson – the elder, I mean, not our lovely Matty.'

He issued a relieved sigh and said, 'Yes, of course. But I hadn't thought of Matty being another Miss Maddeson. It seems very strange. I don't think she'll like it, even though she's always seemed more mature and sensible than any of us. Do you suppose it's because she took on her mother's role when Mrs Maddeson died?'

'I do,' she agreed, 'and she was far too young to take on the responsibility.'

'I remember Matty and Julia being brought to our house that day,' he said in a low voice. 'Not Faith, because she wasn't well, and Becca was only a baby. Matty just sat staring into space and didn't want to play any games, and Julia stood next to her, holding her hand; she wouldn't sit down or take her coat off.'

And Julia probably remembers that too, Louisa thought, or some of it, and didn't understand what was happening, and maybe that is why she is cool towards Adam without knowing why.

'And your sister, Eliza, where was she?'

'I don't remember,' he murmured. 'Not with us. My mother and Nanny said I had to look after the two girls until someone came to fetch them home.' He sighed. 'No one said why; we only found out later. Nanny came to fetch Matty home but Julia wouldn't let her go without her; she must have known that something bad was happening.' He stopped suddenly and looked at Louisa. 'I'm sorry. I keep making these awful blunders. She was your sister, wasn't she? I'm so very sorry.'

She patted his hand. 'It's all right, Adam. We have to keep talking about people we've lost. It's how we remember them.'

'Yes, you're right,' he said. 'I felt the same about a dog I had when I was little. He died and I kept talking about him so often that eventually my father got me another one to take my mind off him.' He turned another anguished glance towards his companion. 'Not that I'm saying it's the same thing at all – I mean, there's no comparison.'

He groaned, and Louisa laughed and stood up. 'Come on!' she said. 'Don't let's get mawkish. Let's take that walk! It's going to be a glorious evening and I'll explain what it's like to be a proper grown-up.'

'Could I ask you one more thing?' he said, following her off the grass and on to the drive. 'When you said we have to keep talking about people who have died so that we remember them, I thought . . . well, I thought that I've never heard you speaking of your husband and I understand that you are a widow?'

'So I am,' she said, keeping on walking. 'But there are often exceptions to the rule.'

CHAPTER SEVENTEEN

The following day they were booked to visit Isola Bella, so it was unfortunate that Tim was due to leave early that morning. He had said goodbye to several of the party the night before: Miss Maddeson, whom he hadn't met previously, who was charmed by his courteous manners; Faith, who said she had had such a lovely day she didn't want it to end but couldn't keep her eyes open; Becca, who was also falling asleep in her chair, even though she insisted she wasn't in the least tired. Most of them were flagging; it had been a long, though splendid day.

In the early evening more food had been brought out to tempt them: crisp crostini brushed with olive oil and topped with chicken livers or anchovies, sweet pepper frittata, salads and tender chicken strips, sweet almond biscuits, crunchy biscotti to dip into Vin Santo; light-as-air sponge cake, ice cream, and jugs of lemonade and chianti from the region of Florence. Sparkling wine sat cooling in ice buckets.

'Who's going to eat all of this?' Roland had slurred and Louisa had shaken her head; Adam and Tim with young men's appetites had bravely taken up plates and begun again. Matty picked up a plate too and helped herself to crostini.

'I don't think I ate much at lunchtime,' she said. 'I was far too excited. Such a lovely birthday, Papa. Thank you so much.'

'Well deserved, dearest daughter,' her father said, and swivelling round in his chair waved a hand at Julia. 'Your turn next, Julia. Next year, is it?'

'No, Papa,' she laughed. 'I've just turned sixteen, remember?'

'Ah, yes,' he said sleepily. 'Of course. We had a tea party, didn't we?' He rose from his chair. "S no good,' he said, swaying a little. 'I can't keep up. Too much *vino*, I'm afraid.' He bent to say goodbye to Tim, who couldn't stand up as he had a plate of food on his lap and a glass of wine in one hand. 'Don't get up,' Roland garbled. 'Shafe journey home.' He patted Matty's head, then Louisa's, then Eliza's and Dorcas's, and nodded to Adam. 'You're staying, aren't you? Not going home yet?'

Adam wiped his mouth with his fingers. 'No sir, I'm staying awhile.'

'Goodnight, then. Louisa, you'll lock up, won't you?' He peered at her. 'Or somebody will, I expect.'

Matty giggled. She had never seen her father inebriated. Too much sun and too much wine, she thought, but why not? Today has been special.

Adam put down his plate and jumped to his feet. 'I'm popping upstairs, sir,' he said, putting his hand on his host's back. 'Can I assist you? The stairs always seem steeper at night, don't you find?'

'Well, what a wise young man you are,' Roland slurred. 'You're quite right. They do.'

When Adam came down again, after pointing his host towards the right bedroom door, he said eagerly, 'There's a moon and millions of stars. Would anyone like to come up on the roof and take a look?'

'Oh, yes, do let's,' Matty said, getting up, and Julia agreed. Louisa looked at the young people and declined, making the excuse that she was ready for her bed, even though she wasn't. Moonlight and starry skies were for the young and they would have much to talk about; and who knows, she thought, glancing at Timothy who had seemed to have had eyes only for Matty during the whole day, what might come of it.

She walked to the French doors, which were still open, and looked out across the lawn. She could hear rustlings and murmurings in the trees and saw the reflection of the moon in the lake; there would be a good view of it from the roof. She wished that Stephen had come; he would have been a pleasant companion. She didn't often feel lonely, but tonight she did. Perhaps it was because of the young people, and Matty in particular on this her birthday, who were on the cusp of life and would be eager to embrace it.

Timothy, clever and articulate, would join his father in their family firm of solicitors once he had finished at university; she had heard a murmur that Adam wanted to be a teacher. He would make a good one, she thought, kind, patient and understanding; look how he had jumped to help Roland upstairs when he was clearly incapable of getting up them alone. He obviously adored Julia, who seemed to be totally unaware of it. Julia, who had some long-held problems, she considered, needed a young man like Adam in her life to keep her steady.

Listen to me, she thought, as she closed and locked the doors. Such a wise sage as I am, offering advice and guidance to those who don't need it. Young people grow up and find their own path. Or some of them do. I didn't. She sighed, and headed towards the staircase. On reaching her floor she heard the muted sound of laughter coming from the roof and smiled. Yes, she considered. They'll be all right with whatever life throws at them, unlike me. I seem to have taken the wrong track and can't seem to find the right one.

On the roof, the young women wrapped their shawls around their shoulders and gazed down towards the lake. A sweet smell of honeysuckle and something lemony like viburnum, daphne or cistus wafted towards them. The road beyond the garden was empty and all they could hear were soft chirruping noises from the trees.

Timothy, who had been leaning on the balcony rail, suddenly turned to face them. He still had a wine glass in his hand, as he and Adam had brought an opened wine bottle up with them. 'This has been one of the best days of my life,' he said, and raised his glass to each of the young women in turn. 'Thank you, Matty, for inviting me. What shall we drink to?'

Adam raised his glass too. 'Friendship!' he said. 'There can be nothing more worthwhile.'

CHAPTER EIGHTEEN

Matty and Dorcas both rose early to say goodbye to Tim, who'd already had breakfast and was about to leave when they came down in their dressing gowns at six o'clock. He gave his sister a hug and took Matty's hand in both of his, and she felt that she wouldn't have minded having a hug too, but quite properly that wasn't offered.

'I'll be home in the summer, Dorcas, so I'll see you then, and I'll hope to see you too, Matty, if possible? I won't be so pushed for time then, as university will be finished and I'll be waiting for my exam results.'

'That would be lovely,' she said, filled with delight to hear that they might meet again so soon. 'You'll be out in the big bad world,' she said jocularly, to hide her pleasure at the thought.

They waved goodbye from the terrace as he reached the end of the drive and turned to lift a hand in farewell, then stepped back inside. 'Shall we have breakfast now?' Matty said, lifting the lids of containers on the dining room table. 'I don't know why Cook would think that Tim could eat so much.'

'He might have eaten more if he hadn't been travelling so early,' Dorcas said. 'Would it matter if we ate in our dressing gowns?'

'Of course not,' Matty said. 'We're on holiday – we can do whatever we like. I would think that everyone else will be late for breakfast after last night in any case, although we have to be ready by ten o'clock to get the boat. I'm so excited about the visit to Isola Bella; can you imagine someone building a palace for you to show you his love?'

'I can't,' Dorcas said prosaically, picking up a plate and forking up rashers of thinly sliced prosciutto and then a slice of melon. 'But I suppose Italians are more romantic than Englishmen – if the story is true. It might be just a romantic tale.' She sat down at the table and looked about her. 'Do you think the coffee is hot?'

Matty was spearing her own prosciutto and indicated the brass bell on the table. 'Ring for it,' she said, 'and ask for bread too. I love Italian bread.'

A maid came in answer to the bell, bringing in fresh bread, and they asked for another pot of coffee.

'We are so lucky, Dorcas, don't you think?' Matty murmured.

'To be here?' Dorcas said, melon juice dripping down her chin. 'Yes, I do, and thank you for inviting me, Matty.'

'Oh, I didn't mean that particularly,' Matty was quick to respond. 'I meant generally. We have so much compared with other people. I feel sometimes that I should be doing something useful now that I'm old enough. It was different when we were children and being educated and couldn't do anything without permission, but now . . .'

Her thoughts drifted away. But what could we do? Our governesses have taught us numeracy, literature and art, but that doesn't equip us for making a living, as so many people have to.

'Mama used to take us with her to visit old people in Beverley,' she went on. 'She generally took a basket of groceries, eggs and butter, that kind of thing, which she said they might not be able to afford to buy. We stopped going of course, after . . .' She hesitated. 'I asked Papa once if we could start again, but he said we couldn't, not on our own. But I could now. I'm old enough, but I wouldn't take Julia.'

'Why not?' Dorcas asked.

Matty shook her head. 'She'd be upset.'

Dorcas sighed. 'I'm expected to marry well, so there isn't much time to do anything else now that I'm almost eighteen,' she said lazily. 'Tim is having all the fun away at university, and I expect he'll become a successful lawyer and make important contacts through the people Papa knows.'

It's not enough, Matty thought guiltily. We should do more.

They finished their breakfast and went up to get ready for the trip to the island, feeling virtuous when they woke Eliza, Julia, Faith and Becca and told them they had already had breakfast.

'I think I'm suffering from having eaten and drunk too much,' Becca said sleepily from beneath her sheets, covering her eyes from the sunshine pouring in through the window.

'But surely you didn't drink alcohol, did you?' Matty exclaimed.

'I don't know, I might have done.' Becca stretched her arms above her head. 'Something sweet from a jug,' she said. 'A sort of reddish brownish colour, tasted of lemonade.'

'Punch!' Matty said. 'You weren't supposed to drink that! It has rum and other spirits in it, I think. Was it nice?' she added, rather spoiling the effect.

'Lovely!' Becca threw back the covers. 'I had two glasses.'

Adam was ready for the trip and having his breakfast when the young ladies came down, wearing comfortable shoes and carrying their sun hats and parasols.

Next to come down was Aunt Gertrude, and then Louisa. Adam went upstairs to knock on Roland's door in case he had overslept, which it seemed he had, for he looked pale when he came down, refusing food and only drinking strong coffee. Nunny was last to come in for breakfast, even though she had been busy since seven o'clock, which was very late for her.

They walked down the drive to where the boat was berthed off the promenade close to the villa. The boatman and

Roland helped Gertrude and Nunny on to the vessel and they sat together in the small saloon so that they were under cover.

'It isn't far, Nunny,' Matty told her. 'You can see the turrets of the palace from here.' She pointed across the deep blue lake to where the green island seemed to be floating. 'I was reading that a few hundred years ago it was simply a rocky place with few inhabitants and little cultivation.'

'Well, my word,' Nunny said. 'I can see tall trees, and . . .' She peered ahead as they steamed towards the island. 'Can I see people standing on the edge of the cliff? That's very dangerous,' she said in some alarm. 'We must be very careful when we arrive.'

'I believe they're statues, Mrs Nunnington,' Adam broke in. 'Seemingly there are hundreds of them.'

'Good heavens!' Aunt Gertrude scoffed. 'How ostentatious! Why would anyone want so many? Surely one, or perhaps two, would suffice for anyone to show off their wealth.'

The party was silenced, until Becca piped up from where she was leaning over the bulwark watching the island. 'Perhaps it was built as a kind of playground. There are a lot of steps, and balustrades with urns on top of them.' She turned to look for Faith. 'Have you brought your sketch book, Faith? There are lots of things you can draw. Look.' She pointed up to a cliff top where they could see a stone wall and above it a marble statue of a man on a horse. 'I'd love that. Papa?' She looked around, but her father was talking to the captain. 'That's what I'd like.' She pressed her lips together. 'Though I'd rather have a real one.'

'A man on a horse?' Julia said curiously.

'No, just the horse, silly!'

A guide was waiting to greet them as they docked. The boatman helped Aunt Gertrude and Nunny to disembark, Roland and Adam helped Louisa and the girls, but Becca jumped off herself. 'Look, Papa,' she said, pointing up to the top of the terraces. 'Look at the man on the horse. Oh.' She shielded

116

her eyes. 'No! It isn't a horse, it's a – what is it? It has something sticking out of its head!'

The guide came towards her. 'It is a unicorn, signorina. A mythical creature. A special animal for beautiful young women. We will look at it more closely in a leetle while, yes?'

'Yes!' she whispered, completely mesmerized.

'Well,' Adam murmured to his sister, 'that's taken care of Becca. She's completely captivated. She'll tell her father that's what she wants for her next birthday. I wonder what her sisters will want to take home?'

'It's very romantic,' Eliza said, her eyes roaming over the gardens, the flowering trees, the colourful blooms. 'And what is that glorious scent? It's enough to make anyone fall in love.'

'Heavens, not you too?' he said. 'What a pity that Tim has gone home. He'd be more your kind of fellow than the Italians, I'd think.'

She looked at him, her eyebrows arched. 'Then you'd be totally wrong, brother dear! And besides, I rather think that Tim might have other ideas that don't include me.'

Adam gave an inward groan. Not Julia! Tim's eyes had followed Matty yesterday, but Matty treated him only as a friend; she wasn't a coquettish kind at all. Later, he'd seen Julia and Tim in earnest conversation. But she's too young, he reflected uneasily, and she's surely not his kind or he hers. He's serious and deep thinking and Julia is – Julia is . . . He couldn't possibly describe Julia's characteristics; he only knew that he would be glad to get away to London, to fill his life with study and not see her at all, for she always made it perfectly clear that he was never in her thoughts, ever.

They were given a two-hour tour of the palace and gardens, from the lower floor of the palace, with its cool cobblestoned grottos of black and white stone and marble arches, through the gallery of art that made Faith smile in wonder and delight and her father draw in a breath, to the room where Napoleon and his lady, it was reported, once spent the night; and then they ascended the wide steps flanked by huge pots holding

117

sweet-smelling shrubs of oleander and camellia, magnolia and roses, which filled the air with perfume and led them to the very top of the numerous terraces with its statuary and wonderful views.

'It's like being in a magical fairyland,' Julia murmured to no one in particular as she gazed from the highest terrace and looked out over the blue lake.

At her side Louisa nodded, but didn't comment. She thought her young niece was right: it was extravagant and flamboyant, but beautiful enough to take the breath away from anyone with only half a romantic heart, and she felt a sudden loss, not of her husband, but of any other man by her side to share in the wonder of it. Her thoughts switched to Stephen; he hadn't come as he had said he might. He would have been a good companion to be with, she mused again.

She glanced across at Roland. He looked pale and drawn as he gazed into the distance. The guide had left them now to make their own way back to the boat. She heard a church clock strike on the mainland. Gertrude and Mrs Nunnington were sitting quietly on a bench resting their legs, for there had been a lot of steps to negotiate.

'Roland,' she said quietly, 'I think our time is up. The boat will be waiting for us.'

'Ah! Yes.' He gave her a quick acknowledging nod. 'Best gather everyone up.'

Dorcas was talking to Adam, Matty to Eliza. Julia was still gazing at the view, Faith sitting on a low stone wall, lost in whatever she was sketching in her pad, and Becca staring upwards at the man on the unicorn's back.

'Is everyone ready?' Roland called. 'Time to go. It's time for departure and lunch.' He was trying to sound jolly, but there was a strain in his voice that Louisa intuitively caught.

They were all quiet on the journey back, exhausted and bedazzled by the sights they had seen. Louisa strolled to where Roland was standing with his arms crossed, looking without seeing at the incoming shore.

'You've been here before,' she said softly.

'Yes. We came here on our honeymoon.'

'Italy – yes, of course! I remember, though I didn't know it was here.'

'We took a boat down from Switzerland and Constance was so taken by the island we decided to stay,' he said. 'We found a taverna in Stresa which was glad of our custom and we stayed for three days. It was the most wonderful time of our lives.' He turned an anguished expression towards her. 'It was my fault she died.' His voice broke as he spoke in little more than a murmur. 'Like many men I wanted a son, but I should have waited; there was plenty of time, we were still young enough. But I loved her and was too eager, and she had already had four pregnancies in quick succession, and I shall never ever forgive myself.'

CHAPTER NINETEEN

Nunny was packing for home and making heavy work of it. Matty sat on the bed in her room up on the roof and watched her.

'Who's going to pack for you all, Miss Martha, when you're ready to leave? That's what I'm worrying about.'

'We'll just have to manage, Nunny. That's why I'm watching you,' Matty said, and smiled a little because Nunny kept forgetting to call her Miss Maddeson as she'd said she would. 'We are old enough to do this for ourselves; you just spoil us.'

'Young ladies like you and your sisters shouldn't have to do things like this. That's why people like me are here to do it for you.'

'You'd better stay then,' Matty responded. 'Tell Aunt Gertrude that you can't possibly leave us and she'll have to travel home alone.'

'I can't do that.' Nunny put both hands on her ample hips. 'You know I can't. How would the poor lady manage?'

'Then you're completely torn, aren't you, Nunny?' Matty climbed off the bed.

'Indeed I am.' Nunny clicked and closed the clasp of her portmanteau. They were not leaving until the day after tomorrow, but she was ready apart from packing food for the journey, which she would do the following evening. 'I have had such a wonderful time – that palace . . .' Words seemed to fail her, but then she went on, 'There is one more thing I was looking forward to, and I'm afraid I might miss it.'

'What's that, Nunny?' Matty said affectionately, hesitating by the door.

'That painting yon Italian fellow is doing. I'd like to see that when it's finished. Will it be coming home?'

'I certainly hope so.' Matty leaned against the wall. 'I understand that Papa has offered him a commission; I think he wanted to in case Grandmama did and then wanted to keep the painting here.'

'Ah, so it'll come home and we can put it up on 'drawing room wall or somewhere?'

'Yes,' Matty agreed. 'Of course,' she said thoughtfully, 'we don't know if it will be any good or not, but . . .' She hesitated. 'He did ask if he might call tomorrow, so we can ask him when it will be ready. We've had several sittings – or standings, at least – and I know he's started with his brush, for I noticed the paint on his fingers.'

'Hmm,' Nunny said, and raised a finger. 'You will watch Miss Julia with that young man, won't you, Miss Martha? He might be a bit forward, if you understand my meaning; don't let her go out alone with him. Get young Adam to keep an eye on him, we know we can trust him, or Mrs Walton might be better. You just don't know wi' foreigners.'

Matty nodded and smiled. She could imagine Julia's face if it were suggested that Adam should be her escort; and whatever would Adam think about it?

Adam, however, was at that moment in serious conversation with Mr Maddeson, after some consideration and a discussion with his sister, who had advised him that he should do whatever he thought best.

'So you see, sir, I worry that I should be back at school, to be sure that if I am offered a place at university I am there to accept it.'

'I quite understand,' Roland told him, 'even though we should be sorry to see you leave. But are you likely to hear yet? Isn't it a little early?'

'It probably is, sir,' Adam answered. 'But I always like to be prepared for any possibility.'

'What subjects are you looking at?'

'History and English; and then I'd like to teach.'

'Really?' Roland was surprised by this. 'At university level?'

'No, sir,' Adam said, and raised his chin as if he had been used to derisory comments about his choice of career. 'I'd like to teach locally, at either a National School or a Ragged School: children who perhaps won't get much of a chance in life. I'd like to help them at least get one foot on the ladder of education, so that means I'll need a teaching diploma.'

Roland gazed at him and wished that he had had such a son. 'Most commendable,' he said softly. 'A most worthy ambition. Your father must be proud.'

'I don't know about that, sir.' Adam stood up tall. 'I rather think he'd prefer me to go into law or politics, but neither subject interests me.'

'No,' Roland murmured, knowing Cecil Chapman as an influential man, who apparently hadn't put his own desires above his son's moral aspirations. 'You have the human touch.' He put his hand out to shake Adam's. 'You must do as you think best. It's your life; do with it what you will and be satisfied. That's all any of us can hope for.'

Adam gave a huge grin. 'Thank you, sir.'

The following morning he went to see Matty, who was sitting outside on the terrace, and apologized to her for deciding to leave early. 'I've enjoyed myself tremendously. I love it here, and I'll never forget my room on the roof, but there's always a plus side to everything, and it means I can offer my services to your aunt and Mrs Nunnington as chief luggage carrier.'

'They'll be delighted to hear it, although I think Nunny was quite looking forward to the challenge of being in charge,'

Matty told him, laughing. 'Will you be able to change your tickets?'

'Yes, I think so. Your father said there was an agent in Stresa so I'll go there after lunch and ask them.'

'I'll walk in with you then, if I may?' she said. 'It's such a nuisance that young women aren't able to walk alone, even along the side of the lake. We walk into Beverley, but the Italians are so protective, especially of their daughters.'

'But everyone knows you in Beverley,' he said. 'They don't here, and, well, you could be anyone.'

'A bad influence?' She smiled. 'Tempting their sons away from the *signorine* they have chosen for them?'

'I'm not sure it's quite like that, but maybe something of the sort.'

'Nunny said I shouldn't let Julia be alone with Antonio,' Matty teased him. 'She says you can't always trust foreigners.'

He tutted, but she saw that she had touched a tender spot. 'We're the foreigners!' he said. 'That's the trouble with the English we think we're so wise.'

'So you think she'd be quite safe with him if they went for a stroll along the lakeside?'

He gazed at her, cottoning on to her wit. 'No,' he said emphatically. 'I do not! You must accompany her.'

He left her then to ask Miss Maddeson and Nunny if he might escort them on the journey home; they were both extremely pleased to consent, and when he left them to go upstairs and pack they agreed that he would be the perfect companion.

When Matty told her sisters that Adam would be leaving the following day along with their aunt and Nunny, both Faith and Becca expressed their disappointment, but Julia said little except that she was sure he shouldn't have any doubts about being accepted at university. 'Tim said he was an exceptional candidate,' she murmured.

'Did he?' Eliza said, her forehead creasing. 'At one time Papa would have liked him to study politics. He thought he would have a great future, could even become Prime Minister! But he's come round to the idea of him being only a school-teacher, I think.'

'He'll be a very good one.' Louisa was sitting in a deckchair with a sun hat over her face and they'd forgotten she was there. 'He's patient, intelligent and understanding, and any one of the children he might teach in future could go on to great things because of his influence.'

She lifted the hat and squinted at them through one eye. They all remained silent. This was Adam she was talking about, and she seemed to know and understand him better than any of them, including his sister, who nevertheless glowed with pride at the praise she had given him.

It was getting warmer each day, and that evening they sat out on the terrace to eat. Roland opened bottles of prosecco and poured freshly made lemonade to wish Aunt Gertrude, Nunny and Adam a safe journey home the fol-lowing day. A bowl of olives was placed on the long table, along with sliced tomatoes drizzled with olive oil on a bed of rosemary and garlic. Cook had excelled herself with Crostini di Casali, of which Nunny had prior knowledge having watched her make it from hot and tender chicken livers mixed with anchovies and capers and served on crisp grilled olive bread. There was salad with ripe avocados and ricotta, paper-thin *crespelle* filled with chopped spinach and sheep's milk pecorino cheese and served with tomato sauce; and inevitably there were several bowls of pasta, fol-lowed by sweet dishes: tiramisu, brioche, zabaglione.

They had finished eating and were chatting over their drinks when they saw a figure coming up the drive struggling with an extremely large parcel.

'It's Antonio,' Matty said. 'Is he – he's brought the painting!'

Adam got to his feet. 'I'll give him a hand,' he said, and set off down the drive.

'He should have asked,' Roland said, also standing up. 'We could have met him and helped him with it.'

'How exciting!' Matty said. 'I can't wait to see it. He's been very quick.'

'He has, hasn't he?' Louisa said languorously.

'*Buona sera, signore,* forgive my intrusion.' Antonio was breathless, but he bowed to the older ladies and Roland. '*Signorine.*' He put his hand to his chest as he looked at the young ladies. 'Forgive the lateness of the hour.'

'Come and sit down, please,' Matty told him. 'Get your breath back. Papa—' She was about to ask him to pour Antonio a glass of water, but he had done so already, and given him a glass of prosecco as well. Antonio sat down whilst Adam propped the parcel carefully against the villa wall, keeping his hand on it in case it fell over. He glanced at his sister and raised his eyebrows.

They waited in silence until Antonio had drunk the whole glass of water and taken a gulp of prosecco. Matty passed him a plate of biscotti, which he refused.

'It is finished,' he said, waving his glass towards the parcel. 'I show it to *la nonna* yesterday and she like it very much, but I wish to bring it for your – your *opinione.* That is right word, yes?'

'Yes.' Matty nodded. 'Should we go inside? The sun is going down.'

Antonio agreed, so he and Adam took one side of the parcel each and they all trooped inside. Antonio went towards the stairs and began to carefully unfasten the string that held it and then unwrap the painting, keeping the back of it facing everyone as they crowded into the hall. Julia and Matty glanced at each other; Julia's cheeks were pink.

'Ah, *mamma mia,*' Antonio was muttering. '*Mamma mia.*' Then the brown paper fell away to the floor. Adam stood back as he caught his first glimpse of it.

Eliza looked at him. He doesn't like it.

Antonio swivelled it round to face them, and giving a short bow announced: '*Belle Donne.*' Beautiful Women.

Except that it wasn't them. The images were of four young women, one brunette, two blonde, and one with jet-black hair.

125

If that is supposed to be me and is how I look, Julia thought, then I'll throw myself in the lake.

The faces were all the same, without a single characteristic to denote the young women who were staring back at them. Not a smile, nor a single expression. They could have been made of stone.

'Vanity,' Aunt Gertrude muttered. 'Sheer vanity to have an image made of oneself; I shall give up on art altogether,' and she turned round and walked out of the front door.

Nunny stood and stared, then looked at her employer's face. He was stroking his beard. I know that look, she thought, and she too turned and walked out.

'Which one is me?' Becca was heard to say. 'Is it the one with the braid and short skirt?'

'*Si, signorina.* Can you not tell, mmm?'

Becca shook her head. 'No. I didn't realize I looked like that.' She sighed and turned away, heading for the door as her aunt and Nunny had done.

Matty wanted to giggle, whilst Faith was bitterly disappointed. With her interest in art she'd been eagerly awaiting something exceptional. Not his fault, she thought sadly. He just hasn't the talent for it. The backdrop of the painting was a show of bright colour, representing the light from the dome which had shone so beautifully on the day they had posed for the sketches, but here there were no swathes of delicate rainbow shades, only garish reds, greens and purples. Even their pretty gowns which they had chosen so carefully were unrecognizable, the whites were grey and the subtle flowers embroidered on the skirts were lost completely in the brash and gaudy display of the background.

The final affront, Louisa thought, was Julia's rose-coloured gown painted deep red, the colour he had asked her to wear. Whoever was it who had persuaded this young man that he had talent?

CHAPTER TWENTY

A cabriolet had been ordered to take the three travellers to the railway station and everyone had got up early to see them off. Roland was travelling with them to the station to reassure himself that his sister and Nunny had everything they needed for the journey; he was extremely relieved that Adam was escorting them the whole way home, and he slipped him some money, Italian, French and English, to cover emergencies if there should be any.

Once on the train Gertrude gave one final wave goodbye but Nunny waved and waved from the window until she was shrouded in steam and smoke and Roland could no longer see her; she was upset over leaving behind her young ladies, he could tell, and indeed they were sad too, and Becca, still in her dressing robe, wept a little and said she wished they were going home, for she was missing Pug and knew he would be missing her.

Perhaps a month is too long, Roland pondered as he turned away to head for the cabriolet stand, and then stood stock still as he saw a family group also waiting for a cab.

Recovering from the shock, he walked slowly towards them. 'Albert!' he said, forgetting that his brother preferred to be called Fisher.

Albert turned. His mouth opened and closed. 'Roland!' He put out his hand to shake his brother's. 'How did you know we'd be on this train?'

Roland greeted his sister-in-law by taking her hand and murmuring 'Caroline', and then nodded to their son and daughter who were standing lethargically beside her. 'I didn't,' he answered. 'We'd given you up. I've just seen Gertrude and Mrs Nunnington on to the train for their journey home. You've missed them, I'm afraid.' He heard a little grunt from Caroline. She would be pleased to have missed Gertrude, he deduced. The dislike between them was mutual. 'You've also missed Matty's birthday, which is why we came.'

He looked at Ralph and Rosalind. 'We had a splendid celebration. I'm sorry you weren't here for it. Erm, have you booked accommodation, or are you staying with Mother? We could fit you in our villa, in Gertrude's and Mrs Nunnington's rooms at a pinch, though they are rather small.'

He didn't mention the rooms on the roof; his daughters were already planning what they were going to do with them. Faith had said she would drape sheets over the windows of one of them if it became too hot and use it as a studio so that she could paint; Matty and Julia were set on having the other as a garden room.

'Oh, we couldn't possibly intrude on your family,' Caroline began, just as Albert put up his hand to hail a cab, shouting, 'Cabby! Cabby!'

'You won't get one like that,' Roland said, and set off to the cab stand where, in hesitant Italian, he asked if there were two cabs available. They came immediately, and Caroline and the two children went in one and Roland and Albert in the other, with the family's luggage piled inside and on top.

'By the way,' Albert said as they bowled away, 'can you call me Fisher and not Albert? Especially in front of Caroline.'

Roland sighed. 'I'll try to remember, though it's not a proper name, is it? I can't conceive why you were given it in the first place, and there's nothing wrong with Albert. However, about accommodation? What would you like to do? I don't think Caroline will enjoy being swamped by a bevy of young

ladies; they've all brought friends to stay,' he said menda-
ciously, 'and then there's Louisa.'

'Louisa? Constance's sister, do you mean?'

'I know no other.'

Albert gazed at him incredulously. 'You've brought your
sister-in-law? Won't people talk?'

Roland stared back. 'Talk? Who? And what would they talk
about? Louisa is a good friend; my daughters adore her and
she was a great support when Constance died, even though
she was grieving for her sister too.'

His voice had risen and he felt angry with his brother; how
dare he insinuate there was anything questionable about a
normal family relationship? Albert's wife had done nothing
to help him or his daughters when they were overwhelmed by
their mother's loss, saying that she had her own young children to think of; she had never invited them to stay, nor had
she ever come to their house to comfort them, but only written a formal letter of condolence.

The cabriolet turned on to the road by the lake and Roland
looked out at the water. He was furious and he didn't want
Albert or his wife to stay with them; the children could come,
if they wanted to, but not to stay: the son in particular was very
like his mother.

They trotted on, his eyes barely seeing as he stared out of the
window, until he noticed a man sitting on a bench, one arm
stretched across the back. Roland sat up and leaned towards
the window. It was the beggar he'd seen the first night, when
he hadn't any money in his pocket. He rapped on the roof.
'*Fermare!*' Stop.

The cab slowed and he opened the door to get out. 'I have
to speak to someone,' he told his brother. 'You'd better drive
on to Mother's. I'm sure she'll have room for you there. You've
stayed plenty of times.'

Albert didn't answer, just nodded his head. Roland
slammed the cab door and called up to the driver, telling
him Henrietta's address, and then walked back the way they

had come. He can damn well pay for the cabs, he grumbled to himself. Albert wasn't known for his generosity and he'd be peeved that he had to pay for two vehicles instead of one. Not that I care, Roland thought. I'll give the money for the fare to the beggar.

He walked on until he came to the bench, and sat down, leaving room so that the beggar didn't have to move his arm. The man looked towards him and nodded. '*Buongiorno, signore.*'

Roland glanced at him and returned the greeting, then continued looking out at the water. He was still seething and crossed his arms in front of him. I mustn't let this spoil things for Matty; it's her birthday treat. Though I don't suppose Caroline or Albert will want to visit us in any case, and especially if I continue to call him Albert, which I will.

His companion on the bench was speaking to him, something about the beautiful view. '*Bella bella,*' he was saying, and pointing to the '*bella vista*'. Then he leaned towards him and Roland glanced up.

'You are *inglese, signore?*'

Roland nodded. The man didn't sound like a rough beggar, although he looked like one. His hair was long, as was his beard, and his boots and coat were shabby. Neither was he old; about his own age, Roland guessed, and wondered what had brought him so low.

'You are erm – *vacanza?* Erm – 'oliday?'

Again Roland nodded. '*Si.* With my daughters. *Con le mie figlie.*' He held up four fingers to show how many, and then put his fingers round his face. '*Bella. Bella.*' He smiled, his spirits lifting.

The man smiled too, then tapped his chest and lifted one finger. Then, his smile fading, he indicated that she was far away, and Roland couldn't decide if she lived a long way away or if perhaps she had died.

They continued in this manner for some time and it seemed as if the man had no wife, and Roland indicated the same; the

Italian's name was Matteo and Roland told him his and then, as if of one accord, they both rose from the bench to go their separate ways. They shook hands. Roland patted his pocket and then rubbed his fingers together to indicate money, but Matteo shrugged, pointing to the sky and the deep blue lake as if that were sufficient. However, Roland was determined to give him at least the price of a meal, and insisted. They shook hands again after the transaction and moved off in opposite directions. Roland walked towards the villa for a minute or two and then turned. Matteo hadn't gone far and was leaning on the rail looking out at the water. As Roland watched he lifted his head, saw Roland looking in his direction, and put up his hand in salutation.

Roland heaved a breath as he strode on. I must remember how lucky I am.

As expected, they didn't receive a visit from Roland's brother or his family; Matty and Julia asked their father if the two of them could visit their grandmother and he agreed that of course they could. They found her in the company of Rosalind, who had decided not to accompany her parents and brother on a shopping trip into Stresa. 'It's not as if it's a big town,' she said. 'Not even as big as Beverley, and in any case I've been before.' She asked about Faith and Becca and said she might ask her mother if she could call on them.

'I hope they're not going home at the same time as us,' Julia said afterwards, as linking arms they walked back to Vista Lago. 'I dislike Uncle Albert's wife intensely. She's so cold and cynical.'

As they reached the drive they saw Mario Alfonsi coming towards them. He greeted them courteously and said he had called to see their father. 'I am travelling to Florence soon,' he said. 'I am – I have, er, a place at school of art and I would like to take with me my painting of you and your sisters. I call it *Quattro Sorelle* and I ask Signor Maddeson's permission first.'

'Oh,' Matty said. 'Where is it? May we see it?'

'It is not yet finished, signorina. I have more work to do yet, but I ask when you go 'ome and then I will almost finish it. You must come to my room to see it.' He hesitated. 'It is my best work, I think, and cannot – er – cannot – *rischio . . .*'

'Can't take the risk?' Julia suggested.

'*Si*, yes. It is too—' He widened his eyes and, shrugging, laughed and said, '*Qualcosa di preziosa!*'

Both Matty and Julia chewed over this for several seconds, and then Matty said, 'Precious!'

'Yes,' Julia agreed. 'That's what I was going to say. Very precious, or . . . something precious?'

Mario laughed again, and they agreed later that he was probably the most handsome man they had ever met.

'He's not even a fully grown man yet, is he?' Matty said. 'I think he's only about eighteen, the same as Adam probably. They're all going away to university or somewhere to carry on their education,' she continued gloomily. 'There will be no young men to talk to.'

'We couldn't talk to the Italians in any case,' Julia commented. 'We'll be going home soon, and actually I shan't mind in the least. It's always when I'm away that I wish I could be at home, and when I'm home I can't wait to escape.'

'I wonder what Mario's painting will be like?' Matty mused that evening when they were all sitting cosily inside. The door into the front loggia was open to let in the scented air and the smell of a cigar that their father was smoking outside, but there was a fire burning in the grate and they all had blankets over their knees.

'Better than Antonio's, I think,' Faith piped up; she was turning the pages of a book of art that she said Mario had brought to show her the type of art that interested him. 'He said that Antonio would be better as a draughtsman than an artist. This,' she indicated the slim book, 'is what Mario has to emulate for his studies, but he says that when he leaves for Florence he hopes to create his own style. He has only lent it to me,' she said, when she realized everyone was looking at her. 'He knows I'm interested in art.'

'What kind of artistry was he indicating?' Louisa asked. She was curled up in a chair with a thick blanket wrapped around her; although she wasn't cold it was very comforting.

'Well, for instance,' Faith explained, 'he showed me the difference a brush can make and that there are all kinds. I tend to only use two or three – a flat brush, a stubby one or a very fine one – but he said that all brushes can be used in different ways, the point of the brush or the edge or the flat, to convey different effects. I shall try it when we are home again.'

'You are already very good, Faith,' Becca said. 'You paint beautifully.'

'Thank you, Becca.' Faith smiled at her sister. 'But I think there's room for improvement. I'm going to ask Papa if Mario can write to me; he said he'd like to once he's started his studies, and he could maybe give me some more ideas.'

There was a short but significant silence, broken by Matty. 'That's a very nice idea,' she said. 'But perhaps you should wait until you've seen his painting and judged his talent?'

'Yes,' Faith agreed. 'I was very disappointed with Antonio's portrait of us when he had been so enthusiastic. Mario is different, I'm sure of it, but we'll know tomorrow, which is when he asked if we would view it. In the morning would be best, he said. When the light is good.'

CHAPTER TWENTY-ONE

It was the work of a young artist, but the talent was immediately apparent. Breathtaking in its simplicity, it portrayed the youth and innocence of the sisters: their unblemished skin, their shining hair, the guilelessness in their eyes as they gazed out at the observer.

Personality, too, shone through: he had captured each and every facet of their character and they wondered how he had done that in a few quick sketches while Antonio was arranging them on the stairs. The sisters were silent, not knowing what to say; Roland, overcome, murmured 'Beautiful', and Louisa nodded in agreement, not trusting herself to speak as she took out a handkerchief to catch a tear.

Mario looked at them all, and as no one spoke he said hastily, 'It is not finished, signore, there is much to do – the gowns, slippers, hair. But I must ask *permesso* to take it with me to Florence to finish under – er – tuition, yes?'

'It is not for me to say where you should take it,' Roland said huskily, 'but when you have finished it I would like to buy it from you.'

Mario looked startled. 'Ah – signore, that is not my intent. It is not for sale.'

'Not for sale?' Roland said, astonished. 'But why then would you ask my permission?'

'I would not display such a personal painting without *permesso*, signore. These are . . .' Mario lifted his hands as he sought the words, '*le tue figlie.*'

'Yes, my daughters. I understand. Are you saying that you won't show the painting without my permission?' Roland felt that he had never met anyone who would miss such an opportunity to show off his talent.

'But of course, signore.' Mario drew himself up. 'They are young. I – would not – er – *non li sfruttero!*'

Sfruttero? Not a word Roland had come across and he puzzled over it.

Mario saw his dilemma and sought another description. 'I am male, yes? They are maidens – er – *innocente?*'

Roland hid a smile, and nodded. He meant he would protect their reputations. 'Exploit? You would not exploit them. Is that what you mean?'

Mario's face cleared of a frown. '*Si, signore.* That is the word, I think.'

Whilst this conversation was continuing, Faith and Matty were looking at other sketches pinned to the walls of this small room at the top of Mario's parents' house.

'Oh,' Faith murmured. 'Is that me?' She pointed to a small sketch of a girl's face in profile. Beside it on another sheet was a pair of eyes, and below it a mouth.

Matty drew in a breath. 'I do believe it is,' she murmured. 'And here's another. That's your hair, isn't it?'

Faith nodded, embarrassed. When had he done the sketches? She hadn't noticed; he must have carried them in his head. She looked about her. There were many drawings on the wall, on the table, pinned to the muslin curtains. Many of them were of dainty flowers such as those on their gowns, some of trees, and many simply of swathes of different rainbow shades such as came through the windows of Vista Lago. Then she saw other sketches of her sisters, a drawing of them looking forward as they were in the larger painting.

Another easel stood in a corner of the room, holding a canvas covered by a cloth. Tentatively, Faith glanced around and saw Mario still in conversation with her father. She lifted a corner of the cloth and peeped beneath; she dropped it quickly when she saw what lay below. It was an unfinished painting of her.

Roland received a letter from Nunny a week after she and Gertrude and Adam had departed for home in which she thanked him for a most memorable visit to Italy and vowed that never in her life would she forget it.

At the end of the same week, he received another, this time from Adam, thanking him for his generosity in inviting him and Eliza, and apologizing for having left earlier than originally planned, and then going on to say that he was sure that Mr Maddeson would be pleased to hear that his exam results had been good and he had been offered a place at London University.

By the same post Eliza also received a letter from Adam, relating more details than he had given to Mr Maddeson.

I'm over the moon, Eliza, he wrote. *I received excellent examination results and have been offered a scholarship, subject to an interview. Pa is so very pleased that I think he's forgiven me for not going into politics or the law.*

Everyone was delighted for him, and by now Matty and Julia had begun putting some of their belongings into the trunk ready to go home. They all visited their grandmother and by chance they called on a day when Albert and his wife and family were out. They had only seen them twice since their arrival. Roland took Antonio's painting with him.

'Mother,' he began, 'your protégé Antonio most kindly painted this portrait of your granddaughters, and as it's too big for us to take home on this occasion I wondered if you would like to keep it for the time being?'

She looked at it long and hard through her lorgnette and then commented, 'It's not their likeness, is it? They are beautiful young women and he has not captured them in the slightest. But yes, we'll put it in a dark corner somewhere.'

'Mario has a great deal of talent,' Roland told her. 'He is also producing a portrait of them, which is wonderful, but he says it is not for sale. He's taking it with him to Florence where he is to study.'

'Mmm, yes. I have seen some of his work.' She patted the sofa for him to sit beside her. 'He painted a few small pieces for me, flowers and birds and views of the lake; not for money, just as a gift. He has a good eye. I think perhaps I'll transfer my patronage to him. His parents struggle, I know, to pay for his education. They run a pastry shop and work all the hours God sends. His sister helps in the bakery so that he can paint.'

Roland was delighted by his mother's generosity and by the fact that she had recognized the young man's talent; she gave the impression that she had a butterfly mind, fond of entertainment and idle gossip, when in fact she was shrewd and knowing. He dropped a kiss on her cheek. 'You are kindness personified,' he said softly. 'You will reap your reward.'

She shook her head. 'I don't need a reward,' she said. 'I have enough. I am very fortunate.' She gazed at him. 'Now then, darling Roly,' she murmured, 'what about you? What will make you happy again?'

His mother and his late wife were the only people who ever called him Roly and he had no answer to give her, but simply squeezed her hand.

On the day before their departure, they bade goodbye to their grandmother, and Matty asked their father if they could call on Mario to wish him good fortune in his studies, and ask about the painting. The pastry shop was closed but Mario's mother came to the side door and invited them in. She didn't speak English but called Mario down to greet them, and he took them upstairs to the attic again.

He was working on *Quattro Sorelle*. They had thought it perfect before, but now he had caught other subtleties. A fold in a skirt, an escaping strand of hair in Becca's braid, a hint of merriment in Matty's expression, Julia's discerning gaze, and the exquisite refinement of Faith's bone structure.

'It is not finished,' he protested again when they all murmured their approval. 'I finish it in Florence.'

'And what's under here, Mario?' Becca had been on the prowl and spotted the other easel; she lifted the cloth. 'May we look?'

'No, it is not—' he began, but too late. The cloth slipped from her hand and fell to the floor, and they stood in silence gazing at Faith's image: the fine blonde hair, the high cheekbones, the soft and tender eyes, the slender nose and the slightly parted mouth which they all recognized from when she was earnestly painting or sewing or playing the piano.

But Roland recognized something else. It was a picture of innocence painted with love.

CHAPTER TWENTY-TWO

'There's nothing to worry about,' Louisa murmured to Roland as they travelled on the first leg of their journey home.

The sisters and their friends were all stationed at the windows, chattering and watching the valley below as the train steamed its way out of Italy. They were all travelling in one coach; it was rather a squash, but Eliza and Dorcas could not have journeyed alone in a separate coach.

Roland, however, once they were safely under way, had stretched out his legs, crossed his arms, and, with his eyebrows drawn together, a pinched mouth and a sour expression, leaned back looking most disgruntled.

'What? Worry?' he replied tetchily, sitting up straight. 'What makes you think I'm worrying about anything?'

'Because I know you: the indulgent and protective father,' Louisa whispered. 'You're going to get a lot of this, you know, with four daughters!'

'I don't know what you mean, Louisa.' Then he turned to her. 'She's a *child*!' he hissed. 'She's just turned *fourteen*.' Faith, the subject of their conversation, had celebrated her birthday quietly as she had said she wanted to do, except for another visit to Isola Bella.

'She isn't a child, but she doesn't know what the painting implies,' Louisa said. 'And maybe neither does he.'

Roland made an extravagant cynical gesture with his eye-brows and grunted throatily.

'He's just a very young man, who has fallen in love with a young and beautiful English girl and has the talent to capture her on canvas,' Louisa continued quietly. 'It happens, Roland: young people fall in and out of love. You surely must remember! He can't have met anyone like her.'

He gave a slight nod. That at least was true. Mario would have known only dark-haired young Italian women, firmly shackled to their mothers. Opposites attract. He did know that; it had happened to him too when he had been not much more than a schoolboy.

'He wants to write to her!' he muttered. 'And I'd agreed, before I saw the painting of her.'

'To discuss art! They have a common interest. It's good, isn't it, young people from different countries, different back-grounds? Besides,' she said softly, 'it's wonderful to fall in love for the first time. It must surely be the same for young men as it is for young women.'

He sighed. It was. He did remember. But it was different when it was one of your own daughters under discussion. Had it been Matty, it would have been different: she was of an age when she might legitimately attract young men; but not Faith, not his darling little girl, who was fragile and delicate and must be cared for.

Maybe he had it all wrong, but in any case, he considered, any letters would come to him first and there would be many miles between Faith and the would-be Lothario. Perhaps Louisa was right: probably Faith didn't understand the mean-ing behind the painting. She was too young to comprehend the nuances that were so obvious to her elders, who recog-nized the ardour of youthful love.

I must be getting old; it's hard to accept that I'm never again going to feel the joyous sensation of being in love with someone who loves me in return.

*

140

Louisa too was feeling introspective. She was happy to be going home even though she had loved being with her nieces, whom she adored, and had thought Stresa, Lake Maggiore and the surrounding area simply wonderful. The truth was that she had missed her home; she hadn't been away from it for such a long period in years.

She thought about Stephen. Had he travelled as he had said he might, and if so, why hadn't he come to see them? He would have been welcomed; everyone knew and liked him. Had he gone somewhere else entirely? Perhaps across to Norway or Sweden and then to Germany and the Netherlands?

Or not gone anywhere at all? I've missed him, she mused. I'm so used to seeing him every day. I hope he's all right. Of course he will be; he's a very active man. I've never known him to be ill, but there's always a first time. For heaven's sake, she chided. Whatever's the matter with you?

Everyone resumed their usual activities once they were home. Roland closed the study door behind him, caught up on his newspapers, considered his shares and his business dealings with his brokers, and resumed his association with like-minded people in the neighbourhood. He forgot about his anxiety over Faith until the first letter arrived, and after reading it he concluded that Louisa had been right. It was quite innocent; a young man's fancy only. Women seemed to understand such things, he decided, whereas men didn't.

Becca had rushed joyously into the house expecting to be greeted by Pug, but he wasn't there. He hadn't been seen for almost three weeks, even though the boot boy and Betty had been sent out to look for him. Becca was devastated and cried that she should never have left him, but on visiting the stables just as soon as she could she found that he had turned up there one morning, and Owen, knowing that the Maddesons were away, had made him a bed in one of the tack rooms.

The dog ran in circles round her in greeting, submitted to her hugs and kisses and followed her home, settling himself outside Faith's door as usual.

'It's been a lovely time, hasn't it, Julia?' Matty said, and Julia agreed, but both said that they were pleased to be home again and back to their old routines. Matty had found a letter from Sybil waiting for her, apologizing for not coming to Italy. *I had been given strict instructions by my father that I must stay at school until the holidays,* she wrote, *but I promise that I will come to see you as soon as I return home. I am, by the way, having the most marvellous time now after that terrible start. We have been introduced to some very nice young Frenchmen who have been called in to help us with our French conversation lessons – I'm much happier about the idea of going to France now* . . . and here she entered a whole line of exclamation marks.

Matty put down the letter with a sigh. 'She won't come,' she said, then handed it to Julia to read. 'She will think our life very mundane.'

'Are we very boring, do you think?' Julia murmured as she read it. 'Not that I think that Sybil's life is exciting; simply learning how to catch a husband, it seems to me! I still meet Miss Hargreaves once a week for general discussion, but you don't; wouldn't you like to do *something*? Apart from play the piano or sew, or paint, which neither of us is very good at. Faith is, though. She has real talent, and I gather from Mario's letters that he encourages her.' Faith always read out Mario's letters, which came frequently at first, but less often once he had commenced his studies in Florence.

Matty was only half listening. She had been thinking of Timothy, who had called with Dorcas a few days after they'd returned from Italy; he had come home for a weekend, and she was almost sure he had singled her out.

'Yes,' she said, 'I think you're right. She's very talented.' She thought for a moment, and then said, 'And you're also right that we live useless lives and I'm going to do something about it. I'm going to speak to Mrs Chapman. She's always busy – joins groups and gets things going. I'm going to ask what she might suggest.'

Matty asked her father if she could visit Mrs Chapman for this purpose, but he said he had a different proposition to talk over with her. Louisa had told him in Italy that she had always been a much better organizer than her late husband.

'What I might suggest, Roland,' she had said, 'is that you teach Matty how to manage the household expenses. It will occupy her mind and prepare her for the future if, or more likely when, she marries. It can only serve her well, and help her keep the domestic staff happy. Servants don't really like dealing with a male head of the household who might not understand the want of candles or household soap.'

'Good heavens,' he had said at first. 'I manage very well, thank you!'

'*Mrs Nunnington* manages very well,' Louisa said wryly. 'She keeps all the household bills, I imagine, and pays the butcher, the grocer, the coal man and everyone who comes to the door, and then presents you with the account.'

He was silenced. Yes, that was what happened. So it was Nunny who kept the house running smoothly, not him. Drat Louisa, he thought, why does she have to be right every time? But it's true. Constance used to look after domestic expenses, and did it well. She knew where every penny went whilst I just hand over whatever Nunny asks for. Which is all well and good with someone you can trust.

So he told Matty he had something else in mind and invited her into his study. He had always been very casual with accounts but now realized that it might not always be so for his daughters, although they would all have a good dowry if they should marry, and Matty already had a sum of money left to her by her mother for when she turned eighteen. He had never asked her what she would like to do with it and realized that he had been very remiss not to do so.

He took out a sheet of paper, wrote *Household Expenses* with the date beneath, and drew three vertical lines to make columns to the bottom of the page.

'Here you are, Miss Maddeson,' he said jokingly. 'Your first task to prepare you for the time when you are mistress of your own household.' He saw the dismay on her face, and said consolingly, 'Your aunt Louisa suggested that this would be very useful to you.' He leaned back in his chair. 'I'm happy to hand over this important duty to you.'

He handed her a newly sharpened pencil. Told her how much money she would have to manage and suggested she put in the first column the servants' wages, starting with Nunny, then Cook, the general domestic servants, the groom, the laundry woman and the boot boy.

With the tip of her tongue protruding she did this in her neatest handwriting and then began another column: fuel, food, clothing, shoes and haberdashery.

'Haberdashery?' he queried. 'What kind of thing?'

'Sewing cottons, needles, embroidery silks, ribbons and sometimes material if one of us needs another dress. We do pass on our clothes, Papa,' she explained, 'and poor Becca gets all of our hand-me-downs, but fortunately she's not very interested in clothes so she doesn't complain. However, they are well worn by the time they get to her and we have to do quite a lot of patching, or put in new sleeves, or a collar or something.' She smiled. 'I don't suppose you notice?'

He shook his head. 'No,' he said, 'I don't,' and thought how lucky he was to have such thrifty, accommodating daughters. They are more practical than I have given them credit for, and I don't know where they get that trait from, for their mother didn't live long enough to teach them. And how much more she would have taught them, he thought, in preparation for their lives to come.

CHAPTER TWENTY-THREE

When Louisa arrived back in Scarborough, there was a chill east wind blowing and she shivered. It should be warmer than this, she mumbled to herself; still, it's always good to come home. She was pleased to see that her housekeeper had opened all the windows at the front of the house; she had given Mrs Birch a rough date for her return, and she would have known to let some good sea air into the house after it had been shuttered during the whole month she had been away.

Louisa looked up at Stephen's house adjoining. The windows and curtains were closed and there didn't seem to be any sign of life. He must be away still, she thought. I wonder where he went?

Mrs Birch had also been away but had arrived back two days before in order to take the sheets off the furniture, open the windows and prepare some food. 'I'm not a cook, as you know, ma'am,' she said, 'but I've made some bread and a meat pie and scones, just to tide us over. We'll manage until the butcher and baker turn up on the doorstep.'

'What a blessing you are, Mrs Birch. Whatever would I do without you?'

'I expect you'd manage, ma'am.' The housekeeper smiled. 'You wouldn't starve.'

'Have you seen anything of Mr Nielsen? I noticed his windows are closed and the curtains drawn. He must have been away too.'

'Don't think so, ma'am. He came into the garden after you left; was doing a bit of spring pruning, he said. He was home all the time I was here, at any rate.'

'Oh,' Louisa said. 'Well, perhaps I'll have a prowl around later. It's not like him to leave the curtains drawn.'

'Mmm,' Mrs Birch poured Louisa a cup of tea as she sat at the kitchen table. 'Maybe he's not well. There's been influenza about,' she said. 'Which is very odd for this time of year, though I gather it hit mostly older people; them as live down in the town where the cottages are packed together cheek by jowl, not healthy gentlemen like Mr Nielsen.'

Louisa nodded. Mrs Birch often spoke of the fisher folk who lived down at Sandside as if up on the castle hill she was a touch superior, forgetting her own roots. Her grandparents, parents and siblings used to live down there and hardly ailed with anything, being so close to the sea as they were.

'I'll get out of my travelling clothes,' she said when she finished her tea. 'Are we too late for fish for supper? Will there be any? I know you said you'd made a meat pie, but I've been longing for fresh Scarborough fish since we set off for home.'

'I'll pop down the hill,' Mrs Birch said compliantly, 'and see what's left. You don't mind what? Codling, whiting, mackerel?'

'Anything,' Louisa said. 'I'll take a look at my garden to see what's come up and pop next door to check that all is well, and I'll tell you about the beautiful gardens we saw on Isola Bella when you come back.'

She took off her travelling gown and corset and changed into a skirt and blouse, then draped a warm shawl about her shoulders; she looked in the cheval mirror in her dressing room and thought she looked well. She had a rosy glow to her skin and her hair had lightened with the sun.

She breathed in deeply and then expelled a long breath. 'It's so good to be home,' she murmured. 'Delightful though it was in Italy, it's wonderful to come back.' She looked around her. 'Hello, house. I'm home again.'

In her comfortable shoes she ran down the stairs, unlocked the side door and slipped into the garden. It was simplicity itself, unlike the magnificence of the Italian gardens they had visited; the apple and pear trees were bearing fruit and some of the rose bushes were in flower, but the daffodils were finished and the grass was in need of cutting and she wondered about that: Stephen kept it immaculate as a rule, treating her garden as he would have done his own.

He must be away, she considered, and looking up at the back of the house saw that an overflow pipe was dripping, leaving a damp trail down the wall.

I'll go round to the front and knock, she decided. Surely Polly will have been in even if Mrs Harris hasn't. Stephen employed his domestic staff on a daily basis; neither his house-keeper nor the maid stayed overnight.

She knocked on the door and rang the bell, but there was no sound from within. She put her ear to the heavy oak but heard nothing. Knocking again, she looked up, but there was no response, no twitch of a curtain. His dog would be in kennels if he were away, but where is his cat, she wondered. Someone must be feeding him. She rang once more, long and hard, and heard the peal inside, and then she turned away and was halfway down the path when she heard a bolt being drawn back and a key being turned, and the door opened a crack.

'Stephen,' she called. 'Is it you?'

His white and black cat suddenly wound himself round her skirt; he looked fat and healthy, and she wondered if he had been living outside.

She walked back towards the door. Someone was just inside. 'Stephen?' she said again.

'Yes,' a voice croaked. 'You can't come in. I'm sick.'

Her heart plummeted. 'With what?'

'Influenza, the doctor said.'

147

She could hardly hear what he said, his voice was so gravelly. 'How long have you been like this?' She approached the door, peering inside.

'I don't know. The doctor came and then sent a nurse. She says she won't be back again as I'm over the worst. She said I've just to rest now. Fat lot she knows. I think I'm dying. Polly brought some soup. Her mother's, I think. God, it was awful.'

'What was?' She went up the steps.

'The soup.' He began to cough. 'I have to go in,' he said. 'I'm cold.'

'Go back to bed,' she said, seeing that he was wearing only a thin dressing robe and his legs were bare. 'Leave the door unlocked and I'll bring you something to eat and drink. I've only just arrived home.'

He gave a humph that could have meant anything. 'Go on,' she said. 'Get into bed. Have you plenty of blankets?'

He turned back to face her again. 'Who do you think you are?' he muttered grumpily. 'My mother?'

He closed the door and she listened; he didn't lock it. She bent down and looked through the letter box and saw him walking slowly across the hall floor towards the staircase. She smiled and shook her head. He'd be all right.

She left Mrs Birch a note to say she was next door and had taken a slice of meat pie for Stephen and a buttered scone. She also took the tea caddy, as she thought he might have run out of tea, and a jug of milk.

His kitchen was very untidy, with cups and plates piled in the sink; she looked in his larder and there was nothing there but a jug of sour milk and a mouldy loaf of bread.

'Oh dear, oh dear,' she muttered. 'Where is Polly? That's the trouble with young maids, they don't always know what to do.'

She made a pot of tea, found a tray and put all that was needed on it, and climbed the stairs, hitching up her skirt with one hand so that she didn't trip.

'Stephen,' she called outside one of the front bedrooms. 'Where are you?' He'd once told her that his bedroom overlooked the front as hers did next door, but his voice came from one of the ones at the back. She pushed it open with her foot and found him sitting on a single bed with a blanket wrapped round his shoulders. His hair was long and dishevelled and his beard was thick and unkempt.

'Why are you in here?' she asked.

'I thought it easier for Polly to clean,' he said huskily. 'But her mother told her not to come whilst Mrs Harris was away; she said it wasn't proper for a young girl to look after a man on her own with no housekeeper.' He gave a short, gruff laugh. 'If she'd known how I felt she wouldn't have had any worries whatsoever.'

Louisa put down the tray and turned to open the curtains.

'Don't let the neighbours see you, Louisa. You'll ruin my reputation.'

'I'm pleased you haven't lost your sense of humour,' she said, opening the curtains and the window. The sun was shining and immediately the room looked brighter. 'Just don't tell Polly's mother I've been up here.'

He pulled his legs into bed and drew the blanket round him. He looked at her. 'You look very well.'

'I feel well,' she said. 'Unlike you. You look dreadful. How long have you been ill?' She poured his tea and handed it to him.

'Since you went away,' he said grumpily, sipping the hot tea. He closed his eyes for a moment and gave a deep sigh. 'Don't ever do this to me again, Louisa. I might have died and you wouldn't have known.'

She gazed critically at him. 'You want me to be your nurse, cook and housemaid?' she said with sarcasm.

'No.' He stopped speaking to cough. 'I want you to be my wife and then I can demand that we go away together or stay at home together.'

She sat down on a basket chair near the window. 'You're delirious,' she said mildly.

He shook his head and took another sip and closed his eyes as if the tea was soothing. 'Not now I'm not, though I have been, and whilst I was in my death throes,' he said dramatically, 'I knew that I must tell you what I've always wanted to tell you and then I'd die, either happy or ready to go if you refused me.'

'You're an idiot,' she said, and wondered why she always felt uplifted when they met, even now when he looked so terrible.

'I know,' he wheezed. 'But I can't help that. I had an idea, whilst in my delirium.' He paused for breath. 'For when you agree to marry me. I know you won't want to give up your own home, and I'd quite agree because it's a lovely house, so what I thought we could do is knock a hole through the wall in the hallway and put in a door, and you can have the only key on your side if you wish; but we must do it soon, Louisa, for I've realized that I'm mortal, and I love you. I've always loved you, even before that dull as ditchwater Arnold snapped you up before I was ready, and you didn't know that I was waiting for the right time to ask your father, who really, if we're *really* honest, doesn't have much of a clue about love being needed in a marriage.'

He turned his head away to sneeze whilst fumbling for a handkerchief in his pocket. He blew his nose and turned to her, his eyes watering. 'So what do you say, dearest Louisa?'

CHAPTER TWENTY-FOUR

During August the Maddesons all trooped off to Scarborough to stay with Aunt Louisa for their annual visit. Becca in particular loved the seaside. She was still young enough to enjoy watching the Punch and Judy shows on the sands, and although she was too big to ride on the donkeys as she used to, she stroked them and fed them on carrots, and asked the donkey man one day if she could lead them when the children queued up to ride them; he willingly agreed, having noticed her sure touch with the awkward stubborn creatures.

'Well, there we are,' her father said to Matty one day as they watched from the promenade. 'That's Becca's future occupation taken care of.'

She laughed. 'You know, don't you, Father, that she'd like to run her own stable one day.'

Matty had recently begun using *Father* rather than *Papa*. She had thought it rather more fitting now that she was older; he'd smiled the first time she had used the term, though he felt sad that his eldest daughter was leaving, or indeed had left, her childhood behind.

Julia still used *Papa*, even though he thought that sometimes she seemed older than Matty. His second daughter was an enigma and he didn't always understand her moods; unlike Matty who was such an open book, Julia was a closed one, keeping her judgements to herself on most subjects, yet sometimes giving vent to a sharp retort over something that had upset her or she disagreed with. She had a cool and critical mind and didn't suffer fools in any shape or form. Pity the poor fellow who falls in love with her, he often thought, and knew there would be many, for she was as beautiful as her mother had been.

Faith hadn't come down to the sands today, preferring to sit in Louisa's garden sketching the flowers and chatting to Stephen, who, Roland noticed, seemed to pop in more often than he used to.

'I don't think that that will be an option,' he said in answer to Matty's comment about Becca. 'She'd better marry the Lawrence boy, if that's her desire. I expect he'll manage the stables when he's finished his schooling.'

Julia arrived with four ice cream cones and giving two of them to her father to hold and two to her sister, she took off her shoes before taking the cones back from Matty and trudging across the sands towards Becca to give her one.

'Ooh, thank you,' Becca said, and held the ice cream above her head as the donkey bared his teeth. 'He's a devil mule, this one,' she said. 'He almost had a little girl off his back just now. He's not well trained at all.'

'They must get very bored walking up and down the sands all day.'

Becca nodded. 'Yes, they're not at all like horses. Must go,' she said, as she saw that all the donkeys had riders on their backs. 'Don't go without me,' she called. 'I've almost had enough of them.'

Roland didn't stay the whole fortnight in Scarborough, but went home after a few days. The seaside wasn't his favourite place, though he could understand his daughters loving it and the freedom they enjoyed away from home; and of course Louisa was their special aunt, so much more amenable than his own sister, who, he was certain, was fond of her nieces but unable to be less than formal with them; or his brother's wife, who rarely had anything to say to them at all.

He wanted to get home to look at his banking concerns. He had recently bought shares in a London company that his broker had recommended; he had taken a risk with them and as he was normally a prudent investor he was checking on them regularly through the *Manchester Guardian*. That was his excuse for leaving, but knowing his daughters were safe with Louisa he was rather looking forward to having some time alone, going to his club and meeting up with some fellows he knew.

Louisa and Stephen took them to the Spa, which was presently undergoing building work to make it one of the most elegant and prominent buildings in the country. Few people took the healing spa waters as they had once done, and to satisfy the holidaymakers who came in droves to breathe in the sea air Italian-style terraces on the hillside were being created with floral beds and a delightful band-stand outside the main hall, which Faith particularly loved, where they sat listening as the band played, and they drank tea or lemonade and ate little cakes and then took the long walk back along the promenade and up the cliff steps to Louisa's house.

On other days, Becca and Faith walked alone to the nearby castle and sat on the broken ancient walls and gazed over at the scene below, the harbour and the fishing boats coming in with their catch of the day, and the north bay, with its fine sands and high waves, which was only accessible by the town road or boat.

Stephen Nielsen came to eat dinner with them on most evenings, making them laugh with his ripostes but also talk-ing to them of general affairs and asking their opinion on many matters. He was a Scarborough man born and bred and had been part of the fishing and shipping trade when he was a young man; he had known of the Hull fishing com-pany which had belonged to their paternal grandmother's parents, and although he had now sold his own company, he kept up to date with what was happening in his home town, being on committees and local groups and making sure that Scarborough would always be an elegant town to visit.

'I'd like to live here in Scarborough,' Becca said eagerly one evening. 'I'd have horses and ride on the beach every day.'

'Are you going to marry someone rich enough to buy the horses for you?' Stephen asked.

'No,' she said. 'I'll ask Papa.'

He smiled. 'And what about you, Faith?' he asked. 'What are you going to do when you're a proper grown-up?'

'I'll be an artist,' she said, quite sure in her response. 'I won't be a burden to anyone because I'll sell my paintings and live on the money.'

'Most commendable,' he said, glancing at Louisa and solemnly nodding his approval. Then he turned to Matty and Julia. Julia stared stonily back at him; she wasn't giving anything away. Matty didn't say anything either, but shyly lowered her head and shrugged. She hated it when anyone questioned her about her future, for how was she expected to know; surely it would depend on so many things. Preferably, she silently debated, I'd like things to continue as they are. She considered herself very fortunate to live the life she did. She didn't really want it to change.

They wanted to travel home by train, so Louisa and Mr Nielsen agreed to go with them to Hull's Paragon station where Aunt Gertrude would meet them and take them out to tea before they returned to Beverley.

As they waved goodbye and watched Aunt Louisa and Mr Nielsen getting back on the train, Faith turned to Matty and Julia, checked that Becca was out of earshot, and excitedly exclaimed, 'Did you see? Did you see?'

'What?' Julia asked, whilst Matty raised her eyebrows, looked back and saw nothing more exciting than the guard waving his flag.

'Mr Nielsen. He was holding Aunt Louisa's hand! His fingers kept creeping to hers and she kept pulling them back and trying not to laugh.'

'No! Are you sure?' Matty said.

'I am sure,' Faith said unfalteringly. 'Absolutely. Oh, isn't that wonderful? They must be in love!'

'But they've known each other for years,' Julia said. 'Besides, aren't they too old to fall in love?'

'Oh, no,' Matty and Faith said simultaneously. 'Of course not!'

There were many cafés and hotels in Hull where they could take afternoon tea. Some of them were still coaching houses, though Aunt Gertrude eschewed those, saying they were not suitable for young ladies, and took them to a café which served afternoon tea with sandwiches and cake.

They spent an hour with her, and as they were gathering their belongings together Julia, who was sitting next to her, murmured, 'Aunt Gertrude, do you think I might visit you sometime? On my own, I mean?'

Her aunt gazed at her. 'I'd be delighted if you would, my dear. Of course; that would be very nice, very nice indeed.'

'I don't know Hull very well,' Julia said. 'And I'd quite like to explore it. I'd like to see the Humber and the docks, and see the shops too.'

'Let me tell you of a little known secret,' her aunt whispered. 'A little bird told me' – she gazed about her and lowered her voice – 'I have it on good authority that an invitation has been issued to a most royal personage to visit this fine town.' She tapped her finger to her lips. 'It won't be this year, of course; maybe not even next, because she must receive many such invitations.'

'*She*?' Julia whispered. 'You mean . . .'

Her aunt nodded. 'So if it is to happen,' she murmured, 'the whole town will be scrubbed, painted and polished to within an inch of its life. So do come this year and see it before it's prettied up, because it's a fine town in any case. But not a word,' she whispered, and Julia solemnly nodded, and without thinking made the sign of a slit across her throat, which she immediately regretted, thinking that it was such a childish thing to do.

The year quickly passed. Julia went to stay with Aunt Gertrude and found her good company with a sharp sense of humour and was invited to come back whenever she wished; their father took the train to London to visit his new investment company and Faith received occasional letters from Mario and wrote back sporadically and continued with her painting, building up a portfolio which she hid at the bottom of a cupboard that she knew no one would look into. Becca, whenever she could, spent her leisure time at the stables; the governess Miss Hargreaves was working her hard in English and history and wrote in her reports that Rebecca was inclined to be lazy and didn't concentrate on her learning.

Matty was rather enjoying her new role of keeping the household accounts in order, and Nunny was now coming to her regularly on a Monday morning so that they could decide on the week's menu and agree on what household items were wanted.

Christmas was almost with them and Aunt Gertrude was invited, but regretfully declined as she had been invited to spend the day with Albert and his family; Louisa also declined and gave a lame excuse about her parents coming to visit, but Faith, Matty and Julia rolled their eyes and were sure there was more to it than she was admitting.

'She would tell us,' Matty pointed out. 'She wouldn't keep it a secret from us.'

'Who wouldn't keep what a secret?' Their father had caught the tail end of the conversation, but all three pressed their lips together and refused to say; so he laughed and sat down with his newspaper.

CHAPTER TWENTY-FIVE

Matty was about to turn nineteen; Julia had become seventeen, Faith's fifteenth birthday would follow in June, and the three of them had decided that instead of going to Italy again for their joint birthdays, as their father had suggested, they would ask if they might visit London. Matty wanted to see the royal parks, Julia to look in some of the fine shops; both wanted to visit museums and Faith to visit art galleries, whilst Becca, who seemed to Roland to still be the baby daughter, even though she had grown taller and more assertive as she longingly waited for her thirteenth birthday in November, wanted to ride in Rotten Row.

Becca had been taken into her sisters' confidence over the mystery of Aunt Louisa and Mr Nielsen, and the four of them could hardly contain their curiosity: would they, wouldn't they become engaged to be married? But there was still no news.

In Scarborough, Stephen was also suffering, as Louisa wouldn't give him an answer one way or another.

'If I say no,' she said, 'you won't give me a moment's peace.'

'Quite right, I won't,' he said.

'And if I say yes, you'll—'

'Shout it out from the rooftops,' he said. 'Of course I will! You're killing me, Louisa.' He dropped dramatically to his knees just as Mrs Birch knocked and opened the door. He scrabbled about on the floor as if looking for something and

Louisa clasped her ear lobe, muttering, 'My earring! I've dropped it. It's one of a pair that Arnold gave me. I must find it,' whilst trying to hold in her laughter.

Stephen looked up, his mouth half open, and got up again. 'I can't see it. You'll have to ask the maid to look later.'

Mrs Birch looked from one to the other and then turned round and went out again without saying what she had come in for.

'You're driving me crazy,' he hissed. 'And don't think that Mrs Birch doesn't know, because of course she does.'

'Of course she doesn't,' Louisa answered back. 'Now go home before she guesses.'

In truth, she loved these little games they played. He made her laugh so much. But she was afraid of making a mistake as she had done with Arnold. Yet if she said this to Stephen, he would take her hand and say, as he had said on the day he first asked her, when he was ill and she said delirious, that she had been young then and didn't know how marriage would be.

'And neither do you,' was her retort, 'because you've never been married.'

'I didn't *want* to be married after you married Arnold. There was no one else for me, Louisa.' She had seen the look of love in his eyes and didn't know how she could refuse him, especially when he pleaded. 'There was only you. There has never been anyone else.'

Roland took them all to London for a few days as they had asked, and on their return they continued with their everyday lives. Julia saw Eliza often and her friend told her that she had decided to go to finishing school in Switzerland in September as her parents wanted her to.

'To be honest, Julia, I'm really bored now that Adam is away at university. He absolutely loves it, he says his subjects are so interesting; and of course when he finishes he will then be almost qualified to teach. Pa isn't all that happy that Adam wants to teach in the Ragged Schools, but he's set on it. He's quite a socialist, I think, but he says he's not political at all; he just wants to make a difference and give a chance to children who have nothing.'

'Where are the Ragged Schools?' Julia asked. 'Are they here or in London?'

'There are some in Hull,' Eliza said idly. 'He says he wants to come back to teach here.'

'Like Tim,' Julia said. 'He's coming back to join his father's company.'

Eliza nodded. 'The men have their lives mapped out, don't they? It's just the young women who flounder. We live idle lives, Julia. That's why I've decided to go away to find out what else there is. Would you like to go? Would your father allow it?'

Julia shook her head in dismissal. 'I don't want to. I think you'll find it's the same in Switzerland as it is here. You'll be mixing with other idle young women just the same as us, and you'll be learning how to chat to rich young men without any brains.'

'Possibly.' Eliza fiddled with the ribbon in her hair. 'I might enquire about nursing,' she murmured. 'Except that I faint at the sight of blood.'

Roland had visited the London financial company and was pleased with how things were working out. They were not averse to taking small risks with their clients' finances, they had told him, but they would never take a big one without consulting him. His profits and interest had increased, but he was inclined to be cautious; this was his daughters' inheritance, he often reminded himself.

It was the early part of October when he received an invitation to another meeting along with other clients to join in a discussion about financial matters and a possible merger with another company. They'll probably invite us to re-invest more money, he thought, and decided he would go and hear what they had to say.

'I should be back tomorrow night,' he told Matty early on the morning of his departure, as he waited for Sam to bring the cabriolet to the front. 'But don't worry if I'm not. It will depend on how long the meeting takes. I'll book a room tonight that's handy for King's Cross and catch the first train home I can.'

'What is the meeting about, Father?'

'Just financial matters,' he said. 'Nothing to be concerned about. I just like to keep on top of things.'

He seemed very perky, she thought as she waved to him from the window. He probably likes to get about and mix with his peers from time to time, rather than being at home with his daughters. It wasn't a grumble; she realized that he spent time with them because they hadn't a mother who would have done so.

Julia wandered down about half an hour later. 'Has Papa gone already?' she asked.

Matty nodded. 'He's catching the early train. Sam has taken him into Hull. What shall we do today? It's a lovely day; we could walk down to the Beck and look at the boats. Or have a walk on Swine Moor.' This was another green and grassy area on the eastern boundary of the town, with a spa and bathing facilities, which although old were used often, particularly by young people.

'We could.' Julia helped herself to toast and marmalade and felt the coffee pot to see if it was still hot. It wasn't. She picked it up and wandered to the door. 'I'll make some more coffee. Would you like some?'

'Yes, please. I'll give Faith and Becca a shout. Becca will have forgotten the time and Miss Hargreaves will be here at nine.'

Faith appeared at the door, still in her night clothes. 'I'd forgotten what day it was,' she sighed. 'It's my piano lesson this morning.'

'You'd better get dressed then,' Matty said. 'Go on, quickly. Julia's gone to make coffee; she'll be back in a minute.'

'Where's Papa?' Faith asked sleepily.

'You've missed him. He's set off for London.'

'Oh, of course he has.' She turned for the door again. 'I should have got up early to say goodbye.'

'It's only a short trip,' Matty said. 'He'll probably be back tomorrow.'

Except that he wasn't, and as there had been some question whether he would be, there was no concern. The following evening, Matty asked Nunny to leave some cold meat and pickle and bread and butter out for him in case he was late, and they went to bed as usual.

But the food was still on the breakfast dresser the next morning, and Matty kept watch from the front windows and wondered what had been important enough to keep him.

Eventually she went out to the back garden adjoining the stables where Sam was chopping wood. He looked up as she approached. 'Master not back yet, Miss Martha?'

'No, he's not. Something's kept him. Did he say to you when he'd be returning?'

He shook his head and then pushed back his cap. 'No, he said he wasn't sure, but that he'd catch 'Beverley train and then walk home.' He grinned. 'Reckon he's seeing 'sights of London.'

He wouldn't be, Matty thought, but perhaps the meeting has gone on much longer than he expected. I wonder why he hasn't sent us a postcard to let us know, though. But as she walked back into the house she reconsidered. Poor Father, she thought. He doesn't have any time to himself; he's always surrounded by his daughters. He's always thinking about us, steering us through life; I suppose he feels that we are his responsibility, which we are, at least until we marry, if we do.

She went to her room and sat by the window and gazed across the green meadowland. There were people with dogs, an occasional single rider, and then a group of riders heading towards the racecourse. The leaves on the trees were turning a pale gold and some were falling already, making a thin carpet below the trunks.

I won't get married, she thought, even if I'm asked, unless Father meets someone that he would like to marry, which is doubtful after so long; I'll stay here and keep house for him. It's the least I can do, when he has cared for us so fondly. I'm sure there can't be many men who would elect to bring up four children without a wife to help him.

Julia will marry for money, I'm quite sure. She won't find a man who will marry her for love, with her sharp tongue and acidic humour, in spite of her beauty. Faith . . . well, she sighed. It will have to be a very special person who will love and care for Faith. As for Becca, her harum-scarum youngest sister would love her horses better than any young man, Matty thought, except perhaps for Owen Field, but Father wouldn't allow that, I'm sure. I don't suppose Owen will have a penny to his name, which is a pity because he's so very nice and patient with Becca.

She'd met Owen several times when she'd gone to fetch Becca home for supper and found her sharing a sandwich with him as they sat on a bench outside the stable block. He always rose to greet her and touched his cap. Becca had told her that Owen would run the stables one day when he was old enough, but Matty had disbelieved that piece of information, thinking that it was a flight of fancy on Becca's part.

She put on her coat and hat, deciding she would take a walk into town; she'd look in the shop windows and buy a few bits and pieces from the haberdasher.

'Julia,' she called up the stairs and waited for her sister to appear, but her door remained closed. Faith opened hers; she had a paintbrush in her hand and a streak of paint on her cheek.

'Julia's gone out to meet Eliza,' she said. 'She looked for you but couldn't find you.'

'I've been outside speaking to Sam. I'm going into town; would you like to come?'

'No thank you, I'm busy, but could you get me a new pencil sharpener and some gold watercolour paint? I want pale gold, Matty, not garish yellow or I'll have to mix it with white; and get me the Winsor and Newton metal tube if you can, please, rather than the cake. You can get a better colour with the liquid.'

'What are you painting?'

'The falling leaves,' Faith enthused. 'Have you seen how they're drifting down on to the grass of Westwood and making pools of pale gold beneath the trees? I'm going to paint a small canvas of our view from the house and send it to Mario. I don't suppose he's ever seen an English autumn.'

'I don't suppose he has.' Matty smiled. Pools of gold, she thought. How apt. It conveys a lovelier image, so much more than carpet, which was my first thought.

She stepped out towards town, and going through North Bar nodded to a few people she knew and stopped to speak to some. She continued onwards towards Saturday Market and looked up at the building that housed the offices of Dorcas's father's company, pausing to let a horse and cart pass as she was about to cross over the road.

She looked over her shoulder as she heard her name. 'Miss Maddeson.'

Who would call her that? She turned and put her hand to her forehead to shield her eyes. The sun was very bright. Approaching her was a tall broad man wearing a bowler hat, the kind of fashionable hat that young men wore to business.

'Matty, it's me, Tim Garton. Sorry to startle you. I saw you from the office window and thought I'd come out and say hello.'

'Oh, Tim, hello! I couldn't see for the glare of the sun. How are you? It's so nice to see you.' She could feel herself blushing. She hadn't seen him for a while.

'Absolutely fine,' he said. 'What about you? Erm . . .' he looked about him, 'have you time for a cup of coffee or tea? Or am I being very forward?'

She laughed. 'Isn't it ridiculous?'

'It is,' he agreed. 'Ludicrous that two friends can't meet without rumours circulating. Tell you what, why don't I pretend that you're a new client and we're meeting to discuss various matters?'

She laughed again. 'Wouldn't we do that in your office?'

'Yes, probably.' He raised his eyebrows enquiringly. 'Is that a no, then?'

'No,' she said, 'it's a yes, and I see you have your briefcase with you, so I'm sure that you have some papers that you could show me.'

He took her arm and led her off towards the small café in Dyer Lane. 'How very clever of you,' he said. 'You've done this before?'

'Oh, no, I haven't,' she claimed. 'Never!'

He ushered her inside. 'I was joking, Matty,' he said quietly. 'But I see no reason at all why you shouldn't.'

There was no one else in the café, and the proprietor came for their order. 'Good morning, Mr Garton.' She turned to Matty. 'Morning, miss.'

'Do you know Miss Maddeson, Mrs Grainger?'

The woman looked at her. 'I didn't recognize you, Miss Maddeson. I've seen you in here with your sister, but I didn't realize it was you. You young ladies grow up so fast.'

Matty nodded. 'Yes, my sister Julia and I come in from time to time. We used to come when we were very young and pretend to be grown up, and with Dorcas too.' She turned to Tim and sighed. 'And now we are grown up.'

Mrs Grainger took their order and moved through an inner door to the kitchen.

'You're not quite grown up, though, are you?' Tim said. 'Neither you nor Dorcas.'

'Not yet. Old enough to marry, but not to take charge of our own lives!'

He shook his head. 'Nor ever will be unless the laws are changed. It isn't right, is it, that a woman has to rely on her

164

father or her husband to give her permission to make important decisions about her own life?'

She gazed at him and saw that his dark brown eyes were thoughtful and candid as he looked back at her. My goodness, she thought. How good to know that there are young men who hold such beliefs. The world is changing, even in a small town like Beverley.

CHAPTER TWENTY-SIX

Matty walked back towards North Bar in a complete daze. She was unused to such attention; Tim seemed genuinely interested in her, asking for her opinions on many subjects. She had known him for most of her life, but until he arrived at Vista Lago she had only ever thought of him as Dorcas's older brother. He told her about his life at university and made her laugh at the things he and his fellow students had got up to.

He also told her about his decision to come back to Beverley and agreeing to take a junior position in his father's company. 'It seemed to make sense,' he said. 'There was a place here for me. I'm a pretty dull fellow really, but there's plenty of work here; I'll never be idle. I've not seen your father since Italy,' he continued, rather awkwardly, she thought. 'Would he mind if I call sometime? My father says I must make a point of keeping in touch with people I know.'

She said she was sure her father would be pleased if he visited, not wondering why he would want to. But that reminded her that her father might have arrived home and she made her excuses for leaving, and he too said he hadn't realized how the time had passed and walked her back as far as his office, where they said goodbye. It wasn't until she was halfway up to North Bar that she remembered Faith needed her paint and she turned round and went back again.

When she arrived home, Julia asked her where she had been. 'I heard that you'd been seen with a gentleman,' she said slyly. 'It's all over town.'

'How ridiculous,' Matty protested. 'It was only Tim. We went for a cup of tea. Wasn't that daring of me! Who told you that?'

Julia laughed. 'I saw you,' she teased. 'I was coming up Toll Gavel when I saw Tim run across to catch you.'

'Oh, well, I'm doomed now,' Matty said fatalistically. 'I'll be a scorned woman.'

'You will,' Julia said in a scandalized voice. 'Papa will insist on him marrying you!'

'Is he back?' Matty asked eagerly. 'I was getting worried.'

'No,' Julia responded. 'Why? Is he late? Did he say how long he'd be away?'

Matty was suddenly alarmed. 'He – he was expecting to be back on the second or third day after leaving. He went on Tuesday and thought he'd be back either Wednesday or at the latest on Thursday.' She looked at them. 'It's now Friday. The meeting must have taken longer than he expected.'

Becca looked up. 'I wonder why he didn't send a postcard to say he'd been delayed. I don't like him being away and us not knowing where he is.'

'He'll be fine,' Julia said heartily. 'He's probably met some fellows and they've things to discuss. He'll probably be on the afternoon train.'

'Of course he will. It's not long, is it, and London is such a busy place,' Matty interjected. 'He'll be enjoying a break from female chatter.'

But he wasn't on the afternoon train, nor the Saturday morning one, and when Monday came round and then Tuesday and he'd been away for a week, there was cause for concern for his daughters; why had he not sent them a postcard or telegraph message if he had been held up, or, worse, if he had been ill or in an accident.

'What can we do?' Matty and Julia whispered to one another, and both shook their heads. They didn't know. They could only wait.

CHAPTER TWENTY-SEVEN

Roland had disembarked from the train at King's Cross and walked out on to the concourse. He would first of all book in at a lodging house. He'd seen one near the station when he came to London with his daughters. They hadn't stayed there – he'd chosen a better class of hotel right in the heart of the shopping district as a treat for them – but this small and neat lodging house with its clean curtains and a window box and flowering tubs outside the door looked good enough for him for this short trip. The board above the second storey proclaimed *The Regina Hotel.*

An hotel it was not, but it was clean and the landlady welcoming and they had a room, so he booked and paid for two nights. He had brought only his night attire and a clean white shirt with a high collar for the next day, and after washing his hands and face he put on his grey thigh-length coat over his tailcoat, adjusted his cravat, pushed his small attaché case under the bed and went out in search of his supper, for the landlady said she only supplied breakfast and not an evening meal.

The next morning, during breakfast he asked the landlady to send out for a cab, for the company office he was visiting was on the south bank of the Thames, situated in Southwark close by St Thomas's hospital.

There was a huge amount of early morning traffic: hired cabriolets such as he was using, wagons and handcarts, carrier carts, and every conceivable mode of transport, including horse buses, barouches and broughams, lumbering coaches and smart, fast-moving single-horse chaises and curricles.

The noise was deafening. Traders were shouting, drivers were yelling at other road users and it seemed to Roland that there was a general uproar. After half an hour he looked at his pocket watch. Was he going to be late? Perhaps he might be; but then they moved on again as the traffic eased.

Fifteen minutes later the driver called down to him. 'A road jam building up again in front, sir. 'Ope you're not in a hurry.'

Roland leaned his head out of the window and looked in the direction they were travelling. They had crossed the river and he could see St Thomas's hospital in front of them, but they had slowed down again almost to a stop. It might be quicker to walk.

'Drop me here, if you will,' he called up to the driver. 'I'll walk the rest of the way.'

'Righty ho, sir, as you please.' The cab drew up close to the roadside; Roland got out and held up his hand to give him the fare.

'Take care, sir,' the cabby said, taking the money and grinning his thanks as Roland waved away the change. 'Keep your hand on your pocket book. There's some ne'er-do-wells about.'

'Thank you.' Roland smiled, patting the inside pocket of his outer coat. 'I will.'

Although there was a breeze coming off the river, the air felt muggy and he unfastened the buttons on his overcoat and took it off, putting it over his arm as he walked on. There was a traffic jam, as the driver had said, and he now saw the cause: in the centre of the road and coming from the opposite direction a driver was unhitching a mule from its traces on a cart that had a wobbly wheel. The lopsided cart was in danger of depositing all its cargo on to the road and other road users were becoming increasingly impatient as they tried to get past. A horse bus full of passengers was stuck behind the cart and the driver was shouting for the muleteer to get a move on.

Roland was almost opposite the hospital entrance and wondering how he could safely cross the road when a great shout went up. The horse-bus driver had taken a chance and tried to overtake the mule cart, squeezing through the narrow gap between the two lanes of traffic, but the driver of the cart had lost his grip on the mule and the animal had set off, taking its escape route right in front of the two horses that were pulling the omnibus.

They reared and panicked. The driver couldn't hold them and they set off at a great rate, the bus swaying from side to side, with the passengers yelling and screaming as they tried to hold on and not be thrown out.

Roland saw the horses and the vehicle behind them as they headed towards him, and other people outside the hospital entrance began to run. He saw the vehicle sway, the horses rearing almost on top of him, and as he fell backwards he saw the underside of a horse's belly, a pair of flailing hooves and a swinging door. He reached out for purchase as he fell, failed to find any, and felt a blow on the back of his head which turned everything black.

There are always onlookers at the scene of an accident, and the man leaning on the wall outside the hospital knew that those who were nosy enough to stop and watch but didn't run to assist were concentrating only on the drama in front of them. He had gained many a pocket book by being observant.

He saw the gentleman fall and his coat fly from his arm and hurried towards him, looking about him as he went. Others were slightly injured, those who had run and then tripped, but he was the only one near enough to help the unconscious gentleman as other people caught the horses, assisted the driver, who had toppled from his seat, and helped trapped passengers out of the vehicle, which had fallen on to its side.

'Let's get you covered up, sir,' he mumbled. 'Looks to me as if you've been hurt. And you've lost your 'at. Ah, here it is.' He reached for Roland's top hat, placed it on his own head, and yanked the coat from under the injured man's arm, hearing a muffled groan.

'What you up to, Bert?' A voice he knew came from behind him.

'Nuffink to do wiv you, so clear off,' he said. 'Find your own punter.' He carefully covered the gentleman with the summer overcoat and with the smoothest sleight of hand removed the timepiece from the inside pocket of the black tailcoat the injured man was wearing: any minute now the coppers would be here, as would the hospital staff once they heard about the commotion. It wasn't a hospital normally used for accidents, but he guessed they would come anyway.

''Ere, Matron!' he called to a young woman in a nurse's uniform who was running down the hospital drive towards the gate, followed by other women similarly clad. 'Come an' have a look at this gen'leman. He's in a bad way. I reckon he's a goner. I've put me coat over 'im; that's the right thing to do, ain't it?'

'Yes, thank you.' The nurse bent down to the unconscious man. 'You can leave him now, the stretcher bearers are coming.'

'Righty-ho,' he said. 'I'll take me coat, though; it's the only one I've got.' He peered down at the silent figure on the ground. 'Don't fink he'll be needin' it, do you?'

He gave her a saucy wink, threw the overcoat over his shoulder and left. When she looked up again, he was nowhere to be seen.

Roland opened his eyes. There was an excruciating pain across the back of his head. It hurt if he turned it so he swivelled his eyes. He was in a long room and he was lying on a bed. There seemed to be a multitude of people coming and going and many babbling voices, though he couldn't understand what they were saying.

A woman came and spoke to him but he couldn't make sense of the words. It was all a muddle. She was wearing white and had a large white hat on her head. He tried to sit up but was hampered by something wrapped around his arm. She pushed him down again and he was bothered by that. Who was she? Where was he? He touched his head with the unwrapped arm; there was a hat on it. He touched it all over. It covered the whole of his head and it was sticky. He stared down at his fingers. They were dirty and bloody. He tried to count them but he couldn't remember how to.

Another woman came by. She smiled at him. He frowned. Who was she? She stopped. She had reddish to fair curly hair with a thin scarf tied around it, knotted at the top. What were they called, those things? They had a name but he couldn't remember.

'*Comment allez-vous?*' Her eyes creased as she gazed at him.

He nodded. He didn't know how he was, if that was what she was asking. '*Je vais bien, merci,*' he muttered. He thought he was all right, but couldn't be sure.

'*Vous voyagez?*' She put her head on one side as she spoke.

What? He didn't understand. She was indicating with her hand that he should get up, and signposted to the door. Yes. He could leave. Could he stand? He felt dizzy. If someone helped him he could get up. She put out her arm for him to hold on to and he noticed then that she had cuts on her hands and strips of white gauze across her knuckles. He took her arm and, trying not to put all his weight on her, for she was only slight, heaved himself up. He let out a deep sigh. What had happened? Why was he here? He looked about him. He didn't know this place or the people in it.

The woman was looking about her. She called to one of the women dressed in white with the hat on. Was that what he was wearing on his head, and who were they? The woman in white came across and looked under the bed and shook her head, raising her hands and shrugging.

She was speaking to him. '*Un manteau chaud?*'

A coat? He gazed at the two women. The fair-haired woman was rubbing her arms as if she were cold. Did he have a coat? His mind was a blank. He wanted to get out of here. He took two steps forward and the room began to disintegrate, the beds shifted, the door tilted sideways. A man came running at the young woman's call.

He spoke rapidly to her, shaking his head, but she spoke urgently back at him, calling him Louis and pointing to the clock on the wall. '*Rapidement*,' she said, and pointed to the door. He shrugged and then nodded and collected other people who were bandaged, and Roland and the woman and everyone else moved forward, down one corridor and then another and on towards the door.

A horse-drawn omnibus was waiting with a group of people beside it. The sky was grey. 'Jeanette!' someone called, and indicated for the woman who was holding on to him to hurry. She and the man called Louis helped him up the few steps of the vehicle and he sank on to a seat and closed his eyes. Someone put a blanket over his knees and a black coat. He held his left arm with his other hand. It ached almost as much as his head. Jeanette came and sat beside him and the vehicle moved off.

Some of the other passengers were asking questions. Were they speaking about him or to him? Some of the words and sentences were beginning to join up and make sense. Something about a train? Yes, he had travelled by train, but from where? He couldn't recall. He looked down and saw that his shirt wasn't fully buttoned; he touched his head again. Was this his hat? His sleeve was rolled up and a white – what was it called – a cover, which was white but not bloody. That was it, there was blood on his head and the white covering wasn't a *chapeau* – it was – it was – he sought for the word but couldn't find it. He touched his throat. He wore no cravat. He was only half dressed.

He frowned as he tried to concentrate, to make sense of where he was and who he was and what had happened to him.

Who were these people? Who was this woman? She seemed kind; he thought he could trust her, but wasn't quite certain. He felt anxious; where were they going? He heard their chatter; they seemed excited about something, but he couldn't understand everything that they said. It was very confusing and he wanted to sleep but each time he closed his eyes this Jeanette woman wouldn't let him, but shook his arm to wake him up, his good arm, the one that wasn't painful, or at least not very, though his whole body ached as if he'd been punched all over.

He was taken off the coach with Jeanette on one side of him and several others he had seen in the place with the beds . . . what was it called? They were taken across a large paved area where there was a lot of engine noise and doors banging. Where are we going?

A man was asking his name, but he didn't know it. Jeanette interrupted and pointed to one of the women who had been on the coach and jabbered something to her. The other woman shrugged as if she didn't know and both looked at him as if they were expecting him to answer, but he didn't, because he didn't understand the question.

CHAPTER TWENTY-EIGHT

He was on a train, although not a long journey, not like, not like – what? Where were they taking him? He wanted to ask, but wasn't sure what words to say. They were speaking in a language he knew but didn't properly understand. His head ached if he did too much thinking, so he had just followed or been led across another area where again there was a lot of noise and shouting. Why did they have to shout so much, so that their voices echoed up into the high roof of metal and glass?

He saw birds, big white ones, as they went outside and climbed aboard another vehicle. He could smell something different from the acrid odour of smoke and steam inside and then he saw the water and a ship and they were being taken towards it.

When they got off the vehicle, he and Jeanette, the man called Louis and three other men, all with various white dressings on their heads, arms or hands, were taken to a building where someone in a blue uniform came to talk to them. He was asked questions but only stared at the man who was asking them and wished he would hurry because he really wanted to sleep, and he kept closing his eyes which made him sway, but Jeanette kept shaking him by the shoulder to keep him awake.

Eventually the man in the uniform wrote on several sheets of paper, stamped them and gave them to Jeanette, then pointed to him, saying something, and they were allowed to leave.

They all walked towards the ship and Jeanette handed out the sheets of paper to everyone but him, and he wondered why. One of the sheets fluttered to the ground from one of the other travellers' hands and he bent, unsteady and giddy, and picked it up, patted his side looking for a pocket to put it in but there wasn't one, so he pushed it up the sleeve of the black coat which he was still carrying.

Everything was a blur. He followed the other people up a narrow walkway and was shepherded on board the ship. He felt confused as people kept coming up to him to look into his face as if he were a child or a curiosity. He leaned on the ship's rail and closed his eyes so that they would go away.

He jumped when a loud noise startled him and he felt the vessel shudder and begin to move. It seemed a vaguely familiar motion and he clung to the metal rail as if to a memory, feeling it cold beneath his hands; when he looked at his fingers again he saw that he had scratched blue paint off the rail and flakes of it were beneath his nails.

They went inside and sat down in a group and he took the sheet of paper from inside the coat sleeve. It was mostly blank with indecipherable writing but at the bottom was a name. Jacques Dacey. Was that his name?

Someone brought him a drink and he took it gratefully; he didn't know what it was but it was hot and sweet and soothing. He must have been allowed to sleep for he remembered no more until he woke up on a bench seat with a blanket over him. They were guided off the ship on to land and he thought it was morning, because there was a freshness about the day, a bright blue sky and gulls, he remembered that was what they were, wheeling high above them. They stepped into another vehicle and then another train and again he fell asleep and no one tried to wake him.

The train screeched to a halt and most people got off, as did the woman called Jeanette, so he followed them. A group of people were waiting on a platform to meet the travellers, several of them bandaged as he was; *bandage,* that was the word he had been seeking; he heard some of the train travellers talking of *accident* and *'ospital.* A question was asked and people turned to look at him and some frowned and shook their heads, murmuring, '*Non, je ne le connais pas,*' they didn't know him; or they simply shrugged in a negative manner. Someone else appraised him and murmured '*Bon drap.*' Good cloth. He didn't understand what they meant by the remark.

Everyone dispersed into wagons and carts and some into traps, except for Jeanette and Louis, and they seemed to be arguing. Louis looked angry and was waving his hands about and Jeanette was shaking her head. They came across to him where he was just standing waiting to be given directions.

'We don't know your name,' she said softly in her own language, and he thought what a pretty accent she had. French, he realized, and he understood her because she spoke slowly, unlike Louis who spoke quickly and impatiently. 'Or where you live. Can you remember which village you are from?'

'*Non!*' he said, feeling muddled.

Louis interrupted and said something about *commissariat de police,* which alarmed him. Had he done something wrong?

But Jeanette seemed to be on his side and said, '*Non, non, non!*' and something about its not being his fault, it was theirs, and when Louis objected to this she said '*Pff! Le mien*', and turned her back on him.

'Do as you like,' Louis muttered. 'We don't know who he is and I'm not getting involved. He could be a felon, for all we know.' Then he walked away and out of the station.

She shouted after him. '*Merci beaucoup!*'

He drew the paper out of the sleeve and showed it to her. She read it, then looked at him, shook her head and lifted her hands in denial. 'Jacques Dacey,' she murmured. 'The port steward!'

She stood for a few minutes, biting her lips and scrutinizing him as if making a decision. She looked about her. It was a

177

single platform station and all the other passengers had gone. Then she walked across to the station office and knocked on the door and peered through the window.

'Tsk!' she muttered, and walked off the platform and round the back of the station house where she knocked again on another door, but there was no answer there either. She stood for a few minutes, running her hands across her cheeks as she pondered, looking at him from time to time, for he'd followed behind her.

Then it was as if she'd made a decision and she indicated for him to come with her. Behind the station house was a small stable and inside was a donkey. Jeanette spoke quietly to it and brought it outside, and gave the reins to him to hold whilst she pulled out a lightweight wooden cart; he saw that she was going to hitch the donkey to it and he moved the animal towards the cart, manoeuvring it so that it could be backed between the shafts. He picked up the leather traces and fastened them, then handed the reins back to her. She thanked him, and taking a carrot from a deep bag that was in the back of the cart gave it to the donkey, who chomped on it with large yellow teeth.

'I have never known such a good-natured donkey,' he murmured, feeling pleased with himself that he had remembered how to find the words. 'Only bad-tempered ones.'

She looked at him and smiled as if she too was surprised, but she didn't make a comment.

They drove for three or more miles, passing an isolated farmhouse, a derelict barn without a roof, a lake where he spotted a heron standing motionless on the opposite bank, and then onwards towards a thickly wooded area. A narrow path took them through the trees and they drove on for perhaps a mile towards a clearing, where they came to a fenced-off area where chickens were scouring the ground in front of a single-storey brick and timber building with a pantile roof.

'*Maison!*' she said, with an air of gladness, and climbed down, indicating to him to do the same.

So this is her home. Does she live alone, he wondered, and if so, why am I here?

He waited for instructions. She put two fingers to her lips and gave a piercing whistle. Then she put her head back and shouted, 'Chien.'

She has a dog. Of course she has, living out here. He frowned a little; someone else has a dog. Who?

There came a crashing through undergrowth, a cracking of wood and the sound of barking. 'Chien,' she called again. 'Come on!'

A huge dark brown dog came hurtling out of the forest, heading towards her, and then, seeing a stranger, skidded to a stop, a low growl coming up from his throat and his teeth bared.

'It's all right,' she said softly. '*Ami*.' Friend. She called the dog to her and put her hand on his collar, which was festooned with trailing goose-grass, twigs and leaves.

'He won't hurt you,' she said. 'Unless you hurt me. He's my guardian.'

He shook his head. 'I won't hurt you,' he said softly, and put out his hand for the dog to come and sniff. Chien came stealthily and nosed his hand, his bandaged arm, his trousers and boots, and seemed to be satisfied, though wary.

'Please, come inside.' She pushed open the cottage door and beckoned him to come in. The door opened straight into a room with a dirt floor; two old easy chairs were placed by a roughly made slate and brick hearth where kindling and dried moss were laid in the grate with a pile of logs and a kettle to the side of it. She took a match from a jug on the mantelshelf, struck it on the hearth and put it to the moss, which smouldered before catching, and then a yellow flame licked at the kindling, setting it alight.

A bonfire, I think it is called. It was good to see it, as he had been feeling rather cold; he had put on the black coat and wore a linen shirt beneath it but it wasn't meant for warmth. She must have had the same thought, for she opened a cupboard door and brought out a large knitted jumper, much too big for her, he thought, and handed it to him.

He slipped out of the tailcoat and pulled the jumper over his head; instantly he felt warmer. Then she pulled a blanket out of the same cupboard and invited him to be seated and gave him the blanket to wrap around himself.

'I will make coffee,' she explained, 'and then soup when the fire is hot enough. Something simple, potato and onion and some herbs; and bread.' She smiled. 'Always we have bread.'

That was all he wanted, something warming to eat or drink, and then to sleep. He was so very tired. Would he be able to sleep here? Was there a room with a bed? A large soft cushion was behind his back and he sank against it, bringing the blanket up to his neck. 'Hah,' he breathed out. He felt safe now and not as confused as he had been, surrounded by so many people and so much noise. Where had he been? Where had he come from and where was he now?

Something was not quite right. What was that place with the beds? Who had wrapped up his head and arm? And who was Jacques Dacey? Is it me?

Jeanette came back with something in a cup. He sniffed at it and looked up at her. The drink had a spicy piquant aroma and he took the smallest of sips.

'Drink,' she said. 'It is good. It will help you relax, and then later we will talk.'

She was right, it was good; it was warming, sharp, yet sweet like apple, sending a tingling down his throat. It reminded him of something, but what? He drank it all and then ran his tongue round the inside of the cup so as not to miss any of it. He closed his eyes. He could hear noises echoing in his head, hear shouts, the neighing of startled horses; saw the great wall of water as the ship ploughed through it; and then nothing. Just a deep black veil of comforting silence.

CHAPTER TWENTY-NINE

Matty was trying to hold herself together but anxiety was threatening to tear her apart. As another day dawned, she told herself that she must keep steady for the sake of her sisters, especially Faith and Becca. Julia, of course, had drawn into herself as she always did, taking it personally that their father had not yet come home.

Faith said little. She would go to the piano and begin to play, but then abandon it and pace the room. Her painting on the easel had also been abandoned; she had no further interest in it, she said.

Becca cried; she wouldn't do her lessons, but kept getting up from the desk when Miss Hargreaves came to teach her, to stand by the window. She rushed downstairs if she heard the slightest sound from the hallway and alarmed the postman whenever he came.

'You will be the first to know when we hear something.' Matty hugged her, trying to be the one in charge when she didn't want to be; she wanted to lock herself in her room and climb under the bed sheets and hide until someone came to tell her that her darling papa was safe and all this worry was a simple misunderstanding, that she had got it wrong and he had said he would be away for a week.

Except that now it was longer than a week.

Nunny knocked and came into the room. 'Now, m'dear, I think it's time to take some advice. The postie has passed 'door and not delivered any letters.'

Matty's face creased as her lips trembled, and she pressed them firmly together. 'Who would I ask? I don't know what to do.'

'Your uncle comes to mind, and your aunt Miss Maddeson,' Nunny suggested. 'It's time they were informed, beggin' your pardon, Miss Matty.'

All formality had gone: she was Miss Matty again, not Miss Martha or Miss Maddeson, and Nunny was there to help and advise her again, just as she had been once before. She was upset too. All of the staff were anxious; Matty could tell by the way everyone tiptoed about and Cook made warming soup and rice puddings, knowing that no one had any appetite for anything solid.

'I'll write to Aunt Gertrude,' she said, 'and I suppose I could drop a note to Uncle Alb— Fisher,' she corrected herself, 'and ask him to call.'

'Yes.' Nunny nodded. 'There you are, you see, you are a very capable young woman. You write your letters and I'll get Betty Brown to take them straight away. And I think it would be a good idea to ask your uncle to come here; that way you won't disturb his wife.'

Her mouth turned down. She had no time for Mrs Fisher Maddeson and her condescending manner. She had much more for Miss Gertrude Maddeson, especially after travelling with her. She liked her spiky humour, never directed at the lower orders but only at those who considered themselves a cut above others, like Mrs Fisher Maddeson, who, Nunny thought, could generate trouble.

'I think it best if you include Miss Julia in your decision, so that she's prepared, and perhaps tell Miss Faith and Miss Becca later in the day?'

'Julia won't want to hear of it,' Matty claimed. 'You know she doesn't like bad news.'

'Whether she wants to hear it or not is of no consequence,' Nunny answered gently. 'Miss Julia is old enough to be aware of any decision being made; she's not a child any more. You can't protect her from everything she doesn't want to hear or know. Besides,' she added more heartily, 'it won't necessarily be bad news. You'll be doing something positive.'

Matty climbed the stairs to speak to Julia before she wrote the letters. Perhaps Julia would like to give her opinion on what to write. She had come down for breakfast in her dressing robe, had said nothing but good morning, eaten some toast and then taken a cup of coffee back upstairs to her room. They had their own bedrooms now, having decided a while ago that the time had come to have their own private places, though they often joined one another when there was something they wanted to chat about.

She knocked on the bedroom door. 'Julia, I need to speak to you. It's important.'

Julia opened the door immediately. She still wasn't dressed. 'What? Has something happened?' Her face was white, her eyes wide.

'No. May I come in? We must speak, Julia; we can't go on pretending that everything is all right, for it clearly isn't.'

Julia stared at her and then opened the door wider and turned her back, going to sit on the side of her bed. She swallowed. 'What?'

Matty sat next to her. 'I'm thinking of writing to Aunt Gertrude.' She mentioned their aunt first, knowing of the antipathy Julia felt towards Uncle Fisher's wife. 'And of asking Uncle Fisher to call.'

'With what intent?' Julia asked; her voice was devoid of any emotion.

'Why – to ask their advice! Papa is missing, Julia. He wouldn't leave us not knowing where he is.' Her voice broke. 'I have gone over our last conversation time and again to determine whether I've misunderstood his intentions.' Tears began to flow down her cheeks. 'And I haven't! I haven't! I *didn't* mishear him. So why hasn't he written to us? There's not even a postcard. Something is wrong. It's nearly two weeks!'

Julia put her arms round her sister. 'You're blaming yourself,' she murmured. 'I didn't know.' She was choked. 'I'm sorry. I'm so sorry. What a selfish pig I am.'

They both wept, the release of tears and anxiety somehow drawing them closer. They sat side by side on the bed and Julia reached for clean handkerchiefs from a drawer and handed one to Matty.

'What I thought was,' Matty blew her nose and took a deep breath, 'was that I'd write to Aunt Gertrude; she's so sensible, she'll have some advice, I'm sure. And Uncle Fisher – I thought I'd ask Nunny to send a note round to him asking him to call.'

'As long as he doesn't bring his *charming* wife,' Julia said bitterly. 'She'll have plenty to say, I don't doubt!'

'Why do you hate her so?' Matty had never asked the question before; she always thought that Julia would rebuff her if she did and Matty preferred a quiet, hassle-free life.

'Because of what she said after Mama died. I remember it so well.'

'What?' What had been said to a six-year-old child to make her recall it after so many years?

'It was some time later, I think. I remember it was raining. We'd been taken to their house, I don't recall why.'

She paused and wiped away her tears. 'Uncle Fisher was waiting in the hallway and Aunt Caroline was dressed to go out; she was wearing something dark, in mourning for Mama, I suppose, and she was leaving us with the nursery maid, who asked her how she should treat us.

'Aunt Caroline said, "Oh, don't bother about them too much. Let them do as they will as long as they don't break the china. They're poor little orphan girls; they'll never amount to much now that they've no mother to guide them. They'll grow up without manners or decorum, I expect, and it's not my place to counsel them. I have my own children to advise."'

'Was I there?' Matty had no memory of it.

'Someone was, either you or Faith, I don't recall. Faith was only little. Perhaps you didn't hear.' She shook her head. 'I can't get rid of it; it's there every time I see her, which is not often, thank goodness, or even if someone mentions her name.'

She has to have someone to blame, Matty pondered. Just as I blame myself for not being good enough for Mama to live with us. Faith and Becca were too young to understand, and there was always someone there to feed them or put them on a loving knee – Nunny came to mind immediately – but Julia and I, well, we were vulnerable and we missed our mother – and now, and now . . . Her tears began to flow again as she thought of her father: this time we have no reason to blame ourselves and yet we still do.

CHAPTER THIRTY

Uncle Fisher came later the same day. Their house was in the centre of town, only five minutes' walk away, yet clearly he was disgruntled at being asked to call.

The maid showed him in and closed the drawing room door quietly behind him. 'Now then,' he said. 'What's this? Where's your father?'

Matty and Julia had risen to greet him and sat down again, straight-backed, their hands folded in their laps.

'Won't you take a seat, Uncle?' Matty said. 'There is something we would like to discuss.'

He sighed and sat, drawing up the knees of his trousers with his fingertips.

'We wouldn't have bothered you,' Matty went on, 'but we are very concerned.'

He crossed his legs and said smoothly, 'Something you can't discuss with your father?' and raised his eyebrows.

'Our father *is* our concern, Uncle,' Julia slipped in coldly. 'Otherwise, as my sister said, we wouldn't have bothered you, knowing how very busy you are.'

She can be so very cutting, Matty thought.

The sarcasm was wasted on him. 'Why? Is he sick? He looked very well last time we met.'

'We don't know if he is sick,' Matty began, and felt her throat constrict. 'We don't know where he is. He left for London

186

almost two weeks ago, saying he would be back the next day, and he hasn't returned.'

'Really? So where do you think he might be?'

Julia turned to Matty with an expression of derision, and then explained to their uncle with the sweetest of smiles, as if he were a halfwit, 'That is why we asked you to call.'

'To ask if you can shed some light on our disquiet,' Matty continued.

Fisher pouted. 'I suppose it depends on why he went to London in the first place. Do you know why he made the journey? Or perhaps he didn't tell you.'

Somehow, he had the knack of insinuation, which neither of them completely understood and yet they both squirmed.

'He had gone to a meeting, a – something about a broker.'

'Oh, well, I can't help you there, I'm afraid. Your father doesn't discuss business matters with me.'

'I don't suppose he does,' Matty responded impatiently. 'We wondered merely if you might have a suggestion as to what we might do; we are very anxious.'

He must have finally sensed their apprehension for he glanced at them both and then teased his fingers through his beard. 'I'm sorry,' he mumbled. 'So what are you thinking? That he's had an accident and hasn't been able to get in touch?'

Matty turned quite pale. To hear her worst fear spoken out loud was dreadful, and yet it could be even worse. 'Who should we turn to?' she whispered. 'The police?'

'No, no! We don't want that. Think of the rumours,' he said. 'Who would know of his broker? His bank? His lawyer, maybe? Doesn't he deal with Garton?'

'Yes. Would they know?'

He shrugged. 'You could ask them, but if it's only a matter of two weeks they probably won't think it important yet.' He looked from one to the other. 'What about money? Does your father pay the accounts, servants' salaries and so on?'

'Yes, but they are not paid weekly,' Matty answered, thinking it was just as well that her father had taught her about expenditure. But why had he thought to do that, she wondered. A small doubt crept in. He was surely not thinking of going away?

'No, of course not,' he agreed. 'And in any case, we leave those matters to the lady of the house to deal with, don't we?' Then he realized his blunder and harrumphed loudly and stood up.

'I'll, erm, I'll have a think about what to do,' he offered, 'and try to come up with a solution. Try not to worry,' he pattered on, edging towards the door. Julia and Matty stood up and Julia rang the bell on the wall for someone to escort him out.

'Thank you for coming,' Matty murmured routinely. 'Sorry to have troubled you.' Betty knocked on the door and opened it. 'Would you see Mr Maddeson out, please?'

When he had gone, they both sat down again. 'That was very helpful, wasn't it?' Julia said sarcastically. 'He's just the kind of man you would run to in an emergency.'

Matty heard the tremor in her sister's voice. 'Aunt Gertrude will help us,' she said. 'She'll receive our letter by the first post in the morning. I'm sure she'll come as soon as she can.'

Becca heard the cabriolet outside the house as she was dressing the next morning and rushed to the window. 'Papa?' she breathed, but it wasn't. It was Aunt Gertrude, who had received their letter first thing and sent the boot boy out for a cabriolet to drive her to Beverley rather than take the train.

'I haven't had any breakfast, Mrs Nunnington,' she said to Nunny, who happened to be in the hall when she heard the loud ringing of the bell and had hastily opened the door. 'I came immediately I received the post. Whatever has happened to my brother?'

What a contrast to Mr Fisher Maddeson, Nunny thought. He couldn't get out of the house fast enough. She didn't make a habit of listening at doors but she had heard enough of the muted conversation to know that he hadn't been helpful.

'We are completely in the dark, ma'am.' She helped Miss Maddeson off with her coat. 'The young ladies are trying to be brave, but it's very difficult for them; a most unlikely situation. Mr Maddeson would never let his daughters worry so.'

'He wouldn't. You're quite right.' Aunt Gertrude looked up as Becca ran down the stairs, flung her arms round her waist and burst into tears. 'Now now, Rebecca, let's have no hysterics. We must remain calm.'

Matty opened the dining room door. 'Oh, Aunt, thank you for coming so quickly. Please come in, we're in here. Nunny, will you . . .?'

'Of course.' Nunny didn't have to be told. 'Fresh coffee, Miss Maddeson, and you'll have breakfast? Eggs, bacon, kippers?'

'I'll have two poached eggs on toast, please, Mrs Nunnington, and a rasher of bacon. Tell Cook I like my bacon crisp.'

Matty ushered her into the dining room, gave her a seat at the table and set her a place. She felt a huge sense of relief now that her aunt had arrived. She would tell them whether or not their anxiety was warranted.

Nunny brought in a fresh pot of coffee and poured it, and put jugs of milk and cream in front of Miss Maddeson for her to help herself. 'Breakfast is being cooked now, ma'am,' she murmured, and left the room again.

'Now, my dears,' Aunt Gertrude was saying when Faith slipped into the room, dipped her knee and greeted her.

'I won't give you a kiss, Aunt,' she said. 'I feel as if I'm starting with a cold.' She sat down at the other end of the table.

'Then you must go straight back to bed after breakfast,' Aunt Gertrude told her. 'Use plenty of pillows so that you can sit up and the cold won't settle on your chest; and honey with a thimbleful of whisky and hot water will send it on its way. I have great belief in whisky as a cure-all.'

'I will, Aunt,' Faith murmured. 'Thank you. I don't want breakfast, Matty.' Matty was hovering by the dresser, about to serve her with something. 'I'll just have a cup of tea when Nunny comes back.'

Their aunt sipped her coffee and heaved a sigh. 'That's better. Now, tell me from the beginning: when did your father leave and where was he going?'

'Two weeks ago, Aunt,' Matty said. 'He told me that he was going to a meeting in London on the following day; he had business with a new company. He had met them before, but had been invited again for a discussion on some matters. He told me that the time the meeting finished would determine when he came home, but he expected to return on the third day if not before.'

'And you don't know the name of this company?'

The door opened. Nunny brought in Aunt Gertrude's breakfast and placed it in front of her before discreetly leaving the room.

'I don't,' Matty said, 'and of course I haven't looked on Papa's desk for his address book.'

Aunt Gertrude began her breakfast, and after making headway into it paused and patted her mouth with her napkin. 'Then that is the first place we must start, and if we find them we must write to them.'

She gazed at them all in turn. 'I realize that you are good and honest young women and wouldn't dream of looking at your father's diary or papers in the normal way, but this is not the time to be fastidious. We must find out who he was meeting and write to them accordingly.'

Faith excused herself after drinking her tea and went back to bed. She knew what to do, having suffered so many illnesses when she was a child, and for her, bed was always the answer. She would be warm and comfortable, and Nunny would be up as soon as breakfast was over with the stone hot water bottle, a strip of willow bark and a cup of honey and hot water. She wasn't sure about the whisky; she'd have to ask Nunny about that.

Becca asked Matty if she should cancel her lessons today. It was geography and mathematics, neither of which was her best subject, but Matty said no, it wouldn't help at all, and the main thing was for them to keep busy and then they wouldn't worry as much.

'But I *am* worried, Matty,' Becca said tearfully. 'I can't concentrate when Papa is missing.'

Matty took a deep breath. 'He isn't missing, Becca. We just don't know where he is!'

'It's the same thing.' Becca began to cry. 'It's exactly the same!' She flounced out of the room, almost crashing into Nunny, who was coming in with a tray to clear away the breakfast crockery.

'I'll see to her, Miss Martha,' she said, remembering her position in Miss Maddeson's presence, and put down the tray to follow Becca, who she thought was in the throes of something other than worry over her father.

'I'm ill, Nunny,' Becca cried. She was sitting bent forward on the stairs, her head in her hands. 'I think I've got what Faith has, only much worse because I've got a pain in my middle as well.'

'Come along, Miss Becca. I know what it is and we'll soon put you right. Pop upstairs to your room and I'll be with you in a minute.'

'If it's not one thing, then it's another,' she muttered as she went back to the kitchen and drew out a small pair of steps to stand on to reach the top shelf of a cupboard.

'Let me do that, Mrs Nunnington.' Betty Brown took the steps from her and climbed up, handing a tin box down to her.

'How did you know what I wanted?' Nunny asked.

'It's 'most used box in the house, and if you'll pardon me for saying, Mrs Nunnington, I think that with four young ladies in the house it should be in 'bottom drawer so that it's easier to get at. Or,' she added, 'put some of the requirements in their bedroom drawers so they can get their own when they're needed.'

Mrs Nunnington nodded rather wearily. 'You're quite right,' she said. 'It's just that I've always taken care of such things.'

Betty Brown looked round to make sure that Cook wasn't listening. 'There's no need,' she said. 'They're all very capable young ladies. They'll manage. Well, mebbe not Miss Becca just yet, but,' she lowered her voice, 'why don't I talk to her and explain that all young women have to go through this palaver every month and we just have to put up with it.'

Nunny gazed at the plain-talking young maid. 'Yes, that's a good thought, Betty.' She handed the box back to her. 'Would you do that, please? It will be something less for me to think about. Tell Miss Becca it's just about growing up, and mebbe she'll be pleased about that.' And I can take care of Miss Faith, she thought. She doesn't look at all well to me, and we don't want her being ill just now.

CHAPTER THIRTY-ONE

He stirred as daylight filtered into the room. 'Jacques!' Someone shook him gently by the shoulder. 'Wake up. I have made breakfast, and there's coffee.'

He looked round and didn't know where he was. It was a small room and he was curled up on a chair, covered by several blankets; beneath his head was a large soft pillow which was stuffed with feathers, the shafts of some of them sticking out of the cotton cover. A merry fire was burning in the grate with a steaming kettle on it.

He pulled himself up and remembered eating soup and bread and nodding sleepily over it; and a dog. A dog that had parked himself outside the woman's bedroom door. He recognized the woman who had spoken to him, but could not think of her name. His mouth worked to ask a question. 'Excuse me, do I know you?' He asked the question in the language she was using, though it didn't come so easily to his tongue.

A shadow flitted across her face. 'Jeanette. Do you not remember me? Do you not recall the accident with the 'orse bus? The 'ospital, no?' She patted the back of her head. 'You hurt your head.'

He gingerly touched his head; did he remember something? He was wearing a covering, a – *bandage*, someone had said. 'I – I'm not sure.' He looked down at his left arm, which was also wrapped up; like a parcel, he thought.

'Was there a – horse?' He had an image of flashing hooves.

'Yes, and a mule.' She smiled. 'Good. You were on the omnibus, yes? A mule escaped from a cart and frightened the horses. The bus overturned and we were taken into the 'ospital.'

He shook his head. There had been a lot of noise and shouting, and then the horses. He didn't recall anything else.

'Come, I have made gruel,' she told him. 'Can you get to the table?'

He said he thought that he could, but first – 'I need . . .' He looked about him. 'I need – to go outside.'

'Of course.' She helped him up and walked him to the door and opened it. 'Watch out for Chien,' she warned. 'Just stop if he comes up to you. Don't let him think that you're a threat. If you can walk to the back of the house – hold on to the wall – then later I will show you where the latrine is.'

He walked unsteadily in the direction she had said, found a convenient tree where he relieved himself, and then looked about him. The back of the cottage faced on to a garden which was divided up into small plots. A wooden fence, clumsily fashioned, with a gate, led out into a grassy area with a washing line tied between two trees, and beyond that was woodland. There was no sign of Chien, but he could hear a chorus of birdsong: a blackbird with its melodious refrain and maybe a chaffinch; the coo of a dove, whilst above him he saw a buzzard circling.

He went back to the house. His legs felt less wobbly than they had done, but his head was fuzzy and ached and he couldn't recall how he had got here.

Jeanette had placed a washbowl and a towel on a bench outside the door near to a water pump; he washed his hands and rinsed his face to try to wake himself up, for he felt as if he were sleepwalking.

He sat down at the table and she placed a bowl of gruel in front of him, with a dish of honey to sweeten it.

'The gruel is made with goat's milk,' she explained. 'Not everyone likes it, but the honey is very sweet; it is from the sweet chestnut trees. I have beehives nearby. In summer we also have lavender honey, as I grow lavender bushes in my garden.'

Like a schoolboy he licked the spoon after letting the honey trickle into the gruel. He nodded. It was good. 'Do you keep a cow?' he asked.

'*Non*,' she said. 'I cannot afford a cow, only a goat. The milk is good and the meat is very tender.'

He turned his eyes towards her. 'You eat the meat?' He was confused. It seemed strange; who was this woman who seemed to live alone in this isolated place?

She gave a small smile. 'Not often, only when they finish producing kids and milk. And I ask someone to slaughter them. I don't do that myself.'

He scraped the bowl. He had been very hungry. She placed a baton of bread on the table and fetched him a plate, indicating that he should eat more honey with the bread.

'Do you – erm, have a . . .' He paused. What word did he want? He seemed to have lost some of his vocabulary. 'Erm . . .' He pointed a finger around the room and then pressed his own chest. 'Husband?'

'*Mari? Non.*' She frowned a little at the question, and then showed him her ringless hands.

She poured coffee into a tin mug and handed it to him, and poured one for herself. He took a sip. It tasted nutty, nothing like anything he had drunk before. 'Acorn,' she explained. 'Out here I have nowhere to buy food. I make what I need. It is good, yes?'

He nodded. Yes, it was. 'Where am I?' he asked.

'Cerisy Forest,' she said. 'Near Calvados. You must know of it? In Normandy?'

'I don't think so.' He was beginning to feel anxious again. Nervous. What was happening to him? Did he live here?

She seemed to pick up on his unease. 'Can you recall where you are from?'

As she spoke she leaned across and took hold of his un-bandaged arm and held his hand, running her fingers over his skin. It was very soothing. 'You are a gentleman, I think?' She turned her own hands over to show him her workaday palms. 'Perhaps from Paris, or one of the big cities?'

Paris? Have I been to Paris? Paris is in France. Is that where I'm from?

She was asking him something: about the ferry and where he had embarked, who he had travelled with, or had he travelled alone? He watched her lips as she spoke and it was as if he couldn't hear her; he simply watched her expressions, the upward tilt of her mouth, the softness of her lips as she paused to consider what to ask next, the rise of her eyebrows. He saw the reddish gold of the curls on her forehead; what were they called? A fringe! A small miracle: he smiled at the thought that he'd remembered what the curls were called. She ran her long fingers through them, brushing them away from her face, which had a trace of sun on it and a band of freckles on each cheek.

'Can you recall?' She'd asked the question twice before he realized.

'What?' he asked. 'I'm sorry, what was the question?'

'Why were you in England? Did you travel with our group? We stayed only one night. It was a special excursion, a ferry and train journey to London, to an exhibition of mechanical engines. Some of the others had saved up for a whole year, but I was asked if I would take someone else's place, someone who was sick.' She gave a little shrug as he watched and listened. The act seemed to be characteristic of her. 'I speak a little English, you see, that is why I was asked. I travelled for free. I wouldn't have been able to afford to go otherwise. I didn't look at the engines,' she went on, and again he watched her facial expressions rather than listening. 'I walked by the Thames. I hadn't been to London since I was a girl and so I explored and visited art galleries. I don't have the chance to do that in France, which is a pity when we have such wonderful galleries full of beautiful paintings. Especially in Paris, of course.'

Something clicked in his mind as she talked; something to do with paintings. But it came and went as a fleeting image and he couldn't catch hold of it.

'If you have finished your breakfast,' she was saying, 'I will take off the dressings on your head and bathe your injury and wash the bandage. I have others. They are clean; I keep them for when I injure myself.' She gave a little laugh. 'Sometimes I cut myself when I'm sawing wood.'

He drew in a breath of concern. 'You have no one to help you?'

'*Non*. I am very strong and able.' She got up to clear away the table and put the kettle back on the fire, then went to the cupboard he had seen last night and busied herself bringing out a small metal bowl and a tin box, which she opened to reveal rolls of bandage and jars of ointment.

'Shall we take the bandage off your arm first of all?' She rolled up the jumper sleeve. 'This is warm, yes?'

'Yes,' he said. 'Whose is it? Not yours?'

'My brother's,' she said. 'He leaves it here for when he visits. He says my house is cold. He and his wife live in Paris. He says it isn't so cold there, but I know that it is!'

'Why do you live here? You are very far from other people.'

'I can be independent here,' she explained. 'No one questions why I choose not to be married, or why I like to grow my own food.' She paused. 'Here I answer to no one. In towns and cities, women must do as their husbands, fathers, brothers even, tell them. Village people here accept me as I am.' She put her head back and laughed. 'It is true, some think I am a little mad, but they still come and ask for help or advice.'

She finished unwinding the strapping on his arm. There was a deep cut with congealed blood and a large purple bruise that had spread up his arm and on to his elbow. She asked him if he could straighten it, which he did, gingerly. She felt carefully around his wrist and then his elbow, which elicited an intake of breath from him.

197

'It is not broken,' she said. 'I think you fell backwards on to your elbow – perhaps caught it on something.'

'And my head?' he said.

She nodded and went outside to fetch the washbowl, and he heard the clank of the pump and the gush of water and guessed there must be a spring nearby. She took the kettle from the fire and added warm water to the bowl, which she had placed on the table, and then bathed his arm and washed off the blood, dried it on a clean towel and put a thin strip of bandage over it.

'That will soon heal,' she said. 'A few days and you can take off the bandage.'

'You're very kind,' he said. 'To a stranger.'

Again she gave the characteristic shrug. 'I think perhaps it is my fault you are here. Perhaps if we had left you at the 'ospital, someone would have come to look for you?'

'I don't know,' he said, and thought that he would prefer being here than in that room with all the beds and the women with the strange headwear.

She began to carefully undo the head bandage. He felt the tenderness as she eased the bloody dressing from where his hair was matted at the back.

'There is a large cut and a bump on the back of your head,' she said. 'I will clean it and put on another bandage; we must take care not to get any dirt into it.'

Patiently she cut away the matted hair, bathed the sore place, then threw the dirty water outside and refilled the bowl with clean warm water, bathed his head again, patted it dry and then carefully creamed ointment over the wound with her fingertips before covering it again with a clean dressing.

She searched again in the bottomless cupboard and brought out a woollen beret. 'Hah!' she said, holding it up to show him. 'Breton onion seller!'

He nodded. 'Your brother's?'

'*Exactement!*'

She placed it carefully on his head so that most of the bandage was covered, and then pulled it to an angle. 'So! It will keep your head safe from dirt and dust and protect it too.'

There was a mottled mirror hanging on the wall and he turned to look in it. He didn't recognize the image staring back at him. The man in the mirror had deep dark shadows beneath his reddened eyes, an untrimmed beard and bedraggled hair peeping from beneath the beret. Is this what I look like? I don't know this person. He turned to Jeanette and said in a broken voice, 'I don't know this man. If this is me, then I am truly lost.'

CHAPTER THIRTY-TWO

Aunt Gertrude had come prepared to stay and Nunny made her up a bed in a guest room. She had already attended to Faith, who, when Nunny touched her forehead, was burning hot and probably had a high temperature. Nunny had decided that if it hadn't gone down after she had bathed her forehead, neck and shoulders with cool water and given her honey and water to sip, she would suggest that the doctor should be called. She wondered if anxiety over her father had brought on this bout of fever, but Miss Faith was a resilient young soul in spite of her former childish illnesses. I don't want to worry Miss Matty, Nunny thought. Everything seems to fall on her shoulders, bless her, so I'll just mention it to Miss Maddeson.

Aunt Gertrude and Matty were at present going through papers on Mr Maddeson's desk. Neither was happy about it, but Matty took her aunt's advice and made the decision that it was the right thing to do.

The first thing they did was look in her father's desk diary, but on the day of his departure to London all that was written was the train departure and arrival times, plus the initials D.F.H. with no indication of what they referred to.

'I think, my dear,' Aunt Gertrude said, after a deal of harrumphing and clearing of her throat, 'it might be best to make an appointment to see your father's lawyer, Joseph Garton. It is still the same, isn't it? Our father used to deal with his father Mathias Garton.'

'Yes,' Matty muttered; she was beginning to feel sick. 'And now his son Timothy has joined the firm. You met Tim in Italy, do you recall, when he came to my birthday party?'

'Of course he did!' Her aunt saw the flush on Matty's cheeks. 'I'd forgotten. A very nice young man. Good,' she added approvingly. 'I believe in continuity of family tradition. So will you send a note to make an appointment? With the elder Mr Garton, not the son. It won't be appropriate if he's a friend of yours.'

Matty put her fingers to her lips to stop them trembling. This, she thought, is becoming far too real. 'Yes,' she croaked. 'Yes, I will, but Mr Garton is also a friend of my father's.'

Aunt Gertrude gave a small encouraging nod. 'That is quite different in the present circumstances. Joseph Garton will be acquainted with your father's business dealings, if in fact he has discussed them; if not, then you must make an appointment with his banker. We must find out if any monies have gone out of his account.'

Matty turned a distraught face to her aunt. 'You mean, in case something has happened to him? Someone has – has attacked him – or . . .'

'No, I don't mean that at all, but to ascertain whether your father has drawn out any amount larger than normal and if so from which branch. We can then enquire at the branch concerned and find out if they remember him. But first things first,' she said firmly. 'There might be a simple explanation.'

'Will you come with me, Julia?' Matty asked the next day, when a quick response to her letter to Mr Garton invited her to visit his office that afternoon.

'Is Aunt Gertrude not going with you?'

'Yes, she said she would, if we wished, but I'd like you to come too, Julia. You have a sharp mind and I feel as if I'm floundering.'

201

'But you're not.' Julia clutched Matty's arm. 'You're so steady, and you think things through. I tend to jump in with both feet and then wish I hadn't.'

They both gave a wry grimace. It had been a trying morning. Dr Laybourn had called to take a look at Faith and he found that the cold had gone on to her chest. He had left a bottle of medicine and recommended that she stay in bed, propped up on pillows, with an extra blanket and the window opened a crack to let in some air.

Aunt Gertrude had taken a sniff at the medicine and announced it to be rubbish, and commanded Nunny to give her a spoonful of whisky in hot water. This she had done and Faith was promptly sick, bringing back the spoonful of porridge she had had for breakfast and a quantity of whisky, water and mucus, to which Aunt Gertrude had said, 'There you are, what did I tell you?'

A young clerk opened the door to them in the Saturday Market office of Joseph Garton and Richardson and asked them to take a seat. Matty wondered when Timothy's name would be added to the shiny brass name plate.

Tim came through to greet them in the reception, addressing Aunt Gertrude first of all and saying how nice it was to see her again, and then welcoming 'Miss Martha' and 'Miss Julia', as would have been expected of him.

'My father will see you now,' he said. 'If you'd like to come through to his office.' They followed him down a corridor to the rear of the building where he opened a door with a frosted glass panel, announced them, and closed it behind them.

He must be wondering what the matter is, Matty thought. He won't have the slightest idea; it's quite preposterous and absolutely unbelievable that someone could just disappear.

But Joseph Garton, when he had heard them out, said that he had been told many unlikely tales in his time and most had been resolved sooner or later. 'We know that your father would not go missing of his own accord, do we not? He was quite of sound mind, was he not?'

Matty and Julia nodded their agreement on both counts.

'He had no money worries, had he? No one chasing him for overdue accounts? No, I think not,' he added before they could answer. He seemed to have the answers ready for his questions almost before he had uttered them.

He is giving us optimism, Matty considered; reassuring us that Papa hasn't disappeared of his own volition, which means . . . She paused to consider; which means that something has happened to him, and that also means, she thought and gave a little shudder, that he is not in a position to let us know where he is.

'You said in your letter, Miss Martha, that your father was travelling to London for a meeting with a broker? A new broker, was it? Nothing to do with his usual one in Beverley?'

'So I understand,' she replied in a low voice. 'But that is as much as I know. In his diary he has written the letters D.F.H. I don't know what they mean. He had visited them on a previous occasion.'

'So he is familiar with their London situation; he wouldn't have become lost and wandered into an unsavoury area?'

'No,' she said clearly. 'He is well acquainted with London.'

'Very well; I will make some enquiries. If you will allow, I will ask his local broker, Bennet, if he can shed light on this . . .' – he looked down at his pad, where he had written the initials – 'this D.F.H. company and find out who they are and where they are based, and then I'll write to them on your behalf. If they don't exist we must involve the police, and if they do then they might possibly shed some light on the mystery of his disappearance.' He stood up and came round to the front of the desk and leaned forward to take Matty's hand and then Julia's.

'Try not to worry,' he told them. 'We will find out about your father, one way or another. We are old friends, you know,' he said kindly. 'Boys together, school together . . . mischief together,' he added with an impish smile. 'We will find him.' He turned to their aunt and took her hand too. 'It's very nice to see you again, my dear Gertrude. You are looking exceedingly well; you don't change at all.'

She gave him a piercing and frosty look. 'Nor do you, Joseph,' she said. 'Nor do you.'

Timothy came down the corridor to escort them back to the front office and let them out.

'I trust all is well, Miss Martha, Miss Julia?' he said quietly. 'Please don't hesitate if there is anything we can do for you. We are at your service at any time.' He gave a short bow as he opened the outer door. 'Miss Maddeson,' he said to their aunt. 'Good day to you.'

Matty turned her head as they left and saw him through the glass panel, watching them. He inclined his head. How kind he was, she thought, and her eyes were wet with tears.

Julia slid her arm through Matty's. 'It will be all right, Matty,' she whispered, squeezing her sister towards her. 'We've got good people helping us. We'll find Papa now.'

And it was those positive words from her frequently sceptical sister, who didn't often have confidence in anyone or give them the benefit of their concern or trust, that sent her tears flowing.

Becca had popped her head into Faith's room and found her sleeping. She didn't know what to do. She had had her lesson with Miss Hargreaves, who had left early as she said she had a headache. Becca wondered if she was having her monthly headache, as Betty Brown had told her that all young women faced the same situation every month, and she supposed that Miss Hargreaves was still a young woman: a lot older than Matty, but not as old as Aunt Louisa or Aunt Gertrude. They were her guidelines as far as ages went.

I don't know what to do now, she thought. I wonder how long Matty and Julia will be. From the front window she peered out to look up and down the York Road, but apart from a horse and wagon trundling up the slight rise between the meadowlands on either side it was a fairly quiet afternoon.

She saw that the leaves were turning a rich golden colour and most of them were falling rapidly.

She wondered if the Lawrence twins were home from school. She rarely saw them, as their mother took them out visiting quite often when they were home, even though they didn't always want to go. I might go across and ask if they're there, she thought. Owen will know. I can ask him without disturbing Mrs Lawrence.

Mrs Lawrence always made her welcome at the house and Mr Lawrence had told her that she could come to the stables whenever she wanted as long as she didn't distract Owen from his work. She was never quite sure what Owen's position was. He had a room above one of the stables, but ate with the Lawrence family every evening. She'd noticed too that some of the other stable hands and riders who came to exercise the horses always tipped their caps to Owen.

She changed into an old skirt and warm jumper, put on her coat and took the back stairs, popping her head into the kitchen to tell Nunny she was going out, but both Nunny and Cook were asleep in their chairs. Betty was washing up at the sink, but she decided not to tell her she was going out in case she said she shouldn't.

Pug was in his kennel outside the back door; her papa had insisted that he have one so that he could guard the house. Becca had made it very comfortable for him with an old pillow – at least, she had considered it to be old, but Nunny had said that it wasn't, and had given him a thin rug instead, saying that he was a dog, not a child to be mollycoddled. Becca had retrieved the pillow when she thought that Nunny wasn't looking and put it back in the kennel, and nothing more was said.

'Come on,' she called now. 'Walkies!' Pug yawned, and then reluctantly got to his feet. 'You're supposed to look after me,' she told him. 'I'm going to see Owen; are you coming or not?'

The dog stretched, and then broke into a trot as soon as she set off in the direction of the Lawrences' stables.

'I haven't seen you lately,' Owen said when she arrived at the yard; he had a dandy brush in his hand and was brushing the mane of a dark bay stallion. 'Where've you been?'

She stroked the smooth coat of the stallion, thinking that she hadn't seen him before, and shook her head in answer. 'Nowhere,' she said miserably. 'Just at home. We're all very worried just now, so I didn't feel like coming out. Faith isn't well either; we had to call the doctor in to visit her.'

He paused and turned to look at her. 'Did you? I'm sorry to hear that. So you're worried about her, is that it?'

She nodded. 'Yes. But something else as well. I don't know if I'm supposed to talk about it, but I'm very upset.'

He put down the brush and folded his arms over his chest. 'Is it about your father?'

She put her hand to her mouth. 'I thought no one knew!'

'Word gets about, you know. Do you want to tell me about it?'

Her bottom lip trembled. She could trust Owen, she knew that. He was older than her, but not like a proper grown-up person, though she supposed he was Matty's age. 'I don't know,' she muttered. 'I don't know whether I can.'

'Mrs Lawrence is at home,' he said. 'With the twins. Would you like to talk to her?'

She began to cry. 'Yes, I think so. You see, we don't know where Papa is. He went to London and hasn't come back.' Her shoulders began to shake. 'And I'm really really worried about him.'

Owen put the horse back into its stall and closed the door. 'Come on.' He held out his hand to her and she let him lead her to the back of the house. He scraped his boots on the iron scraper attached to the wall and opened the door into the large kitchen. At the table eating cake were Roger and Frances. Frances squealed and scraped back her chair. 'We were just coming to see you,' she said.

'I wasn't,' Roger mumbled, his mouth full of cake. 'I'm going to help Owen groom the new horse.'

'Well, *I* was coming,' Frances retaliated. 'We don't have to do everything together and we've only got one more day left before going back to school! We've been visiting!' She pulled a face, her mouth drawn down in displeasure.

'Becca wants to talk to your mother,' Owen told her. 'Will you take her up?'

Frances put an arm about Becca's shoulder. 'Yes,' she said. 'Of course I will.'

CHAPTER THIRTY-THREE

Owen and Frances walked Becca home, with Pug following behind. They went to the back door, where Nunny rushed out to greet them.

'Where've you been, Miss Becca? We've been worried about you.'

'No need for you to worry, Mrs Nunnington. She came to see Frances and Mrs Lawrence. She was a bit lonely, weren't you, Becca?' Owen smiled and gently tugged on one of her plaits. 'Is Miss Matty at home? I'd like a word, if it's convenient?'

'Come in, Master Owen,' Nunny said. 'You needn't have come to 'back door. Hello, Miss Frances. It's nice to see you. My, how you've grown.'

Frances nodded. 'I'm taller than Roger now.' She gave a grin. 'He's really cross about it.'

'He'll catch up, I dare say,' Nunny said vaguely. 'Come this way, Master Owen, I'll take you up myself. Miss Becca, take Miss Frances to your room for five minutes, will you?'

Becca and Frances raced ahead of them and Nunny took Owen into the sitting room, where Matty, Julia and Miss Maddeson were drinking tea. He gave a short bow of his head to Aunt Gertrude and nodded a greeting to Julia, and refused Nunny's offer of tea.

'Becca came across to the yard,' he said without preamble. 'She was in rather a state over her father's disappearance. So I took her in to see Mrs Lawrence.'

'Oh! Did Becca tell you?' Matty was astonished.

'No, we'd heard a rumour that he hadn't returned home as expected.' Owen didn't mention that it was Sam, their father's groom and handyman, who had told him and he had passed the news on to Mr and Mrs Lawrence himself. 'It's only to be expected in such a small community,' he went on. 'But what Mrs Lawrence asked me to tell you was that even though Frances and Roger are returning to school in a couple of days' time, Becca would be welcome to stay with her and Mr Lawrence if it would take her mind off the worry, and especially if Faith is unwell too, as Becca said. She could help in the stables if she'd like to.'

'She loves to come to the stables,' Matty said. 'She wouldn't be a nuisance?'

He smiled. 'She's not a nuisance at all; she can help to exercise the horses too. She's an efficient rider, and we'd make sure she was safe.'

'She'd love it,' Julia broke in. 'She's very worried over Papa, as we all are.' She turned to Matty. 'I think she should, if she wants to, Matty. What do you think, Aunt Gertrude?'

'Hm.' Their aunt gave a grunt. 'Horseback riding isn't the kind of desirable pastime I would recommend for a young lady,' she pronounced, 'but I realize I am quite behind the times.' She gave a little sigh. 'I suppose she's still young enough to be inclined to fear the worst about her father, so perhaps she should accept Mrs Lawrence's kind invitation.'

Mrs Lawrence said she would help Becca with lessons herself if they would like her to, but Matty and Julia said they would prefer her to come home every night and have her usual lessons with Miss Hargreaves in the mornings and then spend the afternoons at the Lawrences', either playing the piano or sewing and chatting with Mrs Lawrence, or with

Owen at the stables where she could make herself useful, mucking out the stalls or riding with him and the professional riders on the racecourse. She was thrilled when she was told this, as this was the first time she had ever been allowed to do so and it was infinitely preferable to sewing or playing the piano.

Matty was pleased to see the difference in her outlook even after only a few days, and realized that Becca couldn't have been expected to cope with the apprehension and uncertainty over her father's disappearance, or with the worry over the illness that had left Faith weak and exhausted, without such a distraction.

It was almost a week later when a messenger came from Mr Garton's office asking them to call at their earliest convenience. Aunt Gertrude had already left for home, being driven by Sam to save her the train journey, and he was happy to be occupied and out of this unhappy household.

Matty and Julia dressed quickly when the message came; they had told the boy they would be but half an hour. It was that exactly when Tim opened the office door to them.

'Please come through,' he said quietly, his face giving nothing away. 'My father is waiting for you.'

He took them through to the inner office and Joseph Garton stood up as they entered. 'Please do sit down,' he said, adding to his son, 'If you would stay, please, Timothy.'

They were both glad to sit; Matty felt faint, and Julia wore an icy expression on her face which hid her uncertainties.

Mr Garton clasped his fingers together, and then opened them. 'The news we have is not necessarily bad,' he began, which alarmed them even more than his urgent summons. 'We must try to be positive. Through the broker, Bennet, we have discovered that the letters of D.F.H. belong to a new, though reputable, company with their headquarters in London, as was suggested.'

He paused to clear his throat. 'What we have discovered is that your father did have an appointment with them on the day indicated in his diary, but according to their records he didn't arrive. They gave him half an hour in case of any traffic hold-ups, as seemingly there were problems on the road that morning, but as they had a long agenda with other clients they had to begin without him. They have heard nothing more from him.'

Matty and Julia sat as if frozen to their seats; Julia gave a huff of breath and then Matty said in a tight voice, 'So something must have happened to him on the journey there—'

'Or after he arrived in London,' Mr Garton said solemnly. 'Did your father make a habit of using the same lodgings? If so we can make enquiries, but,' he hesitated, 'I'm very much afraid that we will have to inform the police that your father is a missing person.'

Matty began to breathe hard, and Julia clutched the arms of her chair. Tim left the room and came back a moment later clutching two glasses of water, which he handed to them. 'Take a breath or two,' he murmured to Matty. 'Don't speak. Take your time.'

She wanted to cry, she felt so desperate. Had their father been involved in an accident? Was he injured and unable to get home? What would they do without him? Uncle Fisher was their guardian; he would want to take over their lives, or at least his wife would. I must speak to Aunt Gertrude immediately. There must be something we can do. I'll go and look for him myself if necessary; I'll comb the streets of London until I find him. And then another thought struck her. What would they do about money? Their father paid all the bills. Another month and the staff would need to be paid, and what about the butcher, the grocer, the dairyman? Would she be able to draw money from their father's bank account? Common sense told her that no, she wouldn't.

When Mr Garton finished speaking and had said he would do all that was necessary concerning police procedure, they thanked him and rose to leave; Tim took them into the outer office and asked them if they would wait a few minutes whilst he fetched his coat, and he would walk them home.

Both were pleased to accept his offer; both were shaky and apprehensive, wondering what was the next step. 'I'll write to Aunt Gertrude, and also Aunt Louisa,' Matty murmured as they waited. 'She knows nothing of this. She'll be most alarmed; she's very fond of Papa.'

'He's not dead,' Julia hissed. 'We would know it if he were.'

'We would,' Matty agreed. 'Of course we would. But we must now tell everyone we know in case they can shed some light on the matter.'

Tim came back, opened the front door and asked if they would care to take his arm. Matty was glad to lean on someone, and Julia, after a moment's hesitation, did the same.

'I'm so sorry,' Matty said to him. 'We're keeping you from your work.'

'I often escort elderly ladies home,' he said gallantly, 'so why should I not see two lovely young ladies home too, especially in distressing circumstances. But don't give up hope, either of you. We must put on our thinking caps and come up with ideas of where your father might have got to. I have some thoughts of my own, but I must think them through before acting upon them.'

'What kind of thoughts?' Julia asked.

'Well, one that was triggered by the remark in the letter from the manager of the D.F.H. company, that there was a problem on the road that morning; we could perhaps ask the police to look into that to find out what kind of problem there was.'

'Oh!' Matty licked her lips. 'Some kind of accident, do you mean?'

'Perhaps.' He looked down at her. 'We should take nothing for granted. London is always busy with traffic, with horse buses and carriages, and he was probably going to the meeting at the busiest time. Do you know what time his appointment was?'

'I – I don't recall if he mentioned it,' she said slowly. 'Or perhaps I've forgotten.'

212

'Well, don't worry about it now. It might come to you when you're not thinking about it at all, and if it does, then we can act upon it.'

He guided them through the narrow footpath beneath the North Bar and they turned left for the short distance home.

'We can manage now, Tim,' Matty said, glancing at Julia. 'We're in sight of home; unless you'd care to come in for a cup of tea?'

He shook his head. 'I won't, thank you. I'll get back to the office if you're both feeling all right,' he said compassionately. 'You are both so courageous and sensible.'

'Thank you, Tim.' Julia's voice was tight with emotion. She couldn't wait to rush up to her room, where she could let free her feelings of fear and panic without upsetting Matty, who was being so brave and sensible and planning what they should do next, whereas she was in danger of falling apart into a million little pieces.

The door was locked, and neither had brought a key. Julia rang the bell and Betty came to let them in. She looked as if she wanted to ask them something, but of course she didn't.

'Doctor came whilst you were out, miss,' she mumbled. 'He said Miss Faith seems to have turned a corner.'

Matty let out a sigh. 'Oh, thank goodness! Did Nunny speak to him?'

'Yes, miss, she did; she's just mekkin' a pot of tea for her, Miss Faith, I mean. Shall you want 'same?' She looked from one to the other.

'I'll have a cup with Miss Faith,' Matty said. 'Julia – do you—'

'I – I'll be down in a few minutes.' Julia tore off her coat and bonnet, dropped them on the floor and rushed upstairs.

'Just for me, then,' Matty said. 'Thank you, Betty.'

Faith was sitting up in bed, supported by pillows and with a shawl draped about her shoulders. Her face was waxy pale but she managed a wan smile at Matty.

'Nunny said you'd gone to see Mr Garton,' she said weakly. 'Did he have any news for us about darling Papa?'

Matty swallowed hard. 'Not as such,' she said, her voice steady and bright, 'but he explained however slow it might seem they are busy exploring all avenues of enquiry and will tell us just as soon as there is some positive news, which he hopes will be very soon.'

She took hold of Faith's thin white hands and, gently stroking them, said softly, 'I hear Dr Laybourn is very pleased with your progress, and has said how much better you seem today. You will soon be up and about again.'

Faith put her head back on the pillows. 'Yes,' she murmured. 'That is *exactly* what he said.'

CHAPTER THIRTY-FOUR

Each day he felt physically better; his head didn't hurt or ache quite as much as it had, although it was still very sore each time Jeanette bathed it. She had taken the bandage off his arm and thought it would be good to let the air to it to help the healing; it was still raw where the skin had been scraped off, so each evening she put some ointment on it and wrapped it lightly again with thin gauze so that he didn't knock it. So, too, did she bathe and re-bandage his head, trimming his hair around the wound.

His awareness remained the same, with the memory of past events hazy or non-existent. 'What has happened to me?' he asked time and again. 'Who am I? Do you know me?'

She would shake her head, and blamed herself for she was sure he had travelled with their group when she saw him in the same ward in the hospital as the others from the horse bus, although she had wondered about his accent, for it was almost too perfect, with a different inflection that she couldn't quite grasp.

Sometimes, especially on waking in a morning, he found he had flashes of memory, but they were mostly of beds in a long room and the noise of frightened rearing horses and jangling leathers and screams. Why were people screaming?

He asked her, this woman Jeanette who was looking after him, bathing his head and giving him soup, and she repeated each time that the omnibus had overturned and passengers had been injured. He remembered being driven and also travelling on a train and then on a ship, but not how he came to be there or where he was going.

'What would you like to do?' she asked him one day. 'Would you like to go back on the ship and to the hospital to ask if anyone remembers you?'

He became anxious. 'No, I'd rather stay here until my head has healed,' and he pulled the beret over the top of the dressing as if he were hiding beneath it.

She hadn't the heart to send him away, but said softly, 'It's getting colder; the clothes you are wearing are not suitable.'

He was still wearing the large woollen jumper and his own black tailored trousers, and although she realized that the trousers were of fine cloth they were not appropriate for country wear, and so she made a decision.

'I have some items that I can sell at market. I make curios and trinkets from wood, small things that tourists like to buy, and the money would buy you a warm jacket or breeches.'

He looked at her. 'May I see the trinkets that you make?'

She nodded and went to the deep cupboard where she had found the woollen jumper and brought out a box from it. Inside were many pieces of bric-a-brac, wrapped in brown paper bags or sheets of paper she had saved from when she had bought goods for herself.

Amongst the bits and pieces were plaques and small plates roughly hewn from pieces of beechwood and oak, but polished and buffed and adorned with carvings of leaves and flowers carefully cut into the wood. There were wooden puppets, their arms and legs attached by string, their faces painted with black eyebrows, a spot of carmine on each cheek and an upturned smiley mouth. Wooden necklaces and bracelets made from knots of wood, polished like the plaques, were threaded together with fine oiled rope.

'Who made these?' he asked, fingering the puppets and wondering what they reminded him of.

'I did,' she said, as if surprised that he should ask. 'It is my income. I gather suitable wood in the summer and make them in winter when I can't get out.'

He looked up at her. 'When you can't get out?'

'When the rain or snow comes,' she said. 'The streams sometimes overflow and it's difficult walking without getting my boots very wet and muddy. I must gather some wood soon and dry and prepare it.'

He fingered the shiny surfaces of the plaques. 'How do you do this, make them shiny?'

'I collect resin from the pine trees. Just a little cut and the resin trickles out and I use it as polish.' She smiled. 'I waste nothing.'

'Does no one ever come?'

'People? Here?' she said. 'No. The forest is dark in winter and people are afraid of getting lost or of being attacked by animals; there are wild dogs and cats in the forest, and packs of wild boar as well as beaver and stag.'

'Are you not afraid?'

'No,' she said. 'I know the forest well, but I don't go far in the winter. If I should fall or injure myself no one would know.'

He was silent for a few minutes. The forest was huge; he had only ventured a short distance into it and Jeanette had always insisted he take Chien with him.

'Are you never lonely?' he asked. 'With no one to care for you?'

'Sometimes,' she admitted. 'I have my dog for company, but our conversation is limited. But,' she lifted her chin, 'I can take care of myself.'

'So you sell the things you make and buy – what – blankets, food?'

'Whatever I need to help me through the winter, but this time I will buy you something suitable to wear. There is a market once a fortnight in the next village and a stall where they sell men's trousers and coats and working boots that are no longer needed.'

'Should I come with you?'

She shook her head. 'It is a long day,' she explained. 'Sometimes the market is busy and everything sells quickly, but if there are no tourists to buy my trinkets I wait the whole day until nearly dusk, in the hope that local people will buy them for themselves or as gifts, and then I must sell them more cheaply.' She shrugged. 'We must help each other to survive; some have no money at all, and live only on what they can make or produce: butter, honey, cheese . . .' Her voice trailed away. Then, taking a deep breath, she said, 'It will be too long a day for you, I think. You have not yet recovered.'

It would be too long, he realized. There were days when he had to lie down on the small sofa and sleep; he never seemed able to get enough sleep.

'I'll go tomorrow,' she said. 'I'll set out as soon as it is light. Chien will stay with you. Don't feed him. I will do that when I return. There is bread and cheese for you when you are hungry; and you can make tea or coffee.'

She made bread most days from flour and water mixed with goat's milk and a knob of butter, and a small amount of yeast that she took from a bowl on a warm shelf above the fire which she kept growing with a daily top-up of flour and honey. She told him that she was feeding it. He had watched her make the dough into a round shape and punch, knead and stretch it into small rounds which she placed one by one in a small flat pan and baked over the hot fire, the aroma making his mouth water.

When he woke the next morning, she had gone and the dog was outside. 'It's going to be a long day, Chien,' he said, opening the door. It was a bright autumn morning, yet he could feel sharpness in the air. The dog wagged his long tail as if he was pleased to see him, and he patted the top of his head. He saw that his water bowl was empty and took it to the pump and refilled it and was then curiously conscious of the existence of another dog, smaller than Chien, who yapped a lot.

He tried to bring up the memory, but it remained hazy. Was it my dog? Do I have a dog? But the remembrance slid away, out of reach, and he remained frustrated.

He ate the bread and cheese that Jeanette had left for him, put the big warm jumper over his shirt and trousers and wandered outside and down to the fenced-off area where vegetables had been growing. He recognized the discarded potato shoots lying in a heap and the rich soil recently dug, and searched in the rickety tool shed for a spade and dug up a root, putting the potatoes in a metal bucket and storing them up on a shelf. Then he saw what he thought were small marrows, the yellow flowers fading and the stalks disintegrating, but he wasn't sure about pulling them in case they were needed for something else, and so he left them alone.

He noticed that there were broken lower planks on the fence surrounding the plot, as if someone or something had pushed up against it. Jeanette had said that there were wild boar in the forest, so it might have been them trying to get in among the vegetables. Pigs are notoriously greedy animals, he thought. They'll eat anything.

He stood up straight and pondered. How do I know that? Am I a farmer? He looked at his hands. They were not working hands, Jeanette had told him, and she was right. His fingers were long and white, his skin smooth, and any nicks or rough patches were clearly due to whatever had happened to him just before he came here.

He sighed and went to look for wood and a saw: he'd attempt to repair the fence to keep intruders out. Whether he could do it remained to be seen.

There were many small pieces of wood in the shed, small knotted branches of peculiar shapes and sizes, and he guessed these were what Jeanette used for making her knick-knacks, but looking around outside he found a pile of planks, suitable for repairing the fence, which looked as though they had come from a small shed, similar to the tool shed.

How had she dismantled it? She was a slight woman; and who had built the fence? Maybe some fellow from the nearest village had offered to do it in exchange for cheese or honey. Some part of him hoped that he hadn't wanted anything more than that.

He found nails neatly stored in a tin and a hammer hanging on a hook; other implements were hanging from string on nails that she'd hammered into the wooden walls, and his admiration for her aptitude increased enormously. When he opened a box on the floor there were other tools that she must have collected: a carpenter's adze and several planes, the kind that a woodworker might use for smoothing rough edges.

He stood back and admired his handiwork on the fence when it was finished and he was relatively pleased. He was obviously not a carpenter, but he thought that the repair would hold. He walked back to the cottage and went inside for the water bucket and refilled it from the pump, wondering again where the water came from and concluding that there was a spring and that a well had been dug underground at some time to feed the pump. He brought out the kettle and filled that too to place over the fire to make a drink. The fire was burning low and he needed to find more kindling before it went out.

'First things first,' he mumbled. 'Can't boil a kettle without a fire. You should have reminded me, Chien,' he told the dog, who answered him with a small *woof* and a yawn.

He found kindling already gathered at the side of the shed and brought some inside, then ate bread and cheese and when the kettle had boiled made a mug of acorn coffee and looked at Chien, who had parked himself outside Jeanette's bedroom door, his chin on his paws.

I wonder, he thought. It would be nice to stretch out on a bed. Dare I? Would she mind? Will Chien let me? After the exercise, the food and then the hot drink, his usual afternoon lethargy was overcoming him. He decided to try. He stood up slowly, put more wood on the fire, and going towards Jeanette's room he stepped over the dog and pushed open the door.

The bed was tidy, with a patchwork cover over the top and a single pillow. It looked most inviting; he was already in his stockinged feet, having taken his boots off at the door. He sat on the edge of the bed and looked at Chien, who hadn't moved, so he eased himself down on to the patchwork cover and sank into a blissful ease.

He was asleep in minutes. He was somewhere in warm sunshine and bright colours, and young light voices were calling to him. He couldn't make out what they were saying, but they were encouraging him to come to them. And there was someone else too, someone in a further off habitation that he couldn't reach. In his dream he stretched out a hand, over and over again, but each time the image moved further away and the voice became more distant.

A sound disturbed him and he stirred; he heard a regular *thump thump thump* and a soft gentle voice. He sat up in darkness and shouted, '*Constance! Constance! I'm sorry.*'

CHAPTER THIRTY-FIVE

Matty had written to Aunt Louisa to give her the news, and asked her if she would write to their maternal grandparents on their behalf. Her mother's parents rarely corresponded or came to see them since moving up to North Yorkshire, except at Christmas when they sent small presents; on arriving home from Italy after Matty's eighteenth birthday she had found a letter waiting for her giving their congratulations on completing her eighteenth year.

Matty thought that they should be told even if they gave the impression that they didn't care overmuch for family matters. I must also write to Grandmama in Stresa, she thought, and dreaded upsetting her with the news of their father's disappearance.

Louisa was distressed by her letter and dismayed that she hadn't been there to support them. 'I will come on the morning train,' she wrote.

When Louisa told Stephen, he said he would go with her and find lodgings somewhere in Beverley. 'There must be something I can do to help. Who else have they spoken to?'

'Their Aunt Gertrude and Uncle Fisher Maddeson, Roland's sister and brother. Gertrude is very practical and has been with them to see Roland's lawyer. Those poor darling girls,' she said, 'for that is all they are, they must be terrified that something has happened to their father. Whatever can it be?'

'He's had an accident, that's for certain,' Stephen said, running his fingers through his beard as he pondered. 'If he's alive, but sick or injured, then maybe he's not able to contact them. He could be in hospital – he might have lost his belongings, been robbed, anything! London can be a forbidding place if you don't take care.'

'Oh, Stephen! You're not being positive. Don't say that to my nieces, will you?'

'Of course I won't! But if they give me details of where he was going I'll travel to London and do some detective work for them.'

'Would you really?'

'I spent a good deal of time in London when I was young.' He wagged a finger. 'I'll take a bag with me and stay a few days, if they'd like me to, and make some enquiries.'

She saw that he was quite fired up and thought his idea was a good one. It wasn't something her nieces could do on their own, but a man could, and it would be quite fitting for him to ask questions on their behalf.

She decided that they could travel together rather than separately when they caught the train to Hull; it was bizarre that a grown woman should pander to society's rules on what was right and proper. When they arrived at Paragon station Matty and Julia were waiting for them, having come in the brougham with Julia's luggage for her visit to Aunt Gertrude's.

'It occurred to us that she must be very worried too,' Julia said. 'She is Papa's sister after all.'

'I think it is extremely kind of you both to think of her,' Louisa told them. 'Of course she's bound to be anxious, and you may tell her, Julia, that Mr Nielsen, Stephen, has offered to travel to London and make enquiries.'

'Oh, would you really? Thank you, that is so very kind.' Matty's eyes glistened as she thanked Stephen. 'That's just what I wanted to do, but I'd only be considered to be a foolish young woman and no one would listen to me.'

Julia nodded in agreement. They had discussed this between them.

'It's best if you're at the steering end, Miss Matty,' Stephen told her tactfully, seeing her distress and frustration. 'You are the director, the planner; tell us mere men what you'd like us to do and we'll carry out your instructions.'

'You will be the only man, Mr Nielsen,' Matty said, as they walked towards the brougham. 'Our lawyers are being very helpful but naturally they can't chase off to London. They can only write to make enquiries and do the legalities, and we're bound to abide by their instructions.'

'We'll discuss it later, shall we?' Louisa suggested as the three of them stepped inside the brougham. Stephen sat up next to Sam, and they set off to Albion Street to drop Julia at Aunt Gertrude's house.

'I wish I was staying at home now,' Julia murmured to Matty as they pulled up outside the house.

'Nothing much will happen yet.' Matty stepped down beside her in order to greet their aunt. 'If you think of something that Mr Nielsen could do, send me a postcard and I'll draw up a list for him to take to London.' She gave her sister's fingers a squeeze. 'I feel more positive now that Aunt Louisa is here with us, and Mr Nielsen is very positive and helpful. He might be our uncle before long, don't you think?'

Julia gave a deep sigh. 'I do hope so. But you're right. In spite of knowing what needs to be done, and believing ourselves capable of doing it, our hands are tied, simply because we are women, and it's *not* fair!'

Stephen joined Matty and Louisa inside the brougham for the journey back to Beverley, and when they were moving said, 'If I might bring up a point, Miss Matty, regarding the remark you made about your lawyers?'

'Yes, by all means,' she said, 'but please call me Matty. There's surely no need for formality? You have known me and my sisters for many years – most of our lives, in fact!'

'Indeed,' he said jovially, glancing at Louisa. 'We're practically related, aren't we, give or take one or two obstacles?'

Matty smiled; she liked this man and would welcome him as an uncle. 'What was the point you referred to?'

He folded his arms. 'With regard to your lawyers, you said that they would arrange all the legalities and that you were bound by their instructions; and it is to the latter that I refer, because your lawyers are bound by *your* instructions, not the other way round. You and your sisters are paying them to act on your behalf and they must – as long as it is legal – do whatever you ask. So if you wished to hire a private investigator to make enquiries about your father, for instance, that is what they would do, or anything else that you wanted, no matter how bizarre. You, Matty, in particular, probably not your younger sisters, are in charge!'

He watched her expression as she digested this fact, and then went on: 'As it happens, you do know of someone, practically a relative, with a knowledge of the London area who is willing to perform this service without a fee, but perhaps a cigar if his investigation proves successful!'

She smiled; as she had said to Julia, she felt more positive now that Louisa and Mr Nielsen were here, and what he had said made sense. She might not legally be able to make some decisions as she was not yet old enough, but she could direct a search for their father and that was what she intended to do. Stephen Nielsen, it seemed, would be more than willing to follow her instructions or act on his own initiative.

She felt tears welling in her eyes again, but she fought them back. I am *not* going to cry again, she told herself. Or at least not until we reach a conclusion. I am an adult capable of making decisions, and my decision is that we will find Papa.

A pony and trap was tied up outside the house. Matty didn't recognize it. They climbed down from the carriage and Stephen lifted down Louisa's travelling bag just as Nunny opened the door to them, her face grim. 'Your aunt Mrs Fisher Maddeson is here, Miss Martha. She has only just arrived, and Miss Faith is with her.'

Matty knew by Nunny's voice, and the way her mouth turned down, that it was not good news, but Nunny welcomed Louisa and said how nice it was to see her again, and bobbed her knee to Mr Nielsen, who told her he would be staying the night at a local hostelry.

'I'll get Betty to take your bag up, Mrs Walton, and organize a pot of tea for you all. Mrs Fisher Maddeson is in the sitting room, Miss Martha.'

Matty turned to Stephen. 'Don't leave yet, will you?' She glanced at Louisa. 'Please, come in, both of you.'

Mrs Fisher Maddeson was standing by the unlit fireplace as if she were the hostess. Faith was sitting in a chair with a warm shawl about her shoulders, but she got up to greet Louisa and Stephen, giving them her hand but not a kiss as she might otherwise have done.

Mrs Maddeson came forward to greet Matty, to whom she said 'You poor dear child', and then Louisa, whom she hadn't met in many years, expressing surprise at seeing her there, to which Louisa remarked that she often visited her nieces and then introduced Stephen as an old friend of the family.

'You must be exceptionally busy, Caroline,' Louisa went on, sitting down on a small sofa and drawing Faith next to her. 'I never see you when I come over.'

'Well, of course I have children to attend to,' Caroline replied, rubbing in the fact that Louisa hadn't.

'Are they still so young that they cannot be left?' Louisa said in mock surprise. 'My goodness, I thought they'd be almost grown by now.'

'Have you had tea, Aunt Caroline?' Matty interrupted.

'No, thank you. I can't stay long, but what I came to say was that your uncle and I have had a discussion, as we are very conscious of how difficult it must be for all of you without your father here. Indeed, you should not be living alone without an adult relative in attendance, and so we have decided that we will come and stay with you. Your uncle can then direct proceedings as to what should be done regarding dear Roland's disappearance.'

'How very thoughtful of you, Aunt,' Matty replied. 'But we have already made arrangements and put them in hand. Our lawyers are working on my instructions and Mr Nielsen is ready to go to London when I have finalized the guidelines. Aunt Louisa has kindly agreed to stay and look after household matters for as long as we need her, whilst I will continue to liaise with our father's lawyers and bank manager.'

'Matty has had a lot to do,' Louisa put in, 'and with Faith being unwell, Becca being too young, and Julia attending Gertrude at the moment, I don't know how she has managed everything, but manage she has, and quite remarkably. I thought the least I could do was give her some household relief, and I certainly can't do that whilst living in Scarborough.'

Faith's lips parted as she listened. She slowly crept up to Louisa and putting her head on her shoulder sighed as if in gratitude and closed her eyes.

'Well!' Caroline gave a small gasp. 'We spent most of yesterday evening planning for the best. We agreed it would be a tight fit for us all, and of course Ralph and Rosalind have to have separate bedrooms, but I – we had thought through all the alternatives and – well . . .'

It seemed as if she had run out of things to say, so Matty apologized politely, and added quietly, 'But you see how it is, Aunt,' with a nod towards her sister, who appeared to be fast asleep tucked under Louisa's arm. 'Above all, we have to be sure that Faith is not disturbed.'

Nunny knocked on the door. 'Beggin' your pardon, Miss Martha. I know it's late, but could you say how many it will be for luncheon? Miss Becca has been invited to the Lawrences'.'

'Has she? How very thoughtful of them. Five then, I think; will you be staying, Aunt Caroline? No? Four, then. Something light will suffice, thank you, Nunny, and I'll speak to you later about this evening's meal.'

Matty took in a deep breath and marvelled at how she had play-acted authority, rendering Aunt Caroline temporarily speechless, although she would no doubt have plenty to say to her husband on the subject of his brother's ungrateful offspring.

Faith opened one eye as a disgruntled Aunt Caroline left the room with Stephen, who had offered to turn the pony and trap round to face the direction of her home, and whispered, 'Has she gone?'

When Matty said yes, Faith heaved a relieved sigh and sat up. 'You would not believe what she was planning! She is so devious. Blaming Uncle Fisher when it had been her idea. Rosalind was going to have my room until I said that the doctor had said I should be isolated in case of infection, so Aunt Caroline said she would have to have the guest room. Ralph was going to have your room, Matty, and you would go in with Julia, and she and Uncle Fisher were going to have Papa's. She had a nosy amongst the ornaments and fingered the curtains and said they were not thick enough for winter, especially as the room had such an open view of Westwood. I was so pleased to see you drive up, for I couldn't think of any reason why they shouldn't come!'

They ate a lunch of baked ham and sliced beef, mustard and pickle with fresh bread, and Matty murmured that perhaps their uncle and aunt's motives were well meant.

'I was pleased that Julia wasn't here, for we all know how she loves Aunt Caroline,' Faith said. She had some colour in her cheeks and Louisa, looking at her, hoped that the blush was there because she had been so animated and not an indication of any illness that might be in waiting.

Faith said that she was quite well, and that her sleep on the sofa was deliberate, but Louisa was not too sure about that and thought that if tomorrow was a dry day she might suggest a short walk with her across Westwood, to ensure that Faith was as well as she said she was.

CHAPTER THIRTY-SIX

Stephen had asked Matty for the name and address of the London brokers, even though her father hadn't arrived for the meeting. 'I can take a look at the district and try to discover any reason why he didn't arrive at the broker's office.' He didn't mention that his first call would be at a local police station to enquire if there had been any fatal accidents on that day.

Matty had given him the name and address of their lawyer and a covering letter from her to verify who he was and that he was looking into her father's disappearance on her behalf. He had gone to see the Gartons immediately and asked for an appointment.

He left for London early the next morning, telling Matty that he would stay as long as necessary and come back when there was something to report. It was late afternoon when he arrived in London, and thinking of what Roland Maddeson might do first, he assumed that he would have looked for accommodation for that first night.

The new King's Cross station from which he exited was different entirely from the station he had used as a young man when returning from his overseas travels. The Great Northern Railway was a poor relation of what it had hoped to become as the gateway to the north, and was already considered to be inadequate to support the amount of passenger traffic using it.

There were many lodging houses to be seen as he left the station, and, as he recalled from his student days, many of them were to be avoided at all costs by vulnerable young men. However, he was not a young man any more, and walking a short distance away he eventually found a suitable one: a modest hotel in Somers Town which was in the midst of the building of new roads and housing.

Not that it matters, he considered. I'm here on a mission of rescue and not as a holidaymaker. To this end, he had dressed appropriately in a plain three-quarter coat with a checked waistcoat over his shirt, a plain cravat and matching checked trousers, and a shorter top hat than he would normally wear so that he would look like an ordinary townsman making enquiries and not the gentleman he actually was.

He set out early the next morning, walking at first in the direction of Southwark and then hailing a cab to take him there. He called first of all at the broker's office but they couldn't tell him anything more than they had already indicated. His next stop was at a local police station to ask if there had been any incidents or fatal accidents on the day in question, and explained the reason for his interest.

At first the sergeant at the desk shook his head and said not that he could recall but that he would look in the incident book; a new and eager recruit, however, who had been listening from his desk behind the sergeant, came forward.

'There was that accident with the horse bus that overturned, sir,' he reminded his superior. 'There was nobody killed, but some of the passengers were taken to St Thomas's.'

'Check it out then,' the sergeant told him, and left to attend to a miscreant who had just been brought in.

'It's here, sir.' The constable brought the file to the desk. 'It wasn't public transport. It was a hired vehicle and the horses had reared. Something had frightened them and the vehicle overturned. Oh, I remember it now! A mule escaped from its traces and the horses panicked. The mule driver was charged.' He looked down at the file and turned a page. 'Causing an obstruction and creating mayhem. I recall now, the passengers who were injured were taken to St Thomas's to be patched up as it was the nearest 'ospital. They were foreigners.'

Stephen looked up. 'Who were?'

'The passengers, sir, that's what it says here. The bus was on its way to Dover for them to catch the ferry.'

'Was anyone else injured?' Stephen asked. 'Any onlookers or pedestrians?'

'Can't help you there, sir. You'd have to enquire at St Thomas's. They'd know, I expect, but if your friend was injured he'd have been sent on elsewhere. St Thomas's isn't the kind of 'ospital you'd send injured folk to.'

Stephen thanked him for his help and didn't ask which hospital would have taken injured people; he'd enquire at St Thomas's for that. He knew what kind of hospital St Thomas's was now and thought it highly unlikely that Roland would have been admitted there if he had been caught up in the debacle.

He remembered St Thomas's. It was a huge building over six hundred years old, and used, he recalled, as a pauper hospital and for the incurables. He'd read in newspapers over the years that it was no longer considered fit to be used for general purposes, even though it had amalgamated with Guy's and money had been pumped into it.

It wasn't far from the police station; just a ten-minute walk, and he paused outside the gates to write in his notebook just what the young constable had said about the incident that had happened on that day.

Two men sat on the pavement leaning on the stone pillars at the entrance and looked up at him with a disinterested air. That they were not disinterested he knew very well: they looked everywhere but at him and they were clearly summing him up. He had a briefcase, it was true, but there was no money in it; his pocket book, which did contain money, was firmly buttoned down in an inside pocket of his coat.

One of the men was extremely scruffy, wearing boots with the soles hanging off and a battered straw hat on his head, whilst the coat he was wearing had seen better days in the distant past. The other man wore what had not long ago been a smart top hat and a passable coat which, though soiled and stained, was not worn and looked like a good wool cloth.

'Good morning, gentlemen,' Stephen greeted them. 'Are you familiar with this area?'

'Might be.' The man with the top hat shifted his position. 'Where do you need to be, guvnor?'

'Oh, I know where I am, but I'm making enquiries about an accident that occurred hereabouts just a few weeks ago. Some French people were involved in a horse-bus crash.'

They both lifted their heads, mouths open, showing few teeth. 'Frenchies, were they?' said the man with the top hat. 'Huh. If I'd known that, I might not 'ave given them an 'and.'

'Aye, hero of the hour, weren't you?' The other man grinned, and dug his elbow in his comrade's ribs.

'Don't know about that.' The top-hatted man got to his feet. 'But you got to do what you got to do to help your fellow man, ain't you? Come on, Sid. Let's be off. We got work to do.'

He looked Stephen up and down, his eyes resting on his checked trousers. 'Fancy get-up,' he said. 'Very nice. I like a bit o' style m'self.' He looked his scruffy companion up and down and then turned back to Stephen. 'Some of us 'ave it, ain't we, and others don't.' He hitched up the lapels of his coat and left, leaving his fellow vagrant to follow him.

Was here, but doesn't want to talk about it, Stephen mused. Still, even if he'd told me anything I wouldn't have believed him. There are some who live by their wits and he's one of them.

He walked down the long drive to the hospital entrance and made himself known to the porter who was standing by the door, giving him details of his task though not mentioning the French. He was directed inside and warned that this was a place for paupers and to watch his pockets.

He enquired through a glass window about the horse-bus incident, and although the man behind the glass knew nothing of it, another clerk had been on duty at the time and came out to take him to one of the wards.

'We're only allowed to bring in a certain number of paupers each day,' the young man said. 'It's one of the rules. We don't usually deal with emergencies, but as the crash was outside the gate and the injuries weren't serious, on that occasion we did. This is where they were brought, sir,' he went on. 'As you see, at the minute they're all old people in here. Nurse Williams,' he called. 'Will you fetch Sister, please?'

There were some beds in the room but few people in them, and as the clerk had said they were indeed old people, or, if not old, somewhat ravaged either by hunger or by something more sinister. Some were sitting on hard wooden chairs, others on the floor waiting for attention. The young nurse who had been diligently looking after an old lady had gone to fetch Sister.

'Yes?' Sister, wearing a crisp starched white headdress and a long white apron over her dark dress, was obviously short of time and exceedingly short-tempered.

He told her about his enquiry and she replied that she was extremely busy and hadn't time to look through the diary for something that had happened weeks ago.

'Not so very long ago, Sister,' he said pleadingly. 'And this gentleman's daughters are deeply worried about him.'

'An Englishman, you say?' She frowned. 'But these were French people. They were travelling in a privately hired omnibus, from what I was told, and the only reason we allowed them in here was because the accident was right outside our gates; they had minor injuries, so we simply bathed their wounds, bandaged them up and then let them go on their way.'

'I see. Well, thank you, Sister,' he said resignedly. 'I'm sorry to have troubled you.'

She nodded and moved away and he went out of the ward and headed for the door.

'Behind him, Sister called for Nurse Williams, who hurried across. No dawdling was allowed with this Sister, and no running either. 'You were on duty on the day those travellers were brought in from the omnibus accident?'

'I was, Sister.'

'French, weren't they?'

'Erm, most of them were, I think, though they were almost too shocked to speak.'

'That's what I thought. There's been someone enquiring about a missing person.' She frowned. 'There were no Englishmen, were there?'

The nurse hesitated. She hadn't known any of the patients were French until they were all being strapped up or bandaged and began to talk to each other. 'There was one who might have been,' she said, 'but he didn't speak, as he was knocked over by one of the horses and cracked his head and elbow. He was unconscious when he was brought in, but recovered. We were looking for his coat before he left, if you recall, Sister, but we couldn't find it. He went out with the others in just his tailcoat suit, and no hat or gloves.'

Sister pursed her lips and nodded. 'Very well. Carry on with whatever you were doing.'

But as the young nurse continued caring for the old lady, who was covered in bites and sores, she thought of the injured man she had tended outside on the footpath and the other man, a vagrant she often saw at the gate, who had been kneeling over the gentleman when she arrived by his side, and left with a top hat and a warm coat, which he said were his own. The gentleman, she now realized, couldn't have been in the overturned vehicle with the French people, as he'd clearly been knocked over by the horses.

She put down the cloth she was using to bathe the patient's legs and walked quickly out of the ward, then rushed to the outer door. She spoke to the porter but he shook his head, pointing down the long and empty drive, and she went back inside, disappointed.

CHAPTER THIRTY-SEVEN

Jeanette was so startled by his shout that she jumped. She had thought that he might be asleep on the sofa and had come in quietly, surprised to find Chien inside.

'Jacques, what is it?' He was in her bedroom. 'Are you ill?'

'I'm so sorry. So very sorry!'

Though the light was fading and there was no window in the bedroom she could see that he was weeping; his face was wet with tears and she thought he was apologizing for being on her bed.

'It's all right, it doesn't matter. I should have said you could; the bed is much more comfortable than the sofa.'

He stared at her as if he didn't know her and put both hands over his face, then drew them away, his expression telling her that he had thought she was someone else.

'*Constance?*' he whispered, speaking in French; this woman who had looked after him, had she told him he was French? He shook his head. 'You're not Constance, are you? Constance is dead.' He drew his legs on to the floor and sat with his hands on his head. She sat at the end of the bed.

'Who is Constance, *chéri*?' she asked softly.

'My wife – *was* my wife.' His words seemed forced out of his throat. 'Mother of my children; my little girls.'

'I see,' she murmured. 'And – she died?'

He nodded, and turned towards her. 'Her hair is dark, not like yours. *Was* dark. It was my fault that she died.'

'How was that?'

'I – wanted a son. We have little girls.' He frowned, as if puzzled. 'It – was too soon, I think. They died; she and the child. A boy.'

'Sometimes it happens,' she murmured. 'There should be no blame. Did you love your wife?'

'Oh yes.' The words came out on a sigh. 'But it was too soon, the doctor said.'

'And where are your children now?'

'I don't know.' He shook his head. 'I can't remember.'

'Is someone looking after them?'

Again the puzzlement was etched on his face, but then he said, '*I* look after them.' He put his hand to his head again. 'I have a headache.'

She stood up. 'I will make some tea. Why not wash your hands and face under the pump to refresh yourself and then we can talk some more. Perhaps then you will remember.'

He did as she suggested, and when he came in again she had made a pot of tea and put bread and ham on the table and a fruit cake that she had bought.

'I sold most of the things I took,' she said, picking up a rucksack that she'd dropped on the floor. 'And bought some warm clothes for you.'

'You have spent your money on me!' he murmured. 'That was kind.'

'You are a guest,' she said brightly. 'This might be a long cold winter and your clothes are not suitable.'

He pondered on this but didn't answer. She had bought a wool jacket, cord trousers and a woollen jumper.

'The jumper is cashmere, I think,' she said. 'It is very soft. The jacket is well worn around the cuffs, but it is clean.'

He nodded. 'What am I to do?' he asked wearily.

'Eat and drink,' she said. 'Then we will talk.'

She built up the fire and lit a small oil lamp; they ate the ham and bread and drank the hot tea, then she went to the cupboard and brought out a bottle of thick pale liquid and two small glasses and half filled them, and placed slices of fruitcake on small plates to eat with it.

'This is made from apples,' she said, handing him one of the glasses. 'It is made not far from here, in Calvados. If it is kept for a long time it tastes something like cognac but sweeter. I think you will like it.'

'From apples?' He sniffed it. 'Like cider?'

She frowned a little at his pronunciation. 'Stronger than *cidre*,' she said and lifted her glass in salutation. '*Santé!*'

He toasted her and took a sip. It was good. The amber liquid slid down his throat. It was like cognac and had a kick to it. When have I had cognac? The thought ran through his head.

'How long is it since your wife died?' She broke the silence as they sat and sipped their drinks. 'Can you recall?'

He thought of Constance every day and it seemed like only yesterday that he had sat by her bedside and watched her slip out of reach. But was it perhaps a long time ago? Their children – he frowned again. One not much more than an infant, who cried and cried until someone – who was it? – picked her up and gave her milk from a bottle. And another small child, blonde like her baby sister, who searched every room in the house for her mother and then put herself to bed.

He forgot her question and closed his eyes, trying to make sense of his jumbled thoughts. That day, the day Constance died, so many people came and I didn't want to see them; I only wanted to be with Constance. Another image came to mind: an older child, sweet-natured, who held his hand and stood beside him. I shouldn't have allowed that, he thought; no child should see death so close. I should have been comforting her, but she was comforting me. He remembered small soft fingers that gently stroked his wrist.

'Matty,' he breathed, not realizing he had reverted to his mother tongue. 'Matty – and Julia; the doctor said that Julia shouldn't be allowed to see her mother because she was too young.' Dark-haired Julia, with her mother's beauty, but aloof and distant with everyone but her sisters.

He gazed at Jeanette. 'How did I come to be here?' He asked the question in English and she put her hand to her throat, silenced.

'There was – erm, an accident, I think,' he went on. 'But I don't know where. A horse – horses?' He recalled rearing animals and the sense of falling, holding his arms across his face to avoid being struck by flailing hooves.

'London,' she whispered, speaking in broken English, her expression stunned as she comprehended that she had brought him to France under a misunderstanding. 'The horses pulling our – conveyance – *transport* – bolted, frightened by something, and it turned over. *Mon dieu!*' she mouthed. 'What have I done?'

They sat until late, dusk turning to night and the lamp sputtering until she turned it out and they sat in semi-darkness, the room lit only by the fire, which she fed bit by bit with small pieces of wood and bark. He recalled little of the incident except for waking up in the hospital where the nurses were dressed in white; he'd followed other people outside and been helped on to a conveyance of some kind where he slept; he'd seen deep water from a ship's rails and been reminded of another voyage which at present eluded him.

'You will remember when you least expect to,' she advised. 'Perhaps you travelled abroad, maybe on holiday?'

'Yes, perhaps so,' he agreed, but there was something else bothering him and he couldn't bring it to mind. 'I visit my mother; she lives in Italy.'

'She is Italian?'

'*Non.*' He reverted to French, as she had too. 'She is English. She likes the weather, the food, the way the Italians live. We went to visit her.' He raised a smile, no longer so anxious or afraid. 'It was Matty's birthday—' He stopped. We were there to celebrate, he thought. A party of us: my daughters and their friends; my sister; who else – sister-in-law. Mrs – Mrs – no, not Mrs . . . Nunny! She it was who gave Becca a bottle of milk to soothe her when she cried.

'They are not small children,' he declared, running his fingers through his hair and making it stand on end. 'They will be missing me, worried for me. Why was I in London? How long have I been here?'

He let out a barrage of questions as recollections came trickling back, but Jeanette could answer none of them.

CHAPTER THIRTY-EIGHT

Matty waited eagerly for Stephen Nielsen's return. He'd been away for several days, and although she knew she was foolish for expecting that by a major miracle he would find information immediately, she lived in hope that there would be some news.

She missed Julia, who was still with Aunt Gertrude, even though Louisa was an excellent companion and each evening, after they had eaten, they and Faith and Becca sat by the fire and chatted, sometimes discussing their father and sometimes answering Louisa's gentle probing as to what Faith and Becca would like to do in their adult lives, her intention being to take away their worries for at least a short time.

Faith had already formulated ideas; she didn't say *if I live long enough*, for she was optimistic, even though she often felt tired and washed out and would retire to her room or even to her bed during an afternoon.

'I will become an artist,' she said. 'I feel the most joy when I'm creating on a blank canvas. Perhaps I will go to live in Italy; I love the warmth and the sunshine and I feel vital and alive when I'm there. I will ask Papa when he returns,' and a stubbornness came to her lips, daring anyone to suggest that he might not come home.

'Perhaps you could live with Grandmama,' Becca suggested. 'I should think she'd like that. You would be good company for her.'

Faith didn't answer. Much as she loved her grandmother, she wouldn't have the freedom to paint if she lived with her, for she had such a busy social life and might expect Faith to join her in it. Neither she nor Becca had given thought to their grandmother's age.

'And what about you, Becca?' Louisa coaxed. 'What will you do when you're grown up? Will you find some handsome prince, rich enough to buy you a string of thoroughbreds?'

'I'd have to choose them,' Becca answered solemnly. 'The horses. A prince might not know about breeding or what to look for in a thoroughbred. But best of all I'd like to run my own stable; and I'd like to be a trainer. I don't see any reason why I shouldn't, just because I'm a girl; and Owen said there was no reason why I shouldn't either as long as I have enough money.'

Matty sighed. Money! There was the difficulty, she thought. She would soon have to talk to their father's banker about money to pay the household staff. She had already calculated that if she wasn't allowed to dip into his account, which seemed likely, then she would have to use her allowance. She didn't mind doing that, but in the long term, if Papa didn't— but no. I won't contemplate that at all. And then there's the house. Uncle Albert would inherit it and they would have to move out and find another house, smaller than this one, depending on what they could afford.

Her mind wandered even though she had told herself not to think of it, for she couldn't help it, and every night she tossed in her bed as she tried to plan a future for them all. In her subliminal considerations she arranged that Julia would live with Aunt Gertrude and be her companion, and eventually someone would fall in love with her beauty and come to appreciate the exceptional character beneath. Faith would live in Italy, as she herself had outlined, and the climate would

242

suit her health. Becca could live with the Lawrences, for they were very fond of her, and she would find a cottage in Beverley for herself.

She had already earmarked one: an empty terraced two-bedroomed cottage in a narrow street off Butcher Row. She knew that no one would want to marry her, for she would have no dowry to speak of. She couldn't bring herself to think of her father's having been run over by a train or killed in any other way, so therefore neither would she consider that there would be a dowry for any of them.

'Matty?' Louisa said, having said her name already. 'Come back! We're discussing your possible futures, in the merriest way of course, and we've come round to yours.'

Matty looked up and gave a wan smile. She didn't think she'd have much of a future as a single spinster; she would be a person that everyone would come to if they were in difficulties and she would have to find satisfaction in that.

'I'd rather discuss yours, Aunt Louisa,' she said, with a playfulness that she didn't feel. 'Are you going to marry Mr Nielsen? We hope you are, because we all like him and think him very kind and suitable for you; and I personally think that you would make a very happy couple because he makes you laugh. I've noticed how your eyes sparkle when he's in the room.'

'Goodness, do they really?' Louisa was taken aback that Matty should notice such a thing. It was true that her spirits were lifted when she was with Stephen, but then they always had been, even before he had made the unbelievable and dramatic offer. It was also true that she had been exceedingly impressed when he had offered to go to London to search for Roland. That was an offer he didn't have to make, but he had, showing what a good heart he had. But did she love him as he had said he loved her? Perhaps – she gave an inward sigh – perhaps I am too old for love.

They heard someone knock on the front door and Betty's pitter-patter of footsteps down the hall and sat still, waiting in expectation. It was rather late for visitors and they hoped for good news.

Betty tapped on the door. 'It's Mr Timothy Garton for you, Miss Martha,' she said. 'He's apologized for the late hour.'

'Show him in, please, Betty,' Matty said.

He seemed embarrassed to see them all together and apologized again for disturbing them. He refused Matty's offer of tea or something stronger, and, sitting down, said it was an impromptu visit. He was on his way home from the office, and thought he would call to ask how they all were. 'Mr Nielsen called in to see us before he left for London and we were able to give him details of the broker company and give him our letter of introduction. He knows London well, apparently, so will have no difficulty finding his way around. I don't suppose you have had any news from him yet?'

'No, no we haven't,' Matty murmured.

'It does take time,' he advised. 'Our clients sometimes think we are exceedingly slow, but collecting information from various sources is time-consuming. However, we always put in extra effort when we are working for friends.'

'I'm getting a little anxious, I must confess,' Matty told him, after deciding the worry was better out than in. 'I shall soon have to pay the household staff and the tradesmen's accounts, and as I can't take money from Papa's account I shall have to use my personal allowance.' She knew that her father had put it into the safe custody of his lawyers until she reached twenty-one.

Louisa gave a soft murmur of disquiet, but Timothy said immediately, 'There's no need for that, Matty. Tell me when you need to make the payments. Martinmas, is it? Did your father use that traditional period?'

When she told him he did, he said, 'I will send a note across to the bank; you don't need to worry about it. Besides, Mr Nielsen will more than likely bring us good news, and your father will be home well before then.'

He stood up to leave, and she walked with him to the door. 'Thank you for coming, Tim. It's very – kind of you to think of us. I'm – *we* are grateful to be in your safe hands.'

He took hold of one of her hands in both of his. 'It's the least I can do, Matty,' he said gently. 'I'm sorry that you are so unhappy. Rest assured we will do all we can to find your father and bring him safely home.'

She composed herself before returning to the sitting room, and as she sat down again Louisa spoke up. 'Matty, you mustn't worry over money. I can pay out for the household expenditure until all is resolved. Arnold left me very well provided for and I have no debts except for everyday ones. Please, I want to do this for you. I have only all of you as my family, so what else would I do with my money?'

'What would Mr Nielsen think?' Matty said in a choked voice.

'It has nothing to do with him. But if it had, he would be agreeable,' Louisa added. 'And if he was not, then I wouldn't marry him!'

'Does that mean that you are going to, Aunt Louisa?' Becca burst out. 'Could I be one of your attendants, please? Cos it will be ages before Matty or Julia get married; they haven't even met anyone suitable yet.'

'How do you know that?' Faith asked her. 'They might have secret admirers that we don't know about.'

Matty listened to the chatter and thought that the conversation had lightened considerably. She hoped that Faith was right and there might be someone who could care for her and she for him, but at the moment the idea was not even a pipe dream.

It was late afternoon of the next day when Stephen Nielsen arrived back in a very despondent mood. He had found nothing, he told Louisa, who was the first to greet him. She took him into the sitting room to wait for Matty, who had gone upstairs to change for supper.

'I have scoured the streets of London, called at several hospitals and police stations, talked to tramps and itinerants, shopkeepers and lodging-house keepers . . . do you happen to know what Mr Maddeson was wearing when he left for London, by any chance? I would have asked before but I didn't want to risk upsetting anyone.'

'I have no idea. A tailcoat, top hat and gloves, presumably, or maybe a coat, but I wasn't here; you'd have to speak to his daughters. Why do you ask?'

'A police station near St Thomas's hospital said they would be willing to put a *Missing* poster up if we sent a description of what he was wearing.' He felt in his coat pocket. 'I have a note of their address. They told me that there was a minor accident near the hospital that day when a vehicle turned over, and some of the passengers were taken in for treatment. I went in to enquire but apparently they were all French visitors here on an outing and were discharged once they'd been patched up.' He sat down, his chin in his hands. 'I am so disheartened. I really did want to solve this mystery. Those poor girls. Not knowing must be the hardest thing to bear.'

Matty came in as he was speaking and he stood up to greet her, but it was as if she knew that his search had been unsuccessful even before he said so.

'You have found nothing, Mr Nielsen?' She sat down and folded her hands on her lap. 'Well, he is out there somewhere, I am convinced of it.'

He told her of his visit to the police station and their request for a description of what he had been wearing.

'I suppose he would be indistinguishable from any other gentleman,' she murmured. 'He wore his second best tailcoat, black trousers and silk plush top hat, not his beaver. Oh,' she added, 'and he took his grey wool coat in case it became cold.'

Stephen nodded, remembering the vagrant sitting on the pavement outside the hospital gates who had remarked on Stephen's own clothes. He was wearing a grey coat and a top hat which had once belonged to someone else, though no one would want them back. The odds against finding him again, he thought, were minimal; then he recalled the man's words when asked about the injured people taken into the hospital. *Frenchies, were they?* he had said. So not Roland Maddeson after all, for he would be immediately recognizable as a typical English gentleman.

CHAPTER THIRTY-NINE

'How can I get home?' he asked Jeanette the next morning. 'I have no money.'

She had worried over that all night since he had recalled some of what had happened. Foolishly, it seemed to her now, she had brought him back with them to France, thinking that it was his home. No one else wanted to be responsible for him, certainly not Louis, even though he too had thought he was with their party. She had argued with Louis that they couldn't possibly leave him behind when he was injured.

'I am so very sorry,' she had wept, realizing her mistake, but then she asked herself what would have happened to him if they had left him behind. He didn't appear to have any form of identification with him, and she had wondered at the time why he had come to England without coat or hat.

'You did what you thought best.' Roland patted her hand. 'You were being kind and thoughtful to a stranger.'

She wiped away her tears. 'I spoke to you in French and you understood me, even though you had some concussion.' They were alternating between French and English as they talked.

'I didn't know where I was,' he said. 'I still don't. I don't know why I was in London. I don't think I live there. But French comes easily to me; perhaps I was taught it at school.'

He obviously still had amnesia; dare she even think of his travelling alone, and indeed what would he do for money to pay for the ferry? She knew no one who would lend them any, and she could never pay it back, though it would be up to her to do so.

'We must make more artefacts, *objets d'art*,' she declared. 'There will be another market in two weeks. You will have to help me.'

'*Objets d'art?*' He wondered how they could do that with the kind of material she had previously used. 'Two weeks? And then I shall travel?'

'You must leave before winter sets in. If we have snow you can't make the journey. I told you, I stay at home in the winter. We must make things to sell to pay for your fare, but what will you do when you get to England? How then will you get home? You will go to the *Gendarmerie Nationale*, perhaps?'

'The police? I don't know. How can I prove who I am? Tell them my name? Say I am Roland Henry Maddeson and I don't know where I live?' He stopped abruptly and they stared at one another.

She put out her arms and clasped him to her. 'Roland Henri Maddeson? Is that really your name?'

He picked her up and swung her round in the small room. 'Yes. Yes! It is!'

'So, *chéri*.' She wiped her eyes. 'You remember your name. The rest will follow as surely as night follows day. All we need to do now is make some money.'

They went into the wood store and Roland carried back the sack containing the small pieces of wood and tipped them on the floor. Then they put on coats and woollen hats, before going out again, this time into the forest with the empty sack, Roland with an axe over his shoulder and Chien following closely behind, as they tried to find interestingly shaped branches to carve into objects.

'It's beautiful, isn't it?' he murmured. Though the morning was briskly cold the sun shone brightly, dappling the few remaining leaves on the treetops, and as the last stragglers swirled down to the ground they were caught in a gold and amber shower.

Roland smiled as he picked them out of Jeanette's hair and woollen hat. He thought that her hair was almost the same colour as the leaves, and dared to tickle her nose with them. She had freckles too, caught by the summer sun, which he hadn't noticed before.

She showed him where a narrow stream trickled through the undergrowth and then stopped him with her hand on his arm, putting a finger to her lips. A creature had emerged from the undergrowth; at first he thought it a squirrel, but it wasn't: it had darker brown hair and a creamy white bib and throat, a narrow face and pointy ears and a long and bushy tail. It stood on its back legs for a moment looking at Chien, whose hair had bristled as a low growl rumbled in his throat. Then the little animal leapt past them, ran up a tree and disappeared into a hollow, higher than they could reach.

'What was it?' he asked.

'It is, erm – *Martes martes*. I don't know the English.'

'Pine marten? I've never seen one before. They are in Scotland, I think, not where I live.'

'Which is where?' she asked casually.

'An old and busy market town in Yorkshire,' he said, as they continued to walk. 'That's in the north of England, a long way from London. We need at least two trains, sometimes three, to travel to London.'

'Really?' She turned a brilliant smile towards him. 'And what is the name of this delightful place?'

'Beverley,' he said. 'It's where I was born—' He realized what was happening, and he took her hand and led her towards a fallen tree by the stream, where they sat down. 'Jeanette,' he murmured, 'you have saved my life for a second time.' He lifted her hand and gently pressed it to his lips. 'How can I ever thank you?'

She gazed at him for a second and then slowly retrieved her hand. 'There is no need,' she said huskily. 'We must do what we can for those in need, and we will be rewarded; we always receive back in kind whatever we give.'

'It is a good maxim to follow,' he said, looking away and down into the clear water. The stream was wider here and ran faster over the stones and rocks in its path, tossing up a sparkling shower. 'I will try to do as you do when I eventually arrive home.' He took a deep and profound breath. 'I have led an idle life. I realize that now after seeing how you live, yet you seem happy with your lot.' He turned his gaze back to her. 'Are you happy?' he asked.

The question seemed to unnerve her, for she paused before answering. 'I have had happier times. I was happy as a child with my mother and father and brother.'

'Ah!' He fingered the jumper he was wearing. 'The owner of this fine thing.'

'*Non!* That was not his. My brother Leo died when he was young. He didn't live long enough to fill clothing of that size.'

Roland frowned, puzzled. 'So whose was it?'

'It is a long story. I will tell you later. It's a pity to spoil such a fine day.'

She rose to her feet and then so did he, and they continued their search. She pointed out the fruits of the forest, the different trees – mostly beech, but some birch; she showed him the horse-hoof fungi growing on dead trunks, which she said she used for her winter fires as it was hard and burned slowly but well. He gathered acorns and dried mast husks from the forest floor as if he were a boy again, smelled the sweet pungent vegetation as the leaves rotted into the ground and gave dense richness to the soil; he stopped to listen to the tap-tap-tapping of woodpeckers and saw their bright flashing colours, and heard the crashing of hidden animals, boar or deer, as they sped away from the invading humans. Then there was silence, except for the faint coo of doves, the throaty *whoo hoo huh* of pigeons and the chorus of birdsong high in the treetops.

He carried the sack, full now of small branches and twigs, holly and trailing vines, and Jeanette said they had enough, until they found a fallen beech with a thick branch hanging from it which

Roland chopped off with the axe and trailed back. Tonight they would plan what to make and tomorrow they would start.

For their supper she made potato and onion soup from the onions that were hanging in the shed; she sliced courgettes, which Roland had called small marrows, and cooked them with garlic that she had grown in a pot by her door, and told him that come winter she would plant some more from those that were already sprouting green shoots.

Chien appeared at the door with a rabbit in his mouth. 'Good boy!' she exclaimed and his tail whipped back and forth at her praise. 'Will you hang it outside?' she asked Roland. 'There's a hook by the door. I'll skin it and cook it tomorrow. Perhaps we will also make a fire outside? It will be quicker than over the kitchen fire. We can wrap ourselves up warm and eat outside too.'

For Roland, who had only ever eaten outside at his mother's villa in Italy when the sun had shone, it would be, he thought, an experience.

She had caught his interest in her suggestion and said softly, 'Now that your memories are returning, *chéri*, we must make some more, for soon you will be gone.'

He heard what she said and knew that leave he must, one way or another; but in place of the happiness that had returned with his memory that day, a cloud of sadness descended upon him, dank and cold, and he thought that she felt it too.

The next day, remembering he had seen a granite rock on the forest floor nearby, he searched out the saw that Jeanette used for sawing logs for the fire and took it and some knives and sharpened them on the rock. He brought out the other tools that he had found and she told him that she had bought them for a few francs from an old widow long ago, but had never been sure how to use them.

He handled the large beech branch that he'd hauled back, turning it every which way to find the best side of it. He trapped it between two large stones, packing it in place with moss, and began to slice and saw until he had an almost round wooden plate. The inside of it was beautifully marked and he smoothed it with his hand and blew the sawdust from it. 'That's lovely,' Jeanette said from over his shoulder. 'I love the way the colours of the wood blend so well.'

'I remember a carpenter telling me long ago that beech was better buried underground for a few years and then dug up again when it had aged,' he told her. 'The worms and other creatures put their mark on it, adding to its beauty.' He sighed. 'We haven't time for that, but I'll smooth out the edges with the plane, and with some of your resin to polish it we will have a fine plate to sell.'

He sat back on his heels. 'I'd forgotten about that old man who gave me the gift of his wisdom,' he murmured. 'Who would have thought, certainly not he, that such a piece of information would come in useful one day?' He turned to her. 'If I saw several pieces from the branch,' he said, 'you can polish them over the winter to sell next year.'

'Perhaps I will bury them as your man did and see if he was right.'

'Yes.' He looked up at her. Behind her the low sun was bright and lit up her hair like a halo, and he smiled. That would be a good memory to keep.

Jeanette lit the fire outside beneath a trivet that she had fashioned out of some old ironwork, a gate or fence or something similar that she had found some time before, and once again he was astounded at her ingenuity, at her foresight in keeping something that might one day come in useful.

She jointed the skinned rabbit whilst he was sawing and planing, and scattered herbs over and inside it and covered it with bracken to let it slowly cook over the heat. She scrubbed potatoes and when the rabbit was halfway done she placed these on the fire too.

He watched her. They would have a feast tonight. These were the memories she was making and inviting him to share.

*

253

The night was cold and sharp but it was warm by the fire. The sky was clear, with a quarter moon and endless stars. As they ate their meal of tender rabbit, with bread to dip into a sauce she had made from goat's milk and herbs and thickened with flour, she told him how she came to be here.

'You know of my brother Leo. He died when he was eight and my father was inconsolable. We all were, my mother and I too, but my father had lost his son and heir, and although we were not rich he had a good living and now no one to hand it on to. He chose, therefore, once I was old enough, to search out a husband for me, and he found one. A man the same age as him.'

She paused, and gazed into the fire. 'Unfortunately for me I had fallen in love with someone else, who was considered to be unworthy; and as I was thought to be a wild child my father locked me in the house so that I couldn't meet him secretly. I escaped, and we ran away together.' She shook her head. 'My father was quite right. He was unworthy, for he had no good intentions towards me, and returned to his home having sown what my father called his *wild oats*. Do you have this saying in England?'

'We do.' Roland nodded. 'It is the same.' Many of his friends had been encouraged by their fathers to do it, but not his own. Henry was an honest and upright man and expected his sons to be the same.

'My father wouldn't have me back. He said I was soiled goods.' She lifted her chin defiantly. 'I was eighteen years old and I made a living as best I could. I left my father's district and became a chambermaid, constantly looking for somewhere I could live in peace on my own and earn money for bread, just as men do.'

She smiled. 'I arrived in Cerisy Forest one summer and found the hut and spent the night here. I wasn't frightened, even though I could hear animals snuffling about outside, and I decided that I would find out whose it was and ask if I might live in it.'

She lifted her shoulders in the shrug that he had come to know so well. 'But no one knew, not any of the villagers around, and so I stayed. I was given old furniture and here I am still, twelve years later. I am part of the forest and I make my living as you see, by making things to sell to tourists who come to look at the flora and fauna and buy from the markets. They don't bother me, for the villagers tell them not to come this way as there is a strange old woman in the forest.'

'And this?' He fingered the jumper he was wearing.

'Ah! It is the only thing that my lover left behind and so I kept it. I make-believe that it was my brother's. I have in my heart,' she swallowed, 'made a life for him, even though he is long dead. I have given him a wife and children, so he left this behind on their last visit. I wear it myself in winter and it gives me comfort.'

She's lonely, he thought. How I understand that.

CHAPTER FORTY

Julia spent over a week with Aunt Gertrude and found her quite genial, though she realized that she was still worried about her brother, for she mentioned him quite frequently, reminiscing over their childhood and the behaviour of their younger brother.

'Ridiculous,' she snorted. 'Nothing wrong with Albert. I blame his pretentious wife with her bizarre ideas.'

Aunt Gertrude was happy to allow Julia to walk out alone in Hull once she had shown her which areas should be avoided and which were perfectly safe. 'But of course you must come back before dusk, as I expect you do in Beverley. Hull is a pleasant town; at least I like it here. There are meeting places, museums, and many theatres. I mainly go to matinees if I am alone, and as the managers know me they make sure I have a good seat. You must tell me if there is anything that you'd like to see whilst you're here. I know Beverley does not have the same choices.'

Julia didn't want to go to the theatre. She didn't think it right to be enjoying herself when she was so anxious about her father, but she allowed herself the indulgence of visiting the market in the centre of town, browsing amongst the stalls, and then walking on towards the pier, where she sat on a bench and looked over the Humber estuary.

There was always a breeze here which tangled her hair, unloosing it from its usual tight chignon coiled at the back of her neck. The Humber surged in front of her, tossing spray towards her feet, and she felt its shower against her face as well, which she didn't mind. The turbulence of it reflected her own state of mind: a turmoil of unrest which she knew wouldn't settle until her father returned and brought back stability.

She walked slowly back again and on a sudden impulse went towards Holy Trinity Church and sat inside for a few minutes. There was no one else there except a verger who was putting out fresh candles, lighting two and leaving tapers for others to use if they felt the need; he nodded to Julia but didn't speak. When he had gone she walked down to the table and lit a candle for her father, closing her eyes and praying for his safe return and putting coins into the box.

It was almost lunchtime by the time she returned to Aunt Gertrude's house, having walked about the town admiring the elegant old buildings. My aunt is quite right: it is a lovely town, she thought as she came to the street of Georgian houses where she lived. Some had basements which seemed to be used mainly as kitchens; there was also the Catholic church of St Charles Borromeo further down, on the edge of the green and pleasant Kingston Square in Jarrett Street.

How strange, she thought. He must surely be related to the same family who own the Borromeo Islands. What a coincidence!

I could live here, she thought, if I didn't love Beverley so much.

After lunch Gertrude wondered aloud whether to have an afternoon nap or take a short walk to waken herself up.

'What would you do if I were not here, Aunt Gertrude?' Julia asked. 'Please do not think that you must consider me. I'll be happy to sit and read a book whichever you do.'

Before her aunt could reply they heard the front door-bell and the maid scurrying to answer it. Moments later she tapped on the sitting room door. 'Beg pardon, ma'am,' she said. 'There's a young gentleman asking for you.'

Gertrude sat up straight and glanced at Julia. 'A young gentleman! Well, that will be the first time in many years. Did he give his name?'

'Yes, ma'am. Mr Adam Chapman, ma'am.'

Gertrude tutted. 'Well, why did you not say so, foolish girl! Show him in at once.' She turned to her niece. 'He won't be coming to see me, of course,' she said with a gleam in her eye. 'But I'm pleased to know that he has good manners.'

The maid knocked again and opened the door. 'Mr Adam Chapman, ma'am.'

'Show him in, then,' Gertrude said sharply. 'Don't keep him waiting.'

Julia, turning in her chair, saw Adam give a swift grin to the hapless maid as she ushered him in, and hid her own smile as she stood up to greet him.

Adam bent over Aunt Gertrude's hand and murmured he was pleased to see her again, and then turned to Julia and touched his hand to his chest. 'Julia,' he said softly. 'I hope you are well?'

'I am, thank you,' she responded. 'Do you bring any news?'

Aunt Gertrude invited him to sit, and as he did so he answered, 'Sadly no. I called in to see . . . your sisters this morning.'

He would have expected to see me, she thought. Eliza will only recently have returned home from Switzerland too. Their mother would have given them any recent news, so there is none. She drew in a breath. I must go home, not hide away.

'I am very sorry, Julia; you must be so anxious,' he said. 'And you too, Miss Maddeson.' He turned again to Julia. 'My mother wrote of your father's, erm, disappearance, and I did write to ask if there was anything . . .' His voice faltered and tailed away.

She nodded. There were letters, and I opened none of them. What a coward I am.

'We are hoping for good news soon,' Miss Maddeson told him. 'Someone is in London even now making enquiries on our behalf.' She paused for a moment. 'Adam – do you mind if I call you Adam? I feel as if we became friends on the way home from Italy.'

'Of course.' He gave her a broad smile. 'That was a very happy time, wasn't it?'

She said that it was, and then went on, 'I must ask if you will excuse me. I was about to take a nap, and Julia will be much better company than I. Julia, perhaps you will ring for coffee or tea for Adam?' She rose to her feet without waiting for an answer, and Adam stood up too until she had left the room.

'I don't need coffee or tea, thank you, Julia,' he said. 'I'd rather talk, and Nunny told me you were still at your aunt's.'

'Is Matty all right?' she asked. 'I should go home, really.'

He nodded. 'Your aunt Louisa is returning to Scarborough today, I understand. Mr Nielsen has returned from London.'

Julia licked her lips, which were suddenly dry. 'And – anything? Anything at all?'

'I understand not, but that is not to say it's bad news, Julia. London is huge, and Mr Nielsen said he will go again.'

'I must go home,' she muttered. 'I can't be skulking here when Matty is alone.'

'She's not alone,' he said softly. 'Faith and Becca are there, and Nunny, and Mrs Walton has only just left for home.'

'But if Aunt Louisa has returned to Scarborough . . .' Julia's voice rose and she put her fingers to her lips. She stood up as if she were about to fly off immediately.

'Listen.' He stood up too, took hold of both her hands and made her sit. 'Stay here for the rest of the day, and then why don't I come back tomorrow and we'll catch the train together if you insist on returning? Your aunt Gertrude won't mind, will she?'

She shook her head. 'No,' she whispered. 'She won't. She'd be willing to come back with me if I asked her to, but she's anxious too, and at least whilst she's here at home she can occupy herself.'

'So shall we do that?' He was asking her to make a decision and she knew that she must.

'Yes, please,' she whispered. 'If you don't mind?'

'Of course I don't mind. It's the least I can do.' He pressed her hands in his. 'I'll leave now. I'm glad I came, Julia, but I'm sorry to see you so worried and upset. Your father will turn up; no news is good news, isn't that what we say?'

She blinked to keep back the tears that threatened to engulf her, even though she nodded in agreement. I am losing control, she thought. What is happening to me?

Adam headed back to the train station feeling a pulse of excitement in his throat. He had been aghast when he had heard of Roland Maddeson's disappearance and wanted to help in any way he could, but especially he wanted to see Julia, who he knew, in spite of the aloof and unapproachable manner she had maintained since childhood, would be crumbling inside and needed someone to take away the hurt. And she had not rejected his offer to bring her back home.

When he had first arrived back in Beverley for the holiday he had called at the Maddeson house as soon as he could, only to discover that Miss Julia was staying with her aunt in Hull, and Miss Martha was not at home to visitors because their other Aunt Maddeson had arrived without warning and was 'worring her to death', according to Nunny, who was tight-lipped with fury at Mrs Maddeson's descending without notice. He'd left a message that he would call again in a few days and walked back down the path, wondering why Matty should be so upset by her aunt's visit.

It wouldn't matter normally, I suppose, he deliberated, but Matty and Julia don't trust this uncle and aunt because they think they want to move in to claim the house. Surely that can't happen, he thought, except . . . they are all under age, and if the uncle is their guardian . . . I wonder, do the Gartons know of their worry, and can Tim help to put their minds at rest?

He decided to walk home through Saturday Market in the hope that he might meet Tim Garton leaving his office, and sure enough he was coming out of the door just as Adam drew near.

'Tim,' he called. 'Have you got a minute?'

The two young men shook hands and continued walking together, as they lived in the same direction. 'Are you finished for the holidays?' Tim asked. 'The year has gone by so fast.'

'It has,' Adam agreed. 'Not that I'll be having much of a holiday apart from on Christmas Day. I've brought loads of work to do.'

'Snap!' Tim laughed, holding up a packed briefcase. 'It never ends.'

'I wanted to ask you something,' Adam confided. 'I've just called to see Matty Maddeson. But she's tied up with her aunt at present, and, erm – well, seemingly she and Julia are worried that their relatives want to move into the house and live there with them until the matter of their father's disappearance is resolved.'

Tim stopped walking. 'I can't discuss it, Adam,' he said. 'They're clients of ours.'

'I don't want to talk about the Maddesons,' Adam told him, 'but I wondered if, hypothetically, young women who are not yet of age could have their home taken from them by their guardian so soon after their father's alleged disappearance.'

Tim frowned. 'I can't—'

'It's a hypothetical question only,' Adam said quickly. 'I mean, how long does anyone have to be missing until they are declared – erm . . .'

'Death in absentia, I think you're trying to say,' Tim answered wryly. 'And it's seven years, so we don't have to even think about it at present.'

'Oh, that's good news!' Adam said. 'But I wasn't speaking about anyone in particular, you know, just adding to my general knowledge for when I become a teacher.'

Tim didn't comment, but Adam knew that he was listening. Unable to contain his elation any longer, he blurted out: 'I called to see Julia in Hull today. She's been staying with her aunt, Miss Maddeson, and I'm returning tomorrow to bring her home.'

'*You* are bringing her home?' Tim stopped in his tracks and grinned. 'Am I out of touch? Do you and Julia have an understanding?'

Adam gave a dry laugh, suddenly deflated by the question. 'The only understanding that I have, is that I don't stand a chance of having any understanding at all.'

CHAPTER FORTY-ONE

Adam arrived at Miss Maddeson's house at ten thirty the next morning; he would have been there earlier but he didn't want to appear too eager.

Julia was ready with her luggage packed, but her eyes were moist as she kissed her aunt goodbye. 'Will you come to visit us soon, Aunt Gertrude?' she asked. 'We would like you to.'

'I will, my dear. Perhaps in a week or so, and maybe by then we will have news.'

Julia nodded. 'I hope so,' she murmured. In truth, although she longed to be home, she was also dreading it, for when she had left Beverley to come to her aunt's she had felt that a dark cloud was beginning to seep through the house where they were left in limbo. To keep her mind off the subject whilst on the short train journey she questioned Adam about his time at university and his hopes of becoming a teacher. He was more than willing to discuss his plans and delighted that she was interested; he had, he told her, visited some of the London Ragged Schools, of which there were many.

'They're desperate for teachers,' he told her, 'but they don't get many applicants as the salary is poor. However, those who do go are totally committed to giving their pupils a chance in life by teaching them to read and learn their numbers. I met one couple, a man and wife, who even use their own home as a school; they set aside a room for teaching

and another as a dining room, and gave the children breakfast every morning.'

Julia listened, her eyes wide open. 'Do you mean they don't
have breakfast before they go to school?'

Adam shook his head. 'They live in poverty, Julia.' With a
wry smile, he added, 'Some come only for their breakfast, and
then disappear. After they have done that a few times they
are refused breakfast until they have learned their alphabet.
Generally, though, after they have eaten their porridge the
children can smell the dinner being cooked, usually something like a stew with dumplings, and they want to stay. But
they're not fed unless they have learned their lessons first.'

'And are there any women teachers, or only men?' Julia
asked as the train slowed at a junction.

'There are some.' He glanced out of the window and
saw they were passing Cottingham and would soon be in
Beverley. 'The ones I met were the wives of the head teachers, although I understand that there is no barrier to employ-
ing women. They pay them less, as is the general rule, but
there is little money available in any case.' He stood up
and picked up Julia's sparse luggage. 'We're here,' he said.
'Home again.'

When they reached the house Julia rang the doorbell, as
she hadn't her key, and when Betty Brown opened the door
Adam put her bags in the hall.

'I won't stay, Julia,' he said, hoping she would press him to.
'You'll be anxious to see your sisters.'

Betty Brown dipped her knee. 'Miss Martha is with Miss
Faith, Miss Julia,' she said. 'She's not well.'

'Faith isn't or Matty isn't?' Julia said in alarm, whilst Adam
hovered in the doorway.

'Miss Faith. She's caught a chill.'

Julia turned to Adam and he saw the panic in her face.
'Thank you for bringing me home,' she said, and paused,
as if not knowing what else to add. He had been so kind, so
thoughtful.

He reached for her hand and gave it a gentle squeeze. 'Think nothing of it,' he murmured. 'I'll call later. I'll see myself out,' and with a nod to the maid he backed out of the door and closed it behind him.

'Are they upstairs?' Julia asked.

'Yes, miss. In Miss Faith's room. Mrs Nunnington is there too.'

Things really can't get any worse, Julia thought. And where is Becca?

She tapped gently on Faith's door and opened it. Faith was in bed, propped up on pillows with Nunny bathing her forehead with a cool flannel, but she turned her head when Julia came in and Julia saw how very pale and listless she was despite the bright spot on each cheek. Matty was sitting on a low chair next to her bed. She too turned as Julia came in, and Julia immediately saw the tension on her face.

'Oh, we're so glad to see you, Julia; aren't we, Faith?' she said brightly.

'Yes. You've been away for ages,' Faith said huskily. 'Or at least it seems like it.' Her voice was cracked and hoarse and she gave a chesty cough. 'I'm so pleased you're back home again, darling Julia.'

Julia blew her a kiss, knowing that Faith wouldn't thank her for giving her a proper one. 'I would have come earlier,' she said. 'You should have sent for me.'

'It's nothing,' Faith said quickly before Matty could answer, though her voice was weak and her breathing strained. 'But I'll feel much better when dear Papa returns home; he will come, won't he, Nunny? He won't stay away much longer, will he?'

'Now you know he won't stay away longer than is necessary,' Nunny answered with a catch in her voice. 'He's been detained longer than expected, but you know that your papa won't leave his girls alone unless there's been something particularly urgent or unexpected to hold him up.'

'Where is Becca?' Julia asked. Her voice was wobbly. 'Is she at her lessons?'

'No,' Matty answered. 'Mrs Lawrence came over yesterday with Roger and Frances. They're home for the holidays, and she asked if Becca would like to stay with them for a few days. They're being allowed to ride on the racecourse.'

'Becca will enjoy that,' Julia said half-heartedly. 'Matty, I'll sit with Faith for a while. I'm sure you have lots you need to do.' Even have a sleep, she thought, for Matty looked exhausted.

'And I'll see how Cook is getting on with lunch,' Nunny broke in. 'She's going to make chicken soup. You'll have a little, won't you, m'dear?' she said to Faith as she mopped her forehead with a soft towel. 'It'll mebbe help clear your chest.'

'Just a small bowl then,' Faith said to please her. 'And I might have another sleep if Julia will sit with me, but first I want to know what you've been up to whilst you were in Hull.'

'I'll be two ticks,' Julia smiled, using one of Nunny's expressions. 'I'll just take my coat upstairs and put my bag in my room.'

'I'll get Betty to do that, Miss Julia, save you the bother,' Nunny said.

'It's no bother, Nunny.' Julia reached for the door before the housekeeper could. 'I need to wash my hands after the train journey.' She headed upstairs, knowing that her bag would already have been taken up, but wanting to reach the sanctuary of her room before she burst into tears, for seeing her elder sister worn out and anxious and her younger one looking so weak and ill that she could barely lift her head had so alarmed her that she felt physically sick.

She dropped to her knees by the side of her bed and put her face in her hands. What was happening to them? Their lives were crashing down around them. Papa, she called to him in her head. *Papa.* Where are you?

Matty tapped on her door and Julia turned, tears streaming down her face. 'I should never have gone to Aunt Gertrude's,' she said brokenly. 'I should never have left you to cope alone.'

'I wasn't alone,' Matty said pragmatically. 'Aunt Louisa was here till yesterday and she would have stayed but I told her you were coming home soon, and we weren't to know that Faith would go down with another chill. She was so much better, but then yesterday afternoon she went out for a walk over Westwood. It was a lovely sunny day but the wind was very cold and she went too far, all the way to Burton Bushes and beyond. She was out so long that I sent Sam to look for her and he had to practically carry her home.' She stifled a sob. 'I should have gone with her; I wouldn't have let her walk so far.'

'Don't blame yourself.' Julia got to her feet. 'We all know how independent Faith can be; she doesn't like to be considered weak. Now listen, Matty,' she said. 'I'm going to sit with Faith so you can rest in your room, then after lunch why not lie on your bed for an hour and try to sleep. There's nothing so urgent that it can't wait.'

Matty nodded. 'Dr Laybourn will probably call,' she said. 'He came last night and said he'd come again today.'

'There's no reason for you to see him. I can do that.' Julia was getting into her stride. 'It's time I stopped running away when things are difficult.' She took a warm shawl from her wardrobe. 'I'll have my lunch with Faith; she might take some soup if someone is with her.'

Matty shook her head. 'She won't,' she said morosely. 'I've tried that. But I'm pleased you're home, Julia. Having you near does lessen the burden – not that Faith is a burden, she's *not*. She's *not*. But I'm so afraid . . .' She started to weep. 'I'm so afraid that we'll lose her, and I just can't bear it.'

Julia took a comfortable cushion and a book with her to Faith's room; the book in case Faith fell asleep, for she intended to stay there with her for the whole afternoon. They had just finished their lunch of chicken soup, of which Faith ate a little, with some persuasion, and then a spoonful of ice cream that Cook had made especially for her, when Dr Laybourn called.

He listened intently to Faith's back and chest, his bristly eyebrows going up and down as he concentrated. 'Hmm,' he muttered. 'No worse.' He turned to Julia. 'This young lady needs to be kept warm, but not hot. Plenty of cooling drinks, and' – he turned now to Faith – 'plenty of rest and no going out now that winter winds are almost upon us. In another few days, if you remain the same, you can get up out of bed and sit in an easy chair to look at the world out of the window, providing you are well wrapped up in a blanket.'

He took Julia to one side. 'And what about you, young lady? You're very pale, as is Miss Martha. I suppose you're worried about your father? Which is perfectly natural, but worrying about him is not going to bring him back any quicker. You and Miss Martha need your fresh air, so providing you don't overdo it, you must take a short brisk walk at least once a day.'

She didn't make him aware that she had been staying at her aunt's and had walked out every day, but only nodded and said she would tell her sister, and she knew he was right, as Matty wouldn't have been out, but would have stayed at home waiting for news that didn't come.

He told her he would visit again in a few days, but to send for him if he was needed before then.

'Do we have to pay Dr Laybourn each time he comes, Julia?' Faith asked hoarsely when he had gone. 'If we do, what a huge bill we'll have to pay.'

'It doesn't matter if we do,' Julia replied. 'We must get you well before Papa comes home or he'll think we've neglected you.'

'No, he won't.' Faith slid further down into bed and pulled the sheets under her chin. 'I shall tell him how well you and Matty looked after me when I was being such a nuisance.' She smiled at Julia, who she knew would protest, and quickly said, 'I'm going to have a sleep now. Nunny gave me a powder before lunch and it always makes me sleepy. You don't mind, do you?'

'No.' Julia bent over and kissed her on the forehead. 'Would you like me to read to you? I found this old book on Aunt

Gertrude's shelf and she said I might borrow it; it was Papa's originally, when he was a boy, and she borrowed it and forgot to give it back, and then he said she might keep it. It was written over a hundred years ago and it's by Daniel Defoe. It reads like an adventure story: a man called Robinson Crusoe sets out on a voyage from Kingston upon Hull, so it seems very real.'

'Then read it aloud, if you will,' Faith said sleepily, 'and don't mind if I fall asleep, will you, for it is very soothing to be read to. Did Mama read to us, Julia? I can't remember.'

Julia put her hand to her mouth and swallowed. 'Yes, she did. Not such a book as this, as it might seem like a book for boys and young men, but she read from books more suited for girls.'

It was a memory she had suppressed. The reason, she had once thought, was so it would not give her pain; but as she began to read, in a low voice, for Faith was almost asleep and the first few pages were descriptive of the character – the narrative became more vivid as the ship pulled out of the Humber and became embroiled in a storm at sea – she recalled the low timbre of her mother's voice, and as the tears ran down her cheeks she felt not sadness at her loss, but the glow of love that their mother had given them all.

As Faith drifted off into a comforting sleep, her eyes flickering and almost closed, she saw her dark-haired mother sitting nearby with a book in her hand and felt safe and cared for.

CHAPTER FORTY-TWO

'Mrs Lawrence.' Becca stood in front of her hostess, who was sitting in an easy chair letting down a hem on one of Frances's dresses. 'I'm afraid I have to go home.' She had been with the Lawrence family for three days, but now she was feeling homesick and uneasy.

'Must you, dear?' Mrs Lawrence was very kind and motherly. Rather like Nunny, Becca thought. 'Has my wicked boy Roger been tormenting you?'

'Oh, no! He never does that. We're really good friends, although he doesn't always want to play games with Frances and me like he used to. Not hide and seek or tag or things like that, and Frances and I don't always want to play games either. We all like to ride together, though, and we had such a good time on the racecourse when we went out with the other riders.'

'So why do you want to go home?'

Becca hung her head. It was difficult to describe, and she didn't want to upset Mrs Lawrence or let her think she wasn't enjoying herself, for she had been, and she would again, but she had a deep-seated worry about her father and wanted to see her sisters, especially Faith, who hadn't been very well when she came away to the Lawrences'.

'I'm just worried,' she said. 'You see, I thought that Papa would be sure to be home for my birthday, or at least by

Christmas, but now I'm not sure of either, so I don't really want to have my birthday if he isn't here and I don't know what we'll be doing for Christmas or where we'll be; if we'll stay at home or perhaps go to our aunt Louisa's in Scarborough or Aunt Gertrude's house in Hull or even to Uncle Fisher and Aunt Caroline if they invite us, though I hope they don't, because they're not very good company and we'd rather be at home on our own than with them and our cousins.' All her worries poured out to this kind lady.

Mrs Lawrence inclined her head but didn't comment. She could understand that, for Caroline Maddeson was not well liked generally.

'You can all come here, you know,' she said hospitably. 'You and your sisters. We're generally in a muddle, for we have aunts and uncles, cousins and second cousins and goodness knows who else, but everyone is welcome.'

'Does Owen come too?' Becca asked.

'Owen? Yes, of course,' Mrs Lawrence said. 'He's family, isn't he?'

'I don't know. Is he?'

'Why yes, he's Mr Lawrence's nephew, his late sister's boy. He's lived with us since he was ten, when his father died; we're very fond of Owen.'

'I didn't know that,' Becca said. 'So why does he live above the stables? My father's groom, Sam, who looks after his horse and the carriages, lives above our stable and tack room, but he eats in the kitchen with Cook and Nunny and Betty Brown.'

'Oh, well, that's quite different. Sam is a paid employee of your father, whilst Owen chose to live above the stable once he became sixteen. He hasn't always lived up there. He lived with us until then, and went to the grammar school. Minster House he was in, and he was very well thought of. He could have gone to university but he wanted to work with the horses; it's in his blood, I suppose.

'But then he said he'd like to try out independence and Mr Lawrence said it was totally up to him. We've made his room very comfortable for him, but he always eats with us of an evening, we insisted on that. He'll be going away to college soon to learn about horse management, even though he knows so much already, but he needs certification, and when he's finished we hope he'll come back to us, unless he goes to another stable as manager and trainer.'

'Oh,' Becca murmured. 'I didn't know.'

'Well, no, you wouldn't, dear, because he's only just decided that's what he wants to do. We gave him the option of deciding in his own time, you see, but he's taken advice from Mr Lawrence, who hasn't rushed him at all. It hasn't been easy for the boy, losing both his mother and his father at such an early age.'

She stopped abruptly, as if seeing the connection for the first time; she had often wondered why the boy had been so patient with Becca, who was forever hanging about the stables. Now she knew it wasn't only because of the horses, although the child obviously had a passion for them; it was a generous consideration given by Owen to Becca, who had been left motherless as little more than an infant and without even a memory to keep in her heart.

She had called at the Maddeson house to offer assistance as soon as she'd heard the news all those years ago, and a few days later Mrs Nunnington had brought Rebecca, as she was known then, to be with her children, who were of a similar age. They were all too young to play, but they trotted towards each other. Roger, who was late in walking, fell over a few times in his haste to reach the newcomer and had promptly smacked her. She hadn't cried but only looked at him as if surprised, and then he'd given her a hug. They had been friends ever since.

She smiled at the memory, and added, 'You know that you can come and go as you wish. You are always welcome, my dear. You don't have to ask.'

Becca nodded. 'I know,' she whispered, and felt hot and scalding tears falling down her cheeks. Mrs Lawrence had always been kind and she wished that she could be her mother, but then she would miss her sisters.

'I'm afraid of not being at home when Papa comes back,' she confided. 'And I want to be the first to see him.'

Louisa told Stephen that she would marry him and he'd stretched his head back and given a silent bellow of *Hallelujah*. He'd promised that he would shout it from the rooftops if she said yes, but they were in her house having supper when she told him and he said it would be difficult getting on to her roof as there wasn't a skylight big enough for him to climb through.

She'd laughed and told him he was an idiot and then she had kissed him, properly on the mouth, and said that she loved him; and then she announced that they must wait until the spring for a wedding, because the mystery of her brother-in-law's disappearance would surely be resolved by then and her nieces could be her attendants. 'They won't want to be making merry if their father is still missing,' she explained.

He was disappointed but understood, and said he was willing to go back to London and search again in the hope that something fresh had come up. Louisa dropped a note to Matty to tell her and a reply came immediately asking her to come and stay with them if she would.

There seemed to be a note of urgency in the request so she decided to travel the next morning, telling Stephen that he could come later if he wished, which he said he would.

When she stepped off the train in Beverley it was a brisk cold day and so she decided to take a cabriolet from outside the station rather than walk. As she approached the stand she heard someone call her name.

She turned, and it was Gertrude Maddeson. 'Hello,' she greeted her. 'Are we heading in the same direction?'

'I imagine so,' Gertrude answered in her usual sober manner. 'I received a note from Julia telling me that on returning home from my house she found that Faith was ill and she had been sitting with her to give Matty a rest. So I decided to come and assist if I could.'

'I didn't know about Faith,' Louisa said worriedly, 'but I invited myself. Mr Nielsen has offered to go to London again and make more enquiries about Roland, and I wrote to Matty to tell her so in the hope that she would ask me to go back, which she did. Poor darlings,' she said, as she allowed Miss Maddeson to climb first into the cab. 'They must be feeling desperate.'

Miss Maddeson heaved a sigh as she sat down. 'They must,' she agreed. 'It's bad enough for me sitting at home waiting for news, but so much worse for them. So much responsibility at a young age, and especially when dear Faith is still unwell. I worry for her.' She nipped her lips together, restraining herself from adding that she had always thought that Faith wouldn't make old bones, and hoping against hope that she would be proved wrong.

'Of course.' Louisa was truly sympathetic to Gertrude's feelings. In her anxious state of worry over her nieces, she sometimes forgot that Gertrude would be anxious about her brother too. 'Does your brother Albert Fisher keep in touch with you about what is happening?' She was never sure whether to call him Albert or Fisher and so used both names.

'Tsk!' Gertrude showed her irritation. 'He has been only once to see my nieces to the best of my knowledge, and then sent his wife who suggested they should move in with them. What good will that do?' She turned to Louisa with fury in her expression. 'How does that help?'

Louisa smiled, even though it was not in the least humorous in the circumstances. 'I was there at the time,' she told Gertrude. 'And the best thing was hearing Matty give out all the reasons why they couldn't come, and letting Caroline know she had everything under control, and then Faith hinting that the doctor had said she might be infectious!'

'Well,' Gertrude pronounced. 'Albert *and* his wife will get a flea in their ears when I see them, which I will, for I'll call unannounced. There'll be no calling card from me!'

Nunny opened the door to them and was delighted when she recognized the visitors. 'Oh, Miss Maddeson, Mrs Walton, it's so nice to see you both.' She put her hand to her chest. 'Such a relief.' She dropped her voice. 'What a worry it all is, and what – oh, and here's Miss Becca coming home too.' She had spotted Becca hurrying across the York Road. 'She's been staying with 'Lawrences. So good they are to her.' Her voice went husky as she spoke. 'Mrs Lawrence is an angel in disguise, treats our Miss Becca like her own. Come along, dearie,' she called out. 'Look, see who we have here.'

Becca began to smile when she saw her two aunts together in the doorway. 'I knew there was a reason why I wanted to come home,' she greeted them as she rushed up the path and put an arm round each of them before remembering to dip her knee as she should. 'Have you both come to stay? I do hope that you have.'

'Yes, indeed,' said Aunt Gertrude. 'For as long as you wish.'

Becca knew that wasn't true. Aunt Gertrude would go home when she was ready to, if she thought there was no need for her to be there.

'I will stay as long as you need me,' Louisa said. 'And Mr Nielsen is coming to see everyone tomorrow and is then travelling on to London again.'

Nunny had called Betty to take the aunts' coats, hats and travelling cases when they heard a commotion upstairs that made them all lift their heads. Matty was at the top of the staircase, trying to urge Pug down.

'Oh, how lovely,' she said, and lifting her skirts ran down to greet them, kissing each of her aunts in turn. 'It's so good to see you. Come in, do. There's a lovely fire in the sitting room and I expect Nunny will be organizing the coffee and tea things already.'

Which she was; and within ten minutes she and Betty carried in two trays of crockery for the tea and coffee, milk and sugar and slices of buttered tea cake.

'Becca!' Matty gave her sister a hug. 'Missed us, did you?'

'Yes, I did,' Becca admitted. 'I explained to Mrs Lawrence that I wanted to come home and she said I should come and go just as I wanted and I didn't have to ask.' She sat down on the rug. 'I discovered something whilst I was staying with the Lawrences. Did you know, Matty, that Owen is Mr Lawrence's nephew? He's the son of Mr Lawrence's sister and she died when he was little and then his father died too and so he came to live with the Lawrences.'

'I don't think I knew that,' Matty murmured. 'I only knew that he had been living there a long time.'

'Well, so you see I was right when I told you that he would be in charge of the stables one day.'

Matty nodded. 'I see,' she said vaguely, wondering where the conversation was going.

'So when I'm old enough I'm going to ask Owen if I can work there with the horses.' She crossed her arms defiantly, waiting for someone to say that she couldn't, but they didn't. There were other things far more serious that they needed to discuss, so she went quietly out of the room to tell Julia and Faith that their aunts had arrived.

Julia came down to greet them whilst Becca stayed with Faith, who was sitting up in bed sipping honey and hot water, and repeated the story about Owen and his parents and how he was going away to college to learn how to be a manager. Pug, who had followed her back upstairs, stretched himself outside Faith's door.

'I'm going to stay at home now,' Becca told Faith. 'I'll call to see the Lawrences because Mrs Lawrence says I can come and go as I please, but I won't stay overnight, not until you are feeling better and can come downstairs.'

She considered for a moment or too, holding her fingers in a steeple then slotting them together as if she were playing cat's cradle. 'And then . . .' Faith gazed silently at her sister. 'And then,' Becca went on, 'not until Papa comes home, however long it might take.'

CHAPTER FORTY-THREE

Roland went with Jeanette to market. They took all the things they had to sell in the donkey cart and set up a stall that they had fashioned from planks of wood on a trestle that they borrowed from another stallholder. No one took any notice of him, thinking him a Frenchman; he wore his woollen hat pulled over one ear to hide and protect his head wound which was healing well, and his country clothes, cord trousers and jacket.

As well as making the wooden plates, he had split long strips of wood and painted on them a caricature of a Frenchman with a turned-up thin black moustache, wearing a striped jumper and a black beret. Jeanette had told him that foreign visitors sometimes came walking in the forest and she thought they might buy them as souvenirs. 'They are Breton, of course,' she told him teasingly. 'Frenchmen don't really dress like that!'

'Foreigners won't know that,' he laughed, and wondered if any English people might come and he could ask them for help. But none came; it was too late in the year, but they sold all the other things they had taken, selling mainly to French visitors from nearby towns who liked the artisan products.

As they drove back with an empty cart he asked her if she had paper and pencil or pen and ink, that he might write home to his daughters. 'They will be so anxious, and wondering if I am dead or alive. How long has it been since I came here?' His memory was still hazy.

'Mid-October when the group went to England. When did you travel to London?'

He didn't know, nor could he remember why he had gone. 'Perhaps when I arrive in Le Havre I will find a post office. I must keep enough money to pay for a stamp.'

She nodded. There was nowhere to post a letter in the nearby villages, though occasionally she had seen shop-keepers accept letters and give them to visitors to post when they arrived back in their home town. She had never had to do such a thing since she had come to live in the forest; if they'd thought of it before they could have been prepared and asked a visitor to the market to do that for them, but then again, could they have been sure of trusting a stranger to post it?

After they had eaten that evening, she searched in her many boxes for paper and an envelope. She had plenty of paper, for she saved every scrap for writing reminder notes or for making the fire, but finding an envelope was impossible. Eventually they fashioned one out of plain paper and stuck the sides with the sticky pine resin.

He began to write. *My dearest daughters, I am safe* – but then he put his head in his hands and began to weep. 'What will they think of me? That I have deserted them? That I am dead?'

He began again. *I have had the strangest experience that you would not believe could happen. I have been ill and lost, but now I am almost well.*

Jeanette took the pencil from him. 'Let me,' she murmured. 'It upsets you. Do you trust me to write for you?'

'I have trusted you with my life, Jeanette; I can surely trust you to write a letter on my behalf.' He wiped the tears from his face; whatever was the matter with him? *Am I fit to travel alone? Will I find my way home?*

She started to write, giving the basic facts of the accident and of being brought to France and saying that he was about

278

to leave on his journey home. She read it aloud to him when she had finished.

'Thank you, Jeanette. That is exactly right.'

'I must say to you that you must take great care on the way home, for you are not yet fully recovered.' She put the letter in the envelope, sealed it with the resin and addressed it to *Mes demoiselles Maddeson, Beverley, Yorkshire, England.* That was what he had said and so she had written it.

She handed it back to him, and told him again, 'If you stay longer to recover, you will not be able to travel until the spring. But if you wish to go I will drive you in the cart to the ferry in Le Havre. It will be quicker than walking.'

'Will you do that for me? Will you be safe coming back alone?'

She smiled. 'I will take my trusty Chien,' she said, and the dog looked up and thumped his tail. 'He will take care of me.'

He nodded. 'Then it is time,' he said softly. 'I will miss you, Jeanette. You have been a true friend and I will never forget you.'

'Nor I you,' she murmured, and thought how strange fate was that they should meet in such a way only to part and never see each other again. 'I will be sad to say goodbye.'

'When shall it be?' he asked, for he was in her hands until they reached Le Havre.

'Tomorrow?' Better immediately, she considered, than wait a few days, not knowing what to say to one another.

He took a short sharp breath. So soon. But yes, better this way. He nodded. 'No long goodbyes?'

'*Non!*' she said, and rose from her chair. 'I will prepare food for your journey. Bread and cheese will sustain you until you reach England. You must change your French francs into English currency and then buy food. You will walk, yes? Or perhaps have a ride in a wagon if someone will stop?'

'I don't know,' he said. 'I've never done it before. I have always had a vehicle or travelled by train.' He gave a Gallic shrug and she laughed.

'There will not be enough money for either,' she said. 'Not once you have bought your ticket for the ferry.'

They rose early the next morning and he dressed warmly, putting on the woollen jumper which she said he could keep. He was doubtful about this, protesting that it contained her dreams of her brother, but she brushed that aside, saying it was no matter; she would keep his memory always in her heart.

She cooked him eggs for breakfast and plenty of bread, and gave him a parcel of food for the journey, bread and cheese and some ham that she had bought in the market; and then they were ready.

He brought out the cart and put the donkey into the traces. Chien came and sat watching him as if something different was happening this day. Roland patted his head and murmured that he would miss him and went inside to pick up his belongings.

'Take this,' she said, handing him a rucksack which she had brought out from the back of the cupboard. 'This is also something that he left behind. I have no use for it.'

He thanked her and asked, 'Does he have a name, this scoundrel of a man?'

She gave a small smile. 'If he had, then I have forgotten it. I have other more cherished memories to keep.'

'I wish I had something to give you to remember me by.' He spoke softly. 'But I came with nothing.'

'You did.' She nodded, keeping her words brief. 'Except for your black coat. I will keep that and wear it in summer and remember you.'

His tailcoat. Covered in dust and blood from his injuries. It was no use to him.

'Come,' she said briskly. 'We must be on our way, as we have no timetable for the ferries.'

He took a deep sighing breath, and as they went outside he turned and looked back at the cottage: not really a cottage at all, just a wooden structure, a shed, a hovel some might call it, but she had made it into a home, and made him welcome.

Chien jumped into the back of the cart and nuzzled into Roland's sleeve as he took up the reins. Then, sighing, he put his head on the rucksack.

'Chien will miss you,' she murmured, and he had no words to answer.

They spoke little on the journey, discussing the weather, that they were lucky it was such a fine morning: trivialities only to break the silence. It didn't take long, as the donkey was sprightly on his first outing of the day and there was no one else travelling on the length of the road until they came nearer to the port, when there was more traffic. They saw the funnel of a steamer from a mile away.

They drew up outside the ticket office and Jeanette jumped out to do the talking to the man inside. Roland watched her as she spoke, though he couldn't hear what they were saying. Instead he watched the tendrils of her hair bobbing about as she nodded or shook her head.

She came back to the cart and climbed in; she took a breath and said, 'There is a ferry leaving for Portsmouth in ten minutes. For Dover you must wait for the next sailing which will be late afternoon.' She indicated over her shoulder to the ticket office. 'He said that you can buy a ticket on board. I do not know which will be the best for you.'

He gave it only brief thought. He didn't want to wait until the afternoon. It was not yet eight o'clock. Portsmouth would be a good road to travel on; a major port, there might be a better chance of getting a lift from a wagon. He didn't need to go to London: he could just head north.

'Portsmouth, then,' he said. He nodded to confirm and looked at her, then clicked the reins and they moved off towards the ship.

Neither of them spoke as he took the rucksack from the cart and Chien jumped down and stood by Jeanette's side. She put her hand on the donkey's back and gathered up the reins.

'Well,' he murmured. 'What can I say? Thank you doesn't seem enough.' He felt the most awful sadness, depression and loneliness coming over him, drowning him almost in its intensity. 'I'll miss you, Jeanette. I cannot think of a single person who would have done for me what you have done.'

She shook her head, pressing her lips together. 'We have had a special friendship, *chéri*,' she said, her voice tight. 'One we will not forget.'

'Never,' he said, and putting his hand on her shoulder bent to kiss her cheek. 'Take care on the way home, and think of me sometimes and know that I am thinking of you.'

She gave him a brief kiss in return, one on each cheek, and then gave him a little push away. He walked towards the gangplank. It was empty; all the other passengers, if there were any, were already on board. He took a step on to it and then turned. She was moving the donkey to face the way they had come; Chien was standing stock still, poised, watching him. Roland stood as Jeanette climbed into the cart and called to the dog to get in, which he did, but with his eyes still looking back. Roland stepped on board and leaned on the bulwarks and some other distant memory returned.

Jeanette turned once and raised her arm in farewell and he did the same, and as she moved off Chien lifted his head and began to howl: a wailing, keening lamentation.

CHAPTER FORTY-FOUR

'If you're sure you don't mind?' Matty said to Stephen Nielsen. 'I hate to think we're taking up your time.'

'I don't mind in the least. I might have missed something last time.' He had it in mind to pay another visit to St Thomas's hospital. 'I'll go tomorrow.'

He had whispered previously to Louisa that if they'd been married then she could have gone with him. 'We could have visited a theatre,' he said. 'Or gone to a concert.'

'Well, we're not,' she told him, 'and at least going alone will concentrate your mind! Besides, how could I enjoy something as frivolous as a play when my poor nieces are in such a state of distress?'

'I'm sorry,' he said penitently. 'You're quite right. Poor Matty doesn't look at all well.'

'No, she doesn't.' Louisa sighed. 'She's taking everything on her shoulders.'

Gertrude was on the warpath. The day after she arrived in Beverley she took herself off to visit her brother Albert. *Fisher*, she'd fumed. What kind of Christian name is that? It was early, just after breakfast and too soon for formal visiting, so she knew that her brother and his wife would be at home. She rattled on the door with her walking stick and the maid came running.

'Mr Maddeson, please,' she said, stepping inside uninvited. 'Tell him it's his sister, Miss Gertrude Maddeson.'

The maid knew very well who it was, as she'd once felt the lash of the lady's tongue for dropping her gloves and there was no chance of her ever forgetting.

'I'll just get him, ma'am,' she said, scurrying away whilst Miss Maddeson paced the hall.

'Well, Albert,' she boomed at him when he emerged from the dining room, mopping his mouth with a linen napkin. 'This is a late hour for breakfast, but then I don't suppose you have any reason for rising early. What about your brother, eh?' she went on without giving him time to answer. 'What's to do? Have you instigated any searches? Been to London, or are you leaving it all to our young nieces?'

The questions were fired off one after another. 'Have you written to our mother? No? Martha has written to her but hasn't received a reply. Have you been in touch? Is she ill? Why hasn't she written back? Why haven't you been to see Roland's daughters?'

'Yes, please, I'll have black coffee, no milk.' She caught another maid quite unawares as the girl passed her on her way to the kitchen. 'Are you going to invite me in,' she barked at her brother, 'or do I drink my coffee out here in the hall?'

'Erm, sorry, yes, please come in.' He led her into a downstairs sitting room where the fire was not yet lit, and she gave an exaggerated shudder.

'Can you not afford the coal to light fires in all the rooms?'

'We don't usually have callers so early,' he managed to get in. 'If you'd let us know you were coming . . . Caroline has been to see Roland's daughters,' he added. 'They didn't seem to need any help. They told her that decisions were ongoing.'

'Decisions that they made themselves, because there was no one else to make any for them, apart from their lawyer,' she barked at him. 'A little advice, Albert, might have been helpful, and would have reassured them that someone cared. Telling them that you were going to move in with them was not helpful at all. So have you written to Mother? If she did receive Martha's letter she will no doubt be very worried about our brother.'

'No,' he said. 'I haven't. I, erm, I thought it would be better to write when there was something to tell.'

She snorted, not believing him at all. He had either not thought of writing to their mother, or had put it off for someone else to do.

'Is there any news?' he asked, after he had belatedly invited her to sit down and the maid had brought in the coffee.

'None,' she sighed, taking a sip of the coffee and pulling a face at its bitterness. 'He seems to have disappeared off the face of the earth. A friend of Mrs Walton's has gone back to London today to chase up on another idea. He's been already but drew a blank. It's a bad business, and those poor gels are suffering.'

'I'll do what I can,' he said eventually. 'I'll call in to see Martha, or go with her to see Garton. I suppose they are looking into all eventualities?'

'They are,' she said, putting down her half-full cup on a nearby polished table. 'I'll be going then,' she said, rising from the chair. 'Give my regards to your wife and tell her I'm sorry to have missed her,' she lied icily.

He gave a deep sigh. 'You frighten her to death, Gertrude,' he countered. 'She doesn't know how to react to you.'

She scowled at him. 'What? Does she not know after all these years that I like someone with stamina to stand up to me? That I can't be doing with anyone shilly-shallying and trying to please me? I suggest, Albert, that you take your wife in hand. Good day to you. I shall be staying with my nieces for several days; you know where to find me.'

He hurried after her to open the door. 'Goodbye, Gertrude,' he muttered. 'Thank you for coming.'

Stephen arrived once more at King's Cross station and headed out on to the concourse. What a business, he thought. I've never known anything like it. How on earth can anyone disappear so completely? It's as if he's been transported into thin air.

He looked about him. Last time he was here he'd noticed a lodging house, or it might have been a small hotel; the kind of place where businessmen who couldn't afford anything better might stay. It had looked tidy, and the doorstep and windows were clean; the sort of place he might have stayed in if he only wanted accommodation for a few days, as he did now.

But where was it? London was changing, if indeed it had ever stood still; there was constant building work in progress. It was a place he had loved when he was a young man; it was vibrant and colourful and he loved the busyness of it. Now, he became irritated with the crowds, the absence of cabriolets for hire and the beggars who were always present. Perhaps they had been there when he was a young man, but they had never bothered him; they would have assumed, he thought, that he didn't have any money to give away, and they would have been right. But his demeanour must have changed, for nowadays when he visited he was constantly approached with 'Spare a copper, guvnor?'

He saw a pair coming his way and moved off smartly. They probably knew what time the long distance trains arrived and made a beeline for the travellers spilling out of them. He turned a corner and there was the very lodging house that he was looking for. He went towards it. It was indeed clean and welcoming and he stepped inside.

The landlady greeted him and she too was neat, with a clean apron and cap, and he asked if she had a room for two or possibly three nights. She said that she had and he was welcome to take a look at it if he wished. He said he would and followed her upstairs.

What he saw pleased him and he paid her a deposit as she requested. 'The deposit is the equivalent of one night's stay, sir,' she said, 'and the price includes breakfast but not dinner.'

He left his overnight bag on the bed and left the lodgings. Might as well start immediately, he thought, and then find somewhere for supper. I'll buy an evening newspaper, have an early night and a prompt start in the morning.

If someone wanted to disappear, where would they go? He began thinking through various options. They could stay in London, of course, move from lodging to lodging, but sooner or later they'd need money for food and rent and it would show up in the bank records, and seemingly that hadn't happened.

Then there's the possibility of accident, amnesia, or – heaven forbid – death by means unknown, and if his belongings had been stolen . . . well, no one would know who he was. I could visit the morgue, I suppose, he thought gloomily, but I don't think I'm up to that, and anyway where would I start? There must be hundreds scattered about the city.

He continued walking, and then stopped. Flapping in the wind on a tall lamp post was a poster, and printed on it was *MISSING. Roland Henry Maddeson. Resident of Yorkshire.* Underneath were further details and the name of whom to contact, with a promise of a reward if information proved positive.

Mmm, he pondered. Will anyone stop to read it? I did, because I wrote most of it, but anyone else? Doubtful.

But he was wrong in this instance; he became aware of someone behind him and immediately put his hand to his pocket, even though it was empty. He turned and saw the two tramps he'd seen on his last visit, also looking at the poster.

'Do you know this geezer?' one of them asked him.

Stephen shook his head. 'No. Do you?'

The man peered closer and Stephen stood back as a whiff of gin and unwashed clothing wafted over him. 'Might do. He looks like some toff who got injured in a crash a while back.'

'Oh, yeh?' Stephen said indifferently, affecting a London accent. 'Mebbe worth a tanner from them as is lookin' for him. Where was this?'

The tramp patted the side of his nose. 'Ah, that'd be tellin', wouldn't it?'

'What yeh lookin' at?' his pal asked, looking over his shoulder. 'Is it that feller got knocked over up by St Thomas's?'

'Shut yeh mouth, yeh daft beggar,' he was told in no uncertain terms. 'Come on, let's be off. Cheerio, mate.'

Stephen pondered as he watched them depart. I'd swear they're the same pair I saw outside St Thomas's the last time I was here. That's where I'll head next. Worth another try.

But his enquiries were fruitless; none of the nurses he spoke to knew anything about the incident. He reported the episode of the tramps to the local police, where a young constable took details, but Stephen gathered that they were too busy to do anything about it at present, owing to a murder inquiry that had just come in after a young woman's body had been fished out of the Thames.

He spent another day making enquiries, thanked the landlady for her hospitality and reluctantly returned to Beverley the next morning with nothing more to report than he had on the previous occasion.

'You did what you could.' Louisa patted his hand.

'I just feel that I've missed something,' he murmured. 'Something that is within touching distance. St Thomas's is the key, but I can't turn it to find the answer.'

CHAPTER FORTY-FIVE

It was only a short crossing and few passengers were on it. Roland asked for coffee and a young cadet brought it to him and disappeared without taking payment. He sat on a bench on deck and watched the shores of France withdraw.

He drank the coffee, sipping it slowly and wondering how he would manage the journey home. Portsmouth had a long maritime history but that was all he knew; he had never visited. I'll head east, he thought. I really don't think I need to take the London road, unless by chance I could get a ride on a wagon heading that way and then I could take the Great North Road and head home. If I only had my horse, he mused. Star! I'd forgotten about him. I hope he's being looked after.

He began to feel cold and so went back into the saloon and found a quiet corner. He fell into a despondent mood, thinking of his daughters and wondering if they were managing without him. They would hardly believe what had happened to him. I've been away so long; over a month, Jeanette said, for I can't recall. They must be frantic with worry. He felt in his pocket for the letter to them and thought that he mustn't forget to post it.

It was early afternoon when they reached Portsmouth, and as he walked down the gangway, following other passengers, he saw that some of them were making their way towards a horse bus. I wonder where it's going, he thought, quickening his footsteps. If I could get on it, it might at least take me off the dock area and perhaps into the centre of Portsmouth and save me a mile or two of walking.

He saw the driver looking over his shoulder as if assessing whether anyone else was coming, and instinctively Roland began to run towards it. He climbed aboard and asked the driver where he was going. The driver looked at him and in a loud voice said *Portsmouth*, as if Roland were deaf; it wasn't until he sat down that he grasped that he had spoken to the driver in French. He also realized that not only had he not paid for the coffee he had drunk on board, he hadn't paid for his ferry ticket either.

He was aghast at his omission, but then a guilty elation swept over him: he might have enough money for a meal, or to pay a wagoner to give him a ride for a few miles. I will pay the ferry company when I arrive home, he thought. I'm no thief.

The bus was going as far as the railway station and the driver pulled up there. Passengers were paying him as they got off, and it was then that Roland realized that the only money he had was French: the money that he and Jeanette had made through selling their artefacts in the market.

He stood in front of the driver and showed him what he had in his hands. The driver sighed and shook his head and then waved him away, and although he was pleased not to have to pay, he worried that no shopkeeper or wagoner would accept payment in French francs.

Then the driver pointed him towards a building across the road; he obviously thought that Roland didn't understand English, so he raised his hand in thanks and crossed over. Portsmouth, like many other old English towns, had suffered poverty in its time, and there were many very old ramshackle buildings, but there were also others that were newly built and this was one of them. As he drew nearer he saw that it was a bank, and it was open.

He went inside and explained his difficulty, saying that he had lost his wallet and the only money he had was French and could they change it into English coinage.

He came out barely ten minutes later with English money in his pocket and looked towards the railway station; the driver was still waiting. He fingered the money in his pocket and drew out a coin, walked to the vehicle, and, again speaking in French, passed the coin to the driver, who tipped his finger to his hat.

I'm going to have to live by my wits, he thought as he shouldered the rucksack. Now for the journey home.

Matty and Julia were invited back to visit the lawyer's office. Timothy Garton was behind the desk and rose to greet them as they were ushered in.

'How are you coping?' he asked, looking first at Matty and then at Julia. 'Are you managing all right? Emotionally, I mean?'

'We're muddling through,' Matty answered after a pause. 'Better just now, as we have relatives staying with us; but Mr Nielsen has been on another visit to London and drawn a blank again. He thinks that something might have happened near St Thomas's hospital; there was an accident nearby the day after Papa went to London and he's made enquiries, but there's nothing to link it with our father.' She shook her head wearily. 'He's disappeared entirely.'

'Very well,' Timothy said earnestly. 'This is what I suggest should happen now. We haven't offered this up before as it might be abhorrent to you, but my father and I think that it is worth a try. We will contact the London newspapers. We'll write a short piece telling of a Yorkshire gentleman who has disappeared without trace whilst on a visit to the capital, and saying that his family are very anxious about him. We would need to put in a description of your father's height, colour of hair and eyes and the clothes he was wearing, and,' he paused for a second, 'offer a reward to anyone who can give a genuine lead to his discovery. But we have to be careful,' he added, 'or we'll have all the rogues of London saying that they know him and spoke to him only yesterday.'

'So why haven't you suggested this before?' Julia asked. 'Is there a specific reason?'

'Yes, there is. It's not only because ne'er-do-wells might try to claim the reward. If the newspapers got even an inkling that there might be a story here, they would find their way to Beverley and start poking about in the hope of a scandal over money, or – or something unsavoury that they could pounce upon. We won't put your name to it, or even where your father lives. Yorkshire is a big county, and although our company name will be given to the newspapers, we will ask for professional anonymity.'

Matty and Julia looked at each other and each nodded in agreement. 'Please go ahead,' Matty said. 'We must do something.'

None of them were inclined towards conversation, and the weather was dreary so no one went walking except Becca, who went on her daily visit to the Lawrences' stables to groom the horses but didn't stay as long as she used to, feeling the need to be at home. Faith was feeling a little better, and although pale and weak came downstairs every morning, but was unable or unwilling to paint or sketch. No one hassled her to do anything much, for everyone, including the doctor, agreed that her last illness had been exacerbated by her getting up too early. Stephen had gone back to Scarborough, but Louisa was reluctant to leave her nieces, and so was Gertrude.

Their uncle Albert came to see them as he had promised Aunt Gertrude, and they told him about the London newspaper suggestion. He was rather alarmed about the idea, and worried, he said, that they would have unsavoury people on their doorstep if the name should get out.

'We'll ask Aunt Gertrude to speak to them if anyone should come,' Julia said promptly. 'She'll send them off with a flea in their ear, won't you, Aunt?' She gave her a complicit smile. She was much bolder with Aunt Gertrude since staying with her and discovering that she wasn't as strict as she appeared to be.

'Humph!' came the answer. 'I most certainly will.'

Another issue that was worrying three of the sisters was Becca's birthday, which was coming up in about two weeks' time. She had said quite emphatically that she didn't want a celebration or gifts of any kind, and if her papa wasn't here to celebrate with her then she would forget it completely as if it never happened.

'Not even a cake?' Faith asked her. 'Surely a *little* cake would be all right? And Papa wouldn't like to think you were avoiding your birthday because of him, would he?'

'I don't want to talk about it,' Becca mumbled. 'And I don't want anyone to mention it again.'

Then there was another issue: Grandmama Maddeson still hadn't written in answer to Matty's letter. 'I sincerely hope that she isn't ill or bedridden,' Aunt Gertrude said gloomily. 'That would be the final straw. I don't fancy journeying to Italy in the winter.'

The others agreed, and Faith thought that the wonderful holiday they had all enjoyed so much was a thing of the past; she wondered if they would ever enjoy the like again. Communication from Mario had also faded away, probably because she hadn't written very often even before the worry over their father had obliterated any topic she might have wanted to share with him.

It was almost lunchtime three days later and Matty was in her room washing her hands and tidying her hair. She had asked Cook to bake a ham joint so that they could eat it hot today and cold tomorrow; she was heartily sick of planning meals for a family without an appetite. She had tried fish and various meats and sometimes soup, but everyone just picked at whatever was placed in front of them, eating to please rather than for enjoyment.

She heard the door bang and then running footsteps up the stairs; that would be Becca coming home for lunch. Aunt Louisa and Aunt Gertrude were playing cards in the downstairs sitting room, sitting close to the fire as the temperature had dropped in recent days. Julia was in the kitchen talking to Cook and Nunny, and Faith was upstairs doing who knew what but would be down to join them for their meal.

Matty heard the clatter of hooves and the sound of wheels and then men's voices, and she dashed to the window, ever alert to the possibility of her father's return. But it wasn't. A cabriolet had drawn up outside and a young man had his back to her as he and the driver opened the door to help someone down in a flurry of skirt, cape and shawls. The young man turned slightly and she gasped. Mario!

She ran downstairs, calling, 'Come quickly. I think it's Grandmama arriving!'

There was a bustle of commotion as everyone hurried out from wherever they were and rushed to the front door. Matty was there first, in time to see Mario carefully hand their grandmother down the path to the door.

Nunny appeared at the kitchen door, listened, and then called to Cook to prepare more vegetables, fill the kettle and put it on the hob. Then she summoned Betty Brown and disappeared into the kitchen once more.

'Well, my word, Mother,' Gertrude exclaimed, and kissed her mother's cheek affectionately. 'How pleased we are to see you. We were becoming very anxious.'

She took her other arm and led her inside and into the sitting room, and Matty blessed the fact that there was a bright fire burning.

Their grandmother shook off the restraining hands now that she was indoors and gazed appreciatively around. 'How lovely, my dears, to see you all, and the lovely old house! I haven't been back for so many years.' She plumped down into a chair. 'What news of my dear Roland? Has he been found? I looked for him on our journey here, but have not seen anyone who looked in the least like him. And ah, Mrs Nunnington,' she said, spotting Nunny. 'How kind. We are in great need of refreshment.' Nunny had reappeared with a jug of coffee and Betty Brown was behind her with a tray of china cups and saucers and biscuits.

'You all know my companion, Mario – where is he?' Nunny replied that he'd gone outside again to speak to the coachie, and Mrs Maddeson continued, 'He has looked after me during the whole of my journey. I declare I haven't wished for a single thing but it has appeared. What a good fellow he has been.'

She seemed remarkably sprightly for an elderly woman who had come on such a long journey, and in turn her granddaughters greeted her with a kiss and a dip of their knees. Even Louisa, who although not a relative remembered her hospitality when they had visited her in Italy, dropped a slight curtsey as she shook her hand.

After greeting her grandmother, Faith went into the hallway to find Mario. 'Please do come in,' she said, holding out her hand. 'I'm so pleased to see you, and thank you for bringing Grandmama to us.'

He bowed over her hand. 'I am very pleased to see you again,' he murmured. 'I have thought of you very often. I was honoured to be asked to escort your grandmother.' He turned to an alcove by the front door. 'I have brought this for your father, but I am so sorry that he cannot be here to see it just yet.'

'No!' Her voice cracked a little. 'We don't know where he is at present.' Then, as she looked towards where he was indicating, she said, 'It's a very large parcel you have brought!'

'It is,' he nodded. 'I would not have, erm – affording to have sent it but your grandmother said we could bring it with us. I was very carefully that it did not become damaged.'

His command of English seemed very much better than at their first meeting, apart from the odd word or two. 'What is it?' Faith asked. 'Are we allowed to know?'

'But yes.' He seemed surprised. 'Of course! It is the painting of his beautiful daughters, finished at last.'

CHAPTER FORTY-SIX

Roland found a village post office outside Portsmouth; he'd been lucky enough to get a lift in a delivery cart and this was as far as the driver was going; but he pointed out the cottage which served as a post office and general grocer's shop and Roland bought a stamp and handed the letter to the post mistress. She perused the address and looked up at him, but didn't question him.

The driver was still outside, talking to a wagoner, and Roland asked them for directions for the Great North Road. The men were curious as to where he was going and he just said 'North, near York', thinking that they might not have heard of Beverley.

'I can give you a lift to London,' the wagoner said, in a Hampshire dialect that Roland wasn't familiar with. 'I'm going to old Smithfield market with some sheep, if you don't mind the racket they make. The Great North Road starts there and you'd probably get a ride; the wagoners will have empty vehicles going home. They'll burn your ears off with their chat, though.'

'I don't mind that,' Roland said eagerly.

The first driver laughed and pointed a thumb at his companion. 'As if he won't,' he said. 'And you might not understand all he says. A proper Pompey man he is.'

When Roland looked puzzled, the wagoner said proudly, 'Portsmouth I am, born and bred as my father and grandfather before me. Bill's my name,' and he put out a hand to shake Roland's.

'I'm pleased to meet you, Bill, and I would appreciate a ride.' Roland couldn't believe his good fortune, and hoped that it would continue.

The sheep, as he had been warned, bleated mournfully all the way to London, but as the rain drizzled down the thought of the long walk he would have had to make if it were not for the wagoner's offer made him immensely grateful. Bill hauled a couple of sacks from the back of the wagon which they each draped over their shoulders, and, as Roland had been warned, Bill never stopped talking, but rarely sought an answer except when he asked Roland what had he been doing in Portsmouth, and said he sounded rather a swell, and wondered why he wasn't driving his own vehicle.

'It's a long story,' Roland sighed. 'I was injured and lost my memory, and with the best of intentions someone took me home with them, which happened to be in France. Somewhere on the way I lost my belongings, my coat, my hat and my money, so I was left with nothing.'

The man frowned. 'And have you got money now? You won't get far without it.'

'A little,' Roland confessed, 'which I was given; but that's why I'm walking home. I have nothing to identify me, so I can't go to a bank.' He gave an ironic grunt. 'You wouldn't believe the things I could tell you. I'm even wearing second-hand clothes!'

'Ah,' the wagoner said. 'I thought the voice didn't match the clothes.'

It was late afternoon by the time they reached Smithfield; there were empty pens available for Bill's sheep and he commandeered one of them. Some were filling up already for the next morning's market, while other traders were moving off, having sold their stock that day. Roland eyed these men, wondering in which direction they were heading. He asked the wagoner if he knew any of them and which road they would be using, and in response Bill narrowed his eyes as he looked over the many men who were on the move. Then he put two fingers to his mouth, gave a piercing whistle, and shouted 'Josh Barnes' and whistled again.

A tall, well-built man turned round, put his fists on his hips and looked to see who was calling his name. Bill waved an arm for him to come over and the man strolled across. Heavens, Roland thought. Nobody would want to start a fight with him. He had a shock of red hair, only half hidden beneath his cap, and was built like a prizefighter.

'Is he, er . . .'

'Safe?' Bill chuckled. 'He's a gentle giant. He never has any trouble because of his size, but he's as soft as a feather pillow. I think you might be in luck here. He lives in Alconbury, which is one of the old staging posts. It'll take some time to get there but will save you walking.'

Josh Barnes ambled over towards them. 'How do,' he said, nodding to them both.

'My friend here is looking for a ride to Alconbury, Josh,' Bill said. 'Any chance of that?'

'Aye,' Josh returned. 'As long as you don't want to talk. I'm just about done in.'

'I can take a turn with the driving if you want to have a sleep,' Roland offered. 'Does your horse know his way home?'

'Certainly does.' Josh grinned. 'Just turn his nose in the right direction and we'll be there in no time. You're very welcome.'

Roland shook hands with Bill and thanked him and walked with Josh to his wagon. The big man jumped into the back, stretched out, and promptly fell asleep, and Roland climbed into the driving seat. He was content to sit with the reins loosely held in his hands as the horse ambled home, picking up speed the nearer he came to Alconbury, and then turning down a quiet country lane where Roland drew him in and woke Josh. He thanked him for the ride, but didn't feel inclined to give him a tip as he might have done, considering that he had worked his passage, so to speak.

'Thanks, mate,' Josh said sleepily. 'Much appreciated. Good luck on your journey.'

They shook hands, and Roland once more shouldered the rucksack and went on his way.

Grandmama Maddeson had said she would stay for two weeks, but would not bother them with the making up a bed for her, and would take up residence at the Beverley Arms. They could send their driver to collect her each mid-morning.

Matty was relieved; her grandmother was a late riser and would probably have her breakfast in bed before getting ready to go out. She was obviously used to her own routine and Matty was happy to comply.

'Shall I come over and help you dress, Grandmama?' she asked, but was told no, Gertrude could do that, and surprisingly, they all thought, Aunt Gertrude was pleased to do so.

'But you will look after Mario, won't you?' her grandmother asked. 'He won't be any bother at all; he is very amiable.'

'Will it be all right to allow him to stay, Aunt Gertrude?' Matty asked out of her grandmother's hearing.

'Ye-es,' their aunt said. 'I suppose so.' She seemed just a little doubtful but made no more explicit objection, and later that afternoon their grandmother left for the Beverley Arms, saying she was tired after the journey and would retire early. Sam drove her there and Gertrude went with her to organize a maid to unpack her luggage and be on hand for the remainder of Mrs Maddeson's stay.

'I'm so pleased to see you, Mother,' Gertrude said, as she helped her mother off with her shoes and outdoor clothes and into her nightgown and dressing robe. 'We were becoming worried when there was no word from you.'

'I'm sorry.' Her mother sank down into an easy chair at the side of the bed and accepted the hot drink that Gertrude had asked the maid to bring up. 'I was waiting for Mario to give me a date when he could come with me. He is such a dear and I didn't want to inconvenience him, and I knew that you would be here to look after our girls.' She beamed up at Gertrude and reached to pat her hand. 'You were always reliable,' she said softly. 'Not a flibberty-gibbet like your mother.'

'You have a big heart, Mother,' Gertrude blinked, touched by her mother's words, 'and we all feel much more uplifted now that you are here.'

Towards evening there were two more callers at the door. Adam and Eliza had come to see them and hoped it wasn't inconvenient, which they all said it wasn't.

'We hoped you might have good news for us,' Adam murmured, and seemed dismayed when both Matty and Julia shook their heads and said they had not.

'Now here's a thing,' Gertrude said, as she reclined in a chair by the fire. 'Dear boy' – she was addressing Adam, who seemed startled – 'would your parents be terribly perturbed if we foisted a visitor on them?'

'I shouldn't think so,' he said, glancing at his sister. 'Would they, Eliza?'

Eliza shook her head. 'I don't think they'll mind in the least. Who is it, Miss Maddeson?'

'I don't know his surname,' Aunt Gertrude said. 'I only know him as Mario. Do you remember him from Italy?'

Eliza, catching Julia's eye, affected a swoon. 'I believe I do,' she smiled. 'It will be wonderful to introduce him to our parents, and if necessary he can always share with Adam.' She turned to her brother and batted her eyelashes at him.

Really, Adam thought, as his eyebrows rose. Eliza is learning about things that she shouldn't at that school in Switzerland.

'Where is he?' Eliza went on. 'We must go and say hello and invite him.'

'He's in the dining room with Faith,' Julia said, giving a little smile, perhaps the first in weeks. 'They're discussing art and Faith is displaying some of her sketches on the dining room table for his opinion. Seriously, we are so pleased, as Faith has not looked at any of her sketch books since Papa . . . well, in ages. Mario has managed to renew her interest. His surname is Alfonsi, Aunt Gertrude, and he is the one who is an extremely talented artist.'

'Good,' Gertrude said with a sigh. 'That's one potential difficulty averted.'

'What difficulty did you foresee?' Louisa asked; she had kept rather quiet in Mrs Maddeson's presence, but was now relaxing in a chair opposite Gertrude.

'Well, call me old-fashioned,' Gertrude replied, 'but having a young gentleman in a house full of young ladies, and a foreigner no less, at such a difficult time – well, I believe we must all behave with absolute decorum to avoid the slightest hint of gossip or innuendo, even though there is nothing to gossip about.'

Louisa thought seriously about the possibility, which she considered to be highly improbable, but conceded that Gertrude had a point. She even reflected that perhaps it was fortunate that Stephen had returned to Scarborough, for even though he hadn't stayed overnight at the Maddesons' home he had been visiting an eligible widow.

She nodded her agreement to Gertrude's discourse, but her private opinion was that it was time for change if young women couldn't invite male friends to their homes without a chaperone or their parents being present. Then she remembered that Mrs Maddeson had had no such qualms about inviting Mario to escort her all the way to England, so there was something appealing after all in becoming elderly and being able to do and say just whatever one wanted. Gertrude had managed it, much earlier in life, just by standing up for herself.

There's a knack to it, she deliberated, and you have to be prepared; but I want love in my life more than my independence, so I will marry Stephen, knowing that he will love me and I will love him in return.

*

Early the next morning Mrs Nunnington opened the front door to the postman's knock. 'My word, Jones,' she muttered. 'Whatever brings you to 'front door? No parcel to be signed for, so what's wrong with 'back door? Gone up in 'world, have we?'

'No, Mrs Nunnington, we haven't, but I ain't sure if this letter is meant for this residence.' He peered at the envelope in his hand. 'It says 'ere . . .' He held it away from him the better to see. 'Well, it says Maddeson right enough, but I can't mek out what words precede it.'

'Give it here,' she said, taking it from him, and she too held the envelope at arm's length. 'Mmm,' she mumbled. 'That's a conundrum all right. Wait here a minute,' and she shut the door on him, leaving him on the doorstep.

'Miss Martha,' she called up the stairs. 'Are you about?'

Matty opened the dining room door. 'I'm here, Nunny. What is it?'

'It's a letter. I can't make out if it's – well, it must be for this household as it says Maddeson, but . . .' She handed it over to Matty. 'Is it for us – for you?'

Matty's lips moved. '*Mes demoiselles* Maddeson,' she murmured. 'Oh!' she said, putting her hand to her mouth. 'It is, but who do we know in France?'

'Is it your father's hand?' Nunny spoke in barely a whisper.

'No. I don't recognize it at all, but it is for us.'

Nunny marched to the front door and opened it. 'Thank you, Jones. It is for us,' she called, and shut the door again.

'Julia, Faith, Becca!' Matty called upstairs. 'Do we know anyone in France? This is ridiculous,' she muttered. 'We don't know anyone in France, but – could it be Sybil? I haven't heard from her for so long . . .' She took a deep breath. 'But it isn't her writing, and it has an English postage stamp on it.' She peered at it, attempting to make out the postmark, but it was smudged and partly obliterated, though she thought she could make out a P and an S.

Her sisters hurried down the stairs. 'What?' they said. 'What? Is it news?'

'I don't know,' she said breathlessly, and they followed her back into the dining room. 'Should we wait for Aunt Gertrude and Aunt Louisa?'

'I'm here.' Louisa, fully dressed, came through the open door. 'Has something happened?'

'We don't know,' Matty said. 'Becca, run up for Aunt Gertrude. Ask her to come down; in her dressing gown, if she wishes.'

But Gertrude was halfway down the stairs already, and in her dressing gown, having heard the excited voices. 'What is it?' she said, and stared at the unopened envelope in Matty's hand. 'Open it, then,' she said. 'If it's addressed to you.'

'To us,' Matty emphasized. 'It's not Papa's hand,' she added. 'We mustn't get too excited, and it says *Mes demoiselles*.' She looked at each of them in turn and said with a catch in her voice, 'Papa would never call us that, so it can't be.'

'Open it, Martha,' Aunt Gertrude said gently. 'That's the only way we're going to find out.'

It was the strangest of envelopes, Matty thought as she tore into it with a fingernail. Homemade, she thought, as a child might fashion one, and the single sheet inside was of the coarsest of paper. Everyone clustered round her to see it and took a concerted breath.

'It's written in French!' she said. 'Two different hands.' Tears began to fill her eyes and flow on to her cheeks and her sisters reached out to touch her hand, elbow, shoulder. 'But – I think the first hand might be Papa's.'

She began to sob, and her sisters began to weep with her as she started to decipher the meaning. 'It is,' she said through her tears. 'And he's alive and coming home.'

CHAPTER FORTY-SEVEN

'I don't understand,' Julia said. 'Why would Papa ask anyone else to write for him?'

'He says he's been ill and lost,' Louisa said gently. 'Perhaps he isn't well enough yet to write for himself.'

'Then how will he get home if he's still in France?' Faith asked. 'Will someone bring him, do you think? I know from when I have been ill that I couldn't possibly travel alone, and especially not abroad.'

'Perhaps the person who has written the letter will bring him,' Becca chipped in. 'If it's a man and strong enough to help him.'

It's a woman's hand, I feel sure, Louisa thought. The fine writing and manner of language seems womanly to me, but would a woman travel alone with a stranger?

'We must wait and see,' Aunt Gertrude said positively, 'but I think you ought to show the letter to the Gartons, Martha. We must make sure that it is genuine, although I'm inclined to think that it is; and since that is the case we should tell your grandmother too. I'll go now and visit her; she might still be in bed but she will be pleased to hear that he is at least . . .' She hesitated, and they realized that their stern and sometimes inflexible aunt was as anxious as any of them. 'At least' – she stumbled over her words – 'alive, although not well.'

'May I come with you, Aunt Gertrude?' Becca asked. 'I'd like to, and you ought not to be going alone.'

'That is extremely kind of you, Rebecca,' her aunt agreed, and the others exchanged amused glances, for although no one was in doubt that Becca genuinely wished to escort her aunt, she would also be missing some of her morning lessons.

They couldn't settle to anything, though they tried to concentrate on normal household tasks. Matty told Nunny about the letter, for she was loitering in the hall trying to glean information, and she in turn told Cook and Betty Brown, then Sam, who was dispatched with a note to their uncle and returned with a message that he would call that morning. Betty Brown was then sent out to the Gartons to ask if the Misses Maddeson might call in the afternoon.

'Just as well it's happened now, Miss Matty,' Nunny said, forgetting again to say Miss Martha, as she so often did when she was overwrought. 'Because there's another grocery bill to pay, and then there's Cook and Betty Brown. I don't mind waiting for mine, my needs are few, but what to do about Sam? Mr Maddeson generally sees to Sam's wages.'

Matty had been paying for food, laundry and various sundry items from her own money as the bank manager had suggested she should, saying rather sternly to her, as if she were a child, that it wasn't wise to keep tradespeople waiting for the payment of bills, as rumours of monetary difficulties could spread so easily. Disappointingly, he had otherwise been rather offhand, she considered, and hadn't proposed any other course of action, and the time was now rapidly coming up when she would have to pay the regular household staff or possibly even lose their services.

I can quite see, she mused, that running a household isn't easy, especially when paying household staff, who need their money as desperately as people working in trade or on farms or in any kind of commerce. Our servants have a warm place to work, plenty to eat and work clothes provided. However do workers manage who don't live and work in such conditions?

Her eyes had been opened and she had discussed it with Julia. 'We haven't had to think on such subjects,' she'd said. 'I know we have always given to the poor and taken food to the workhouse, but it's not enough. We've given only tokens.'

Julia had nodded. 'I know. I've been thinking about it since Adam told me about the Ragged Schools. What a derogatory, belittling name to give a school for poor children. What a stigma! How humiliating; it will stay with them for the rest of their lives and they will never overcome it!' Her face had been set with anger as she seethed, when Matty had read out the letter professing to have come from their father. 'I will do something about it, Matty. I swear I will.'

Matty had agreed. 'Yes,' she said. 'We will, but first we must wait for Papa to come home. He is our priority, Julia. We must have him home to make him well again, no matter what has befallen him.'

They waited and waited and another week went by. Each day they watched from their windows and wondered what was keeping him. Julia walked to the railway station to check on the timetable of trains from London, for surely that would be the way he would come; or would he hire a carriage? From which port would he sail? Le Havre or Calais? To Dover, Southampton or Portsmouth? Where in France had he been? They had no way of telling, and once again they began to worry.

Their grandmother too began to be uneasy over the delay. Gertrude said she would take a room at the hotel to be with her; Louisa began to dither about going home but was reluctant to leave. Mario felt that he was overstaying his time as a visitor with the Chapmans even though they said he was welcome, but he was also anxious that he should be returning to Italy with Signora Maddeson before any bad weather began, as it could so easily in Italy.

Mrs Nunnington had the house spotless: every china ornament was washed and the glass and crystal sparkling, the furniture polished. Cook prepared all Mr Maddeson's favourite

307

food: fowl and other meats were bought from the butcher, fish from the fishmonger, fresh eggs from the market, and all placed in the cool larder; fruitcakes and biscuits were baked and stored in tins.

Yet still he didn't come.

He had never been so tired, wet or weary. His lifts on wagons, donkey carts or carriers had been few and, although given freely and mainly willingly, took him no more than a few miles at a time on his journey. The Great North Road was often deserted; travellers nowadays took advantage of the relative comfort and speed of the railway trains that were now criss-crossing the country, particularly north from London. The carriage journey by road was long and arduous.

He had slept in barns and abandoned farmhouses in the company of rats and owls, had taken gulps of water at village pumps and been given hunks of bread by people much poorer than he.

He had reached Stamford and then turned off towards Colsterworth, where he was offered a bed for the night by a cottager for the price of sixpence, a bargain, he thought; and when he was given a breakfast of thin gruel and a slice of bread he gave his hosts a shilling in gratitude, which was made even more pleasurable when he saw their delight. He remembered the name from school as the birthplace of Isaac Newton and thought that now he would always remember it. The traffic was busier here, too, but no one stopped.

He continued on towards Grantham and then Newark, where he bought provisions with his ever diminishing money and was offered a lift in the back of a cart which he shared with a pig that was being taken to market. He scratched it behind its ears and wished it all the best and was dropped off again. He was cheered considerably when he saw a post sign for Bawtry and Doncaster, feeling that he was almost on home ground.

But the rain came down again after a few days of dryness and his progress slowed as he had to shelter wherever he could. He had never felt as alone as he did now, and he wondered if he would ever get home or see his daughters again. He thought of each of them and prayed earnestly that they would keep safe; he prayed as he had never done since his wife had died, and wondered, as he had back then, what evil he had done to deserve this.

He became melancholy and depressed, thinking back to the life he had had, one of comfort and wealth, and the contrast he had seen and endured on this journey. If I ever reach home I will change my life, he vowed, his hands gripped tightly into fists. I will become a better man than I am now. He thought of Jeanette and the sacrifices she had made to care for him. How beautiful she was, both in face and spirit, and he realized how much he missed her.

He curled up into a ball. He had found an abandoned hut in the middle of a field and climbed up into a hay loft. He was so cold and his clothes so wet that he wondered, should he die of pneumonia during the night, would he ever be found.

But he awoke as a grey dawn was heralded by the sound of pigeons on the roof above him, and the rain had stopped. He felt in his rucksack and found one small chunk of dry bread. 'Riches,' he murmured, and tore into it. He shook himself down, descended the ladder and set off once again.

He nodded off to sleep during the next stage of his journey; a cart had pulled up alongside him and the driver offered him a lift. When he woke he was on the outskirts of Doncaster; he gave the driver sixpence and apologized for his poor company.

'It's all reet,' the driver said. 'I'm glad to give a ride to anybody who needs it and I'm not too bothered about yattering on.'

Roland shook his hand and thanked him again and moved on, and within an hour was offered another ride which took him as far as Thorne Moors and Airmyn across the peat bogs.

The further he travelled the more his spirits were uplifted, and he thought that he would possibly survive after all.

He walked for the next two days without seeing a soul except for a woman in a village shop where he bought a penny loaf. She didn't speak to him and stayed well behind the counter; when he thanked her, giving her the penny, she looked sharply at him, and then he caught sight of his reflection in the window as he left and realized that even his own mother wouldn't recognize him, with his long hair and beard and scruffy clothes.

The following morning it had started raining again before another lift came along; he had been walking for three or four hours, and could only guess at the time as he had no timepiece. When he heard the clatter of wheels and the pounding of hooves he looked back to see a two-horse carriage coming towards him. He stepped on to the grassy verge to let it pass, but to his surprise and joy it pulled up a few yards further along. The driver looked over his shoulder and called out, 'Do you want a lift?'

He was unspeakably grateful as he climbed aboard next to the driver, for he had thought he couldn't walk much further. The carriage was empty and the driver said he was going as far as the village of Walkington, near Beverley, to pick up his master at a big house there. 'Not been afore,' he said, 'but I've a rough idea where it is.'

Roland huffed out a breath. 'Oh, I know it well,' he gasped, his voice cracking. 'I know the way.'

They travelled companionably and Roland couldn't grasp how lucky he had been. As they progressed he saw his own county coming gradually nearer; saw in the distance the wooded Wolds with a grey mist hovering over them, and knew that he would soon be home.

He was dropped off in Walkington. Three miles to Beverley. He and Constance, on fine summer's days, used to walk from their house in Beverley past the racecourse and up to the top of Westwood, and on to the village of Walkington to visit friends. He found he was shaking, not only with fatigue but with emotion too, as he waved his new friend goodbye. He watched him drive away down the main street and then turned about. It was not yet dark, but dusk was drifting in. He hitched up his almost empty rucksack on to his shoulders and set off again.

By the time he reached the top of Westwood he was staggering. Exhausted, he sank down on to the grass verge and looked at the town below. In the distance he saw the towers of the Minster dominating the darkening sky. His eyes ran along the skyline and he saw St Mary's where he had been married and their daughters baptized, but his gaze shifted and was now moving down to the green of Westwood and the Hurn, and at its end, with smoke issuing from the chimneys and lamplight flickering in the windows, he saw his beloved home waiting for his return.

Becca's thirteenth birthday hadn't been mentioned; she'd said she didn't want to talk about it, and they all honoured their promise that they wouldn't. But each of them had made cards and gifts, for they considered this a special birthday when Becca was out of childhood and had grown to be on the verge of womanhood.

Becca had wept that morning and then they all did. A birthday without their papa didn't seem right.

As the eldest daughter, Matty had made a decision. She intended, when this week was over, to visit the Gartons with Aunt Gertrude and discuss their position regarding the house. Timothy had already advised her, on the day the letter arrived, that there was no need at all to be worried, but the fact that their uncle and his wife had begun to call more often made them feel threatened.

They had put Becca's birthday cards on the sitting room mantelpiece and arranged greenery and flowers they had bought in the market in vases which they placed on the windowsill and tables. Three of the sisters had dressed in their prettiest dresses for lunch and waited for Becca to come back from the stables as usual, not expecting anything special.

Gertrude and Louisa were still staying with them, and Grandmama was planning on going back to Italy the following week; Mario had to get home again to help in his family's bakery shop and continue his studies for art college. Their grandmother didn't look well. The anxiety over Roland had hit her more forcibly here than it had in Italy.

She had said that she would come for luncheon, and Mario would come too. Matty would have liked to ask Eliza and Adam, but mindful of Becca's wishes, she didn't, although they and Dorcas too had called this morning with cards for her.

Becca was thoroughly miserable and made no comment on her sisters' pretty dresses. Nor did she mention the flowers and the small pile of cards awaiting her, as she knew she would cry and spoil things for everyone else.

Lunch was a forced affair, with everyone putting on a brave face and chatting about everything except what was on their minds. Afterwards Faith played the piano and sang; she had a sweet and gentle voice and many of them noticed how Mario watched her. They were pleased that although she was sometimes tired after her illness she was making more effort with her sketching, with Mario's encouragement. They were all longing to see the painting that he had brought with him, but none of them could find the courage to open it.

Everyone drifted off in different directions. Aunt Gertrude and her mother settled down for a nap by the fire; Louisa went upstairs to put things in her carpet bag, for she intended to go home for a few days, and then return. Matty went to the kitchen to talk to Nunny and Cook about the evening meal and Julia went up to her room. Faith brought her sketch book down, as Mario had said he would teach her the tricks of perspective, and Becca wandered about, took Pug for a short walk in the garden, and then went upstairs to her room.

She tidied her bookshelves and put away in her wardrobe the clothes that she had strewn across the bed, for although she hadn't intended to dress in anything particular for lunch she knew that her sisters had made a discreet effort to make it special for her. But it couldn't be, she'd told herself after trying on one thing after another before finally deciding on a dark blue velvet dress which she knew suited her fair colouring. Shall I change again into an old dress, she wondered now, or leave this on for the evening? I should leave it, I suppose, she sighed; it would be rude, especially as our grandmother is here, and our aunts, and I know the others are trying to make things nice for me, even though I asked them not to.

She wandered over to the window. Dusk was closing in, and the mist gathering above the tops of the trees in Burton Bushes made them look ghostly and ethereal. Faith should see this, she thought. It would make a good painting. The horses that were often to be seen training on the racecourse had been taken back to the stables; the cattle that normally wandered freely over the meadowland had been put in the cattle sheds now that it was coming up to winter. There was no one about.

She glanced down York Road in the direction of North Bar and the town, and all was quiet. She crossed her arms and sighed and looked upwards again to the top of Westwood Road, which a moment ago had been empty.

But now it wasn't. From out of the mist she could make out someone walking down the hill: a man, she supposed, as a woman wouldn't be walking alone at dusk, except perhaps a servant girl; they were allowed to do more things than someone like her, which wasn't fair, she considered. She wasn't even permitted to walk home from the stables at dusk.

Yes, it was a man: she could see that quite clearly now by the way he was walking. He had a peculiar stumbling gait and he kept stopping, and she wondered if he were drunk. And oh, what a lot of hair and a great thick beard she saw as he came nearer. He was a tramp, she decided, and wondered if

313

he would come to their back door begging for food. Should I warn Nunny, she wondered? But Nunny would have locked the door; she never left it unlocked at night, for it would be so easy for anyone to slip in. If he knocked she would give him something, of course, a hunk of bread or a slice of cake; she always did, muttering 'But for the grace of God . . .'

What is he doing? She exclaimed. He's standing by our gate! What is he up to? Who does he— Her heartbeat quickened and she gave a little moan. He looked up as if he had heard her, though she hadn't spoken aloud, and stared at her. She saw his lips move. What was he saying? *Becca*, was he saying? He was. It was – it was Papa! She screamed and ran from the room. '*Papa*,' she shrieked. 'It's Papa!' She ran down the stairs, almost tripping in her haste and catching hold of the banister rail. 'Matty. Julia, Faith, *everybody*! It's Papa! He's come home at last! And it's my birthday!'

CHAPTER FORTY-EIGHT

Everyone who was upstairs hurried down and those who were down or nodding off in their chairs jumped, startled by Becca's screams as she rushed down into the hall. 'Everybody,' she shouted. 'Come quickly!'

She fumbled with the lock and key, and suddenly Mario appeared behind her, grasped the door knob and pulled open the door, then stood back as their father— could this man with a thick and ragged beard and a grey face beneath it, in sodden clothes and worn shoes, really be their father? Unmistakably, it was, and to their great consternation he fell through the door and landed in a crumpled heap on the floor.

They gathered round him, weeping and exclaiming. Nunny took one glance and hurried back to the kitchen stairs where Cook and Betty Brown and Sam were standing, alerted by the commotion. She sent Betty running to fetch Dr Laybourn immediately, whilst she told Sam to go in and help the master.

Sam and Mario picked him up and carried him through into the sitting room, where Matty pulled the blanket from the back of the sofa where they set him down and wrapped it round him. Julia knelt and took off his boots and socks and turned to ask Nunny to bring another blanket and a towel to dry him, but Nunny had gone already, acting on her own initiative as she always did.

He was given sips of hot sweet tea laced with a drop of brandy to revive him, for he seemed to have collapsed from sheer exhaustion. Matty held the cup for him, for he was shaking so much that he couldn't hold it, and Faith and Becca took it in turns to hold and stroke his hands.

'Dearest brother' – Gertrude stood over him with tears streaming down her face – 'wherever have you been?'

Becca looked at her. She had never seen her aunt so emotional, but then everyone was crying, including Grandmama, who had her hands to her mouth whilst Aunt Louisa had an arm round the elderly lady's shoulder and was gently patting it.

Dr Laybourn was enjoying a nap when Betty knocked hard with the knocker and rang the bell too, in case no one heard. He immediately put on his coat and hat and picked up his medical bag and hurried on foot to the house, coming straight in and being ushered into the sitting room by Mario, who had discreetly withdrawn into the hall and sat waiting at the bottom of the stairs in case he might be useful, which he would be, for the doctor ordered a warm bath for Mr Maddeson, when he had recovered a little, before being put to bed.

'He needs rest,' he warned. 'Don't bother him with questions. He has been through some kind of ordeal and received an injury to the back of his head. Be careful when washing his hair,' he told Mario, assuming he was some kind of manservant. 'Don't break open the wound.'

Mario didn't understand all he was saying, but Matty and Julia were both listening and asked if he would help Sam to carry their father upstairs when they thought he was steady enough.

Roland put his head back and closed his eyes. He knew he would wake up in a minute and find himself in a nest of straw; he felt his legs twitching as he walked. 'Is it morning?' he muttered. 'How many more miles to home? Jeanette?' He began to gabble in French, and they all looked at each other. 'How long a journey?'

'He's hallucinating,' Gertrude murmured. 'Confused.'

If his daughters had expected that their father would return home just as he was when he had left, they now knew they were mistaken. He must be given time to recover, Matty thought, and Julia, who had caught sight of the sticky, bloody patch of hair at the back of his head, wondered who or what had caused the injury. Faith and Becca pondered on who Jeanette might be. Was she the woman who had written the letter to say that he was safe?

He was falling asleep, his head nodding, and when Nunny came to say they had hot water prepared for the hip bath in Mr Maddeson's dressing room, Sam and Mario between them carried his dead weight upstairs. They closed the door on the hovering daughters and carefully undressed him, covering him with a bath sheet before lifting him into the warm water, and he sighed, 'Oh, dear God, am I really home, or in heaven?'

The two young men smiled, and Sam said, 'You're home, sir, and we're very pleased to see you back.'

Roland gazed at him through half-open eyes. 'I forget your name.'

'Sam, sir. I'm your groom and look after Star and your carriages.'

Roland blinked up at him. 'Star! Yes, of course. Now I remember. And Chien, is he with you?'

'I don't know a horse called Chien, sir,' Sam answered. 'He's not one of ours.'

Mario looked up and gave a slight frown, but the doctor had said no questions, so he simply asked, 'Is it all right to wash your hair, sir?' But Roland had fallen asleep.

Mario carefully washed his head and beard, cutting away the matted hair but leaving the scab that was covering the injury, whilst Sam washed his body, arms and feet. Roland didn't move until they began to lift him out of the bath, when he tried to put his feet to the floor, but his legs wouldn't hold him; they towelled him, wrapped him in a clean sheet and

317

then a blanket and helped him to the bedroom, where Nunny had the sheets turned back and the pillows plumped up. They deposited him smoothly into bed, then left the room for the sisters to administer to their father.

They each in turn kissed his forehead, and smiled as they saw him returned to the father they knew, in spite of the now clean but still long beard and hair. They stood looking down at him as he lay comfortably sleeping in his own bed, and Matty said softly, 'I think we should bring Grandmama and Aunt Gertrude up to see him now that he is clean and recognizable; I don't believe they thought it was really him.'

'I don't know if he remembered that it was my birthday,' Becca said softly. 'But he was saying something when he looked up and saw me at the window.'

'I think he was trying to say happy birthday, Becca,' Faith said gently. 'He wouldn't have forgotten, but he might have had the days mixed up if he'd travelled far.'

'I wonder why he was coming down the hill?' Julia said, and looked at the others. 'Did someone bring him?' Then she echoed her aunt Gertrude's words. 'Wherever has he been?'

Over the next few days Matty and Julia wrote letters to those who had been concerned. Dorcas and Timothy Garton came to see them immediately to offer their heartfelt relief and pass on their father's good wishes; Uncle Albert Fisher – Matty and Julia had decided they would use both of his first names until such time as he might settle on just one – was told that their father couldn't see anyone yet as he was still sleeping and only waking to take a few spoonfuls of soup; the bank manager bowed and scraped and was all smiles now that he knew his client was safely home, and was left wondering why Miss Martha Maddeson was so cold towards him.

Mario had told the Chapmans, and Eliza and Adam came to call, as did the Lawrences, but they kept the house quiet as Dr Laybourn, who had called each day, had advised.

Their grandmother had decided to return home. Mario had stressed they should because of the imminent winter weather, unless she wished to stay in England until the spring, but he must return to Italy in any case, as he must work. Grandmama told her family that reluctantly she would return now that she knew her son was safe and in good hands. She told Faith she would be pleased to see her in the spring if someone would bring her. 'The weather would be good for you, my dear; the sunshine will warm your bones.'

Faith kissed her cheek. 'I will think of it very positively, Grandmama,' she said. 'But first I must be sure that Papa is well.'

Stephen came to Beverley to escort Louisa back to Scarborough; she had written to him to tell of Roland's safe return and told him she would stay a few more days. When he arrived Stephen asked if he might see Mr Maddeson; it was agreed that he could, as their father was feeling so much better and was now sitting in his room in a chair by the window. Stephen stayed with him for about half an hour while they talked, and Roland told him that he would come downstairs the next day before his mother left for Italy.

Faith came to ask her father a question that same day. He was still wearing his night attire and a warm dressing robe with a blanket over his knees; his hairdresser had been to trim his hair and beard, and although he said he was feeling much better he couldn't yet recall how he had received the injury to his head or how he had arrived in France.

'I have two questions actually, Papa,' Faith said, 'if they're not too taxing for you. The first is, may we look at the painting that Mario has finished and brought with him? He calls it *Quattro Sorelle* and says it is a gift for you. Can you remember it?'

'Yes, I can,' her father said softly. 'It is a painting of my beautiful daughters.' He looked around the drawing room, where he was sitting by the fire and everyone was about to gather before his mother departed. He pointed to the opposite wall, where there was a painting of their mother. 'I shall put it there, and I will put your mama over there.' He pointed to the corner wall by the window on the same side. Looking carefully where he had indicated, Faith realized that the new painting would face the room and be reflected in the mirror that hung above the fireplace. 'That way she will be able to watch you and see how you have all changed from children into adulthood.' He put his head to one side. 'And the other question?' he asked amiably.

'It was when Mario and Sam helped you upstairs and into the bath—'

'Did they?' he asked. 'I don't recall that.'

'You'd just arrived home not two hours before,' she said. 'You had a warm bath and were then put to bed—'

'Like a naughty schoolboy,' he murmured vaguely.

'Sam, the one who looks after the stable,' she reminded him, 'told you that he looked after Star and you remembered, and then,' she added slowly, 'you asked if he also looked after Chien.' She paused. 'And Mario said that Sam said that you'd never had a horse called Chien. But *le chien* means . . .'

Roland smiled. 'Dog! Sam wouldn't know that.' Then his smile faded. 'Jeanette,' he murmured. 'I must write and tell her I've arrived home at last. She will worry.' He gazed at Faith and then at Matty and Julia, who had come into the room followed by Becca. 'How long have I been at home?'

'Less than a week, Father,' Matty said. 'Does it seem longer?'

He didn't answer, as everyone else was coming into the room to bid him goodbye. Stephen had hired a cabriolet to take Gertrude home and he and Louisa to the railway station; Roland's mother had hired one to take her and Mario all the way to Dover, as she didn't like the noise and bustle of the trains.

'Wait, wait!' Faith said. 'You must all see Mario's painting.'

'It is no matter,' Mario said, as if embarrassed by any fuss. 'You may look later at your leisure.'

'No, now!' Matty and Julia said simultaneously. 'Please.'

Scissors and a sharp knife were found to cut the string that bound the parcel and slit the brown paper, and gradually each corner of the plain wood frame was revealed.

'It is a simple gift, signore,' Mario said hastily. 'For your pleasure and mine for the meeting of you and your daughters.'

He carefully pulled off the brown paper and they all drew or exhaled a breath. For the sisters it was as if they were looking in a mirror and seeing their reflections, except that they were standing in Vista Lago at the bottom of the staircase, bathed in the rainbow glow from the windows. Mario had accomplished the finer details of their gowns, the flowers and leaves that were scattered about their skirts, as beautifully as in the sketches that Faith had seen pinned up in his studio. Their slippered shoes had a silky sheen; the colour of the threads on the laces were delicately and finely painted, as were the silky tasselled trimmings.

It looked as if he had noted every single fibre, every stitch, and every shining hair on their heads, each single eyelash and each pair of tender eyes.

'Thank you,' Roland said brokenly, and it seemed that nothing more could be added; any other superfluity would have been excessive.

They waved goodbye from the door, except for Roland who stood by the window with his right arm raised and blew a kiss to his mother.

'Come and sit down with me,' he said, as his daughters came back inside. 'Tell me what you have been doing whilst I've been away, and I will tell you as much as I can remember.'

'We'd rather hear of what you have been doing, Papa,' Matty said. 'We've all been very worried about you.'

He nodded. 'I'm sure that you must have been,' he said. 'I was ill after my injury and I had amnesia. I had no idea of my name or where I was from, but after a time I began to recall several things and I remembered your mother and that I had children. But I don't remember what happened to put me into a hospital bed.'

The sisters looked at each other. It had been worse than they had thought or imagined.

'But first of all,' he continued, 'and most important, I must tell you about Jeanette. The woman who saved my life.'

CHAPTER FORTY-NINE

The following March

Who would have thought? Matty idly flexed the fingers on her left hand and watched the diamonds in her ring sparkle in the sunlight. Who would have thought that so much could happen in two short years? And who would have thought that the change would have begun on my eighteenth birthday whilst we were in Italy, when Tim made the sudden decision to travel to join in the celebration.

I didn't realize, of course, not then, that the spark had kindled and he saw me not as a schoolgirl friend of his sister Dorcas – for we had known each other for years – but as someone else entirely; or that is what he said, when he asked me . . . She put her hand to her mouth to hide her smile from two of her sisters.

'We can see you,' Faith piped up from her corner, where she was idly drawing in her sketch pad. 'Don't think we can't. Showing off your diamonds!'

'Oh, but I'm not, I'm not,' Matty protested; she never could tell when she was being teased.

Faith laughed and then lifted up the drawing for her to see. Matty came across and took it from her. 'How clever you are, Faith. It's so good.'

Faith took it back and sighed. 'You always say that, Matty, and it's not that special. It's very difficult to portray diamonds with a pencil.'

'It wasn't the ring I meant!' Matty protested. 'It's the sketch of me, even though you've only drawn me in profile; look, Becca. You can tell that it's meant to be me, can't you?'

Becca looked up from her book on horsemanship. 'Mmm,' she said. 'It's you all right, but then you're the only one with a ring, so it couldn't be anyone else.'

'Could be someone else,' Faith murmured, pushing a long strand of hair behind her ear and then hovering with her pencil. 'Several people, in fact.'

'Aunt Louisa, I suppose we could count her, but then she's a married woman now, and besides, she's dark-haired.' Becca put her book down and said dreamily, 'Wasn't it a lovely wedding?' Now that she had reached her fourteenth year, Becca's views on life and love were changing. 'She looked so beautiful and Stephen so handsome and happy; and St Mary's church full of flowers. Where did they get such lovely flowers from so close to Christmas?'

Matty gazed into space. 'And how special that they could walk hand in hand across the road from their two houses and down the church path. So very romantic,' she murmured.

Becca raised her eyebrows quizzically. 'I suppose you could walk from here to our own St Mary's when you and Tim marry. Providing it doesn't rain.' She sighed. 'Life is going to be full of wedding talk for *years*! You're all at that age,' she said pragmatically.

'I'm not.' Faith turned over a page and began another sketch. 'I'm still too young, even though I'll soon be sixteen, and besides, I'm not getting married; it's much too complicated. I shall live in Italy or Paris and take lovers.'

Her sisters looked at her. 'Faith!' Matty said, shocked. 'Whatever will Papa say? And what will Mario think?'

'He loves you,' Becca implored. 'You'll break his heart!'

'I know he does, and I won't break his heart. I love him too, but I don't want to marry him.' Faith gazed at her sisters, her mouth quivering in amusement as she teased them. 'He can be my first lover – or even my only one. I can't plan my whole life. Can I, Julia?' she said, as the door opened and Julia came in.

'Can you what?' Julia plumped down into a chair and slipped off her shoes. She was wearing a plain skirt and matching jacket and had her hair in a chignon at the back of her neck but still managed to look incredibly beautiful. She heaved a deep breath. 'I'm exhausted.'

'Plan my life.'

'Shouldn't think so.' Julia was unbuttoning her jacket. 'It's not even worth trying,' she said. 'Because life has a way of turning itself upside down.'

'How was it today?' Matty asked her.

Julia turned to her. 'Wonderful!' She had a beatific smile that lit up her face. 'Absolutely incredible. I really feel that I can make a difference.'

Everything had changed from the time their father came home and began his slow return to good health; and particularly on the evening when he started to tell them about Jeanette and how they had met, or at least what little he knew of that incident. He explained that she had taken someone's place in a group of French people who were visiting London and barely knew any of them; and that because he had been put into the same hospital ward as the French party after an accident she had thought he was one of them, particularly when she spoke to him in French and he answered in the same language.

'I had no coat or hat,' he told them. 'They had disappeared, stolen probably along with my briefcase and money, so I was wearing only my suit – my tailcoat. It was very cold on the ferry. I remember little about the journey and I was confused over another passage across the Channel. I think now that I was remembering when we went to Italy for Matty's birthday.

'When we arrived in France – and I don't know how I got across without a ticket or money, but somehow I did – we took a train, and our journey ended in a small railway station in the middle of nowhere. Everyone, except for Jeanette, then disappeared.' He put his chin in his hands and tried to recall the next sequence, but it had gone; a blur that he couldn't recall.

'Jeanette took me with her as I was alone and bewildered. She had a cart and a most amiable donkey and we drove for what seemed to be miles into the forest.'

His daughters kept silent although each of them was brimming with questions, because they knew he had to tell it in his own way.

'She had a guard dog.' His face softened. 'She called him Chien. I can tell you little more except that for several days she bathed my head and let me sleep and fed me when I woke; and then one night I dreamed of your mother and that I had children. I'd forgotten that you were nearly grown up and not children any longer, but Jeanette eased it out of me day by day until I remembered my name and where I lived.'

He sat thinking of her kindness and how patient she was, and the tenderness on her lovely face. 'She lives such a simple life,' he murmured. 'She makes artefacts from what she finds in the forest and sells them in village markets in exchange for food and things she needs.'

A true gypsy, Julia thought; and unbidden an image of an old gypsy woman wearing a shawl came into her head.

He sat for a moment thinking, and none of them broke the silence.

'And then, as time went on, she said that now that I knew my name and where I lived, and my health had improved, I should return home before winter came, as if I didn't I wouldn't be able to leave the forest, but would have to stay until the spring. But I had no money and neither did she, so we made wooden plates out of a beech log and other simple things, and sold them. They were beautiful.'

His voice was hoarse with wonder when he thought of polishing the beech with resin. 'She bought me warm clothes for the journey, for mine were of no use.'

'Papa.' Matty broke into his monologue. 'She bought you clothes? With the money? How will she live? Had she anything else to sell?'

He shook his head. '*Non*,' he whispered. He'd reverted to speaking in French. '*Rien du tout.*' Nothing at all.

A few weeks later he said that he must try to find her. He'd written to her, as had Matty, but they had no address; he'd simply written on the envelope, in English, *Jeanette, in the Forest of Cerisy, near Calvados, Normandy*. He had also written the contents of the letter in English, in case by chance anyone else should open it and try to read it in an effort to find her. She was a very private person and wouldn't want anyone knowing of her personal life, particularly that a man had been staying with her. He'd put his address on the back of the envelope in case it was returned. But there was nothing.

They had all attended the wedding of Louisa and Stephen during the week before Christmas, when Louisa's nieces had been her attendants and Gertrude, who had also been invited, kept a watchful eye on her brother. Christmas itself they had deliberately kept very quiet. The sisters had gone to church on Christmas morning, but their father had stayed at home, not wanting anyone to question him about his journey, and as he was alone he'd written another letter to Jeanette, then asked Nunny to make sure it was posted as soon as the holiday was over.

After weeks when there was no reply, he said he must go back to France and seek her out.

'It's still winter, Father,' Matty had said. 'Let's wait until the spring.'

When it was deemed to be the right time, Timothy Garton had called on her father to ask if he and Matty might walk out together. 'I have a great admiration for her, sir,' he'd told Roland, and her father was pleased. To Matty, Tim had already said that he loved her.

'The first of my daughters to leave me,' Roland had said to Matty.

'Not yet, Papa,' she answered, and kissed his cheek. 'I won't leave you yet. Not until you are truly well.'

Julia had said she had something to discuss with him and saw him wince. 'Not marriage, Papa,' she said. 'I'm not yet ready for that. But whilst you were away I began thinking that I must do something with my life; and,' she'd hesitated and blushed, 'it was Adam who inspired me to think of it. I would like to become a teacher and teach in the Ragged Schools as Adam is going to do.'

She had looked into it already, she said, with Adam's help. There was the Queen's College in Harley Street in London where young women could gain a registered diploma in teaching, and could then go on, if they wished, to the Cheltenham Ladies' College. 'In time, but not yet, I'd like to take the first course and find out if I'm fit to do it, and if I am then I'll go on to Cheltenham.'

'My clever daughter,' he'd murmured. 'Of course you can.'

She had not yet begun the first part of her plan, as she had enquired at the Hull Ragged School if she might work part time as a volunteer teacher, teaching the children to read and write. The committee agreed and the children loved her, as she was patient but firm and didn't apply the cane, and besides, she was beautiful. They hung on her every word as she read them a story every day before they left for home; on the days she spent there, she stayed overnight with Aunt Gertrude. Her mind was now made up regarding her future and who would be in it.

It wasn't yet time to tell her father the extent of her plans; she would wait until he was truly well, and besides, Matty deserved everyone's full attention as she organized her own wedding to Timothy.

Everyone but Matty had seen the love in Tim's every expression whenever he called on her; Matty had never thought that anyone would want to marry her. She was so intent on everyone else's well-being and happiness that she hadn't ever considered her own.

Julia wasn't going to intrude on that happy occasion with ideas for her own future; she was content, perhaps for the first time in her life.

It had begun on that significant train journey when Adam had brought her home from Aunt Gertrude's; he had known how fearful she was about her father and about Faith's illness and, without her being aware of it, had somehow instilled in her a sense of calm and introduced a scenario of what she could do to fulfil her in life; he had taken her hand as he left her safely at home, and by doing so had shown her how much he cared for her, had always cared for her, as he told her at a later date, since they were only children.

Faith had her own ideas of what she would like to do, but as yet she was too young to leave home. She wasn't really joking about living abroad, but it was too soon, she had decided; she needed maturity, but in the meantime she would keep on painting and corresponding with Mario.

Becca had blossomed once her father had returned to them, and had asked him if she might have a tutor rather than a governess as she felt she'd outgrown Miss Hargreaves; she wanted someone who would teach her languages. Her father was thrilled to hear of this desire, so very useful if she ever wanted to travel. She hadn't yet told him of her aspirations of working with horses or of becoming a trainer, or of knowing the difference between a good runner and a hack; that, she thought, could come later.

It was now early spring of the following year, and as Jeanette had not yet replied to his many letters, and Roland felt well again apart from occasional headaches, he was resolute and single-minded about travelling to France.

'You can't travel alone, Papa,' his daughters insisted. 'We would never settle whilst you were away, particularly as Jeanette has no address and lives in a forest! There will probably be miles of it.'

'Acres,' he corrected. 'Not miles. Or hectares to be exact, as it is in France. All right, which of you will travel with me, for I am determined to go. I'm anxious about her and her well-being.'

But it was more than that, he knew. Quite simply, he missed her. He missed her smile, her sense of humour, her kindness and the caring qualities she had shown to him when he was lost and alone. He didn't say this to his daughters, of course; he had no idea how they might react to his being attracted to another woman after losing their mother.

'I'll come,' Matty said. 'We're not planning a wedding just yet.'

'So will I,' Julia agreed. 'You have no sense of direction, Matty, and we'd have to send out a search party for you.'

'I'll come too, Papa,' Becca broke in. 'I'm too young to stay by myself, and besides, I'd like to see her dog. *Le chien*,' she added, putting on a French accent.

Faith put down her sketch book. 'Well, I can't be left alone,' she complained. 'What if I'm ill? Who would look after me whilst you were all away?'

'You haven't been ill in ages,' Julia said. 'That's just an excuse.'

Roland smiled and shook his head. 'Incorrigible, all of you,' he said. 'All right. We'll all go.'

It was a risk, he thought. What would Jeanette think of his four daughters? Would she be overwhelmed by them? She was used to a quiet life; she'd lived alone for years with only her dog and the donkey for company. Was that the life she wanted? Or did she want more?

CHAPTER FIFTY

Ending

It was a bright though cold morning in mid-April when they landed in Le Havre and picked up a cabriolet to take them to Caen; here they booked in at a small hotel, left their baggage and hired a pony and trap in which to drive to the Cerisy Forest.

Roland was unsure at first of the road that would lead them to the area of forest where Jeanette's cottage was situated, but towards midday he had his bearings and was fairly sure that he was on the right track.

Last year when he had left to begin his journey home, the forest was settling into its winter habit; trees were shedding their leaves, ferns were turning brown, fungi gathering about tree roots and there was a rich, ripe pungent odour of decay. Now there was fresh green growth as the trees unfurled their pale leaves as the sun filtered through the branches, and there was birdsong: a musical harmony of twittering, cheeping and chirping, whistling and piping filling the forest air.

There was movement too: a swift brush of wings above their heads, a flash of colour to startle them and the sound of running water as they approached hidden streams, which finally convinced Roland that they were on the right path.

They came upon the cottage quite by chance as they approached a clearing where small trees had been roughly hacked away, and he realized that the forest was gradually, slowly, yet progressively taking over; that this particular area was not yet being controlled as some of the forest was. If it was not taken in hand, the home that Jeanette had made would very soon be obliterated.

The door was firmly closed. There was no one at home.

'Are you sure this is it, Papa?' Matty said softly. It was a shack, she thought, not really a cottage, and she wondered how anyone, especially a woman, could survive here on her own.

He nodded, but didn't speak as he climbed down from the trap, but his eyes took in the water bowl outside the door which she always left for Chien, and at the side of the house he could see where the soil had been freshly dug over. She had dug up the beech slices she had buried. She had gone to market to make some money.

He put two fingers to his lips and whistled; then he shouted, 'Chien! Chien!' He waited, then whistled again and waited, and then his ears picked up a distant crashing as something tore through the undergrowth. The sisters looked at each other; it could be a deer, or a boar, or what creature was it that their father had told them about? A pine marten?

But it wasn't; it was a dog, a great big dog with a long tail that was thrashing excitedly as it hurled itself at their father. Almost as tall as him, it stood on its hind legs and lashed him with its wet tongue and ran round and round him. And their father! He hugged the dog with his arms around him and they could see that he was weeping.

He brought Chien towards them as they sat in the trap, hardly daring to get out, but Becca was the first and allowed the dog to sniff her hands and her skirts and then he jumped into the trap to introduce himself to the others before he went back to Roland, nuzzling up to him, yapping and whining.

'Where is she, Chien?' Roland asked him, speaking in French. 'Where is Jeanette?'

Chien looked up and then about him. He took several steps away and then came back again. 'Where is she?' Roland asked again and the dog whined. Roland climbed into the trap and picked up the reins. 'Come on. Let's find her. Find Jeanette,' and he wondered if the dog understood, for who else would have used her name for the dog to hear or know, apart from him?

Chien sat up tall and straight next to Roland and the sisters giggled. 'He looks like one of those figureheads at the prow of a sailing ship,' Faith laughed. 'He's leading the way.'

About a mile along, the track divided; Roland drew on the pony's reins. Which path had Jeanette taken? 'Becca,' he said, 'take over the driving, will you, and I'll walk a little way and see if Chien knows which track to take.'

He climbed out and the dog followed him. 'Where is she?' he asked again, and Chien lifted his ears, then put his long nose to the ground and set off down the right-hand path with Roland and then the pony and trap following.

This wasn't a track that Roland knew but Chien did, and presently Roland jumped back into the trap and they followed the dog until the forest thinned out and they came to a small village or hamlet where what appeared to be the only street was crowded with stalls from which villagers were selling their wares as well as bread, cheese and honey to visitors who wore strong boots and carried rucksacks on their backs.

'Walkers,' Becca murmured. 'Come to see the forest.'

'Yes,' her father murmured back, getting out of the trap and casting his eyes over the stalls. He soon found Jeanette's. She had little on it, just a few wooden items that she had painted, but then he saw the plates, roughly hewn but beautifully polished; a man was holding one in his hands and turning it over. A woman at the next stall came and stood beside it; they took care of each other's items if they had to slip away for any reason, for none of them could afford to lose anything to thieves.

But where was Jeanette? He looked about him. And where was Chien? Perhaps he had gone to find her. Then he saw her, coming out of a shop doorway; she had something in her hands and was looking down, frowning. A paper, or . . . no, envelopes? His? His heart turned over as she looked up and then down again as Chien appeared at her feet, pulling on her skirt.

He couldn't hear what she was saying, but he guessed that she was asking him why he was here, but still he pulled on her skirt and she bent to talk to him, patting his great head. Then she looked up again and saw him and an expression of bewilderment crossed her face. Does she recognize me? He'd been a sorry spectacle when she had rescued him. She looked down again at Chien and then back at him, as if checking that he was still there and not an illusion. She murmured something and stepped towards him, and he walked towards her.

'*Est-ce toi?*' Is it you? she whispered, and Chien nuzzled his head against her.

'*Oui,*' he said, not knowing what else to say, but knowing that he wanted to take her in his arms. 'I came to find you. There was no answer to my letters.'

She looked down at the bundle in her hands. 'I have collected them only now,' she said vaguely.

She was pale, and he guessed that she had been inside the cottage most of the winter. This might be her first outing of the spring. He took her hand, and turning it over he kissed her palm. 'I've missed you,' he said softly.

He saw her swallow and she moistened her lips with the tip of her tongue. 'How did you find me? I rarely come to this village.'

He smiled. 'Chien brought us.'

'Us?' she asked.

Without turning round he pointed over his shoulder towards where his daughters would be waiting in the trap; and watching her face he saw she was suddenly anxious.

'Come,' he said, keeping hold of her hand. 'Come and meet my daughters.'

'She's not an old witch,' Julia murmured.

'No,' Matty said. 'She's young and—'

'Beautiful,' Faith and Becca finished for her simultaneously, as sometimes they did.

The woman whose hand their father was holding on to as if he would never let it go was slight of build with a grace that was natural and not contrived; she seemed quite shy as she approached them and they guessed that she had been taken completely by surprise by their father's arrival. Whether she was pleased to see him they couldn't work out.

She could be my mother, Becca thought wistfully, though she's younger than Papa. She has a lovely face. Faith looked at her with her artistic eye and saw warmth and sincerity. I could confide in her, Julia thought: she would listen. And Matty gazed at her and hoped that she would like them.

'They're back.' Becca was once again looking out of the sitting room window. 'I'm the watchwoman,' she said, if ever one or other of her sisters commented on it. She waved now as the carriage slowed and Sam jumped from the driving seat to hold Star's head whilst Roland Henry Maddeson tenderly helped his wife down. They were returning from their honeymoon in Italy where they had rented Vista Lago for a month.

Henri was his wife's preferred name for him. She said she couldn't get her French tongue around Roland, and he didn't want Roly as that had been special to others. But he loved the way Jeanette pronounced Henri: such a special sound that only a Frenchwoman could bring to it.

They had brought Jeanette home to England; she had accepted their offer of hospitality without fully comprehending the scheming wiles of his daughters. One who desperately wanted a mother figure as she couldn't remember her own; another who had only vague recollections of her, a certain

335

fragrance that sometimes lingered; one who subsequently confided that she had always felt as if she had been abandoned when her mother had been taken away from her; and the eldest daughter who needed the presence of someone loving who could take the mother's role as she herself was about to step into her own as a married woman.

Jeanette didn't know this at the beginning, of course; she only knew how lonely she had been when Henri had left, and how she had wept all the way back to her isolated home with Chien howling in her ear, and realized how much she missed him already.

'It was a miracle,' she told him when they were alone. 'When I saw you there at the market I could not believe it. I was about to pack my few belongings and leave and try to get work in Caen or Deauville or somewhere, anywhere, rather than stay in the forest without you.'

Chien? Of course she couldn't possibly leave without him. Little Pug took one sniff of him when they arrived home and scooted upstairs to hide beneath Faith's bed.

She was introduced to the household staff and Nunny approved of her. She would make Mr Maddeson a goodly wife, she thought, though there had been no hint of that as yet. Roland presented her to his brother and his wife when he was good and ready, for he had been displeased that Albert Fisher hadn't been of much help whilst he had been lost in France, and announced her as his future wife.

Jeanette's soon-to-be-step-daughters took her shopping for clothes for her wedding and their outfits as bridesmaids, and a marriage was pronounced in Beverley Minster, which, strictly speaking wasn't Roland's parish, but he had been married to Constance in St Mary's and felt he wanted to keep those old treasured memories separate from these new precious ones.

Roland's mother came over for the occasion, brought by Mario, whom everyone said was more handsome than ever, if that were possible. There were hints floating about that he

336

would marry one of the younger daughters, for it was rumoured that Julia was spoken for.

Julia and Adam were making plans, but no one was telling, and he couldn't believe his luck when the most desirable young woman in Beverley – well, all right, he admitted, he'd had an argument or two with Timothy over that: *one* of the most desirable young women – had agreed to marry him. What they were actually planning was that after they were married they would set up a school of their own where they would offer promising pupils from the Ragged Schools a chance to shine and achieve without the stigma of poverty associated with the name, and call it the College of Learning.

As for Becca, as she grew up everyone matched her up with Owen Field, but he was bound to remain a bachelor and kept Becca as a very special friend who learned from him about horse management and training when he came back from his studies, which made her even keener to do the same. Roger, the young man she would eventually marry, had played a small part in her life when they were young, and she had always been a friend of his twin sister Frances. The Lawrence twins, as they had always been called, would eventually run their parents' racing stables, whilst Becca and Owen bought and trained thoroughbreds and could often be seen on Beverley racecourse putting them through their paces.

Faith did eventually go to Italy to live and study art and Mario was always there in the background; whether or not they became lovers no one knew, because, as everyone knows, lovers should always be discreet.

As for Matty, Roland's eldest daughter, who had held the family together when she was a mere child herself and he in his grief had been unable to, Roland asked her if after her marriage to Timothy she would join with him in creating a charity to help the destitute, who through no fault of their own had had misfortune thrust upon them; he was thinking of the Italian man he had met by the shores of Lake Maggiore without a *scudo* to his name, as well as himself on his long journey home, when he had been met with kindness from many who had so little to offer and yet had given it willingly. And of course she agreed that she would.

When the time came for Nunny to retire as housekeeper, Aunt Gertrude asked her if she would come and live at her house as her companion, so that they might travel together to places abroad without any expense involved on Nunny's part; for as Gertrude explained, she had plenty of money and her nieces were well provided for. Nunny enthusiastically agreed and together they journeyed across Europe and far beyond, to places like Singapore, America and Canada.

Louisa and Stephen had come to meet Jeanette and loved her straight away; Louisa felt that she had regained a sister and told her she was very pleased for them both and hoped they would be as happy as she and Stephen were. She had given birth to a boy and during her second pregnancy, which had come soon after, she came home from visiting friends to find Stephen covered in dust with a sledge hammer in his hand.

'Whatever are you doing?' she asked.

'I'm knocking a hole in the wall through to my house as I always promised,' he told her, wiping from his face bits of the plaster, horsehair and cow dung which made up the wall surfaces in those old buildings, and sneezing in the process. 'Your house isn't big enough for us and all the babies we're producing.'

Almost immediately she went into labour and delivered a girl, which delighted them both.

A year following Roland Henri and Jeanette's wedding, she too became pregnant. Roland was elated when she told him. He told his daughters that he would never forget their mother, and that he saw her each time he looked at them, and that Jeanette too had her own special, but different, place in his heart. They said they understood as they loved her too.

On the day Jeanette gave birth, the sisters had gathered together at the top of the stairs as they used to when they were children, Matty on the top step, Julia below and Faith and Becca holding hands on the third, their faces turned towards the bedroom where their father had joined Jeanette, Nunny and the midwife, for they had heard the first resilient cry of an infant.

Roland Henri kissed his wife and new-born, and vowed that he would love them for ever. 'You saved my life,' he whispered in French, and she smiled and whispered back, 'And you saved mine.'

Nunny wiped the babe's face with a clean cloth, tenderly wrapped the precious infant in a blanket and shawl, once meant for another child, and placed the bundle in Roland's waiting arms. She opened the door for him and he went out on to the landing to greet his daughters.

They rose as one and stood in front of him. His eyes were moist and so were theirs as he said, 'May I introduce your brother? Henri Leo Constant Maddeson.'

AUTHOR'S NOTE

When I was a child my constant favourite book, which I read time and time again, was *Little Women* by Louisa M. Alcott. I didn't realize then that I was reading 'literature', I only knew that it was the best book I had ever read. I took the story of those four American sisters and their mother to my heart as I read of their struggles to cope whilst their father was away in the army.

Jo, impetuous and loving, who wanted to be a writer, was everyone's favourite character, including mine. I didn't think, back then, that their story was influencing me in my own storytelling.

My *Four Sisters* is nothing like *Little Women*, but it is my belief that *we do nothing alone.* We are influenced or inspired by someone or something hovering on the edge of our consciousness, making us what we are and are likely to become.

BOOKS FOR GENERAL READING

The Tragi-Comedy of Victorian Fatherhood by Valerie Sanders, Cambridge University Press (2009)

Beverley Pastures by Barbara English, Beverley and District Civic Society (2013)

Watercolours by Ron Ranson, Brockhampton Press, Hodder Headline (1995)

Costume in Detail by Nancy Bradfield, Harrap Books (1968)

ACKNOWLEDGEMENTS

As this is my twenty-fifth book, a milestone I never imagined I would reach, I feel I must acknowledge the immense support I have received from the multitude of faithful readers who have supported me over the years, giving me the strength and inspiration to write yet another story. Your faith in me has been overwhelming, and along with my family, and my late and much missed husband Peter, who encouraged me at the beginning of my career and was my most ardent supporter, I say to you all an earnest thank you.

Many thanks are also due to Transworld Publishers and the team of editors, copy-editors, proof-readers, cover designers, publicists, and all who have tirelessly produced my books since 1993. It has been an incredibly exciting journey.

Last but certainly not least, the inspirational team who are Divine Clark PR, who put my name out into the world. You are stars that shine.

A Mother's Choice

by Val Wood

For ten years, Delia has had to fend for herself and her son Jack, and as a young unmarried mother, life has never been easy. Every new coat and pair of shoes was bought with what little money she could scrape together as a singer on the stage.

But when the theatre work dries up, Delia faces a dilemma: continue the search for employment with no knowing whether she'll find the stability and security her son needs, or return to the place that should be home . . . where only spite and hatred await them.

Desperate now, a chance encounter suddenly presents a lifeline. But Delia is faced with an impossible, heart-wrenching choice. Can she bear to leave Jack behind, hoping another family will care for him? Will they ever be reunited?

What else can a mother do to give her son the life he deserves?

A Mother's Choice is available in paperback now

A Place to Call Home
by Val Wood

Ellen thought she'd always live in the remote, pretty
coastal village where she grew up. After all, her
husband, Harry, works on a farm where he's
guaranteed a job and home for life.

But when the old landowner dies and the couple and
their young children are forced from their cottage,
the future is suddenly bleak. Rather than stay – and
starve – in the countryside they love, Harry sets out to
find a job in the factories and mills of nearby Hull, and
Ellen must leave behind everything she's ever known to
follow him and build a new life for her family on
the unfamiliar city streets.

The road ahead is full of hardships and challenges.
But with love and determination, they make the best
of things, forging friendships with other newcomers
and refugees; even helping them to succeed in their
new surroundings.

**Then tragedy threatens Ellen's fragile happiness.
How much more can she sacrifice before they find
a place to call home?**

A Place to Call Home is available in paperback now